Something Certain, Maybe

Books by Sara Barnard

Beautiful Broken Things
A Quiet Kind of Thunder
Goodbye, Perfect
Fierce Fragile Hearts
Destination Anywhere

Floored
A collaborative novel

Something Certain, Maybe

SARA BARNARD

MACMILLAN

Published 2022 by Macmillan Children's Books
an imprint of Pan Macmillan
The Smithson, 6 Briset Street, London EC1M 5NR
EU representative: Macmillan Publishers Ireland Ltd, 1st Floor,
The Liffey Trust Centre, 117–126 Sheriff Street Upper
Dublin 1, D01 YC43
Associated companies throughout the world
www.panmacmillan.com

ISBN 978-1-5290-0360-4

3 5 7 9 8 6 4 2

A CIP catalogue record for this book is available from the British Library.

Printed and bound by CPI Group (UK) Ltd, Croydon CR0 4YY

For Rachel, Sarah and Cate.
Thank you.

'Life is unpredictable,
It changes with the seasons,
Even your coldest winter
Happens for the best of reasons,
And though it feels eternal,
Like all you'll ever do is freeze,
I promise spring is coming,
And with it, brand new leaves.'

Erin Hanson

1

The first thing that goes wrong is the playlist.

It's a four-hour drive from Brighton to Norwich — my old home to the new — and I'd spent literal hours collating the perfect playlist. I'd googled 'new-life songs', 'fresh-start songs' and 'student songs' and made a whole list specifically for this one journey, the official start of my new life as a student. It was the right length and everything. I'd called it, very simply, 'Day One'.

I'm just setting it to play in my mum's car — I've even timed this moment for when we cross the city line — when Mum chirps, 'I made a tape! Do you want to put it on?'

'A tape?' I repeat. 'What kind of tape?'

'A mixtape!' she says, like it's 1993 or something. 'For our last trip together,' she adds, very dramatically, pointing at the tape player. (This is how old my mum's car is. Not even a CD player — a *cassette* player.) 'Put it on.'

'I made a playlist,' I say, lifting my phone and waving it at her. 'I'll just play that.'

We've just stopped at a red light, which is why Mum is able to turn to me in this moment with wide, mournful eyes, just like our cat does when he doesn't want to be shut out of our bedrooms at night. 'You don't want to listen to the tape I made for you?'

Historically, I'm not the kind of person easily swayed by this kind of pure emotional manipulation. But this is Mum. Mum, driving me to university in the battered old car she's had almost my whole life, who cheered and cajoled and bullied me into the studying I needed to do to even be on this road, who raised me single-handedly, who thinks — and tells me, often — that I'm the greatest person to ever exist, and truly believes it, even though it obviously isn't true.

So, we listen to the tape, twice, all the way to Norwich. She's put 'Slipping Through My Fingers', the *Mamma Mia* version of the ABBA song, on it *three times*. That's the kind of vibe she's gone for. She keeps getting tearful when she tries to sing along, reaching over to squeeze my knee while she sniffles.

I'm not saying I *needed* to hear the playlist I'd planned for this trip, because obviously listening to it or not won't actually affect how the rest of the year goes. But . . . well, maybe I am saying that a little. I just don't like things not going how they're meant to go, you know? And I was meant to be listening to American Authors singing about the best day of their lives, which was meant to be preparing me for mine. Instead, I get nostalgic Meryl Streep.

Which is fine. Obviously, it's fine. I can adjust my expectations for this one tiny thing, or at least adjust my focus. I push the playlist I'd made into the back of my head and instead think about everything that *is* going to plan. Mum and me in the car. The route we're taking to Norwich and my new university. The fact that I have a university that is *mine*. The thought sends a thrill of pure excitement through my whole body, making my fingers tingle. I know where I am, where I'm going. It's a good feeling.

Everything about starting uni is incredibly overwhelming, so I'm thinking a lot about what I can control, which is something I got taught when I was a kid, after some bad stuff happened and I had to see a therapist for a bit. She told me to list my certainties whenever things felt out of control, and it was great advice. Ever since, it's a way I've kept myself calm when the alternative is panic. So that's what I've been doing all morning, and it's what I do when Mum drives us through the entrance to the university campus and my heart starts going *really* fast.

I am Rosie Caron. I am eighteen. Mum is beside me. She loves me. I have lace-up black boots on my feet, and the rest of me is black jeans and a striped vest top under an oversized hoodie. My hair is the same as it always is – dark brown, short and curly – because it's basically impossible to do anything else with it unless you possess some supernatural hairstyling ability, which I do not. And I am getting out of the car on the campus of my university, where I am starting a pharmacy degree. I will study here for four years, then take a pre-registration year. Then I'll be a qualified pharmacist, and that will be a certainty I'll have for my whole life. My whole life! I love that. Not just that I'm at uni, which is obviously exciting and cool in all the obvious ways, but because of *that* certainty.

I love the safety of that knowledge. Most of my other friends starting uni this year aren't doing vocational degrees, which is what pharmacy is, but the kind with a degree at the end but not a specific qualification. One of my best friends, Caddy, who'll be studying psychology from next week, says she likes that, because it means she's free to choose, but I love the *knowing*. So much of life is so completely out of your control – why wouldn't you want to fix the bits you can? I want to know where I'm going, what I'm doing. And now I finally do.

Starting with today, which is not just the first day of this new life, but also, and perhaps most importantly, the first day of Freshers Week. Today it will be about unpacking, meeting my flatmates, and probably going out for our first club night. Then the rest of the week will be about getting to know the university, registering for stuff, having my first few lectures, getting exciting things like my lab coat and goggles, meeting my coursemates. There'll probably be a lot of socializing and drinking too, because it's Freshers, and though I know it's a cliché, there's probably a lot of truth in it, too. I've basically memorized the list of campus club nights – one every night this week, culminating in the Freshers

Welcome Ball on Friday, which sounds amazing. The pinnacle of the week. I planned my outfit for the ball in July. That's how prepared I am.

A little sick, yes. But still. Prepared.

Mum beams at me, hooking her arm through mine and squeezing tight. 'This is exciting!' she says, correctly. 'What's first?'

'My key,' I say immediately. (So prepared.) 'The student union building.'

We follow the signs that have been put up to guide us there, and Mum waits outside while I go in. I queue up behind a girl with red ombre hair who is muttering – quietly, but distinctly – 'I am stronger than this emotion,' over and over, stopping only when she reaches the front of the queue and the guy sat behind the desk says, 'Hello!'

I wait until she's turning to leave before I say, in my most cheerful but reassuring voice, 'I love your jacket.' I do love her jacket. It's got Life is Strange patches on it.

The girl starts in surprise, looking at me like I've appeared out of nowhere, then smiles uncertainly. 'Thanks,' she says, and I smile back.

I'm feeling pretty proud of myself for this act of kindness – surely a good karmic start to my year – when I collect my key, thank the guy behind the desk and follow the signs back out through the hall into another section of the student union, which is full of stalls in every direction. It's a dizzying array of freebies and general marketing pizzazz; too much to properly take in, which is why I walk right past the stall displaying a huge platter of biscuits shaped like canaries with yellow icing, and that's when the second thing goes wrong. Right when I'm feeling proud, maybe even a little bit confident, most of my attention focused on navigating myself out of the right exit so I can find Mum and we can go to my new flat to unpack my stuff from the car. I register that there's a voice coming from my left, so I look up, confused, to see a beaming man standing beside the stall of canary biscuits, gesturing. He says, clearly repeating himself, 'Take one!' So I do, because I'm polite like that, but I must be more flustered by the general anxiety of the day than I'd let myself realize, and also the number of different thoughts I'm attempting to juggle in my head, because when I take a bite I forget to chew and, promptly, choke on it.

That's right. I choke on a canary biscuit. I don't even mean that I cough a little and go a bit red. I mean I actually choke, and a total stranger has to smack me on the back, and I don't go a bit red so much as a purplish scarlet – I can *feel* my face turning this colour – with full on streaming eyes and everything.

It's mortifying, is what I'm saying. Especially when the smiling man from behind the stall calls out, 'They're not that bad!' and everyone laughs. (I don't know if it's actually everyone, but in this moment, it *feels* like everyone.)

What I should do is laugh along, maybe do something funny like give a little bow, but this only occurs to me after I've already run away, and then it's too late.

Now, I know this isn't a big deal. Obviously it isn't. It's just a little moment of embarrassment. But did it have to happen right when I was feeling confident about myself? It's only tiny, but it's enough to throw me in a way I don't like to be thrown. Spoiling the vibe, just like listening to the wrong playlist spoilt the vibe. And I'd planned to have the perfect vibe.

Maybe that's why it takes me longer than I'd expected to find Mum again, which makes me feel stupidly, ridiculously, a little bit panicky, as if the whole point of her being here isn't to literally drop me off and leave me here. I grip the skin at my wrist and squeeze it hard. *Get a grip. This is all fine. Look, there's Mum. It's fine.*

'What happened?' Mum asks when she sees me, alarmed.

'Nothing,' I say, as if my eyes aren't all red and wet. 'I've got my key. Let's go find my flat.'

My university campus is a maze of grey concrete steps and walkways, but there are helpers in bright T-shirts pointing us in the right direction, so we don't get lost. The flat I'll be living in is in one of the buildings called the Ziggurats, which are the university's most iconic accommodation blocks. They look like stacked concrete pyramids. Suffolk Terrace, my allocation reads. There'll be nine other students in the flat with me, sharing two bathrooms and one kitchen.

'That's a lot of sharing,' Mum had said when we'd talked about it a few months ago. 'Are you sure that's a good idea?'

She'd meant that I'm an only child, and I've never had to really share anything, even her, but I'd shrugged it off. Sharing a bathroom seemed a small price to pay for the Ziggurats being cheaper than other en-suite options, and anyway, I'd have a washbasin in my room, so it wouldn't be that bad. Besides, that was all part of the fun of being flatmates, wasn't it? Mucking in together, sharing it all, even the bad bits?

My room is about the same size as my room at home. It has a bed, a desk, a wardrobe and a mirror, plus a gorgeous view over towards the lake, which I love immediately. It takes a while to bring in all my stuff from the car with Mum, or at least it feels like it does, right up until the moment when Mum says, 'I think that's it. You're all unloaded.' And I realize it was no time at all.

'Already?' I say.

We both look around at my room, the assortment of boxes, the sheets already on the bed. Even though I'm literally standing in it, it still feels impossible that this is mine, my small corner of campus, where I'll be living, studying, sleeping, and everything in between.

'Already,' she says. There's a silence. I don't know what to say, even to Mum. Any words seem like they'll be too big, and also not big enough. 'Well, I think this is it, my love.' She breathes in a shuddery breath, like she's trying not to cry. I'd made her promise not to cry today, and I look at her sharply. She presses her lips together and shakes her head. 'What am I going to do without you?' she asks, squeezing my arm as she looks around. 'My little rock.'

It's what she's always called me. Rosie the rock.

'That's rhetorical, by the way,' Mum adds quickly, releasing me. 'I will be just fine, and I don't want you worrying about me.'

'I won't,' I say. We both know I will. 'I'm going to be way too busy having the time of my life. I'll be like, Mum who?'

She laughs, hooking an arm around my shoulder and pulling me in for the kind of tight hug I'll only ever accept from her. She kisses my hair, then touches the side of my face. She's beaming at me with such pride, such *love*, that my eyes prickle. 'I'm going to miss you,' she says. 'But I don't want you to miss me, OK? I want you to have the time of your life.'

'I will,' I say. 'The time of my life.'

I go with her to the main door of the flat, then wave from the doorway as she walks up the concrete steps of the building, half turns to give me one last wave, then disappears around the corner. My heart lurches and I feel, just for a second, like I'm at nursery again, watching her leave me behind.

Which is crazy, because it's not like I've been any kind of a mummy's girl for years. Maybe even *since* then.

But still, I feel it. That awful tug of realization that I'm alone here, in this brand-new place, so huge and scary. I close the door and head back down the corridor, shaking my head. *I am fine. I'm fine. I can do this, and I'm fine.*

My room seems very quiet with just me in it. Bigger, too.

There's a beep from my phone and I look down to see Caddy's name on my screen. She messaged me twice earlier – **HOW IS IT GOING?????** and then **OMG message me back, this is killing me. I need to know** – but I hadn't replied because I was unloading the car. Now, she's saying, simply, **ROSIE!!!**

Caddy is going to Warwick for uni, but her term doesn't start until next week, so she's almost as invested in my Freshers Week experience as I am. I tap out a quick reply. **Just moved in. Talk later?**

Her reply is almost immediate. **YES! Hope you're OK. I'm at Suze's. We just made a cake. Going to eat it in your honour. Love you!**

My heart gives a pang, standing there alone in my unfamiliar bedroom, the sound of distant laughter coming from somewhere else in the flat. I wish I was with her and Suze, my two best friends, in the comfort of total familiarity, eating cake.

But no. I pinch my wrist. *Don't be stupid.* I'm here at uni, which is the coolest, most exciting thing ever. I worked so hard to get here. There are people to meet, adventures to have. One day not too far from now, I'll look back and laugh at how nervous I was in this moment. (Right?) This is day one of the next chapter of my life.

I take out the bottle of Tuaca that Suze gave me as my going-to-uni present and unscrew the cap to take a sip. *Brighton courage*, I think, closing my eyes at the taste of the familiar liqueur. I can do this. *I can.*

There's a knock at my door and I jump in surprise, Tuaca sloshing out of the top of the bottle and onto my hand. When I turn, I see a girl standing in the doorway, beaming at me. She's gorgeous: tall and lithe, dark hair swinging all the way down her back. Her nails, which I can see because her hand is splayed in a confident spread eagle over her hip, are bright red.

'Hi!' she says. 'I'm Rika. I'm in number seven.' She points down the hall, and I look in that direction as if I can suddenly defy the laws of physics and see round corners. 'Me and Dawn are going to check out the poster sale in the LCR and see what else is going on. Want to come?' She leans a little into my room, craning her neck. 'Your room is exactly like mine. And literally all of them.' She laughs. 'It's so weird, isn't it? We could just swap right now and it's like, who would know?'

'So weird,' I say, even though I haven't actually seen her room, or anyone else's, and the words sound inane out of my own mouth in a way they didn't from hers. I add, 'I'm Rosie.' And then, because it seems like the smartest thing to do at this moment, I lift the bottle still in my hand and say, 'Tuaca?'

'Oh my God,' Rika says, coming into the room, grinning. 'Yeah! What is it? I don't mind. Yes.'

Thank God for alcohol. Thank God for Tuaca. Thank God for forward-thinking friends like Suze who made sure I didn't go to uni without it. I'm about to say that I don't have a cup, but Rika's already taking the bottle from me and sipping gamely from it. Her eyes widen and she looks down at the label.

'Shit, that's sweet. What is it?'

'Sort of a vanilla liqueur,' I say. 'Do you like it?'

'I don't know,' Rika says, frowning. I'm almost surprised by how much her opinion already matters to me. I want her to like Tuaca, as if that will also mean she likes me. 'It's OK.' She shrugs, then hands the bottle back to me and sits down on my bed, kicking her feet out in front of her. 'It's so cool that the rest of you are all here now,' she says. 'It's just been me and Dawn here for, like, the last three days, which is a lot of one person, you know? We got here on Thursday, because we're drama students. I'm not sure if we're going to be friends yet. Like, I think I like her, but I'm not sure she's my kind of person, you know?'

She eyes me, and I let out a knowing chuckle, then hate myself a little, because it's not like I've even met Dawn and I'm usually pretty strong-willed. But Rika is here and Dawn isn't, and right now that seems like the most important thing. Rika glances towards the open door, then lowers her voice.

'She was like, the other day, to me, "You're lucky, you'll get to go for all the diverse roles." *Diverse roles!*' She snorts. 'Say what you mean, Home Counties.'

This time, I laugh for real, and Rika grins, like she's pleased.

'She's not that bad,' she says. 'Now I feel like a bitch.' She says this with a laugh, like she doesn't mind too much about this. 'Anyway, you must be a Southerner too, right, like her? I hope I'm not the only Brummie here.'

'I'm from Brighton,' I say.

'That's OK; Brighton's cool,' she says, nodding. 'What are you studying?'

'Pharmacy.'

Her eyebrows shoot up. 'Oh!'

'Not what you expected?'

She laughs. 'No, but I keep forgetting that not everyone is here for, like, the arts. Wow, pharmacy. That's full on, isn't it?'

I feel a jolt of pride at how impressed she looks, but I try hard to keep it off my face. The last thing I want is for her to think I'm up myself. 'I hope not too much! I'll find out, I guess.'

'So, you're sciency,' she says. 'Interesting.'

The way she says this, combined with the way she looks at me, makes something somewhere inside my chest flicker. Oh. Oh, is this . . . ? Wait, is she being flirty, or just friendly?

The flicker transforms into a wave of anxiety. How am I meant to tell? Is there some secret sapphic code I should know? What if she's giving me a signal and I just don't realize because I'm so dense? I came out this summer, voicing something I'd known for a while, but I don't have much experience in living the actual bi life, at least not in reality instead of just my head. And by 'don't have much', I mean I literally don't have any.

'I really hope we get a good mix in the flat,' Rika is saying, and her voice is so ordinary that I relax. I'm being stupid; this is just a normal, platonic, first-day-of-uni flatmate chat. 'One of my friends started at her uni last week and she says everyone she's living with is doing some version of an English degree. Anyway!' She claps her hands to her thighs and stands up. 'Let's go.'

I follow her out of my room and down the hall to the kitchen, where a similarly tall girl with long, caramel-gold waves of hair is sprawled across two chairs, talking to someone. She sits up when we walk in.

'Hey!' she calls, presumably to Rika, judging by the familiarity in her voice. Her eyes fall on me and her smile brightens. 'Hello!'

'Hi,' I say. 'I'm Rosie.'

'Hi, Rosie!' she sings out, then laughs, shaking her head. 'Sorry. I'm just really excited that everyone's arriving. I'm Dawn. I was talking to Jack.' She points at a boy standing by the cupboards, an awkward smile on his face. 'His parents are still here, so he can't come with us. Let's go.'

The three of us head out of the flat and into the sunshine together to find the poster sale. There's so much energy in the air that it's making me feel buzzy, like my nerves are on tiptoe, trying to reach . . . what? I don't even know. Hundreds and hundreds of people my age, all united in this moment, this first day of uni, first day of the rest of our lives. I want to bottle it. Distil it. Drink it with vodka when I need a shot of adrenaline.

'Oh my God,' Dawn is saying, all of her attention on Rika, 'I was talking to Tammy, and she said that all of her flat, like *all* of them, are science types. No arts! Except Pax, of course, but he doesn't count if he's her boyfriend, does he?'

'Boyfriend? Are they a couple already? I thought they'd just slept together.'

'That's what I mean.'

'It's Freshers. I bet they'll both sleep with at least two other people this week. Especially Tammy. Definitely the type.'

Dawn laughs, and Rika grins, and neither of them tells me who Tammy or Pax are – I deduce they must be fellow drama students – or asks me what I think. Which I guess makes sense, given that I'm not a drama student, but still. Also, for all Rika said about not being sure if Dawn was her 'kind of person', they seem like they're proper friends already. They're talking like friends, laughing like friends. Bitching like friends.

'I hope we get some good options in our flat,' Dawn says.

'I don't,' Rika says. 'My sister said, number one rule: don't hook up with flatmates. It just gets messy.'

'Convenient, though,' Dawn says, and they both laugh again. She looks at me. 'What do you think, Rose? Are flatmates off-limits for one-night stands?'

'Rosie,' I say, and her face flickers, like I've reached out and pulled her hair.

'Rosie,' she corrects herself, her voice slightly flatter than before.

'Messy is probably an optimistic way to describe it,' I say, shrugging. 'You have to live with them for the rest of the year. Don't shit where you eat, right?'

Dawn makes a face, like, *Thanks for that image*, but Rika laughs. '*Right*,' she says. '*Exactly*.'

The poster sale seems to involve a lot of boxes and a lot of fellow freshers, all talking slightly too loudly, occasionally laughing maniacally, high on the excitement and anxiety of pure potential. I lose Rika and Dawn in the crowd as I rifle through the MOVIES section, dithering over a poster before deciding against it. I end up with three posters tucked under my arm: one, a map of the world, which seems like a student necessity; one, a cartoon periodic table; and one with a cat wearing sunglasses that I can't resist.

'I guess you like cats,' Rika says, when I find them both by the till.

'I hate them,' I say. 'This is to remind me why.' They both look at me blankly. I wait a beat, then say, 'Yes, I like cats. What did you get?'

Rika unfurls a poster of a group of naked women from the back, sitting at a pool, painted in different colours, then says, 'And a *Breakfast at Tiffany's* poster.'

'Classic,' Dawn says, nodding. 'Look what I found!' She shows us a portrait of Marilyn Monroe, crouched forward in a tutu.

'Icon,' Rika says.

'Are they your idols?' I ask, instead of doing what I want to do, which is roll my eyes. (Because I'm trying to be nice.) 'Audrey and Marilyn?'

This seems to work, because they both start talking happily about the two actresses, their inspirations, why they've chosen drama, keeping it up until we get back to our flat, which is fuller and louder than it was when we left. The kitchen door has been wedged wide open, and by the looks of things, everyone I'll be living with for the next nine months has arrived and is here. I feel a rush of what could be excitement or nerves or adrenaline or everything at once shoot through my entire body. This is it. Everyone is here and all the parents are gone. Freshers starts now.

I decide to duck into my room to drop off my posters, taking another gulp of Tuaca on the way, then return to the kitchen with the widest smile I can muster on my face. I try my hardest to keep it in place as I pause in the doorway, suddenly seized by an overwhelming wave of anxiety. There are so many people in this kitchen, and whoever they are, I'll be living with them for the next, what, nine months? Anything could happen. Literally anything. These are *total strangers*.

Oh, fuck, I want to go home. I want to go back to sixth form. No, better. Primary school.

'Rosie!' Dawn calls out, appearing out of the throng and grabbing my hand. I'm not a hand-holder in life, strictly speaking, but believe me when I say I take that hand and hold on tight. 'Come meet everyone,' she commands.

'Ah, the enigma!' This comes from a guy in a Saracens rugby shirt and a grin that is more confident than friendly when Dawn introduces me.

'The enigma?' I repeat, confused.

'I'm Freddie,' he says, almost talking over me. 'Frederick Quentin Chiles, bit of a mouthful, haha, my friends call me FQC, but we'll see if you get to that stage, haha, call me Freddie!' This comes out in a bit of a rush, either like he's said it a few times already or he's practised it in his head.

'The enigma?' I say again.

'You weren't in the Facebook group,' he says.

'Facebook group?' I say, alarmed.

'For the flat,' Dawn says. 'Some people found each other on Facebook after they got their allocation. It's OK, though. It's not a big deal. I mean, even Rika wasn't in it.'

In normal times, I'd laugh at this – *even Rika*, like she's some kind of celebrity already – but I'm too shaken by anxiety to even really notice. Thrown, again, in a way I don't like to be thrown. I have a very vague memory of an invite to a Facebook group that I'd ignored because *who uses Facebook any more*, except that was obviously a mistake, a bonding opportunity I missed out on, a way I could have been more prepared.

'Being an enigma is cool,' Freddie says, nodding at me, half appraisal, half judgement.

Somewhere inside me, the real Rosie says, *Do I care what you think is cool?* But she must be buried quite deep because I'm actually, stupidly, relieved. And I hear myself laugh and say, 'All right, I'll take it, then.'

My other flatmates are Matteo (accounting and finance), Marieke (law), Inga (also law – they have clearly already bonded) and not one, not two, but three Jacks. The rest of us spend far too long talking about how we are going to 'tell them apart', as if they look remotely similar, which they don't. Early in the evening, we decide they'll be Jack One, Jack Two and Jack Three. By 7 p.m., they're Geology Jack, Business Jack and Maths Jack. By the time we are all ready to go out for our first club night on campus – the girls ducking out to change while the boys carry on talking loudly in our absence – they are Jackanory, Flapjack and Maths Jack.

And then we're out of the flat and into the dizzying madness of our first night of Freshers, and every coherent thought I have is buried under it all. It's like everything I'd expected, hoped for and dreaded all those times I'd dreamed about what Freshers Week would be like. Loud, manic, giddy, magic, terror, excitement.

I meet so many people that I know even in the moment I won't remember. I dance with total strangers. When I say my name to a blonde girl wearing a trilby by the bar, she screams, 'THAT'S MY NAME, TOO!' with such pure joy that when she hugs me, I hug her back. She tells me we're name soulmates, that we're destined to be best friends, but then it's my turn at the bar and I shout out something even I don't hear or understand about beers and shots, and when I turn around the other Rosie has disappeared, and I don't see her again.

Such is the madness of the night. It's as disorientating as it is exhilarating. At one point, when the two of us lose the rest of the group, Dawn grabs my hand in the crowd and shouts – she has to shout, because we can barely hear ourselves think – 'Don't let go!' with what sounds like real panic. I clutch her hand tightly in response until we find a pocket of space near one of the bars in the corner where we can breathe, and she wraps me up in the kind of suffocating hug I usually hate and shrieks, 'Are you as fucking terrified as me?' right into my ear.

'Yes!' I yell back. 'Fucking terrified!'

She laughs, then starts to cry. Right on my shoulder. 'I broke up with my boyfriend to come here,' she tells me, the words a slightly slurred whimper. 'I wanted to be free to, like, be free. You know?' She looks at me, her eyes expectant under the tears. Oh, fuck, she wants me to comfort her. Say something like, *Aw, I'm here, babe.* And hug her.

'Yeah,' I say. I look around, hoping to see Rika or someone appearing out of the swarming mass of drunken freshers, but there's no one. Just one of the bar staff, who is taking what must be some kind of break in the same air pocket we've found, judging by the cup of water in one hand and a phone in the other. Even though Dawn is almost howling now, she's completely ignoring us, tapping away at her phone screen, her shoulders slightly hunched away from the noise.

'Yeah?' Dawn yells. I can't even remember what she's upset about. I might be more drunk than I'd realized. 'Am I going to be OK?'

'I don't know,' I say, shrugging. Dawn looks at me in clear bafflement, and I remember that she doesn't know me and my bluntness, that this isn't how I'm meant to react. But I'm really not the *I'm here, babe* type. I offer, helpfully, 'I don't know you, remember?'

The bar girl with her cup of water looks up, catches my eye, and laughs. Dawn looks at me like I've just kicked a puppy.

'Yes,' I yell, probably too late. 'Yes, you're going to be OK.'

Dawn starts crying again. I roll my eyes at the bar girl and we share a grin before she pushes her phone back into her pocket, squares her shoulders and disappears into the crowd.

'Where's Rika?' Dawn asks, oblivious to my moment of connection with someone I will never see again.

'Good idea,' I say. 'Let's go find her.'

Later, when the music has faded to a dull throb deep in my ears, after Flapjack has vomited spectacularly down the stairs of our building and Rika has hugged and comforted and 'aww, babe'd' Dawn in exactly the way I hadn't, I lie on my bed under a slightly spinning ceiling and scroll through the photos I've taken – increasingly erratic in angle and subject matter – until I scroll too far and find myself back in the summer with my two best friends, all three of us on the beach, and I start to cry for literally no reason at all. It's like all my emotions have been on such high alert all day that now, in the quiet stillness of this new, unfamiliar room, they've finally burst out of me in the kind of tears I don't usually cry. Brighton feels, in this moment, very far away.

A little voice says, somewhere far off in the depths of my mind, *I don't think I like it here*, which confuses me even in my drunkenness because it comes out of nowhere and isn't even true. A real voice, somewhere far off in the flat, yells, 'I'm fucking bladdered, Nora!'

I close my eyes. I will the sound of seagulls into my ears. I go to sleep.

2

I wake up the next morning nervous, excited, determined and, miraculously, not hungover. I must be the only one because I'm alone in the kitchen, my first stop of the day, eating cereal as I look out over the grass and the lake.

My induction for my course, my first official academic *thing*, doesn't start until after lunch, so I'm planning to spend the morning exploring, hopefully with my flatmates, but when no one appears for a while, I head out on my own.

The campus is busier than I'd expected – it's a bit of a relief to know I'm not the only early bird – with a buzz of the same kind of nervous excitement I can feel in my chest. I get a coffee and wander around, trying to navigate myself. I know it's natural to not have my bearings yet, being that I haven't even been here for twenty-four hours, but I'm impatient for this unfamiliar part to be over. I want to know this place already, to feel confident and comfortable.

I last another ten minutes before I give up on trying to be bold and independent and head back to my flat so I can find some people to hang out with. And then it takes me much longer than that to actually find my way back, because I take a wrong turn down the confusing maze of concrete corridors three times before I end up on the right staircase. In fact, by the time I make it to the door of my flat and let myself in, I actually feel a little bit panicky. It's a relief to walk into the kitchen and see some of my flatmates already there, scattered around the table and chairs.

'Hi!' Rika says, from where she's perched, knees up to her chin, right on the table. 'Have you been out already?'

'Yeah,' I say, nonchalant. 'Exploring.'

'Early bird,' she says, somehow managing to sound both impressed and judgemental at the same time.

'That's me,' I say. 'What are you guys up to today?'

'We're going to check out the Freshers Fair,' Dawn says. 'We're timing it for lunchtime because apparently there's free pizza. Want to come?'

'Yeah, that sounds cool,' I say. 'I've got an induction thing at two.'

She nods. 'Me and Rika have got drama stuff, too. We won't be done until six. But we'll all go out again tonight, yeah? Not sure what the club night is.'

'UV party,' Freddie says immediately. I wonder if he's got the club nights memorized. 'White shirts and glow paint.'

'Cool,' Rika says. 'Day sorted, then.'

It's good to have a plan, but the nervous energy I'd woken up with doesn't dissipate all day. Not when we're exploring the Freshers Fair – which is a sensory overload to such a degree that I actually have to go and stand outside by myself to breathe, blaming it on a phantom phone call from my mother – and not when we all go our separate ways and the campus once again balloons into a labyrinth of concrete corridors and I lose my way *again*, and especially not when I walk into the gigantic lecture theatre and sit down for my first induction session for my literal degree.

People around me seem to be chattering away as if they already know each other, which I try to tell myself is some kind of trick of perception and can't possibly be the reality. I try to talk to the person next to me, who is monosyllabic, then silent.

'Welcome!' the course director, Dr Sam Davenhill, says in greeting, lifting his arms wide as if to take all of us in. 'And congratulations! You made it.'

Everyone cheers, and for a moment I forget my own anxiety and cheer along with them, and it's brilliant. One pure second of, *Yes! I made it!*

'Everyone in this room,' he continues when we calm down, 'is a future pharmacist. Well, almost everyone. Statistically, some of you will decide to go on a different path with your degree, or maybe even switch degrees, or give up on university altogether.' He gives an elaborate shrug. Someone laughs nervously. 'But let's just start with today, shall we? Welcome to the MPharm degree, freshers. Let's talk about the rest of the year.'

I have to keep pinching myself. Literally pinching myself, at the skin around my wrist. I really am here; this isn't a dream. Those lab reports he's describing, the tutorials, the problem-based learning, the calculations – I'm going to have to do all those things, in real life. I try to visualize it all, like I'm sure I did a lot before I got here, but it just feels . . . blurry. Which is weird, because shouldn't it be getting clearer, now I'm actually here?

Life in the overwhelm, I think, then write it down, because it seems like a cool phrase and I want to save it for when I can text it to Caddy during her own Freshers Week in a few days' time. Maybe I could say it to one of my flatmates, but I already get the impression that they might just think it's a bit stupid. I'm not sure we're really on the same kind of level. Which is a shame, because they're meant to be my built-in best friends, aren't they? Maybe I just need to try harder.

The second club night is just as frenetic and manic as the first. This time, I lose every one of my flatmates by midnight, but it doesn't seem to matter in the moment because I'm screaming along to Queen with a group of total strangers that I'm convinced are going to be my best friends and who, by morning, I'll have forgotten all about. When it's time to go back to my flat, I forget where it is, let alone how to get there, and end up crying to a security guard – burly, impatient, Scottish, kind – who transports me along the concrete corridor and to the top steps of my building, where we both encounter Matteo and Freddie, sharing a joint.

'Oh,' Matteo says.

'Shit,' Freddie says.

'Be a bit more subtle, eh, lads?' the security guard says, then leaves us to it.

'Which one are you again?' Matteo asks, eyeing me.

'The Enigma,' I say with a resigned sigh. 'Night, guys.'

And that's Monday done.

3

The rest of Freshers Week unfolds in a loud, confusing, disorientating blur. I don't ever remember a time when I was being so sand-blasted with such unrelenting *NEW!!!* New people, new city, new rules, new no-rules, new *everything*. There are multiple introductions every day – to people, to my school of study, to my personal tutor, to coursemates. And so many things to register for – my campus card, the library, the gym, the medical centre – to the point that I get bored of saying my own name. Amidst all the newness, the only points of familiarity are the photos on the wall of my room: my beaming friends, my mother, my cat. A postcard of the burned-out Brighton West Pier. Sometimes, I glance down and realize I'm clutching my phone like it's some kind of life raft.

I go out every night, because that's what you're supposed to do, right? That's when I seem to spend the most time with my flatmates, because our daytime activities of introductory lectures and welcome activities seem to contradict each other almost entirely. Even our lunchtimes don't overlap. I try my hardest to make up for lost time in the evenings, when we're having dinner in the kitchen or pre-drinking together, and sometimes I feel like I'm making progress, but then Freddie will call me the Enigma again and I'll try to smile but feel, instead, like I'm sinking into myself.

When we're out, we all get drunk too quickly and fall into the relief of lost inhibitions, which is great until the morning, when it's all a bit awkward, actually, and I can't even remember anything we talked about, except that once I told them I was bisexual, which I regret not because I want to keep it a secret, but because it's all they seem to remember about me, which feels strange.

By Thursday, I'm exhausted. I feel like I'm running on fumes. But I can't be exhausted, because it's the busiest day of the week for me: three course-related lectures, an hour each, spaced over the day, and an extra introductory talk from the Pharmacy Society. Tonight, there's a cowboy-themed club night on campus – rumour has it that this night is meant to be the best, and messiest, night of Freshers Week – and I'm going to go, even though all I really want to do is sleep.

I spend the day with half of my head already fast-forwarded to the evening, even as I diligently take notes during the lecture on the role of the pharmacist in healthcare and cheer obediently with all the other MPharm freshers during the talk from the Pharmacy Society, when the two reps – Jade and Nilesh – welcome us with cheesy but sweetly self-aware whoops. Jade, who looks vaguely familiar, though I can't figure out why, is wearing an incongruous leather jacket, sunglasses pushed up over her hair, and has an amazing regional accent I can't quite place. Whenever Nilesh is talking, she puts her hands in her pockets and looks up at us, making eye contact with people, smiling warmly. The enthusiasm that the two of them demonstrate for pharmacy finally ignites the excitement I've been waiting to feel all week.

This is the feeling I try to hold on to when the evening really does come around, and I knock on the door to Dawn's room and ask if she and Rika – who is already sprawled across the bed, face half made – want to get ready altogether. My first few nights in Norwich, I've been getting ready on my own because I've been such a maelstrom of anxiety, but I'm determined to stamp that right down tonight. I need the fun of dressing up with friends. I need friends.

'Of course!' Dawn says, gesturing for me to come in. She's

sitting cross-legged on her desk chair, make-up strewn across the desk in front of her, her face a glistening sheen of moisturizer. 'Gracing us with your presence! We feel so honoured.'

'Honoured,' Rika echoes, without even looking up from where she's focusing her attention on the mirror and the fake eyelashes she's applying.

'I'm sorry I'm not around much,' I say, trying to figure out where I should sit without making it too obvious that I'm trying to figure out where I should sit.

'We're kidding,' Dawn says. She's smiling, which means she must mean it, so I try to relax, even as I feel a pang of sadness that I'm not part of the *we* they already are.

'*I* wasn't kidding,' Rika says, her voice a drawl that she somehow manages to pull off without sounding ridiculous. 'I do feel honoured.' As she speaks, she shifts her feet so I can sit down on the bed beside her, all without looking at me.

Rika is extremely hard to read.

'What have you been up to today?' Dawn asks. 'Did you sign up for any clubs at the Sports Fair?'

I shake my head. I had planned to join the badminton club, but the Friday session clashed with my timetable, and the Sunday session clashed with my part-time job hours. The realization had been another tiny glitch in my plan for my student life, the kind of thing that shouldn't really bother me, but does, a lot.

'*None?*' Dawn says, like she's shocked.

'Not everyone is Sporty Spice,' Rika says, which is the kind of outdated reference only someone as stunning as Rika could possibly pull off. 'Some of us don't like getting sweaty.'

'Even you joined Ultimate Frisbee,' Dawn says.

'Because you made me,' Rika replies. 'And you don't get sweaty playing *Frisbee*.' She turns to me, bronzer brush held aloft in one hand. 'Dawn signed up for *four clubs*. Can you believe that?

She's doing Drama and English Lit and she joined *four clubs*. And about six different societies.'

'You're exaggerating,' Dawn says, her eye-roll not quite distracting from her pinkening cheeks. 'And you only do uni once, right? I don't want to miss anything. Plus, I want to have as many chances as possible to make friends.'

'Smart,' I say. It is smart. And I feel stupid in comparison. Maybe I should look up the clubs and see if any of them fit around my schedule. I could learn how to play touch rugby or something, right? Maybe? I have a sudden flash of myself running through the mud in the rain, clutching a rugby ball. *No.*

'Thank you,' Dawn says. 'See?' She points at Rika. 'Rosie gets it.'

'Rosie didn't sign up for anything,' Rika replies. 'Rosie is just being nice.' She eyes me, then grins. 'How are you, anyway? Where do you go during the day? You're, like, never around.'

'Yeah, my course is pretty full on,' I say. 'But that's just how it is, right?'

'Already, though?' Dawn says, making a face into the mirror. 'It's still Freshers Week.'

'I know,' I say. 'But there's a lot to cover, I guess?'

'Same for us,' Rika says. 'But that's why we started earlier than most other courses. What's your actual timetable going to be like?'

'Busy,' I say. 'Full days of lectures sometimes, and the lab sessions will take a whole day, too, but they're not as frequent. It'll be about twenty-five contact hours a week, on average, maybe? Plus all the work, obviously.'

'I mean, I guess that's how it'll be for us, too,' Rika says. 'Yeah, we won't be in a *lab*, or whatever, but we'll have studio time most days. We're still going to hang out and have fun. Uni's not just about studying.'

'I didn't say it was,' I say, because I didn't. 'I think theatre's a bit different, though.'

I don't mean this in a bad way – I really don't – but I see her face flicker before she glances over at Dawn with eyes saying, *Did you hear that?* and I realize it's come out like I was making some kind of a point about their degree.

'It's all about the balance, isn't it?' Dawn says. 'Like, if you *just* go to uni for the course, why even bother? You have to make time for a social life. All the memories you'll end up with, they're just as important as the degree, right? I want both.'

'Definitely,' Rika says, nodding. She looks at me. 'Don't you think?'

'Sure,' I say. 'I'm a bit worried about all the work, to be honest. Apparently it gets quite intense.' I say this to be generous, hoping they won't think that *I* think I'm somehow better than them, but regret it when Rika nods, almost in satisfaction, like I've proved her right. 'Too late to change now,' I add, as lightly as I can.

'You could if you wanted,' Dawn says, turning to give me a helpful smile. 'I bet you could transfer.'

'It's not about that,' I say. 'I want to be a pharmacist. I've wanted it for years.' This isn't true – I'd never even thought of pharmacy until I was flicking through my first university prospectus in my sixth-form library, and there it was, like the answer to everything. But Dawn doesn't need to know that. I add, 'And I like a challenge, anyway.' I shrug, smiling my most friendly smile. 'Honestly, I'm not really the arts type.'

Dawn sits back, shrugging. 'Fair!'

'What's the arts type?' Rika asks, too casually. The kind of casual that has a hard edge; a challenge.

'Flowy dresses,' I say, leaning back to try and see myself in the mirror as I slide my favourite black headband into place. 'Silk scarves. Reading Jane Austen on a park bench.'

Dawn laughs, and for a second I think Rika is going to carry on frowning, but instead she laughs too, then says, 'With a parasol. And a picnic basket,' and I finally relax.

We meet up with the boys in the kitchen, then all head out together, stopping off at the student bar first to do a round of shots, and then another in quick succession. By the time we get into the actual club, I've already lost track of time, buzzy with tequila, and I find myself having an actual conversation with Freddie for the first time. About cats, of all things. He must be OK, I've decided, if he likes cats. I think I actually say this, because he laughs and puts his hand to his chest, like, *Why, thank you!*

We move from dance floor to bar and back again who knows how many times, separating off into twos and threes, finding each other again. Dawn has found a cowboy hat from somewhere and is line dancing on her own in the middle of a circle of cheering guys, and I'm just wondering whether I should rescue her when Freddie swoops in beside her and joins in. It is, in that moment, the funniest thing I've ever seen, and I'm simultaneously trying to film it and doubling over laughing when there's a hand at my arm, and I look up to see Rika beside me.

'I need some air,' she announces. 'Come with?'

It might be a question, or a command. I must be under the Rika spell because I follow her without hesitation. We go outside to the main steps of the square, which is cooler and fresher but still loud and full of other drunk students. Rika pulls me down onto one of the steps beside her – until that moment, I hadn't realized her hand was still on my arm – and passes me one of the two bottles she's holding. 'Cheers,' she says.

'This is very odd,' I say.

Her perfect eyebrows go up. 'Why?'

'I don't know,' I say, sipping at the bottle. Corona, just like hers. 'You. Me. Here.'

'You think too much,' she says.

'Or the right amount,' I counter. 'And you just think it's too much.'

'Fuck me,' she says, rolling her eyes. 'You're welcome for the Corona, by the way.'

'Thanks,' I say, belatedly. 'How come you wanted air?' She shrugs but doesn't reply, so I say, 'Didn't you want to line dance with Dawn?'

'Freddie was line dancing with Dawn,' she says, and I wonder if the flat delivery of this fact is due to her own competitiveness or if she actually likes Freddie. 'What's it to you, anyway?'

'I'm making conversation,' I say, then add, 'I don't actually care.'

This makes her laugh. She shakes her head, appraising me with one sweep of her eyes. 'You're kind of a bitch, you know that?' she says, taking a swig from her bottle.

'Am I?'

'Yeah!' Something about the way she says it makes me laugh, and she's laughing too, and everything is fine and OK. 'Like, people say I'm a bitch, but you're a bitch in, like, a different way.'

'What way am I?'

'Dunno,' Rika says, then laughs again. Her eyes flicker up over my face, down my body and back again. 'You're a bit cold.'

'And you're what?' I say. 'Hot?'

'Oh my God,' Rika says, pressing a hand to her chest. 'You think I'm hot?' She pretends to fan herself. 'My, my.'

'Not like that,' I say. 'I mean, yes, like that. You are very hot. But you're a hot bitch, and I'm a cold bitch? Is that what you're saying?'

'I don't know,' Rika says. 'I've lost track. Probably?'

We both start laughing again, even though there's a thought somewhere inside me, buried under the alcohol, that this isn't actually a very nice conversation. But she's drunk, and I'm drunk, so it probably doesn't matter.

'You should loosen up a bit,' Rika says. 'Like how you are now.'

'Oh, you like me now?' I say. '*This* is OK with you? Thank God.'

She laughs again. 'Ooh, I like this you. Savage.'

'So, let me get this straight,' I say. 'You want me savage, loose and . . . hot?'

'Hey, you said the hot thing, not me,' Rika says, shrugging with both her arms, causing Corona to splash over my hair and bare shoulder. 'Oh, shit! Sorry.' She rubs at my shoulder, like she's trying to wipe it off. 'I got you all wet.' She snorts with laughter. 'Whoops.' Her arm flops down around my shoulders. 'Hi.'

I raise an eyebrow at her. 'Are you flirting with me right now?'

'I don't know.' Rika squints at me, then grins. 'Maybe. Are *you* flirting with *me*?'

'I don't know,' I say. 'Maybe.'

'You *should* know,' Rika says. 'You're the bi one.'

So she is thinking about it. The bi bit of me; the important bit. (At least, right now.) I knew it, but hearing her say it . . . The way her mouth is curved. The glint in her eye.

'Me?' I say. 'What are you?'

'How rude,' Rika says. '*What* am I.' She tuts, making a face at me that crinkles her nose and pushes out both her lips. She grins again, returning to normal, sipping at her Corona. 'Here. That's what I am.'

'Good,' I say.

'Good?'

'Yeah, good.'

'How good?'

'Oh my God, shut—'

And then she's kissing me. It's happening. She is kissing me. Her arm, still around my shoulder, has pulled me into her in the same moment that she moved her head, and her lips are moving against mine and her tongue is – *fuck* – her tongue *is*, and she tastes like Corona and I am kissing a girl I am kissing a girl I am kissing Rika.

It's a very full-on kiss. The last time I kissed anyone like this, it was a guy, all stubbly chin and aftershave, in his bedroom, in private. It felt pretty good, then, but this? It doesn't just feel *good*. It feels *amazing*. *I* feel amazing. Like I've cracked open the lid of myself. Like I'm expanding, growing, in a way I never even knew I could.

When we break apart, there's a smile on my face that I can't contain. One I don't even want to contain. I let out a breathless laugh and Rika laughs too, her eyes, softer than I've seen them before, sweeping over my face.

'That's cute,' she says, almost quietly, touching her thumb to the corner of my mouth. 'You're cute.'

No one in my life has ever called me cute, not even when I was a kid and cute-sized. Little My, my mum used to call me, after the girl in the Moomins that liked biting people. Snarly, not cute. Never cute.

I'm not sure what the moment is about to turn into – I want to kiss her again, but I hesitate, first-girl-kiss anxiety slowing my reactions. She looks sideways at me, then laughs again. Is she laughing at me? Us? Everything?

'Let's get another tequila,' she says, getting to her feet and brushing off her jeans. She holds out a hand to me and I take it, our hands gripping together for one long moment before I'm steady on my feet and she releases me, smiling a very Rika smile, like an imperial cat.

We end up doing a round of tequila slammers at the bar with Dawn and Freddie, who appear seemingly out of nowhere, whooping for shots. When I slam my shot glass down, Rika is already dancing off into the crowd, and within a drunken second, we're all attempting to line dance to 'Cotton Eye Joe' and it's the best time I've had since I first got here, all that nervous energy I've been carrying around with me transformed into pure *fun*. It's all so good I don't want it to end.

It doesn't even matter that Rika and I don't spend any more time together that night, that we all stay together in a shrieking, laughing crush all the way back to the flat. When I let myself into my room, joining in for once with the 'Goodnight!' bellows around the flat, I'm grinning so hard my face actually hurts. I'm too high on drunken exhilaration to just lie down and sleep, so I call Caddy, but she doesn't answer. I try Suze, who does, and gabble at her for what I will in the morning discover was thirty-five minutes. I tell her I love her, many times, and each time she laughs and tells me she loves me too.

'You sound happy,' she says.

'I'm *so* happy!' I say.

I don't remember what else we talked about, or even saying goodbye and hanging up. When I wake up in the morning, I'm still wearing the same clothes from the night before, no longer drunk, but not too hungover, either. I have a shower, eat a banana, then head out to the two hour workshop I have that morning – an introduction to teaching methods – my bag slung casually over my shoulder, a smile on my face. My workshop group and I get sandwiches together for lunch after, and though we don't exactly bond, it's still nice. The conversation follows the same pattern as the rest of the week – *What A Levels did you do? Where else did you apply? Where are you from? What accommodation do you live in?* I'm so used to this conversation by now that I've started having it in my sleep.

When I head back to my flat with new phone numbers in my phone and a workshop WhatsApp group already underway, I'm feeling pretty good about myself. It may have taken until Friday, but maybe I'm finally getting the hang of Freshers Week.

I let myself back into my flat, already debating with myself whether I should go and knock on Rika's door to see her, or wait to see if she comes to find me, when I hear her voice from the kitchen and head straight in, my heart bouncing, hopeful, in my chest.

'Hey!' Rika calls, her grin wide. It's a friendly grin, but I still find myself thrown by it, though I'm not immediately sure why. She's leaning against the table next to Dawn, who is sitting cross-legged on top of it, eating cereal. Freddie is sprawled across the bench by the window, phone in hand.

'Hey,' I say, instantly regretting my decision to come in here. I should have waited until I could guarantee it was just the two of us, but it's too late now. Just to have something to do with my hands, I go to my food cupboard and pull out the first thing I touch, which is a box of cereal bars. That'll do. I unwrap one at random, taking a bite so I don't have to say anything else.

'Oh my God, me and Rosie got so wild last night,' Rika says to Dawn, who looks at me, eyebrows lifting. That's when I realize what's bothering me about the way Rika is smiling. It's friend friendly. Almost determinedly friend friendly. It's not for me; it's for everyone watching. Somewhere in my chest, my heart gives a confused little kick.

'Oh yeah?' Dawn says.

'Yeah!' Rika says. 'Ro, didn't we?'

Ro. I have never in my life been a 'Ro'. I'm not a Ro. My friends call me Roz.

But it's better than Enigma, isn't it?

'Did we?' I reply, tapping a contemplative finger to my chin.

If she wants to make something that could have been ours into some fun story for everyone, I'll play along, but I'm not going to make it as easy as she clearly thinks I'm going to. 'I'm not sure I remember. It's a bit of a blur.'

'Shut up, no it isn't,' Rika says, laughing. 'You, me, the square, the Corona . . .'

Dawn is looking between us, part baffled, part suspicious.

'You don't forget a kiss like that,' Rika adds, fanning herself dramatically. She grins at me, and now there *is* something conspiratorial in it, something just for us. Which would be nice, but it's not something I'm sure I understand. 'I knew you were fun, really, Ro.'

I look at Dawn in the same moment she looks at me, and for a second I know that we're both thinking the same thing, which is that neither of us have any idea what to do in this moment. Not what to say, or how to feel, or what to do with our faces.

'Wow, Caron,' Freddie says, sitting up straighter, appraising me. 'I didn't know you had it in you.'

It's the first time I think he's called me anything but the Enigma. I didn't even know he knew what my surname was.

'What can I say?' I shrug. 'I'm a constant surprise.'

The longer this goes on, the more I want to cry.

'I can't believe I missed all the fun,' Dawn says, jumping lightly off the table and heading to the sink, empty bowl in hand. 'Save some for me, next time.'

'If we can tear you away from Freddie,' Rika says, with a significance in her voice that I don't understand but that makes Dawn falter in step, glancing back at her. Rika smiles, wide and friendly.

'Hey, I want in, too,' Freddie says.

'No guys allowed,' I say, proud of how light and steady my voice is. 'I've got another lecture. See you guys.'

My lecture isn't actually for another hour, but I don't care. I just want out. I walk around the campus aimlessly until it feels like I can be early to the lecture without seeming weird about it. I'm glad to have something to focus on that isn't that horrible feeling you get in your throat when you want to cry and absolutely cannot, will not, cry. The lecture is on pharmacy calculations, the first dip into what the rest of the course is going to be like, and I concentrate so hard that when I pack up my stuff at the end, I realize I can't remember any of it.

I buy myself a bag of doughnut bites from the on-campus food shop and eat them all, one after the other, dusting sugar methodically off my fingers after each one, then look at my phone to see a message from Suze: **On my break! Call me!!**

Oh God. I'd completely forgotten that I'd called her last night. I feel a white-hot flush of pure, agonizing humiliation. It would be bad enough if the only person who knew how excited I'd been was me, but I'd called Suze and told her. I'd been giddy, even. I *never* get giddy. And now I'd have to admit that it was nothing, that I'd got carried away like a kid with a crush. I can't bear it. I want to shrivel up in the cringe and die.

Sure enough, barely a minute into the call, Suze says, brightly, 'How are things with the girl? The one you kissed?'

A stab at my heart. I close my eyes and twist one of my curls around my fingers as tight as it will go, until it stings. 'Oh, that was just a one-off.'

'Oh! OK, cool.' She's quiet for a moment, like she's listening to the silence. I expect her to move on, but then she says, 'Are you OK?'

'Yeah, fine,' I say. 'Why, don't I sound OK?'

There's another pause on her end of the line. 'You sound like Roz.' I wait for more. 'I miss you.'

'Gross,' I say. 'I don't miss you.'

She laughs. '*Now* you sound OK. And definitely like my Roz.'

'I do miss you,' I say, because even though I know she knows I was joking, it doesn't feel right to not say it. 'Tell me everything about Brighton. How's the weather? How's work?'

We have a nice conversation, the two of us, almost 200 miles away from each other, but when we hang up I find myself feeling confused, maybe even a little guilty. Why wasn't I honest with her about what had happened with Rika? Asked for her advice, even? Or, at least, her support? What's the point in a phone call with one of my best friends if I don't tell her things like this? I shake off the unease, pushing my phone back into my pocket. Suze and I have never been the type of friends who lean on each other like that. That's what Caddy is for, right? Not that I can tell Caddy about any of this, not with her own Freshers Week just about to start. I don't want to give her any reason to be nervous, not any more than I know she already will be.

Anyway. I'm fine, aren't I? So the kiss with Rika didn't mean what I thought it would, so this week hasn't gone how I thought it would, so I'm not feeling like I thought I would. So what? I can adjust. I'm still here, aren't I? I'm still doing it. That's what matters.

Tonight is the Welcome Ball, the highlight of Freshers, the pinnacle of the week, something I'd imagined so many times over the last summer. I bought my dress for it in a boutique in North Laine in Brighton on a sunny July afternoon with my two best friends in tow. We weren't even looking for a dress; we were just spending an afternoon together. Suze had only just moved back to Brighton, and it still felt amazing to spend time as a trio again after being apart for two years, even as I knew that it would be over soon, with Caddy and me so close to leaving ourselves. It had been Suze who'd wanted to go into the boutique, and I'd seen the dress while I was waiting for her and Caddy to get bored trying on ballgowns. A vintage swing dress, burgundy with black detail, in my size.

I'm quite short, which is maybe why I've always found it hard to find dresses that suit me. This one? It felt like it was made for me. Suze even found a silver and pearl hairpiece in the reduced box to go with it. She assured me I could wear boots with the dress, that they would make it look cool. I'd stood in that boutique wearing that dress and the hairpiece, my best friends wolf-whistling at me, and felt happy. Really, really happy. Excited, like I was in the process of my life changing in all the right ways.

Now, I'm sitting on Dawn's bed, a mug of Prosecco in hand, faking a smile. The dress still looks perfect. The boots do look cool. I've sent selfies to Caddy and Suze, who sent back flame emojis. But nothing feels right.

Rika, who is wearing a teal Grecian maxi dress and looks frankly stunning, insists on taking multiple pictures with the two of us, her arm tight around my neck, pulling me close on one side, Dawn on the other. She kisses us both on the cheek and says, with a flourish, raising her own mug of Prosecco into the air, 'To Freshers!' We whoop and hug and dance off towards the kitchen together, and everything about it is exactly how I'd imagined, except that it feels so fake, so empty. I wonder if it feels real to them, or if they're just going along with it too. Does it even matter?

The actual Welcome Ball is an anticlimax. To be fair, this is probably more to do with my mood than the actual event. Everyone around me seems to be drunker than I am, but when I try to catch up, I just end up feeling ill. By 10 p.m., I've got the beginnings of a headache, and by 11, it's throbbing, and I can't keep a smile on my face any more, even a fake one.

I go to the bar to get some water, which is when some guy three times my size comes crashing into me, knocking me onto the sticky, beery floor. There's a howl of laughter from some guys nearby, presumably his friends, but none of them moves to help me up. Someone else near me, a girl, holds out an arm and pulls me up, snapping something at the guys, who start apologizing all over each other, making elaborate sorry gestures at me, their hands clasped under their chins.

There's beer on my beautiful dress and my headpiece has come loose. I shake my head at them, say thank you to the girl, then leave, even though it's not even midnight and I used to think I was fun. I walk back to my flat alone, biting my lip to stop myself crying, messaging Dawn with one hand just in case she happens to notice that I'm not there. In my quiet, still flat, I drink two glasses of water and take a couple of Nurofen, then head to my room.

For the rest of the night, I stay on my bed, watching an old web series adaptation of *Pride and Prejudice* from start to finish, for no reason at all except that it's comfortingly familiar and it stops me from thinking. It also gives me an excuse to cry.

I wake up in the morning in the same position, groggy and disorientated. In the late afternoon, I go to a PharmSoc social and make polite, tired small talk with my polite, tired coursemates, all our social juices clearly, thoroughly drained. I buy a PharmSoc hoodie, eat two lukewarm slices of pizza and leave early.

And that's it, really. That's my Freshers Week, basically done. Did it go how I thought it would? No. But did I enjoy it? Well . . . sort of? Maybe? It already feels like a big, jumbled blur in my head, like there's nothing to anchor a thought on. I guess the thing is that I thought I'd enjoy it more than I have, but now I've experienced the reality of it, I can't even remember why I thought that. Pre-university Rosie already feels like a long time ago.

*

On Sunday, a full week after my arrival, I finally let myself speak to Mum. We've messaged, obviously, but I'd made the decision not to speak to her on the phone, because I was worried about two things happening: one, that hearing her voice would be the final trigger for my overwhelming homesickness/anxiety that I was barely keeping at bay to sweep in, like a tide, and flatten me. And/or the second possibility, the worst one, which was that she'd hear it in my voice and worry about *me*.

'Tell me everything!' she commands. She's already told me that she's sat on her favourite armchair with our cat, Mew – Bartholomew when he's in trouble; Barty when he's being extra cute – on her lap and a cup of tea in one hand. 'Spare no details.'

'You don't want all the details,' I say. I'm sitting on the steps of the main square in the sunshine, hoping the buzz of happy chatter and laughter around me will create exactly the kind of ambience this call needs. 'You want to hear how much alcohol your daughter drank?'

'Lots, I hope,' Mum says. 'Isn't that what Freshers Week is for?'

I laugh, shaking my head. 'Among other things, yes, apparently.'

I tell her about some of the club nights, the first Pharmacy Society social, the Freshers Welcome Ball and then about the lectures I've had so far, the campus, the lab.

'And how is it?' she asks, confusing me until she clarifies. 'I mean . . . *it*. University. Being a student. Is it everything you hoped it would be?'

I'm silent for too long, trying to figure out how to answer. Not because I'm trying to think of a way to lie, but because I really don't know what the truth even is.

'I don't know yet,' I say eventually. 'Still early days. How about you? Are you enjoying having the house all to yourself?'

She laughs. 'Oh yes, I've been having house parties every night. And lots of takeaways.'

I smile into the phone. 'I think we're the wrong way round.'

'It seems like it, doesn't it? Anyway, I've been just fine. Janine was round last night and we drank wine and toasted your brilliance. She says hello.'

'Cool, say hi back from me.' Janine has been Mum's best friend since I first started secondary school, when they met in a flower-arranging-to-help-your-grief class. She's the first real friend I really remember Mum having, and for that reason alone, I love her. 'It's good you're not missing me too much.'

'Oh, that reminds me. I messed up the settings on the washing machine again.'

'How? It's literally pre-programmed.'

'Well, that's the problem – I think I must have accidentally un-pre-programmed it, and then I got a bit flustered and confused. Why do they make those machines so confusing? It should be straightforward.'

'It *is* straightforward.'

'That's easy for you to say!' she says. 'Scientist! University student! Pity your poor, unqualified mother.'

'Just send me a photo of the dial and screen and I'll tell you what to do.'

'Thank you, my love. I'll let you get back to refresher life.'

'Fresher life.'

'What?'

'Fresher. You said refresher.'

'No, I didn't.'

'You did.'

'Well, what does it matter? You know what I meant,' she says, almost a snap, defensive like she gets when I correct her for getting her words mixed up, which is something she does a lot.

'OK, sorry,' I say. 'I'll get back to refresher life.'

There's a pause, like she's trying to decide whether to get annoyed. Then her laugh comes down the phone. 'You do that, Rosie,' she says.

When I hang up, I see six messages waiting for me, all from Caddy, and I smile as I tap at my screen to read them. It's Caddy's first day of Freshers, first day of being a student, and she's kept me up to date with her every thought and feeling since she woke up this morning. Now, it's 2 p.m., so she's reached the point of her first day where she's said goodbye to her family – both her parents and her older sister went with her, because that's the kind of family she has – and is dithering in the empty room she's already sent me multiple photos of – **Trying not to cry!** – psyching herself up to go and knock on doors to introduce herself.

DO IT! I command. And PUT YOUR PHONE AWAY. Don't message me again until you've made six friends. I love you. I miss you. I'm so jealous they all get to meet you xxx

It's a much, much nicer message than I usually send to my friends – much nicer than I usually am in general – but I've never felt so affectionate, being so far away and so worried about her. Caddy is basically family to me, the closest thing I have to a sister. I think her being unhappy at university would be even harder for me to take than *me* being unhappy. That's how protective I feel over her. Caddy's just . . . soft. In a good way, but soft. Easily dented, and prone to being walked over.

EEEEE!!!!!! Send me good friend vibes. I love you too xxxx

I'm about to put my phone away, then change my mind and reopen WhatsApp. I tap out a message to Suze, who I'm worried about just as much. Maybe even more, for totally different reasons.

Rosie:

You doing OK? Xx

Suze:

You mean because I'm abandoned and alone in Brighton, now my two best friends have gone off to live their big old student lives?

Yes.

I'm at work. Some guy just said a girl as pretty as me shouldn't be serving coffee. I'm living my best life, Roz. Who needs a degree? I have coffee beans.

Did the guy say what a girl as pretty as you should be doing instead?

Having coffee with him.

Of course.

I need to go back to work. I'm fine, but miss you both, obvs. Talk later?

Yep! Love you xx

Uni's made you soft, Roz ;) I love you, too xxxxx

I feel so much better – *so much better* – after just a handful of messages with my two best friends, plus the conversation with Mum. Like I'm myself again.

I spend most of the rest of the afternoon in the city centre, because I have an induction at my new job. It's not really a new job, because I worked over the summer at a jewellery shop in Brighton that is part of a bigger chain, including a branch in Norwich, so I've just transferred up here to carry on working part time. The Norwich branch is exactly the same inside as the Brighton branch, even down to the floor layout and where the clock hangs on the wall. It's a comforting kind of familiarity when everything else since I arrived has been so overwhelmingly new.

Caddy has been true to her word, not messaging me at all as the hours pass on her first day in her new life. I message her for an update on the bus back to campus, and she replies in all caps, **I AM SO EXCITED! I FEEL LIKE I MIGHT CRY AND I DON'T KNOW WHY?!!**

This makes me smile. I reply, **It's OK if it's overwhelming! It was for me, too!!**

She replies, **I MEAN IN A GOOD WAY!!!!**

I hesitate, then write, **So did I!**

Immediately after I send it, I feel bad, because I don't lie to Caddy, and why do I think I even need to? I watch the grey ticks turn blue, thinking about adding the truth: **Though also in a bad way, lol, this has all been so much harder than I thought it would be, I miss you so much.**

But I don't.

4

Monday feels like the start of my real university life. Freshers is over, and now it's the start of the routine, the timetable, the predictability. Which is something I'm really, really glad about. I love flipping through my timetable for the next few weeks – helpfully colour-coordinated for me into different modules so I can see, at a glance, whether a lecture will be on pharmacology or medicinal chemistry or medicine management – and being able to see how I'll be spending most of my time. It's reassuring.

OK, maybe that doesn't make me sound like the coolest person in the world, but whatever. Some people like seven straight nights of wild partying; other people enjoy a colourful timetable. I am who I am.

Anyway, I'm determined that this week is going to be the week that I make more friends. I'll get to know my coursemates, and then I'll have friends outside of the flat, and everything will start to feel easier. This is what I'm thinking when I leave my flat at 8.50 a.m. to head to my first lecture of the week and stop to get a coffee on the way to the lecture theatre. When I go to get milk and sugar, I see a girl I recognize from my workshop group.

'Hi,' I say cheerfully. (I know it comes out cheerful, because I make sure it does.) 'You're going to the professionalism intro lecture, right? MPharm?'

The girl looks at me, blinking, like I've walked into a room she was sleeping in and woken her up by yelling in her face. 'Yeah?' she says eventually.

'Cool,' I say, undeterred. 'Me too. I'm Rosie.'

'Laini,' she says. She shakes her head. 'Yeah, I recognize you, actually. Hi. Sorry, I'm so out of it today.'

'Freshers, right?' I say, in my most knowing voice. 'Isn't it just mad?'

And then she bursts into tears. And I mean really bursts. One second she's not crying, and then suddenly she's sobbing. It comes on so fast, she doesn't even get a hand to her face in time.

'Oh, shit,' I say.

'Sorry,' she says, or tries to say. She grabs some napkins and starts rubbing at her face. 'Sorry.'

'It's OK,' I say, when what I should probably do is apologize for being the worst person to cry unexpectedly in front of, because I kind of want to run away. At least when this happened with Dawn, we were both drunk.

'I can't do this,' she says. 'I don't know what I'm doing here. I want to go home.'

I have no idea what I'm meant to do. Should I reassure her that she *can* do this? But what if it isn't true? I don't know her. Maybe she can't.

'It's only the second week,' I say finally. 'It's overwhelming, right? It's meant to be.'

She shrugs, still wiping at her face, sniffling.

Someone behind us gives a small but distinct *ahem*, then steps around us to get to the milk. It's a girl in a belted shirt dress and black boots, clearly a non-fresher – I'm not even sure what gives it away, maybe a particular kind of ease – and I expect, when I move a little out of her way, that she will give Laini an understanding smile, but instead she raises her eyebrows slightly, then says, 'Best to save the breakdown for your bedroom, yeah?'

Laini's distraught expression morphs instantly into one of pure mortification and she turns quickly away, shoulders hunching, head dipping.

'That's really kind, thank you,' I say. 'Really helpful. You have a great day, too.'

The girl rolls her eyes at me, fixing the lid back onto her cup, then walks away without another word.

'What an absolute dickhead,' I say, turning back to Laini.

'See?' Laini responds. 'I'm not cut out for this.'

'Because of *that*?' I ask. 'Oh, please. People are dicks everywhere. Who cares?'

Laini shakes her head. 'I'm going to take her advice and go back to my bedroom.'

'No!' I say. 'We've got the lecture. Come on, we should get going, or we'll be late.'

'I literally don't give a fuck about a lecture,' she says, wiping at her eyes again. 'I hate them.'

'You definitely haven't had enough of them to know that already,' I say.

'I *do*,' she says. 'I definitely know.'

'Well, it's OK if you don't give a fuck about it,' I say. 'But I'm going, so you may as well come with me.'

She hesitates, looking from me to her cup.

'Come on,' I say, picking up my own cup and heading towards the door.

She follows, like I knew she would. This trick has never failed with either Caddy or Suze, and it doesn't fail me now. When I act confident, people follow. It's almost a relief to be reminded that I'm still me.

'Is it obvious I've been crying?' Laini asks me.

Yes. 'No one cares about that,' I say.

We walk up the steps towards the lecture theatre together, which feels nice for me, this first time I've gone to a lecture not on my own, but I don't say so because it doesn't seem like it's a good time. Laini is pulling at her sleeves, taking in long breaths, shaking her head.

'It's really OK,' I say.

She nods. 'It's really OK,' she repeats.

And it is, obviously. I'm wise like that.

The lecture is an introduction to professionalism in pharmacy practice, and though it isn't actually my first lecture, it feels like it is. 9 a.m. in a lecture theatre in my second week of uni. *I am here. This is life now.*

Beside me, Laini stares off blankly to the front of the lecture theatre, occasionally tapping her pen against her notepad, picking at her nails, frowning at the ceiling. After a while, she starts writing and I relax on her behalf, relinquishing my full attention to the lecture. When it's over, I turn to her with a smile as everyone around us starts packing up. The rhythmic flutter of two hundred MacBooks closing at once. 'All good?'

She blinks at me, like she's coming out of a daze. 'Huh?'

'You took notes,' I say, pointing with my pen at her notepad.

'Oh,' she says, looking down. 'A few. But then I was writing out Taylor Swift lyrics.' At the look on my face, she balks. 'This is a lot, OK! And the lecture slides will be online, anyway.' She sighs. 'I don't think I'm cut out for this.'

'Let's get another coffee,' I say.

We go to the Hive together, which turns out to be completely rammed, so we get takeaway cups and go to sit in the main square. She seems to have calmed down properly now, her energy more relaxed, a smile on her face.

'Do you like it here?' she asks me when we've sat down.

I shrug. 'I don't love it yet, but that's OK. It's only been a week. How about you? Do you actually hate it here?'

She sighs again, shaking her head. 'Yeah. I know I'm not meant to say that. My parents get annoyed with me every time I say it. They say I'm not giving it a chance. But I just feel . . . like this is all *wrong*. When I think about being here for another three years,

I feel sick.' Her voice is almost fierce now, her words tumbling out of her mouth, her eyes wet and focused somewhere off past my right shoulder. 'I didn't even want to come to uni. My parents basically made me. They were all, oh, you'll love it once you get there and it'll be the time of your life – they met at uni, so they obviously think it's the best thing ever – and fucking pharmacy, oh my God, I didn't realize it was going to be so much chemistry? I just want to work in a shop and make cakes in my spare time and go on *The Great British Bake Off*. I don't even care if that sounds unfocused or unambitious or whatever else my dad thinks. I love baking cakes. I make *great* cakes. But now I'm here and there's *no oven in my kitchen* and I brought homemade biscuits with me on arrivals weekend for my flatmates and they didn't even eat them? Who doesn't eat biscuits?'

'I would've eaten the biscuits,' I start to say, but she's talking too fast to stop in time to smile.

'And most of my friends either stayed at home to go to Canterbury or just didn't go to uni and I miss them so fucking— Oh, thank you.' She looks embarrassed, suddenly aware of her diatribe. She wipes at her cheeks with the pad of her thumb, trying to smile. 'You're being really nice, thank you.'

'It'll get better,' I say, hoping my voice is as reassuring as I want it to be. 'It's just Freshers. It's overwhelming.'

She eyes me. 'You don't seem overwhelmed.'

'I hide it well.'

She smiles like I'm joking, but I meant it. If there was one single word I'd use for my uni experience so far, 'overwhelming' would be it. I've never felt so overwhelmed in my entire life, and I once had to talk my mother through a panic attack in the middle of a motorway at eighty-five miles per hour.

'Do you like the course?' she asks.

I want to say an immediate and enthusiastic *yes*! But I hesitate, because it doesn't feel true. 'I think it's too early to say either way.'

'Sure, but, like, don't you think it's a lot of chemistry? Looking at the rest of the semester, I mean. You can see it. So much chemistry!'

'Yeah, but I like that. Chemistry was my favourite subject at A Level.'

'Really?' She makes a face, curling her lip. 'Why?'

'Because it's . . . well, it's just cool, isn't it? Didn't you have one of those chemistry sets when you were a kid? I loved mine. Me and my best friend Caddy used to do experiments all the time.'

'Why didn't you just do chemistry, then?'

'Because I wanted to do something vocational.'

'Why?'

I shrug. 'I like knowing where I'm going.'

She sighs. 'Fair. But what if you know where you're going and you don't like it?'

I hesitate. 'I don't know. That does sound a bit shit, though.'

'Doesn't it just.' She shakes her head. 'I don't know what to do,' she says. 'What would you do? If you hated it here like I do?'

'Wait it out,' I say. 'Make changes to make it better.'

'You wouldn't drop out?'

'No,' I say. 'No way.'

She deflates a little, her eyes shifting from mine. 'I'm thinking about it. It's not just one thing, that's the thing. It's, like, every part of it.' She sighs. 'OK, I've talked at you for ages now. I'm sorry.'

'It's fine,' I say. 'You weren't talking *at* me, anyway.' It's been really nice to have a proper conversation with someone that didn't make me feel like I was on some kind of social tightrope. 'How's the rest of your day looking?'

'I can't remember,' she says. 'I was thinking of going back to my room.'

'Your timetable must be the same as mine,' I say, undeterred.

'Organic structures this afternoon, right?'

She shrugs. 'I guess?'

'Come on,' I say, nudging her with my elbow. 'Just get through today, OK? And then tomorrow – which group are you in for the BNF intro?'

'C,' she says.

'I'm in B,' I say. 'But that's OK. We can meet up after you're done and talk it over.'

Finally, a tentative but real smile lights on Laini's face. 'OK, yeah. That sounds OK.'

'I'll take that,' I say. 'That's all you've got to do, you know? Make a plan, see it through. It's as simple as that.'

5

It makes an instant difference, having a friend. Especially one who needs my help and confidence, like Laini does, which reminds me in a lot of ways of how it used to be between Caddy and me. The kind of impromptu pep talks I find myself giving to Laini in between lectures while she doodles cupcakes for me up and down my notebook margins are a lot like the kind I'd imagined I'd be giving Caddy. Which seems ridiculous now, when she's off at Warwick not needing me even the slightest bit. Because if my university experience so far has been a bit of a damp firework, Caddy's is an entire Bonfire Night display, bright and loud and joyful. The kind you can only watch with your mouth open in awe.

As I try to get through my second week without buckling under the weight of it all, I watch Caddy's Instagram fill with photos of her smiling face, usually accompanied by total strangers already hugging her best-friend close, captions about her excitement, hashtags like #studentlife and #lifestartshere. *Life starts here?* I think, staring at the words. What does that even mean?

On Wednesday, Suze messages me with a screenshot of one of these posts, some question marks, a sad face. She writes, **Hashtag left behind???**

Hashtag I haven't forgotten you, I reply.

Suze:

Hashtag lonely.

Rosie:

Hashtag Are you OK?

Hashtag yes, just miss you both. Feel like a bitch for saying this, but kind of sad Caddy seems SO HASHTAG HAPPY to be away.

I want to tell her that I feel the same, that it's worse for me because it makes it all the more obvious how happy I'm *not*, but that feels too exposing, so I don't. **It's the novelty**, I say instead. **It'll calm down.**

And it does, eventually, but the happiness stays. When we talk on the phone, Caddy's voice is full of it. She sounds more confident, too; brighter. She and her flatmates have bonded – it turns out there's a drama student in her flat, too, but they actually get along – and this is the source of a lot of her giddiness, but it's not just that. She loves her campus, loves the lectures ('They're already so interesting!'), loves her bedroom. She keeps referring to the *freedom* of it, how *free* she feels.

'You know what I mean?' she says, over and over, peppering her monologues with it.

It's clear she assumes I'm having a similar time and am just being characteristically understated about it, and that I'd tell her if the opposite was true.

I always say, 'Yeah! Oh my God, yes. Definitely.' And I hear how true it sounds, and I hate myself a bit. For lying to my best friend, for needing to lie because the truth feels shameful in a way I don't quite understand.

It's not that I want Caddy to have a bad experience. Of course I don't. But, if I'm honest, it makes me feel strangely unmoored, watching Caddy live the life I'd expected I'd have. Like we've switched roles, somehow. Who *am* I now, without her shyness to propel my confidence?

While Caddy is having what seems to be the time of her life, I find out that my earlier confidence that the first 'proper' week of university life would be reassuringly calmer, smoother, more certain, is completely misplaced. What I'd apparently forgotten is that while I'm on a course with an average of twenty-four contact hours a week, lots of other people aren't, and some of those people are my flatmates. They, and the people in the flats around us, seem determined to carry on the Freshers Week party into October and beyond.

Which would be totally fine, if I didn't have a 9 a.m. lecture literally every day that week, plus a total of nine lectures overall, five workshops and a three-hour lab prep session. And a shift at my job. And a load of reading and practical prep to do in my 'spare' time. Freshers Week was dizzying, but this – let's call it Normal Week – is dizzying in a completely different way. And I think I might be getting a cold.

'Where have you been?' Dawn says on Thursday, when I walk into the kitchen at 6 p.m. and find her, Rika, Freddie and two of the Jacks sitting around the table together, which is a great question with a boring answer, so I just shake my head and shrug. 'Have you had dinner yet?' she asks. 'We're getting pizza.'

'How did you know I was craving pizza?' I say.

She grins. 'We're getting the student bonanza deal. Any preferences?'

I have a lot of pizza preferences – to the point that I annoy my friends whenever we get pizza together – but I shake my head with a smile. 'Whatever you guys are getting is good.'

'I feel like I only see the back of your head,' Rika says to me while Freddie puts in the order and I've climbed up onto the table to sit with her and Dawn. 'You're always going somewhere.'

'I think our timetables completely clash,' I say.

'You should come out with us, though,' she says. 'That's not timetabled.'

'I will,' I say. 'Maybe not every night, though.'

She rolls her eyes. 'OK, Grandma.'

This is a stupid thing to say, but I bite back a snarky retort and laugh instead, because I want to be friends, and maybe it doesn't matter if it doesn't feel as natural as it did with Laini or any of my friends from home. Maybe this is just how it will be, and that's OK. You don't always have to love your friends, do you?

This is what I'm thinking when my phone lights up and I reach for it automatically, unlocking the screen and opening the message from Laini in one thoughtless motion.

Laini:

Hey, just wanted to let you know that I've dropped out.

Rosie:

What?!

Yeah, sorry I guess. You're literally the only person I'm going to tell lol

Guess that says a lot.

It's just not right for me. Feel so much happier just knowing it's done. I'm already at home.

I don't know what to say?

Nothing to say lol. Thanks for being the
only cool person I met. Have a great year, OK?
Come to Kent sometime and I'll make a cake ☺

'What's the matter?' Dawn's voice.

I look up. 'What?'

'You're making a weird face,' Rika says. 'Did someone die?'

'No, but what if they had?' I say, trying not to roll my eyes. 'Imagine if I had to go, yeah, they did actually.'

She wrinkles her nose at me, which might be affection or annoyance, I can't tell. 'What's happened, then?'

I take in a breath. 'Someone from my course dropped out. I was a bit surprised.'

'Dropped out?' Dawn repeats, looking actually shocked. 'Already?'

'It's only the second week,' Rika points out, like this will be news to me. 'Who drops out in their second week?'

'Who dropped out?' Flapjack asks, looking up from his phone.

'Someone on her course,' Rika says.

'Shit,' Flapjack says.

'Why?' Dawn asks me.

'She just wasn't happy here,' I say. My heart hurts, way more than is proportionate for the loss of someone I'd only met up with a few times. 'She thinks it wasn't right.'

'She knew that after two weeks?' Rika says, looking sceptical. 'Or did she actually know *before*, and so she shouldn't have come and taken the space of someone who would have really *wanted* to come here? Isn't that a bit selfish? Isn't your course, like, really competitive?'

I shrug. I don't really want to talk. Not about this, not to them.

'That's really sad,' Dawn says. 'I feel bad for your friend.'

My friend. 'Me too. I thought she'd give it a bit longer.'

'Sucks to give up so easily,' Freddie says, sliding effortlessly into the conversation. 'Imagine being that much of a quitter, to do it after two weeks.'

'She's not a quitter,' I say, trying not to snap. 'Lots of people drop out. It's normal. And better to do it now than waste money on tuition and accommodation, right?'

'That's true,' Dawn says. 'I guess it's kind of the smart decision, right?'

It's nice of her to try. I want to be more grateful, but I feel all hot and sad and, weirdly, a bit stressed, as if this is somehow my decision, which obviously it isn't.

'And two weeks isn't that short, really,' Dawn adds. 'I know people who didn't like Freshers Week. They're glad it's over.'

'Lame,' Freddie says.

'Don't be ableist,' Rika snaps, surprising me. 'Who says "lame" any more? God. At least say something like *pathetic*. Or *losers*.'

For some reason, this makes me crack up laughing, the kind of hysterical laugh you get when you're suddenly hyper aware of your surroundings, and how ridiculous life is. Rika is such a bitch, and I kind of hate and love her for it at the same time.

We end up spending a few hours in the kitchen together, sharing pizza and beers, and though it never stops feeling like I'm trying, it ends up being a pretty nice evening. When they all go out for a club night, part of me thinks I should go too, but the other part knows the only reason I would is because I think I should, which is the worst reason to do something. So I just wave them off at 10 p.m., taking pictures of Dawn and Rika that they'll plaster all over Instagram later, then go – with some relief – to my lovely, quiet room, alone.

6

Laini's departure affects me more than I want to admit, even to myself. It's not just because I've lost a potential friend – though obviously that's part of it – or even because I feel like I have to start again in finding someone to sit with in lectures and get coffee with before and after. It's because something that I'd always been vaguely aware of but only in an abstract way – dropping out – has suddenly become real. Something someone I know has done. Actively choosing to quit. To leave.

When I look it up, I find out that 6.3 per cent of students drop out during their first year in the UK, which sounds low until I realize that that small percentage is still over 25,000 people. All those different people with all their different reasons to go, contemplating different lives than they'd imagined only a few months earlier. Laini fading into a statistic. I look at the bumps in the year when the most dropouts happen. One bump right after Freshers, one in mid-November, and then not another one until the end of the year. That seems unfathomable to me, too. Dropping out without giving the year a chance seems bizarre to me, but putting yourself through an entire year – and paying for it – and then giving up seems even worse.

But it doesn't affect me, does it? It's sad that Laini's gone, but it's not like I'm going to drop out. Yes, Freshers didn't go all that brilliantly, but it's all in my hands now. I can do better, try harder. Make five new friends in Laini's absence. Be the most competent would-be pharmacist the university has ever seen.

It's a great plan in theory, but by the end of that week, the cold that I'd felt building has run over me like a truck, and I feel utterly crap. And it's not a cold, either. It's freshers flu. Most of my flat seems to have it, too, and, judging by the soundtrack of muffled coughs and sniffles in the lecture theatre, so does about half of my course. Three different lecturers make jokes about it.

I can't find it funny, though, even when I try. I don't get any sympathy from Mum – usually my go-to for exactly that when I'm feeling ill – because she's come down with something too, and she just tells me, irritably, that I've only got a cold. 'I hate it when people stick "flu" on the end of something to make it sound worse. Man flu. Freshers flu. It's just a cold. Stock up on tissues and wait it out.'

This, from the woman who used to take 'bed days' with me when I was even slightly sniffly as a kid, staying home from work so the two of us could watch Disney films all day, snuggled up on the sofa together. 'I love it when you get ill,' she said once. I remember, because she immediately followed it with, 'That sounded terrible, didn't it? I'm the worst mother in the world. Let's get some cake.'

'Well, what's wrong with you, then?' I ask now, angling my phone away from my mouth so I can cough. 'Is yours actual flu?'

'I don't know,' she says. 'But my head is foggy and I keep getting dizzy when I stand up. It's very annoying.'

'Worse than normal?' I ask. Mum's always had problems with dizzy spells when she gets stressed or tired.

'Oh, I don't know,' she says with a sigh. 'I'm sure I'm just overdoing it, and it's caught up with me.'

'Take a day off work,' I suggest.

'I've taken the week,' she replies. 'I'm sure it will help. Anyway, I'll PayPal you a fiver, and you can get yourself some Night Nurse, OK? How's that for long-distance mothering?'

I can't help smiling. 'Stellar long-distance mothering. Thank you.'

I spend Saturday in bed, then get sent home from work on Sunday by my irritated manager, who tells me she doesn't want staff 'coughing all over the customers, looking like death', which I guess is fair enough but makes me feel even worse.

On Monday, I can tell the worst of it is over, but it's still a slog to get through a full nine-to-five day of lectures with just a break for lunch. I still feel too miserable to properly talk to anyone, both because of the not-actual-flu flu and because I still feel sad about Laini dropping out. My third week, and all the weeks ahead, stretch on in front of me, and without any energy left to lift myself, I can't hide from the truth, which is that I don't think I like it here very much. At least, not yet.

Not in the same way Laini didn't like it, obviously, but still. I thought I'd be happier; that's the truth. I thought I'd have made a group of friends by now, that I'd have found my place and my routine, that I'd be loving my course and the lectures and the world I'd be in.

But I don't, which is maybe part of the problem. If my course was going brilliantly, I don't think the rest of it would matter, or at least not as much. But pharmacy in real life looks a lot different than I imagined it in my head when I was seventeen and filling out my UCAS forms. I can't even put my finger on exactly why, but I think, for me, it might have something to do with the combination of chemistry and medicine, which I thought would be the part I would love, but I don't. *It is only the third week!* I tell myself. Yell at myself, really. I have to keep telling myself that, because it feels like so much longer, and it's easy to forget. But I've barely started, and neither has the course. I just need to be patient and give it time.

Except I'm really bad at being patient; I always have been. Right now, it's a Tuesday afternoon in my third week as a student, and I'm sitting in the library, doing my lab prep ahead of my very first practical on Thursday. At least, that's what I'm meant to be doing. I'm actually ignoring the laptop in front of me and my textbook to my left, and instead am looking through my timetable for the next few weeks, figuring out how many hours I have to do everything, and having an existential crisis.

Words keep jumping out at me from my timetable. *Delocalization and aromaticity. Pharmacodynamics. Neurophysiology.* All these words that sounded so cool when they were just abstract, but now I have to learn them. All of them, all at once. And also make friends and earn enough money to live and occasionally be sociable and pass exams and also stay sane and emotionally healthy. *How?*

And one day – I am vaguely aware of how I'm spiralling, like part of me is watching in bemusement as I launch myself down a helter-skelter – all this stuff I'm learning now will be stuff I have to just *know*. Like, off the top of my head. One day I won't be tested on this; I'll just be expected to know it all. And if I don't, if I get something wrong, there'll be actual consequences, actual harm. To other people. What if—

'Hey.'

The soft voice comes from above me and I start in surprise, jerking my textbook away from me, looking up. There's a girl standing at my desk, looking down at me, a squinted quirk of a smile on her face. She looks vaguely familiar, though I'm not sure why. I definitely don't know her. In my confusion, I forget to speak, just frown back at her.

She smiles again, more widely, like she's amused. 'Hi,' she says again, pointedly. She taps a finger to my textbook and rolls her eyes with a tired familiarity that, for some reason, calms my heart, which was still racing from all the catastrophizing. She squats down, resting her elbows on the table. 'You look stressed. Do you need help?'

Who is this girl? A total stranger, appearing out of nowhere, asking me if I need help?

'I'm Jade,' she says, raising her eyebrows as if this should mean something to me. 'I'm in the Pharmacy Society? The equality and diversity rep? I gave the talk with Nilesh in Freshers Week?'

Oh. Oh, OK. Not a total stranger. The tiny part of my brain that always wanted to believe in angels – like my mother does – deflates, then goes back to sleep.

'Listen,' she says, still smiling that amused smile. 'I saw you having a panic. Trust me, I've been there. We've all been there. I'm in my third year. You need a break, OK? I'll get you a coffee. Come on.'

I blink at her, my brain still trying to readjust to the surprise of her appearance. I still haven't said a word, which she seems to find funny rather than weird. She gestures to me to get up, and for some reason, I do.

'Leave your books and stuff,' she says. 'But best not to leave your laptop.' She motions her head towards the exit, and I follow her obediently, reminding myself of Laini that first time we met in the coffee shop, sliding my laptop into my bag as I go. What did she say her name was? Jade? She's taking the steps at an easy jog, hands tucked into her pockets. She glances back to smile at me a couple of times before we get to the Hive, as if to check I'm still following her. 'Are you a tea or a coffee person?'

'Tea,' I say, even though I'd usually define myself as a coffee person more than a tea person, because right now I want tea, and also I'm very confused. 'Um. Thanks.'

'A tea drinker,' Jade says, still smiling like I'm amusing her. 'Cool. Do you want to find us a table and I'll get these?'

'OK,' I say. 'Thank you.'

It takes about five minutes for her to join me at the corner table I've bagged for us near the east-facing window, which is not quite enough time for my brain to properly calm down, but it's getting there, at least. I even manage a proper sentence when she's sat down and handed me my tea. 'So, is this your job? Finding the panicking freshers and buying them hot drinks?'

She laughs. 'Not my job, no. But I do like to try and look out for the Pharm freshers, yeah. We all look out for each other. It's a tough course.'

'It wasn't just because I was looking really pathetic?'

She laughs again. 'Not pathetic, no. You did look like you might combust, though. Properly in the stress spiral.' She takes a sip from her cup, smiling. 'Are you going to tell me your name?'

'Oh God, sorry,' I say, trying to laugh. 'I'm Rosie.'

'Hi, Rosie,' she says. 'Where are you from?'

'Brighton.'

'Oh, cool!' she says. 'I've never been. I'm from Somerset. Burnham-on-Sea, to be exact.' She smiles. 'We have a beach, too.'

'Is that far away?' I ask. I'm actually not sure where Somerset is, beyond a vague understanding of it being somewhere west. My Brighton-affected sense of geography is basically that everything is north of home in one direction or another. It comes with being at the bottom of the country.

'Yes,' Jade says, grinning. 'That was part of the appeal. Nearly a five-hour drive.'

'Do you miss it?'

'Not really,' she says, shrugging. 'I love Norfolk; I've mostly lived here full time since I moved into my house in my second year. And my sister is at Cambridge, so I'm actually closer to her here than I would have been from home, so that helps.'

'Oh wow, Cambridge.'

Jade lets out an affected sigh. 'Always the "wow". Yes, she's a genius. That hasn't had an impact on my self-esteem at all.' I must be making a worried face because she laughs and says, 'She's my favourite person; I'm teasing. I love her to death. Have you got any siblings?'

I shake my head. 'Just me.' I wonder, as I always do when this question arises, if this counts as a lie. Or a betrayal, even. What's the answer when the sibling died? *Just me* is easier. And it feels like the truth. 'Are you a second-year?' I ask, mostly because I want to change the subject.

Another amused smile flickers on her face. 'Still third,' she says, gently teasing. She told me that already, didn't she?

'Oh yeah,' I say, flushing. 'Um. And you're the equality and diversity rep?'

She nods. 'I am indeed.'

'What does that . . . actually mean?'

'It means that I am not straight or white or a guy,' Jade says, rolling her eyes with a grin. 'I am the triple-threat jackpot. My presence says, *Hello, fellow people who are not cishet-white-guys! You are welcome here.*'

'Well, that's good,' I say. 'It's appreciated.' *Say it.* I want to say it. 'As a two-out-of-three. I'm female and, um, bi.' I sound so awkward. Have I ever sounded *so* awkward?

'There you go,' Jade says. 'Welcome, welcome.' She smiles at me, a smile that feels somehow different from her smiles before. Smaller, but realer. 'You know I saw you during Freshers Week?'

'What?' I say, thrown. 'You mean, during the PharmSoc talk?'

She nods. 'There, too. But on the Sunday night. You probably don't remember, but you were with a drunk girl who was crying a lot.'

I blink at her, a vague memory stirring. 'Dawn?'

She laughs. 'Yes? I don't know. But she was wailing about an ex-boyfriend and you were just like, *OK, whatever.* It was so unfreshery. It was hilarious. When I saw you in the lecture theatre when I was giving that PharmSoc talk, I was like, oh cool, she's

MPharm! And so today, seeing you in the library all panicky, I couldn't not say hi.' She grins at me. 'Hi.'

'Well, hi,' I say, embarrassed. And a little confused, to be honest. She saw me? She remembered me?

'So, what got you panicking in the library?' she asks, taking a tentative sip from her cup then curling her hands around it. 'Anything specific?'

I wonder how honest I should be. I don't want to let on how pathetic I am, but then again, the reason she's talking to me is because she gets this and she wants to help. It's not like she actually knows me; why shouldn't I be honest? 'Not really,' I say. 'More like . . . all of it.'

'The course? Uni?'

'Both. It's just . . . you know. Overwhelming?'

She nods. 'Definitely. It's like that for everyone, I think.'

'Is it?' I say, dubious. I think of Caddy, having the literal time of her life somewhere in the Midlands.

'Sure,' Jade says easily. 'It hits people at different times and in different ways, but of course, yeah. It's a huge adjustment, even just the moving-away-from-home-for-the-first-time bit. Add in meeting loads of new people, plus a course as intense as ours, and . . . Well, yeah. It would be weird *not* to feel a bit buried by it sometimes.'

'I guess that's true.' I think about how I said more or less the same thing to Laini, and what little difference it made.

'Of course it's true,' she says. 'You'll be fine.' She says this with such confidence, as if she knows me. 'I can already tell you're made of tough stuff.'

'Can you?' I can't help laughing. 'How?'

She shrugs, grinning. 'I don't know; I can just tell. I'm very good at reading people.'

'And I give off tough vibes?' I'm actually smiling a real smile. I can feel it on my face, like a surprise. 'Is that a good thing?'

'Oh yeah,' she says, still with that same confident voice. 'Definitely a good thing.'

She smiles at me over her cup, and there's something . . . something warm in my chest, a fluttering. Is this a spark? Is that what I'm feeling?

No, I tell myself. I can't go around thinking every girl who makes eye contact and smiles is flirting with me, let alone that there's a spark. Look what happened with Rika. I have to be more careful with myself.

But . . . Jade has already said – volunteered, even – that she's not straight. So maybe . . .

No. Stop it.

'Here,' she says, reaching for her phone. 'Let's swap numbers, and you have to promise that you *will* send me a message if you start feeling panicky about anything pharmacy, OK?' She smiles at me. 'Or, if you just want to chat, I won't ignore you, obviously.'

She hands me her phone, then takes mine, and I obligingly write my name and number into her contacts. It feels strangely intimate, holding her phone. Like I'm holding her life in my hand. When she hands me back my phone, I look down at her name.

'Esfhani,' I read aloud.

'Esfahani,' she corrects, but not in an annoyed way.

'Is that . . .'

'Iranian,' she says, anticipating what I was going to ask, with the patience of someone who has this exchange a lot. 'From my dad. My mum is Spanish. Me, one hundred per cent Somerset.' She grins, all warm and cheerful, and I want us to be friends. I want to be her friend so badly. 'How about you?' She glances down at her phone. 'Caron. That's pretty.'

'It's Welsh,' I say. 'It was actually my mum's middle name. She promoted it, then shared it with me.' That's how she's always put it: 'shared' it.

Jade smiles. 'I love that. That's so cool.' She glances at the oversized clock on the far wall and sighs. 'I have to go to a workshop now. You'll be OK finding your way back to the library?'

This makes me laugh. 'Yes, I'm not so overwhelmed I've lost my short-term memory.'

'That's a good start,' Jade says, getting to her feet, grinning. 'That means you won't forget that you met me. See you, Rosie. Nice to meet you.'

She's gone before I can figure out whether it would be OK to say that even short-term memory loss wouldn't stop me remembering the last twenty minutes.

Jade Esfahani. Maybe it's a name that will become familiar. I hope so.

When I get back to my desk, I open up my laptop again, the timetable still there on the screen, colourful and intense. I feel a stirring of the same anxiety from before, but it's much easier to push away this time.

I allow myself a two-minute daydream of myself in two years' time, a wizened old third-year. I'll be so confident about everything I'll barely remember how I feel now, so lost and uncertain. Maybe Jade and I will still be friends then, and I can say to her, *God, remember when you had to rescue me in the library?* And how we will laugh.

I wish I could just skip ahead to then, actually. Fast forward this part until it's just a memory, when I will know how it all went and even the bad parts will be something I've already survived.

Survived. What a needlessly dramatic word. I roll my eyes at myself as I determinedly take a hold of my pen and press the nib to the paper of my notebook. *Take it down a notch, Roz. Concentrate.*

*

On Thursday morning, I wake up excited – actually excited – for the first real time since I got here. Today is lab day. My first practical as a student. Today I will be in a real live lab and this is everything I've been waiting for, why I chose a science degree, the content of my daydreams.

I love being in the lab. Even though it's all new and clinical and pristine and scary, it still feels familiar, because one of my favourite parts of chemistry at A Level was practical work. Yeah, we didn't have a proper lab – my school was not among the 'outstanding' state schools in the area, let's just put it that way – but the essentials are the same.

It finally feels like I've remembered why I'm here, why I chose this degree: because I love this stuff. I love chemistry. I love science. OK, I don't love the combination of chemistry and pharmaceutical practice yet, but it's still early days. I'm sure I'll get there eventually. For now, I'm just really happy to be here, goggled up and white-coated, about to play with chemicals.

One of the first things we have to do is pick our lab partner for the rest of the year, which throws me because I'd just assumed they'd be assigned to us. There's a full two minutes of awkward jostling as those that have friends in the vicinity rush to claim them and the rest of us try to cover our panic that we'll be the only one without a friend. Turns out, it's most of us, and we seem to end up pairing up naturally with whoever is standing closest to us. I end up with a smiling guy who has the broadest shoulders I've ever seen and a carefully curated goatee.

'I'm Dion,' he says. 'So great to meet you, Rosie.' Which is a nice way to start.

'Are you nervous?' I ask.

'Terrified,' he says, then actually winks at me. It's somehow sweet rather than cringey, though, and I smile back. I think we're going to be OK.

As it's our first ever lab session, it's more of an introduction than an actual practical, which takes the pressure off a bit. Our first assessed practical will be in another couple of weeks, when we'll be synthesizing aspirin. But still, the lab is all set up for us; the chemicals we'll need on our benches, ready and waiting. It flashes into my head that it reminds me a lot of the technical challenge on *The Great British Bake Off*, except instead of food ingredients, it's all chemicals. And that makes me think of Laini, and smile. Maybe I should message her. If we were allowed to get our phones out in the lab, I'd take a picture. Maybe caption it, **On your marks, get set, TITRATE!**

Shit, I stopped listening. *Concentrate.*

I can tell it's not just me that's in equal parts daunted and giddy about being in the lab. There's a kind of energy in the air, like everyone's holding their breath. Even Dion, who seems older and therefore cooler than me, has the same nervous, happy smile on his face that I feel on mine. When we're measuring out salicylic acid to make aspirin, we both handle the weighing boat as if it's made of precious china instead of plastic. Each of us does the measuring once, and then we look at each other and Dion says, 'Again?' exactly as I say, 'Shall we just do it one more time?' And then we laugh, and I know we really are going to be OK.

We're in the lab for three hours, which feels like it goes by in ten minutes. When we get to the titration part, watching the solution turn light pink, then bright pink, then clear, I can feel myself smiling in just the way I used to back in Ashcroft School in Brighton, when our teacher, Mr Lyon, used to say, 'And *that's* chemistry!' every single time, at the point of reaction.

When we're leaving the lab, Dion suggests we get a coffee

together to talk it over and compare our rough notes ahead of the report we'll have to write individually. He tells me he's a mature student living off campus with his fiancée, and I tell him about Brighton, and we make a plan to make post-lab coffee a regular thing. By the time I've packed up my stuff, said goodbye and headed back to my flat, I'm smiling, feeling pretty good about myself. A successful day of my pharmacy degree. About time.

7

That weekend, with three weeks of student life behind us, I decide to make more of an effort with my flatmates. Even though we're all living together in the same space, it's starting to feel an awful lot like being in a Travelodge on the same floor as someone else's birthday party. I can see and hear the fun as I come and go, but I'm not a part of it. I want to be a part of it.

On Saturday night, I go with them for a night out in the city centre, in the Riverside area where there are clubs all clustered together by the waterfront, and it feels like the whole thing was made just for students: unencumbered, with a student loan to burn and no responsibilities.

(Me, I calculated how much I could spend before I even chose what I was going to wear. And I called Mum to check that she'd remembered to book our cat in at the vet's for his vaccination boosters. But still, I'm a student. I count.)

Anyway, the night with my flatmates is fun enough but not memorable. When we talk, they tell me stories not of their home lives — like I still do — but of each other, already. They have anecdotes. Already. Private jokes and catchphrases. Stupid names for each other. (Though, I guess, I have one of those, too. I am still the Enigma.) Dawn and Freddie dance close, his hand on her upper thigh. Flapjack tries to dance with me until Rika slides an arm around my neck, pulling me away, sneering, 'Out of your league, Flappy.' And I expect him to snap at her, but he just looks a bit hurt, and then I feel bad. Rika wants a cigarette, so I follow her, and then smoke with her, even though I haven't smoked since I was fifteen, and she says, 'God, this fucking shitshow,' and I think she'll kiss me again, or at least try, but she doesn't.

In the morning, I lie in bed for the twenty minutes I have before I have to get up and go to work, thinking and worrying, trying to figure out what to do. What if the rest of the year is like this? Me, just a tag-along on other people's nights out. Listening to their anecdotes instead of sharing my own.

I'm so sick of not having anyone to talk to. Not just small talk, but an actual conversation. The kind where you relax into it and stop overthinking. Like I had in the Hive with Jade last week. Maybe I should message her? I've wanted to, ever since. Even brought up her contact card a few times, then chickened out. But she gave me her number, didn't she? She basically told me to message her. But, wait, wasn't that if I was feeling panicky about the course? That's not what this is about. So maybe I should wait until . . .

Oh, for God's sake, Rosie, stop being an idiot.

Hey! Any chance you're free tomorrow? I owe you a coffee. Would be good to have a chat if you're free?

I've sent it before I realize that I've repeated 'you're free', which is annoying. But I shake my head, tell myself it's done, and it doesn't matter anyway.

After another forty-nine seconds, my phone beeps. **Hey! Always free for a free coffee! ☺ I'm free after 2. Meet you outside the Hive if that works for you? x**

A kiss. *A kiss?!* Should *I* have left a kiss? And *three* frees. Is she teasing me? I think she might be teasing me. Which is basically flirting. Which is . . .

Oh my God, oh my God.

No, I'm being stupid. Jade is a third-year, and I'm just a flailing fresher she's decided to be kind to, because she's nice. I reply, **Sounds great, see you then :)**

It's such a chicken move, going for the smiley face instead of a kiss, but I guess student-me is a chicken, because I do it anyway.

And then, almost instantly, :) x

Oh my God.

The next day, when I get to the Hive, I see Jade leaning against a pillar, phone in hand, her head bent slightly as she taps at the screen. I wonder who she's messaging, or what she's looking at.

I walk over to her, waiting until I'm beside her before I say, 'Hey.'

She looks up, already smiling, one hand on its way up to swipe her hair from where it's fallen in front of her face. 'Hey! Happy Monday. How are you?' She rights herself, pushing her phone into the canvas bag she has hanging from one shoulder. Something I should say is that Jade has a nice smile. A very nice smile. She's beautiful, actually. Gorgeous.

'Good,' I say. My voice comes out perfectly normal, and I'm proud of myself. 'You?'

'Better now,' she says. 'Bit of a stressful morning, but now I get free coffee.' She grins at me. 'Always a day-brightener. How do you fancy walking around the lake? I like to walk and talk, and it's a nice day.'

'Sure,' I say. 'How do you take your coffee? I'll just go in and get it.'

'Just a flat white is fine,' she says. 'Thanks.'

When I come back outside, one cup balanced atop the other in one hand and a paper bag containing two cookies between my fingers, Jade is on the phone, frowning slightly off into the distance, drumming her fingers against her knee.

I hesitate, then head over. She smiles in acknowledgement at me, raising one finger in an obvious, *One sec?* I nod.

'Look, I have to go; I can't talk right now,' Jade says into the phone. Her eyes close briefly and she clenches her jaw. 'I know.

Yes, I know. You said that already. Well, you can just talk to her—' She sighs, rolling her eyes at me, like I can hear the other side of the conversation. 'I'll call you later, Mamá, OK? OK. OK, yes. OK, bye. Bye. I love you, too. Bye.' When she finally hangs up, she lets out a grunt of frustration, shaking her head. 'Oh my God. Sorry.' She tosses her hair and smiles at me. 'Ready?'

'Is everything OK?' I ask, gesturing with my chin to the top cup, which she takes.

'Yeah, fine,' she says. 'Thanks. My sister's got a new piercing and my mum is freaking out, which is apparently my problem to deal with. They don't get on, and of course we're all in completely different parts of the country, which doesn't help with the whole communication thing.' She sighs again. 'Anyway, sorry, you don't want to hear about silly family drama. How are you?'

She's asked me that already, but I don't say so. Instead, as we make our way across the grass towards the lake, I tell her about my morning, which was taken up by three lectures, one after the other, spanning drug delivery, pharmacology and medicinal chemistry. She's nodding, listening without interrupting.

'How are you finding it all?' she asks when I stop talking. 'You seem pretty chilled! Are you still overwhelmed?'

I shrug, because the truth is I don't even know what the answer actually is. 'Not as much,' I say eventually, because at least it isn't a lie. 'I had my first practical last week.'

'Oh cool!' she says. 'I still remember my first time in the lab here. My lab partner Vibs spilt hydrogen peroxide all over the floor. It was pretty funny – in an inappropriate way, maybe – because literally before we went in, he'd been trying to calm *me* down because I was so worried I'd make a mistake.'

'Oh God,' I say, not quite able to laugh along with the story, because I'm thinking about how horrible I would have felt if it had been me making a mistake like that. 'Was it OK?'

'Oh yeah, totally fine. Vibs is really easy-going. He was like, *There you go, Jade, I did that for you. Now you see how the world didn't end?*' She smiles at the memory. 'He's a sweetheart. We were flatmates in our first year, and we've stayed living together ever since.'

I feel a surge of jealousy so acute I have to sip at my coffee to stop myself making a very obvious face. Why couldn't I have lucked out with a friend, lab partner and flatmate all in one? Why couldn't Dion have been younger and living on campus and also in my flat? I bet we could have been good friends. It's so unfair.

'Are you OK?' Jade prompts, and I realize I've gone completely quiet.

'Shit, yes, sorry. I was just thinking.'

'About . . . ?'

'How I wish I had a Vibs in my flat,' I say, deciding to be honest. 'But I don't.'

Jade scrunches her face in sympathy. 'That's a shame. How are your flatmates, though?'

'They're fine,' I say. 'But we're not going to be best friends, you know?'

She nods. 'Yeah, I get you. Have you made friends on the course, or in societies or anything?'

'Kind of,' I say. 'I had a friend who dropped out, which was a shame. And I think I'm going to get on OK with my lab partner, but he's a mature student and he doesn't live on campus, so it's not, like, the same, I guess.'

'It's still early days,' she says. 'And hey, next time there's a PharmSoc social, I'll make sure to do the rounds with you. There are some really cool people I can introduce you to.'

'Like a babysitter?' I say, accidentally out loud.

To my relief, she laughs instead of getting offended. 'Yes, exactly like that. Sorry, I wasn't trying to be patronizing.'

'No, I know, sorry,' I say, horrified and furious with myself. 'That would be really nice, thank you.'

She glances at me sideways, a sharp smirk appearing that changes her whole face in a way that makes her sparkle. 'It's OK to be snarky with me. I can take it, even if you are a tiny little fresher, and you should respect your elders.'

I laugh. 'Got it.'

She grins at me, then suddenly veers off the path we're on towards one of the tiny jetties jutting out into the lake, going to stand right at the end of it, the point of her boots hanging over the edge. She smiles. 'God, I love this so much. Isn't it so pretty? I love lakes.'

I smile, going to stand beside her, perilously close to the edge of the jetty. 'Yeah, it's really nice.'

We stand there together for a couple of minutes, both of us quiet, until she spins on the spot and heads back to the path, me following a step behind.

'So, who's at home?' she asks me. 'Tell me what your Brighton life is like.'

'Just Mum,' I say. 'It's been her and me almost my whole life.' Before she can do the awkward ask-or-not-ask, I add, 'My dad left when I was really young, and we haven't seen him since.'

'Gross.'

'Yep. It's not a problem, though. I can't imagine anything but it being just Mum and me.'

'Do you get along?'

'Yeah.' I consider elaborating but decide against it. Too much, too heavy. 'So that's my family, just me and Mum. And then the rest of my Brighton life is my best friends. There's Caddy, who's at Warwick now – she's having an *amazing* time, she loves it so much – and Suze, who's . . .' I pause. How to explain Suze and her complicated life? 'She just left the care system.' I hear how it sounds like I've equated the two things, like I somehow think care leavers don't go to university, and hate myself, but it's too late to take it back, so I add, 'She only just moved back to Brighton, actually. She was away for a while, in foster care. It's kind of a long story. Anyway, she works full time.'

'As what?' Jade asks.

'In a coffee shop,' I say, and even though there's no reason to, I feel guilty, like I've set up my incredible friend to sound somehow lesser than Caddy, than Jade and me, in our university lives. 'She's kind of . . . like, the best person? I miss her a lot.' It's inadequate, but it's better than nothing. 'How about you?'

'Family is my parents, my sister and me,' she says. 'Jasmine – that's my sister. Twin sister, actually. Technically not identical, but similar enough that most people do a double take.' She smiles, proud. 'She's great. My best friend. Not so keen on my parents, but that's also a long story. My group of friends from school are scattered across the country now. We see each other over the holidays and stuff, but we're not, like, close-close.'

'Because you've all been apart?'

'No, just generally, I think. We have a good time when we meet up, but they're not who I call in a crisis, you know? They don't know me like my uni friends know me. Like, Vibs, who I talked about before, and Saff and Aisha, my housemates, I feel like they know my *soul*, honestly. I would basically die for them.' She considers. 'To be honest, I don't really think I have a "home life" any more. I'm not planning to go back to Somerset when I graduate. I'll do my pre-reg year here, then probably stay, I think.'

'Really?'

'Yeah, I love Norfolk. I've been really happy here. It seems a nice place to build a life.'

We've done a full circuit of the lake, both of us slowing our pace instinctively.

'So, was there something specific you wanted to talk about?' Jade asks.

'Specific?' I repeat, confused, then remember I was the one who invited her for a coffee and a chat. 'Oh, no, not really.' Is that actually why she's come out here? Because she thought I needed some kind of pharmacy help and now I've bored her by going on about my life? Have I misread this whole thing?

'Great,' Jade says, confusing me further. 'Have you been to the castle yet?'

'The castle?' I repeat, trying to keep up.

'Norwich Castle,' she clarifies, as if there are multiple castles nearby and I've just got confused.

I look at her. '. . . No?'

'Want to go?' she asks. Her eyes are so bright. 'I'm free if you are.'

'Isn't the castle in the city centre?'

She nods. 'Is that a problem for you? Do you have some kind of agreement with God to not leave campus?'

'I just thought . . .' I deliberately stop myself from finishing this sentence with what I was going to say, which was, *that's a lot of time to spend with me if you don't want to*. Because she clearly does want to, doesn't she? She's offering. 'Are all the PharmSoc reps as nice as you?' I ask.

'No,' she says. 'I'm special.'

'I didn't realize playing tour guide to freshers was part of the job,' I say.

'It isn't,' she says, overly patiently.

'Then . . . why . . .'

'Because I like you,' she says, so matter-of-factly that I really can't tell whether she means it platonically or . . . not-platonically. I open my mouth and she puts an abrupt hand up. 'Don't ask why! I will lose respect for you if you ask why.'

I feel the smile break on my face. 'I would never.' And it's true. The Rosie I used to be, the Rosie I *am*, is not the type to ask, *Why do you like me?* And I love that Jade somehow knows that; that maybe she's seeing past the confidence wobble that I'm experiencing to the bullish, snarkmonster I really am, who doesn't think, *Why?* but thinks, *Of course.*

'Good. I'm not a fan of fishing.' She throws me a grin. 'Let's go.'

There's no queue for tickets at Norwich Castle, and I'm glancing at the prices, already reaching for my wallet, when Jade taps my arm and I look up to see she's shaking her head.

'My suggestion, my money,' she says, so easily, so casually. 'This is on me.'

I know I fail at hiding how surprised I am. 'Oh – are you sure?'

'Of course,' she says. Still so casual, to the point where I still have no idea whether this is just a genuinely friendly gesture or . . . something more. 'Don't say no, or it'll be awkward.' She grins at me. 'You bought the coffee, anyway.'

'OK, thanks,' I say, trying to match her light tone and easy smile. 'That's really nice.'

'I *am* really nice,' Jade agrees, nodding. 'And you're welcome.'

We head down into the Rotunda together, and she gestures in two different directions. 'Art or Natural History first?' she asks. 'We have options.'

'You know this place really well,' I say. 'Are you a tour guide? Do they pay you?'

She laughs. 'No, I just have a very good memory. I've been here twice. It's great, honestly. Loads to see. How many places can you go where there's a teapot collection *and* a bird gallery? The best bit is the Castle Keep, though. We'll do that last, OK?'

'OK,' I say, the only possible answer. 'How come there's so much stuff here? I thought it was a castle, not a museum.'

'It's both,' she says. 'OK, let's go the Natural History route. Art can wait. Isn't taxidermy the weirdest thing? So morbid. Like, it's OK just because it's animals?'

'Imagine if they did it to people,' I say. 'Like a really disturbing Madame Tussauds.'

'That's already disturbing,' she says. 'Nightmare fuel. I should have started with the teapots.' She fake-shudders, and I laugh. She grins at me. 'Tell me something you like.'

I look at a polar bear, stuffed and primed. 'Something here?'

She shakes her head. 'Anything,' she says.

'Peonies,' I say.

'Nice!' Jade says, nodding. 'Good answer.'

'You?'

'Snails,' she says. 'Especially the little ones. So cute. Carrying their tiny houses on their backs like slimy little backpackers.' She laughs, then raises her eyebrows in a clear, *You?*

'Garlic mayonnaise.'

'Mmm, yes. Sunsets.'

'True crime podcasts.'

'Cool! Me too! We'll swap favourites later. Aquariums.'

'Caravan holidays.'

'Cute! Marvel.'

'Specifically . . . ?'

She's led us back into the Rotunda now, heading confidently towards another large, open doorway, and I'm finding myself following without hesitation.

'No specifics,' she says, glancing back at me, grinning. 'All of Marvel. Everything Marvel ever touched.'

'OK,' I say, smiling back. There's art on the walls, but I'll be honest – I'm barely noticing it. 'Is this a good time to admit I've only seen a couple of the Avengers films, and nothing else?'

I say this casually, but she stops dead in her tracks, spinning to stare at me, her mouth dropping open. 'What?'

'Sorry.'

'No, don't be sorry! This is amazing!' She reaches out and grips my arm. 'This means you get to watch them all for the first time. I wish I could do that. If I could choose a special amnesia, it would be that. So I could watch them all again.'

'I'll add them to my list,' I say.

'No, not *alone*!' she says. 'We'll watch them together. They're a collective experience. Way better shared.' She glances at me, then adds, 'My housemates are also solid Marvel people. They'll be excited for an excuse for more watch parties.'

My heart, which had started racing, calms itself. Not a date, but something even better. Friends. 'That sounds great.'

'Doesn't it? Anyway, it's your turn. Something else you like.'

'Cats.'

'A cat person! Nice. That says a lot.'

'Does it? What does it say, other than "not a dog person"?'

'That you value independence,' she says. 'And that you respect boundaries.'

This is pretty true, but I laugh anyway and say, 'You get that just from me liking cats?' She nods, grinning, and so I add, 'You're the same, then?'

'An independent respecter of boundaries? Yes. I like cats *and* dogs, though, pretty equally. I'm a bird person.'

'A . . . bird person?'

'Yep.'

'Is that a thing?'

'Yes! There are lots of us. Sidelined out of the cat/dog binary. It's sad, really.' She sighs an exaggerated, mournful sigh.

'I've never met a bird person before.'

'Well, now you have.' She gives a little bow, right in the middle of the gallery, and an old woman in a yellow coat gives us both a confused frown. 'Hello. We exist among you.'

I laugh. 'Go on then, tell me what a bird person is like.'

'Like me,' she says promptly. 'If I'm the only bird person you've ever met, then that will do, won't it?' She grins at me, her face all warmth and humour, and I suddenly, and completely, want to be kissing her. Right here, in front of frowny yellow-coat woman. I almost feel dizzy with it. I've never in my life wanted to kiss anyone the same way I want to kiss her.

I try and talk normally. 'I don't really know you that well yet, do I?'

'Fair point,' she says, nodding. 'I'll have to work on that, then ask you again.' My heart has leaped at this, but before I can let the words properly sink in, she's distracting my head with, 'Do you want to see a picture of my bird?'

'Wait, you *have* a bird? You mean you own one?'

'Yeah! His name's Dave.' She's pulled her phone out of her pocket and is tapping away at it, beaming.

'Dave?!'

'Yes, Dave.' She waves her phone at me. On-screen, a bright blue bird sits on a wooden stand. 'He's a parakeet. Isn't he gorgeous? I got him when I was sixteen. He's my pal. My dude. I miss him.'

'He looks like an excellent bird,' I say. My head is spinning a little. *I'm* spinning a little. I almost feel like I need to sit down and catch my breath.

'He is,' Jade says, smiling proudly down at her phone. 'Hopefully, when I graduate and live in Norwich permanently, I can bring him here. Burnham-on-Sea is so *far*. Anyway . . .' She looks up and around her, her eyes bright. 'Shall we go and find the teapots?'

*

I'm in such a good mood when I get back to campus, a couple of hours later. It is, by far, the best afternoon I've spent in Norwich since I first arrived. Not only do I finally have a friend – the kind of friend who spontaneously extends a coffee-and-a-chat into a whole afternoon sightseeing – but also a friend with potential for . . . I stop myself. I can't quite let myself think it, because it's too much, too good, too perfect, and the best thing for my mental health is to not raise my own expectations.

I stop off at my flat to pick up some books and my laptop, and then head straight to the library. I don't regret a second of my afternoon gallivanting around a castle, but I've got three full days of labs, lectures and work from tomorrow, and the lab prep I was meant to get done today is still untouched, so I'll probably be up late into the night. Worth it, I remind myself, as I settle into a carrel and arrange my temporary desk.

Ten minutes later, I'm on Instagram on my phone, carefully typing 'Jade Esfahani' into the search and tapping the only result to load. Her life in pictures fills the screen. Not too many selfies; lots of the Norfolk countryside; some group shots; even the parakeet, Dave, makes an appearance the further back I scroll. I also find a selfie of her and her twin, Jasmine. The two of them cheek to cheek, beaming, a near mirror image of each other.

I scroll back up to the top and tap 'follow' before I can second-guess myself. It's totally normal to follow new friends on Instagram, especially when you're a fresher, especially when you've just spent the afternoon together like we have. I don't need to overthink this.

My stomach is still an anxious mess, though.

I go back to my main feed to distract myself and open the story Caddy posted most recently. It's a ten-second video of her and a bunch of her uni friends in what must be a student launderette.

Caddy is actually inside one of the huge tumble dryers, gurning at the camera with the kind of unselfconscious bravado I haven't seen from her since we were about seven. Off-camera, someone shouts in a faux-posh voice, 'Out for a spin, Cadnam?!' followed by laughter that is abruptly cut off when the video ends. I watch it again, searching Caddy's face for the Caddy I know.

Shaking my head, I return to the feed and scroll through a few photos before I find one from Suze. The photo she's posted most recently is of a small dog sitting on an unfamiliar sofa like a human, scowling into the camera like a human. She's written, **Making friends** as a caption, but nothing else. No hashtags, no one else tagged. I wonder whose dog it is, whose sofa.

They feel so distant from me. It's so weird to think of our three lives happening in parallel, so far from each other. I could message them both: *Why were you in a tumble dryer, Cads? Whose dog is that, Suze?* but wouldn't it be embarrassing, somehow, to admit that I'm following their lives on social media, checking up on them, like a distant family member rather than their best friend?

Thinking about this makes me think about my only actual family, Mum, who I haven't spoken to properly for what feels like a long time. I message her, asking if she's free, and she sends back an enthusiastic and immediate, **YES!!!**

I tuck my laptop under my arm and head out into the cool evening with my phone so I can call her, settling myself onto one of the wide concrete steps.

'It's so good to hear your voice,' she says, after we've covered the hello basics. 'I miss you.'

'I miss you, too!' I say. 'It still feels weird to not see you every day. How are you?'

'OK,' she says, her voice a shrug. 'Much the same, really. I'm still getting my dizzy spells; so annoying. I tripped over the back step yesterday, like I haven't walked over it just fine for, what, nineteen years? Embarrassing, really.'

'Did you actually fall?' I ask, alarmed. 'Are you OK?'

'I'm fine. I stumbled, but didn't fall. I'm not quite that decrepit.'

'You should go to the doctor,' I say.

'It's just dizziness,' she says. 'I've had it before. Vertigo, probably. Annoying, but harmless.'

'Are you sure?'

'Yes,' she says patiently.

I frown, not convinced. 'If you're still getting them in, like, a week, will you promise you'll go to the doctor? For me?'

'Yes,' she says again. 'Don't worry. Everything here is fine, including me.'

'Well, good,' I say. 'You're coping without me?'

'Just,' she says.

It's amazing what a difference one good day makes. Maybe all I needed was just one person to make a connection with, and now I can settle, because the next few days after my afternoon with Jade are better than any of the ones that came before. I have a medicinal chemistry tutorial that makes my brain spark and reminds me why I chose this whole degree in the first place, followed by drinks with some of my coursemates. We stay out for a couple of hours, talking and playing pool, and it feels ordinary and nice and studenty in a way I've maybe been hoping for this whole time.

I actually feel . . . kind of happy. Or at least, like I could be. Like there's a life for me here, somewhere I can fit.

On Friday morning, the day Jade and I planned to meet for another coffee, I message the WhatsApp group I share with Caddy and Suze. **Snapshot of your day, please?** I accompany the message with a photo of the page of pharmacy calculations I've been working on. **Sciencing.**

Caddy replies first, sending a photo from a lecture hall, her Mac open in front of her, balanced on the tiny liftable desk at an angle. I can see a lecturer at the front of the hall: a white man with glasses and a full moustache. He's gesturing towards a slide, which is full of letters and branches, like a big confusing tree. **Parsing.**

Suze is last, an hour or so after, with a picture of a coffee machine. **I cleaned this three times today. Oh my God. I'm really living. (Wtf is parsing???)**

I feel bad, then. I'd chosen my photo – and in fact this entire exercise – because I knew how impressive it would look out of context to my two non-sciency best friends. I'd let myself forget how two photos like that in a row might make Suze feel. I hesitate, tapping out an apology, then reconsider. That would probably make it worse.

Rosie:
Just a posh way of saying passing, I reckon. PARRSSSING.

Suze:
Omg, you're right. Cads, are your private school chickens finally coming home to roost?

Rosie:
ORRRR autocorrect mishap. Parsnips??

Suze:
Praising?

Rosie:
Raisin?

Suze:
Rosin?

Rosie:

Aw, Cads, was that meant to be a message of love for me?

Caddy:

1) Parsing is breaking down a sentence into its component parts, 2) that isn't what chickens coming home to roost means, and 3) you both suck.

Suze:

SNARF.

Rosie:

SNAAAARF.

Suze:

Look, you both might be geniuses, but I make the best cup of coffee. That's going to get me so far in life.

Rosie:

Your face is going to get you so far in life.

That sounded like an insult but I actually meant it.

Suze:

THIS FACE?

Suze sends a selfie of herself clearly mid-washing-up, one yellow-gloved hand making the peace sign, her tongue out, eyebrows raised.

Rosie:

Impressive multi-tasking. That + coffee making + THAT FACE = pure marriage material.

Suze:

Fuck off.

Rosie:

Love you too xxx

Suze:

Love you TWO xxxxxx

Caddy sends an eye-roll and a kiss, which is a smaller contribution than she usually makes to our group chat, and for a moment I wonder whether I should feel bad for teasing her. But no, I'm overthinking. This is the dynamic of our friendship, and we all know that. Why should that change just because two of us are at uni now? I don't want it to change. I need it not to change.

8

'So, what made you choose pharmacy?' Jade asks, taking a tentative sip from her cup then wincing, setting it back down on the table. The two of us are sitting opposite one another in the Hive, a coffee apiece. This time, she'd paid. And she'd touched my arm when she told me to go and find us a table. And smiled in a way that was . . . well, it made my skin tingle.

I open my mouth to give her the answer I've given everyone who's asked me this question over the last two years. What I said to Mum when she looked confused as I waved the prospectus in her face, to Caddy when her mouth opened in a little O of surprise, to the interviewers right here on this campus on my interview day. The answer I almost believe myself. *I like science; I like chemistry; I want a secure future* . . .

'When I was in year eleven,' I hear myself say, then pause, looking down at the table. I've never said this to anyone, not anyone. Why do I feel the compulsion to share this with Jade? I look up, and she smiles at me. 'One of my best friends, she . . .' I swallow. 'She tried to kill herself. In the middle of the night, on the beach, on her own. Pills.'

'God,' Jade says. 'That must have been scary.'

I breathe in and out in a long sigh. 'Yeah, it was. It was a shitty time all round. We'd been arguing a lot. We weren't talking when it happened, and – not that her attempt was about me. It wasn't. But yeah, I did get a bit stuck in the mindset of, that could've have been the last . . .' I shake my head, shaking it off. 'Anyway. She's still here. That's the important thing. But it really . . . well, it kind of fucked me up a bit.'

'Of course!' Jade says, eyes widening. 'Of course it would.'

I nod, reassured. I've only ever talked about Suze's suicide attempt with people who also knew her, which meant that talking about how it had affected *me* would be selfish. 'And my head kept coming back to the pills. She had a mix; she'd been hoarding them for a while. I don't know what any of them were, but they were all legit medications, the kind you just take without thinking about it. Nothing dodgy in them, and they're all designed to *help*, you know? I'd always thought of medicine as being this uncomplicated *good*. I'd never thought about what they actually are, how we put this stuff in our body and the reason it stops the headache or helps your blood pressure or whatever is because of how the active ingredients work in your body. And once I realized that, I wanted to know how they worked. On, like, a chemical level? I wanted to understand medication and the body. And how . . . and how those same medications could have killed Suze if we hadn't . . . if she hadn't been found when she was. Because they would have done; she'd have been dead.'

I close my eyes for a second as an old spasm of horror shoots through me, the existential kind, like I haven't felt for a while. When I open them again, Jade's eyes are still steady on me, waiting.

'And it was all mental health and depression and suicidality, and all these things none of us can control. The only things that were concrete and that could make any kind of sense were those pills. I guess I wanted to get some sense of control back, and I felt like, if I can understand that, I . . .' I shake my head, trying to smile. 'I feel like I've stopped making sense.'

'No, I get it,' Jade says. 'Did you think about doing pharmaceutical science?'

I nod. 'I did, but I liked that pharmacy had the patient element as well, not just the science. It's not that I want to be making new medications or anything like that. I wanted to feel like I was helping people, as well as understanding medicine. And, on a practical level, everything I just said kind of tied in with what I really wanted, which is a stable career and a secure future. When I read about pharmacy, it just seemed so . . . so perfect, really.' I remember that, how perfect it felt. Back when it was something abstract instead of my actual life. I keep this part to myself.

'How is she now?' Jade asks. 'Your friend?'

I smile properly, reaching for my phone and unlocking it, opening my photos and tapping, then holding up the screen so Jade can see the photo Suze sent of her washing up, all peace signs and bright eyes and *alive*. 'She's good. I mean, I always worry about her. But she's had a lot of help since that all happened.'

Jade smiles, nodding. 'That's good.'

'What about you?' I ask. 'What was your why?'

She reaches up and curls a few strands of her hair through her fingers, considering. 'Well, I don't have a story as compelling as that. My dad is a doctor and my mum is a clinical pharmacologist. I guess it's not rocket science as to how I ended up here.' She shrugs, a smile still on her face. 'A bit of both, I guess. My sister would say it was because I couldn't bear to let either of them down, so I went with both at once. But she would say that.'

'What does she study? You said she's at Cambridge, right?'

'Impressive memory. Yeah. But she's studying classics.' I must look as surprised as I feel because she laughs. 'I know, right? If I'm the parent pleaser, Jazz is the rebel. If you can be a rebel studying classics. I don't know. She says she feels left out, but she did it on purpose.' She rolls her eyes. 'Families, right? What does your mum do?'

Survives. 'She works in a bank. Nothing exciting.' I feel guilty as soon as I've said it. Why did I feel the need to add that? What's wrong with me? 'Mum's one of those people who's, like . . . life is what happens while you're not at work. You know?'

To my relief, Jade laughs with recognition, not judgement. 'That's kind of how Jazz is, too. She thinks the career mentality is toxic. And maybe she's right, I don't know. But I couldn't imagine not knowing where I was going. I like the certainty of it.'

'Me too!' I say, perhaps too enthusiastically, but it's the first time someone else has voiced how I feel. 'That's exactly it.'

She grins at me. 'I love that you get it. Most people seem to be, like, isn't it boring having everything planned out? No! Besides, I schedule in time for spontaneous fun.' She laughs again, then adds quickly, 'I'm joking. I'm not boring. I hope not, anyway.'

'Definitely not,' I say, again too enthusiastically, but I don't care.

'Speaking of not boring,' Jade says, her smile still perfectly wide. 'Are you going on the Pharm pub crawl this weekend? It's pub golf. Should be fun.'

'I'm not sure,' I say, hedging, because the answer had been no until about thirty seconds ago. 'Are you? I thought it wasn't an official PharmSoc social?'

'It isn't,' she says. 'Which is good. Less responsibility for me when I'm not there in any "official capacity".' She raises her fingers in scare quotes, then laughs. 'I mean, I'm not a big drinker, so I won't be doing the actual pub crawl bit of pub golf, but it'll be fun anyway. You should definitely come. I know this kind of thing can be a bit messy and stupid, but it's fun, too. And I'll look after you.'

My heart gives a kick, the kind that spirits an uncontrollable smile onto my face. 'Well, I can't say no now, can I?'

Her eyes meet mine, her smile wide and almost, but not quite, teasing. 'You can't, no.'

9

I've just started my make-up when I get the wobble. Out of nowhere, midway through a stomach-flipping daydream about what it would be like to kiss Jade, my head goes, *What if this is a mistake?* Which should be a small, easily ignorable question, but my brain decides to seize hold instead of discarding it, and within twenty seconds I'm sat down on my bed, staring into space, lovely daydreams of kisses replaced by increasingly ridiculous worst-case scenarios. Jade, leaning in for a kiss and then laughing at me in front of all her cool third-year friends. Me finding Jade on the dance floor, kissing another girl. No, kissing a *guy*. The two of us kissing and then her pulling back, making a face, saying, *'That's what you think kissing is?'*

Oh my God, shut up, you idiot.

Determinedly, I pick up my mascara again and return to my reflection, focusing on what I know. Which, right now, is how to apply mascara. *One step at a time. This is fine.*

I've done a pretty good job of convincing myself that it really is fine, but then I make the last-second decision to duck into the kitchen for a gulp of cupboard-rum and find that Rika, Dawn, Freddie and Flapjack are all in there, the boys at the table, the girls at the hob, making fajitas.

'Oh my God, are you going *out*?' Rika almost shrieks, which is rude, because it's not like I *never* go out; I just don't go out as much as them.

I glance down at myself. 'Just to the library.'

Rika deflates. Dawn laughs.

'Yes,' I say, reaching into my cupboard and pulling out my

emergency rum, which is very obviously emptier than it was last time. Clearly, at least one of my flatmates has helped themselves. I wipe the top of the bottle with the cuff of my coat, then take a swig. 'I am going out.'

Freddie whoops, which makes me laugh even though I still find him annoying.

'*Without us?*' Rika asks, looking mournful. 'You *actually* go out and it's *without us*? Aren't we your only friends?'

I take another gulp of rum. The gulp is too big, because I splutter on it. 'Shit. No. Yes, it's without you. It's a Pharm thing.'

'Oh, a *Pharm thing*,' Rika says in an affected voice, giving the pan she's standing beside a cursory stir. 'I *see*.'

Flapjack moos. We all ignore him.

'Where are you going?' Dawn asks.

'All over,' I say. 'Pub golf.'

'Oh my God, so cool!' she says. 'We did one last week. It was so messy. I've never been so drunk in my life. Rika had to save me.'

'From what?' I ask.

'A kerb,' Rika says. Her deadpan delivery is so perfect that I laugh properly, raising my bottle to her. She winks at me. This is one of those moments where I think Rika and I could actually get along pretty well if we only decided too, but then she says, in a voice that is all knowing but not kind, 'So who have you dressed up for, then?' and ruins it.

'Me,' I say, but I've hesitated for just a beat too long and made it obvious.

Her catlike grin widens. 'Ro! You dark horse.'

'Your chicken is burning,' I say.

'Your face is burning!' she sings out.

She's right, but I flip her off anyway, rolling my eyes as if I don't care, then saunter off out of the kitchen. (I don't actually saunter. I am many things, but I'm not someone who can pull off a saunter. I just wasn't born graceful.) I can hear Rika laughing behind me, the sizzle of the fajitas they'll all eat together, Freddie's words abruptly cut off by the door closing – 'Do you think she's actually—'

Yes, I think, with a sudden flare of my old bullishness. *I am actually.* I head determinedly towards the first stop of the pub crawl, which is the student bar on campus, my head held high. When I walk in to find that most of the Blue Bar is taken up by a crowd of excitable pharmacy students, not just freshers but second-, third- and even fourth-years as well, a spasm of anxiety threatens, but I try to push it down, smiling confidently. I do wish I had someone to arrive with so I didn't have to do this on my own. I think of Laini, for the first time in a while. I wish she was here to be nervous for me, so I could tell her everything was fine.

'Rosie!' It's Dion, waving boisterously at me, from where he's sitting with three people I don't recognize.

'Hey!' I say, heading over casually, like I could have gone and stood with anyone but was choosing him. 'I didn't know you'd be here!'

'I'm being young and cool,' he says, deadpan, and the guy beside him laughs. 'Rosie, this is Jules, Davis and Martin.' I lift a hand in a wave, and they wave back.

'How do you guys know each other?' I ask.

The woman, Jules, laughs. 'That's very kind of you,' she says. 'But we're all aware of how obvious our mature status is.'

'It isn't!' I say. It is.

'Excuse you,' Martin says. 'I'm only twenty-two. Twenty-two! I'm still a kid.' He looks at me. 'Right?'

'Right,' I say.

'Very kind,' Jules says again. 'Is this why you're friends, Dion? Because she's kind enough to pretend you're eighteen?'

Dion grins. 'Rosie's my lab partner,' he says. 'But yes, very kind.'

'How is Dion in the lab?' Davis asks me.

'Great,' I say. 'Very calm. What are you all drinking?'

I end up staying with them for the next hour, as we all move as a group from the Blue Bar onto a bus, into town and to the first Wetherspoons of the three on the list. Not because I get stuck with them, but because I want to stay. I like Dion, and his friends are just like him: sweetly kind, a little bit serious, relaxed. They don't seem to be performing for anyone, and I feel so much more at ease than I have done on my other fresher nights out. What does that say about me? Maybe I'm prematurely mature. Maybe I should have skipped a few years and started as a mature student.

It takes a while before I see Jade. I've been trying to play it cool, of course, but I've been keeping an eye out for her since I arrived. When I finally spot her, she's with a large group of people I don't recognize, laughing at something, gesturing with one hand and holding on to a bottle of Crabbie's with the other. She looks so completely comfortable where she is, and she's barely dressed up beyond how she usually looks. I could go over, but I don't. All I can think of is Rika saying, '*So who have you dressed up for, then?*' I feel awkward and young and . . . well, scared.

Instead, I concentrate on a story Dion is telling, smiling and nodding. In fact, I make such an effort to not look over at Jade, I don't even notice that she's come up right beside me until her hand is on my arm.

'Hi!' she says, and I jump so dramatically that I spill my rum and Coke all over Martin's shoes.

'Hi,' I say, or try to say. It comes out more like, 'Sorryshithi.'

Jade grins at me while Martin laughs off my apologies, shaking his feet theatrically for effect. 'Sorry,' she says. 'That was my fault.'

'Definitely your fault,' I say, grinning back. I wouldn't be able to explain why, but seeing her grin at me like that has swept all my ridiculous anxiety away, clumsiness or no clumsiness. Instead, I feel . . . I don't even know. A little electric, like something is sparking inside me.

'Hey, Jade,' Jules says.

'Hi,' Jade says, turning what I realize is her Official Pharmacy Society Equality and Diversity Rep smile on her. 'How are you guys doing over here?'

'Good,' Jules says. 'Are you on duty tonight?'

Jade laughs. 'Not officially, no, but it is a pub crawl, so no doubt I'll be babysitting some drunk freshers later.' She gives Jules a conspiratorial eye-roll, and they both laugh again. 'It's fine; I'm used to it. Speaking of drunk freshers . . .' Her eyes meet mine, her eyebrows lifting slightly in a question.

'I won't need a babysitter,' I say.

'Shame,' Jade says, lightly, casually.

That's when the leader of the pub crawl, a second-year wearing both a trilby and a Hawaiian shirt in combination, whose name I have heard is either Jason, Zinc, Jonesy or all three, cups his hands around his mouth and bellows, 'TO THE LAMB!' and everyone is suddenly moving en masse and Jade disappears into the swarm.

The next time I see her is two bars on, laughing with Jason/Zinc/Jonesy by a games machine, shaking her head. This time, there's a J2O in her hand. I head over to say hi, then, 'Didn't you say you'd look after me?' which makes Jason/Zinc/Jonesy look at me like I've just appeared out of a portal holding two cats and a pineapple.

'I did!' Jade says, putting an arm around my shoulder and pivoting us away. 'You're so right, I'm sorry.' Into my ear she says, 'Oh my God, thank you.'

'He wasn't trying to get with you, was he?' I ask, genuinely startled.

'Yes.'

'Doesn't he know that . . . ?'

'Oh yeah, he does. You'd be amazed by how many straight guys can't fathom that lesbian means lesbian. Poor guy. I'd feel sorry for him if he wasn't such a bellend. Anyway!' She drops her arm and leans back slightly to smile at me. 'How are you? Do you actually need me to look after you?'

'I'm good,' I say. I miss her arm. 'And no.'

'I didn't think so,' she says. 'You don't seem like the type. Hey!' She says suddenly and loudly, making me jump, but she's talking to someone behind me. 'Aisha! Rosie, you should meet – Hey! Come meet my friend.' The girl, Aisha, steps over obediently, smiling. 'Aisha, this is Rosie.'

'Oh!' Aisha says, very clearly already knowing who I am, which makes me feel momentarily dizzy by the implications. 'Hi, Rosie.' She gives Jade a look.

'That was subtle, thank you,' Jade says, laughing. 'Rosie, Aisha's one of my housemates. And she's an imposter – don't tell anyone.'

'An imposter?'

'She studies *law*,' Jade says, making a face.

'I do,' Aisha says, nodding. 'I'd be sorry about it, but I absolutely am not. Thank you for letting me gatecrash your pub crawl, though.'

Jade opens her mouth to say something else, her eyes bright, but then someone is calling her name from the bar, and she's rolling her eyes and waving a hand at me, like, *I'll be right back!* But barely two minutes later the whole crowd is crawling on to the next bar on the list, and Aisha is talking excitedly at me about family law, and I start telling her about Suze, of all people, and she's explaining in meticulous detail about how child abuse compensation works, and then another hour has gone by and everyone around us suddenly seems to be very, very drunk and there's no sign of Jade anywhere.

I go outside to get some air, glancing at my phone to see that it's just gone 1 a.m. It's not really all that much quieter outside the club, because we're at Riverside and there are so many clubs clustered in the same area that the combined residual noise is its own bassline, plus there are dozens of drunk students around, some in groups, some in pairs, some talking, some laughing, some crying, some with arms and tongues entwined. Still, the air is nice. I find a bench and sit down, closing my eyes for a moment, breathing it in. I'll give myself a few minutes, then go back in. I'll find Jade, and . . . well, I don't know. But that will be a good start.

'Hey, you.'

I half turn, startled, but already smiling. Jade is smiling, too, her hands tucked into the pockets of the leather jacket she's wearing. She looks, with no exaggeration, incredible. And she's smiling back at me. And sitting down beside me.

'Hi,' I say.

'How are you?' she asks. 'Having a good night?'

'Yeah,' I say. 'You?'

Her eyes meet mine, slow and steady, and it's like an electric current, I swear. It doesn't feel cold any more. And then her eyes travel down to my lips, I watch them do it, and she bites hers between perfect straight teeth. My heart starts going very fast. If I lean forward, I could kiss her, and I think she'd let me. I think she wants me to. She'd kiss me back, and it would be perfect. Can I? Should I?

'Do you want to go back inside?' she asks, and I jolt.

'Inside?' I repeat. My voice sounds a bit weird, which is embarrassing.

'Or do you want to go?' she says.

'Go?' *Oh my God, Rosie, what the fuck is wrong with you?*

'I've reached my Riverside limit,' Jade says. 'I'm good to head back home now. Want to come with?'

I have never, not in my entire life, wanted anything as much as this. I feel myself nod. My face feels hot. She holds out a hand and I take it, the two of us standing in one seamless motion, walking towards the bus stop together. Her fingers thread through mine, and I think I'm feeling every feeling at once. I'm not sure, exactly, how we got here together, the two of us somehow on exactly the same page, even though we've never said anything out loud to get us here.

A big part of me thinks that she might kiss me at the bus stop, but the bus is already there when we arrive. We sit together at the back, our hands still entwined. When the bus lurches away from the stop, she starts tracing her thumb over mine, soft and slow.

'Are you OK?' she asks me after a few minutes, which makes me worry that I'm doing something stupid with my face.

'Yeah,' I say.

'Is this OK?' she says.

We both look down at our hands, currently resting against her leg. No two hands have ever looked as good, locked together, as ours. The nail polish she's wearing is a deep purple, chipped on the nail of her little finger.

'I like your tattoo,' I say. 'Is it Farsi?'

She nods. 'I'm impressed you know that.'

'It was a safe guess; don't give me credit for that,' I say, and she laughs. 'What does it mean?'

'Love,' Jade says. She shrugs a little sheepishly. 'Sometimes I am quite basic.' She grins. 'Jasmine and I both got it when we turned eighteen. Our mother was not amused, but my dad likes it. Do you have any tattoos?'

'Not yet,' I say, which sounds better than 'no'.

I'm about to ask her whether she has any others, but the bus is slowing and she's tugging me to my feet, leading me down the aisle and out – 'Thanks!' we both say together to the driver on the way – and her hand is still in mine.

Her house is a terrace, indistinguishable from all the other terraces on the same road. She lets go of my hand to find her key in her bag and I stand there beside her, waiting, mute. I'm aiming for *cool and chilled*, because it is taking literally all of my concentration to stop my face from revealing how I'm really feeling – excited, anxious, giddy, impatient – so fake-cool is the best I can do.

'Here,' she says triumphantly, withdrawing her key and opening the door. The way she smiles at me then is electric, so full of promise and hope and expectation. 'Come in.'

I follow her through the living room and up the stairs. She pauses at her closed door, her eyes meeting mine again.

'Is this OK?' she asks, just like she did on the bus.

I reach out my hand in response and she smiles as she takes it, opening her door with her elbow, pulling me inside.

Our first kiss is a breathless, heady blaze of fire. All the slow burn of intrigue over the last half an hour burst into life. Her lips and tongue against mine, my whole body alight. Her fingers against my face, in my hair. I've never felt anything like this before, not ever, not with anyone. Kissing Rika wasn't like this. Kissing boys wasn't like this.

When we finally break apart, it's because we have to. I'm gasping for breath, and so is she, and I'm so buzzy with excitement and lust and alcohol that I can't stop myself laughing. I manage, 'Wow,' which makes her laugh, too. We're both still standing in the middle of her room; she's still wearing her leather jacket. 'I love this,' I say, touching her sleeve. I feel emboldened; loose and happy. 'It looks amazing on you.'

She lifts her hand to my face again, smoothing fallen curls

behind my ear, and kisses me again. It's slower this time, intense in a different way. There's a part of me, even while most of my consciousness is focused on how amazing this is, that can't quite believe this is happening. That I'm in this scene instead of watching it, that it's me being kissed like this, me kissing like this. That it's me Jade has chosen. Jade, who is confident and beautiful and smells like vanilla.

Jade, who is moving us backwards, towards her bed. Who is shrugging off her jacket between kisses.

I am, suddenly and completely, very aware of how much experience she must have versus how much I definitely don't have, and the fact that I've never told her that, and maybe she just assumes that I know what I'm doing, even though I don't, and that I'll know what to do, which I definitely will not, and my heart is racing, and the bed is below me, her hand is easing up under my top, I—

'Hey,' she whispers. Her hand stills, then withdraws. She leans a little away from me so she can see me better. 'OK?' she asks. 'I feel like I lost you a bit there.'

'I'm OK,' I say.

'Are you sure?' She reaches up behind her and pulls down a pillow, settling it under both our heads. 'I got carried away. I'm sorry. We don't have to do anything more than this.' She hesitates. 'We don't even have to do this, if you don't—'

'Oh no, I want,' I say quickly. 'Really, really want.'

A smile lights back on her face. 'Good.'

'Very good,' I say. It comes out like a whisper. I know I'm probably looking at her too intensely, her face so close to mine, but I can't help it. It's like I'm mapping it onto my brain, every contour, every line, every eyelash.

'Do you want to talk?' Jade asks, her fingers closing around mine, squeezing gently. 'We haven't, have we? Am I the first girl you've . . . well . . . You're bi, right? That's what you said? This isn't you trying something out, or anything?'

'No!' I say. 'And yes, I'm bi. Definitely, definitely bi.' If I had a shred of doubt before tonight, it's well and truly gone now. 'But I've never . . .' I pause. 'Not just with girls. I've never . . . you know. Never been there. At all.'

She nods, understanding. 'That's OK.'

'What about you?' I ask cautiously.

'Have I *been there*?' She's smiling, that half-amused smile that's such pure Jade. The kind of smile that would be mocking on someone else's face, someone who didn't have her warmth. 'Yes, I have. Only ever girls. I'm not bi; pure lesbian, me.' She seems proud of this. 'I've had two girlfriends.'

'When did you come out?' I ask.

'When I was fourteen,' she says. 'I didn't have the coming-out angst a lot of people have, I think. There was never any doubt. Boys just did nothing for me. You?'

'It took a while,' I say. 'I only came out last summer. And I've never been in a relationship. I've done a few things with guys, but not, like . . . Not anything major.' I can feel a flush in my cheeks, and I hope she doesn't notice. Slowly, unsure whether I'm making a mistake, I say, 'I've never done . . . this.'

'Kissing?' she asks.

'This,' I say, gesturing to the two of us, so close on her bed, face to face, our legs touching.

She shifts slightly closer to me, the tip of her nose brushing mine. 'Do you like it?'

I nod, feeling the smile on my face. 'Yeah.'

10

I feel like I'm high.

Every time I think about how Jade kissed me, that I lay on a bed with a girl and tangled my legs with hers and felt her bare skin under my fingers, it's like an electric shock jolts through my body. The really good kind. I worry that I need to somehow play it cool, that there are rules to this kind of thing and I shouldn't give away how I feel, but she messages me the next day, **I had this dream that I kissed this amazing girl last night and then I was like nope that actually happened, isn't life cool? I love being gay.**

Amazing. She thinks I'm amazing. Even though I'm just a fresher, not just at uni but also in romantic terms, especially sapphic ones. Me. I reply, **Sounds like a great dream. I had one just like it. Don't think it was real, though. Too good to be real.**

Jade:

I'm pretty sure it was real? I'm doubting myself now xx

Rosie:

Maybe we had the same dream?

MAYBE. Maybe we should meet up and compare notes xxx

Good idea. That's the only way we'll know.

Look at you, playing this cool. Withholding kisses. Are you trying to make me actually doubt everything? Xx

How can an x compare to the real thing?

OK, that was a good answer. Are you sure this is your first time on this merry-go-round? Further evidence is required xx

Evidence of . . . ?

The real thing xx

I'm in xxx

xxxx

xxxx

Unfortunately, the next few days are too full on for me to actually be able to see Jade, even though that's the only thing I want to do. But I have four lectures, three workshops, two tutorials and an all-morning lab practical, plus all the prep work and reading that comes with it. Jade, too, has her own schedule to keep to, and so instead we message back and forth every day, sometimes as a conversation, but mostly playing the game we'd started when we visited Norwich Castle together, each of us saying something we like. It's a good second best to seeing her in person.

As well as talking to her, I want to talk *about* her, this electrifying *maybe* that is me and Jade, even as it's moving from the *maybe* to a *probably*. I want to tell my best friends, but, so far, I just . . . haven't. It's not that I'm actively not telling them, but I haven't found the right moment yet. I meant to do it after our first kiss, but Suze went on one of her disappearing acts that week – phone off, no word, no nothing – for the longest blackout since before she moved back to Brighton, five whole days. I was just starting to really panic when she reappeared, chirpy, on WhatsApp, as if nothing had happened. It hadn't felt right to do the big Jade reveal during her absence, but doing it on her reappearance didn't feel right either. And now, it's reaching the point where it feels weird that I haven't told them already.

Also, neither of them has asked. Which is kind of annoying me. It's not like I expect them to be psychic, but I *did* just come out as bisexual, and then go off to university, land of sexual freedom and possibility. It doesn't feel like a lot to ask for one of them to go, *Hey, Roz, how's the love life?*

When I talk to Caddy late on Sunday, for the first time in what feels like a while, I have a vague idea that I'll bring this up, but I get distracted by an elaborate story she tells me – breathless and excited, interrupting herself to laugh – about a Pixar-themed club night she and her friends had gone to that had somehow ended with their photo in the local paper. Even by the end of the story, I'm not sure exactly why, except that the whole thing involved a lot of cardboard – 'It had to be an authentic WALL-E. We used proper industrial paint and everything!' – that almost completely disintegrated in the rain, leaving the wearer – Owen – shivering in his 'literal pants'.

'So who did you go as?' I ask. 'Eve?'

'No, Tess was Eve,' she says. 'I was the plant.'

'How?!'

'Brown trousers, green top, the right pose.' She laughs. 'Honestly, Roz, it was so much fun.'

'Sounds it,' I say, because it really does, and I wish I didn't feel so jealous. 'How's the course?'

'Good! Really good. Everything's great, honestly.'

'And how's long distance?' I ask quickly, before she can ask me about my own life. 'Are you missing Kel?' There's a silence, and I feel a frown of surprise on my own face. 'Cads?'

'It's fine,' she says finally. 'He's fine.'

When Caddy and her boyfriend, Kel, first got together, over two years ago now, Caddy used to talk about him in the same kind of voice she's just used talking about the Pixar night. Now her voice is level, almost flat.

'That was the finest *fine* ever,' I say, teasing.

She sighs. 'Long distance, right? I don't want to talk about that. Have you talked to Suze?'

'A bit. You?'

'A bit. I tried to ask why she disappeared, but – you know what she's like – she just brushed me off. Do you think she's OK? I'm worried about her.'

'When are we ever not worried about her?' I ask, when what I want to say is, *Don't think I haven't noticed that you've used Suze and her constant terrifying fragility to distract me from talking about you.*

'True,' Caddy says. 'Hey. Talk about long distance. Why does everyone always talk about long distance in relation to romantic love? I feel like I'm in a long-distance relationship with the two of you.'

This makes me smile. 'Yeah, I know what you mean. It's weird, isn't it? I wish you and me had gone to the same uni.'

'Do you?' She's so surprised that it makes me instantly regret this moment of honesty. 'Really?'

'Wow, thanks,' I say, laughing to try and cover myself. 'I feel so loved.'

She laughs, too. 'Obviously, I love you. But don't you love getting to do all of this, like, fresh? Accidental pun, but you know what I mean. Freshers, fresh start. Blah blah.'

'A fresh start from what?' I ask. 'You're great. You've always been great.'

There's another pause. It feels, suddenly, like we've stumbled into a conversation that neither of us had intended to start.

'I've never felt like I could be myself around anyone but you and Suze. And, like, my family, obviously. But here . . . I just *am* myself. I really love that. Don't you?'

Of course she assumes I'm having the time of my life, like she is. Like I've somehow found myself, like she apparently has. *Am* I myself? My instinctive answer is yes, but that's a bit worrying, really, isn't it?

'I guess we've always been pretty different,' Caddy says into the silence. 'You've *always* been yourself. This is still new to me.'

I want to ask her what she means, to remind her that we've been best friends since we were five, and is she seriously telling me that she thinks, that whole time, she hasn't been herself? But I can't quite face having this conversation right now; just the thought makes me feel strangely tired. 'I'm glad you're having an amazing time.'

'You are, too, right?' she says. It's the first time she's actually asked me this question as a question instead of a statement.

'Sure,' I say.

'You'd tell me if something was wrong?'

'Obviously.'

There's a pause. And then she says, 'OK.'

And I say, 'OK.'

Seeing Jade again is an anticlimax. Not because of her, or because of us, but because all my anxiety that I've been building up over the last few days, especially in these last few minutes as I watch her walk across the concrete towards me, dissipates the moment she leans over, touches my fingers and drops a sweet, light kiss right by the corner of my mouth. And says, 'Hi, Rosie.'

It all just . . . goes. One big, brilliant anticlimax.

I say, 'Could you do that again?' And she goes to kiss me and I move at just the right moment and we kiss properly, in the daylight, right in the middle of the square.

When we break apart, we both start laughing, and her eyes are bright, and she says, 'Aces.'

We get two coffees and then walk around the lake together. It's only the second time, but it feels like it's already our thing, something we do together. This time, she takes my hand, and when we stop at a jetty, we kiss.

When we start walking again, her hand finds mine, oh so casually, and I must smile really wide because she laughs – with affection – and gives my hand a squeeze.

'So this is your first time doing this, right?' she says, without preamble.

'I've walked around this lake before,' I say, deliberately obtuse. 'With you, in fact.'

'Yeah, yeah,' she says, shaking her head, smiling. 'Seriously.'

'Yes,' I say. 'I'm new.'

'You honestly wouldn't know,' she says. 'You're so confident.'

'Am I?' I'm not confident at all, but this isn't the first time someone's told me I seem confident about something when I'm actually just making it up as I go along. Mum used to tell me that was one of my best traits, that it would be the reason I was successful one day. 'You don't give anything away,' Mum had said. 'That's valuable.'

Sometimes, though – like now – it makes me wonder if I'm just not being very honest. Not deliberately, maybe, but still.

'If I had to guess,' Jade says, 'I'd think you'd had at least one girlfriend before. And I'd never guess that you were a fresher.'

This makes me laugh. 'OK, that one? No. What about that time you caught me panicking in the library – i.e. the reason we met?'

She smiles. 'OK, yes, that moment was very first year. But other than that, no. You just don't act like most freshers. Like how you were when I saw you that night in Freshers Week, with your friend. She was all crying and drunk and you were just like, *OK*.' She laughs at the memory. 'It's a good thing. I like that about you.'

I wonder if this is just another you-look-confident perception lie I am somehow giving off, but something about the idea makes me uncomfortable, so I don't follow it. Instead, I say, a little cautiously, 'So you've had two girlfriends?'

'Yes.' Jade releases my hand to smooth her hair out of her eyes, tucking it behind her ear. 'I had my first girlfriend in year ten, and we stayed together into our first year of uni, which was a bad idea.' She rolls her eyes, then looks at me with emphasis. 'Don't ever try long distance – it's a scam.'

I think about Caddy and her boyfriend, how flat she'd sounded on the phone. 'Is it?'

'Total scam.' She shakes her head. 'Anyway, Marie was a long time ago. She's with a guy now.'

Something about the way she says this makes me say, 'Bi is legit.'

'Oh yeah,' she says, nodding. 'Bi is legit. Marie is a . . .' She half smiles, like she's stopped herself mid-thought. 'An unfeminist word.'

'Wow.'

'I shouldn't talk about Marie. It's not me at my best. Anyway, in my first year, after we broke up, I went a bit . . . well, I enjoyed my freedom. My hometown isn't exactly buzzing with potentials, but here . . . So many options! And then I was with Emma for a while, but that wasn't ever really anything.'

'How come?'

'She was a bit too fresher for me. You know what I mean? I was never really into that kind of thing, even when I was one. She wanted to go out a lot, like all the time, do all the dress-up nights, that kind of thing. It just wasn't me. So we broke up in the end, which was the right thing. How about you?'

'Me?'

'Yeah, like, how come you waited?'

'Waited?'

'To come out, I mean. Until the summer before uni, you said, right? Was your school not great with queer stuff?'

'Oh,' I say. 'It wasn't like that. I mean, I guess it wasn't *amazing*? But that's not why. It wasn't a conscious decision. I just . . . wasn't sure. For, like, a really long time.'

'Why not?'

'God, I don't know. It's all so confusing, isn't it? Like, it took me years just to figure out that when people said stuff like "girl crush", they didn't mean it in the way I did.'

'And how did you mean it?'

'Like an *actual* crush,' I say. 'They just meant it in some weird platonic fun way. I thought everyone got all . . . fizzy around girls they liked. But apparently not?'

Jade laughs. 'Not everyone, no.' She grins at me. 'Just the best ones.'

I grin back. 'Good to know.'

11

It feels like I trip and fall into November, like it's come out of nowhere. When I look around me, nothing is new any more; it's just life. Student life. My life. That should mean I have a pretty solid idea of how I feel about it, but I don't, which maybe has a lot to do with the fact that nothing I like about my student life is what I thought I would like.

- I like eating breakfast alone in the kitchen in the early morning, watching the mist run over the grass and lake, the solitary joggers, the birds in flight.
- I like my job, how those eight hours a week in the soothing calm of the jewellery shop feel, paradoxically, like taking a break when it's literally work.
- I like the flash of pure relief that is talking to my best friends on whatever medium takes our fancy in the moment. WhatsApp, FaceTime, phone calls. When it's always easy, even when it's not; when I don't need to think or question myself; where I make jokes and they laugh; where they call me Roz.
- I like doing my laundry in the laundrette late at night, a course text in my bag and a Dr Pepper from the vending machine by my side.
- I like Jade. (A lot. A *lot*.) This person who seemed to come out of nowhere, who I can kiss, who kisses me.
- I like Jade's house, her cheerful, friendly housemates. Those hours away from the frenetic, non-stop sensory overload that is being a fresher in my flat and on the campus.

- I like coffee with Dion before and after lab sessions, comparing notes and talking about our own lives, listening to him talk enthusiastically about rugby union and *Star Trek* and his fiancée, their Bengal cat named Feist, their house.

They're all great things. I feel lucky to have them, but sometimes I wonder if it's a problem that all the things I love about my student life are the non-student bits.

Everything in my block is loud, whether inside my flat or out of it. Sometimes the bass is so intense I swear it makes my bed vibrate. I can feel it in my teeth. There's usually a flat party happening somewhere nearby, which means groups of people clustered on the stairs, drunk and shrieky, coming in and out of our flat as if the entire building is open to the world. (It is not.)

In the early days, I tried joining in, taking a drink out onto the stairs, starting up conversations with the randoms I ran into, but it was like a weird kind of platonic one-night stand. Even the times I felt like I'd connected with people, I could barely remember who or why in the morning, and they certainly didn't remember me. It got old fast, and after a while, I just stopped trying. Instead, I got used to gathering up my stuff and heading to the library, returning only when I was sure things would be mostly quiet.

Is it always loud in your flat? I asked Caddy.

Yes! In a good way, though.

It's starting to feel like a familiar mantra. *In a good way, though.* It isn't that she's having a completely different life at uni than me; it's just that she *likes* all the bits I don't.

When I talk to Mum, I give her a very censored version of all of this, of course. I tell her about Jade — she is *beside* herself with joy, almost giddy with it — and give her CliffsNotes versions of my lectures and practicals, which she seems to find far more interesting, in the telling of them, than I do.

'Anyway, how are you?' I ask. It's early on a Tuesday evening, and I'm sitting on the top deck of the bus on my way back to campus after a shift at the jewellery shop. 'Have you gone to the doctor yet? About your dizzy spells?'

'I'm fine, and yes,' she says. 'And it's nothing to worry about, just like I thought. The doctor seemed to think I was a bit silly, coming in over something so small. He told me that I could expect the odd "moment" as I got older.'

'Oh my God,' I say, screwing up my face. 'Please tell me you told him off?'

'I didn't. I *felt* silly. Anyway, I'm fine. He says it's most likely what I thought: a touch of vertigo.'

'Vertigo?' I frown out of the window. Basically just a medical term for periods of particularly severe dizziness, something Mum has had before. That should make me feel better, but it doesn't. 'OK, well . . . Did he prescribe anything?'

'No, he says if it's only mild, then it'll pass, but to come back if it gets worse. He says it's probably stress-related, especially as I mentioned I've been having the odd hand spasm, some pins and needles, that kind of thing, and they're apparently all known stress responses. He says I should get more sleep, be more active.'

'Useful,' I say, rolling my eyes. 'More sleep, less stress? Definitely advice worth going to the doctor for.'

'Well, exactly,' she says. 'You see why I felt silly? Anyway, I told him about you, my trainee pharmacist.' Her pleasure and pride shines through the phone, and I sink a little into my seat. 'He was impressed. *That's a tough course*, he said. I said, *I know. She's a tough girl.*'

I try to smile, even though she can't see me, so I might as well have let my face crumple a little, like it wanted to. 'I hope you didn't waste any of your appointment talking about me.'

'It's never a waste of time to talk about you,' she says.

'Seriously,' I say. 'Are you going to try and be less stressed?'

'Yes, Rosie,' she says, and I can hear the patient smile that will be on her face, indulging her overprotective daughter. 'I've decided to take a few more days off to rest up a bit. Janine's going to take some time off, too, and we're going to go to the beach like two old ladies of leisure.'

'That sounds great,' I say. 'Have fun. Tell her I said hi.'

'I'll tell her more than that!' Mum says. 'My trainee—'

'OK, OK,' I say, smiling for real this time. 'I know; you're proud. I love you.'

'I love you too,' she says warmly. 'Speak soon.'

When I hang up, I see a message from Jade waiting, and my heart leaps.

Jade:
Hello ☺

Rosie:
Hello ☺

I had a thought.

Just one?

Yes, singular. Want to know what it was?

Yes xx

It was, I should take Rosie on a date.

☺

Don't you think we should have a proper first date?

I definitely do.

How's Friday night?

Perfect.

Great! Let's say 7 p.m. in the city centre? Xx

Can't wait xx

When I get back to my flat, I head into the kitchen to get myself some food and find Dawn sat alone at the kitchen table, laptop open in front of her, frowning in concentration. When I walk in, she jumps, then smiles. 'Hey.'

'Hi,' I say. I open my cupboard and take out my bread and peanut butter, then go over to the table to sit down opposite her. 'Are you working?'

She nods. 'I'm writing an essay on Artaud's First Manifesto.'

'Cool,' I say, unscrewing the peanut butter, as if the words mean anything to me, which they don't. 'How's it going?'

'OK,' she says. 'I don't love writing essays, but his theories are so interesting. Do you know anything about surrealist theatre?'

I shake my head. 'You can tell me about it, if you want?'

She brightens. 'Is that OK?'

When I nod, she starts telling me about the theatre of cruelty, her voice sparkling with enthusiasm, even passion. That's what I'm listening to more than the actual words she's saying, which don't really mean anything to me: how stimulated she is by all of this. She loves her course, just like Caddy does. Like Jade does.

When she's finished, she's leaning towards me, elbows on the table, hands clasped, and she seems to realize in one moment because she laughs, sitting back. 'Sorry. Tell me something about pharmacy! I don't know anything about it. It must be so interesting.'

Dawn is a nice person, I think, with a kind of distant surprise. Generous with her kindness.

'It's not really that interesting,' I say, and Dawn's face flickers with confusion. 'I mean, it is, but . . .' How to explain that I just don't want to talk about it, that I know I won't match her levels of enthusiasm, and that's something I don't want to face? 'It's really complicated.'

'Oh,' Dawn says. 'OK.' She shrugs. 'I was always so bad at science. Especially, like, chemistry and physics. I get biology, because it's, like, the world, right? But I never got why I had to know about the elements. Like, why? Scientists already know what they are. Why do I need to know, too? I don't need it in my life.' She laughs, and I think about how at secondary school I didn't admit I liked science until sixth form, because I didn't want anyone to think I wasn't cool.

'All of science is the world,' I say, then immediately worry I sound too earnest. 'Anyway.' I try to think of something else I can talk to her about. 'How are all your hundreds of societies going?'

She laughs, pinkening. 'It's not that many. And they're good. I really only go to a couple of them now. But it's nice to be able to hang out with so many people, even though, like, my close friends are all here.' She gestures around the kitchen, as if they're all there, as if I might somehow be a part of it, even though we both know I'm not. 'Do you know who you're going to live with next year yet?' she asks me. 'We're going to go look at a house this weekend. In the Golden Triangle.'

'Already?' I ask. It comes out like a squeak. 'It's only November.'

'Yeah! We thought, like, why wait? We don't want all the good places to go before we get a chance to see them.'

My heart has started racing. If they're already talking about this, other people will be, too. People have already made the friends they're going to live with in their second year. But me? There's no one I know even close to that kind of friendship. The people I get along with – Dion, Jade, Jade's friends – are all older than me and won't be looking for someone to live with.

Oh fuck. What the fuck am I going to do?

'It's OK if you don't know yet,' Dawn says quickly, and I'm embarrassed by how obvious my anxiety must be. 'We're, like, super early.'

'Who are you shacking up with?' I ask, trying to be casual. 'Rika and the boys?'

She shakes her head. 'We thought about it, but we figured, it'll be better not to mix us up like that. It seems smart to not be in the same house as my boyfriend. Just in case. So we're going girls and guys, separate. Rika and me, plus two other girls from our course.'

I'm nodding along before the words snag in my head. 'Wait, boyfriend? What boyfriend?'

'Freddie,' she says, smiling an awkward, shy smile. 'Sorry, didn't you know?'

Wow, I really haven't been around if I've missed this. 'Since when?'

She shrugs. 'Kind of off and on since Freshers. But properly on since, like, maybe a couple of weeks?'

But Freddie's such a basic dick, I manage not to say. 'Yeah, good idea not to live with him, then. You'll probably be broken up by then.'

She laughs like I was joking, which I wasn't.

The kitchen door opens and Freddie and Matteo come in, loud and boisterous, tossing a Coke bottle back and forth between them, knocking into the table, sending the lid of the peanut butter skittering off the table and across the floor. Dawn's face has lit up. I know, even without a mirror, that mine has not.

'The Enigma!' Matteo yells, like a sports announcer with an actual audience, pointing at me. 'She lives!'

It occurs to me, as I try my very best to make my eye-roll friendly instead of just annoyed, that Matteo never speaks to me like this if it's just the two of us in the kitchen. Sometimes, we both have early morning lectures, and we end up having breakfast together at the kitchen table before we head out into campus, and he's usually mellow, even sweet. He calls me Rosie, for one thing. Why do people have to be so different when they're around other people?

'I better go,' I say, leaning over to pick up the peanut butter lid, then putting my plate in the sink. 'See you guys later.'

'She leaves!' Freddie yells.

I can still hear them laughing even after the door falls closed.

12

I meet Jade in the city centre as planned on Friday evening. She's sitting on a stone slab bench, head slightly stooped, phone in hand, and she doesn't notice my approach until I'm right in front of her. I'm hoping to surprise her, catch her off guard, but she barely flinches, just looks up with a smile already on her face.

'Hi,' she says.

'Hi,' I say back. I gesture towards her phone with my chin. 'Family stuff again?'

'What—Oh! No.' She shakes her head, sliding her phone into her pocket as she gets to her feet. 'I was asking for first-date tips from my friends.'

'First-date tips?' I repeat, a pleased grin spreading uncontrollably on my face. For me. She's asking for tips because she's going on a first date with *me*. 'Interesting. Any good ones?'

'We'll see,' she says.

We go to an Italian restaurant on St Benedicts Street, the kind with candles on the table and chunky wedges of fresh bread with oil. I've never been on a date before, first or otherwise, and for the first few minutes I find that I can't even look directly at Jade – who looks unbelievable in the soft light, her dark hair loose around her face – without wanting to laugh or, even more confusingly, cry. She doesn't seem to notice my flustered confusion, even when I spill balsamic vinegar over the tablecloth, just talks happily about how she and her sister went interrailing through Italy last summer.

By the time the waitress has brought us our wine – red, Jade's choice – and taken our orders – gnocchi for me, risotto for Jade – I'm feeling a little more relaxed. I want to enjoy this, and why shouldn't I? This is good.

'OK, I have a question,' Jade says, resting her chin on her hand, smiling across the table at me. 'What is the best and worst thing that's happened to you?'

'Hmmm,' I say. 'I might have to think about that.'

'Don't overthink it,' she says. 'What came to mind for the best thing?'

'My friends,' I say. 'But that feels like a pretty boring answer.'

She smiles. 'It's not boring! It's nice.'

'Is there a more boring word in the world than "nice", though?'

This makes her laugh. 'You're so prickly.' She doesn't say it like it's a bad thing, which makes me sit up straighter and relax all at once. 'And it *is* nice. I've never had friends that I love enough that they'd be the first thing that came to mind.'

'Never tell them,' I say with a laugh. 'They don't need that kind of ego boost. How about you? What's your best thing?'

Jade shakes her head. 'I said best *and* worst. I'll do mine after.'

I take a long sip of wine, stalling. I don't need to think, not even for a second, about the answer to this. I know what the worst thing is. But if I tell Jade this now, won't it spoil the mood? I don't want to be a downer. Especially not when she's smiling like she is.

But I can't lie, can I? That's the bottom line. I don't ever want to lie to Jade.

I take a deep breath and set my glass back down on the table. 'When I was eleven, my baby sister died.'

Jade's whole face drops, just like I knew it would, in horror. The kind of *oh fuck* instant guilt-horror of someone who thought they were playing a cute getting-to-know-you game that's been spoilt by *surprise!* death.

And of course that's when the waitress appears at the table again, beaming, plates in hand. 'Here we are!' she announces cheerfully. 'Careful of that plate there; it'll be hot. Do you guys need anything else, or are we all good? Pepper? Parmesan?'

'This is great,' I say, because Jade still looks speechless. 'Thanks.'

'Fab,' the waitress says. 'Enjoy!'

I wait until she's gone before I turn back to Jade. 'I timed that really badly.'

'No, God, you didn't,' Jade says. 'I'm so sorry. It was stupid to think that was a fun question. So thoughtless. I'm so sorry.'

'It's OK,' I say. It's not OK, and she's right; it *was* thoughtless to assume a person's 'worst thing to ever happen' to them would be some cheery anecdote. But it's not the first time it's happened, and it won't be the last. And I *like* her. 'I was going to tell you at some point; may as well be now, right?' I lift my glass. 'Cheers.'

Even in the dim light of the restaurant, I can see that Jade's cheeks are flushed red. I lean over and touch my glass to hers with a deliberate *clink*.

'It's OK,' I say again, sighing out a small laugh. 'Really. You didn't know. And to be honest, you've done me a favour, getting it out of the way now. There's never a good time to drop that kind of bomb, is there?'

She shakes her head. 'I guess not?'

'Your risotto looks really good.'

She glances down at her plate like she's not sure where it came from. 'Yeah, it does.' She picks up her fork and breathes in a sigh. 'Right. Risotto. Great.' She digs in her fork, clearly still lost in her thoughts, then looks back up at me. 'Do you want to talk about it? Or should I change the subject?'

'Which option will make this less awkward?'

This makes her smile. 'I promise I won't be awkward either way. I'd love to hear about your sister, though, whenever you're ready to talk about her.'

'She was just a baby,' I say. 'She never had time to be my

sister, or for me to have anything to say about her. She was only eight days old. Hadn't even learned to smile.'

I see a flash of alarm on Jade's face and catch myself. *She doesn't know you.* This is the moment when Caddy, who knows me better than anyone in the world, usually reigns me in with a quick 'Roz', or an elbow or a kick in the shin. But Caddy's not here, and I have to learn to spot these moments myself, don't I?

'Sorry,' I say. It's me. I'm the awkward one. 'I get like that when I'm talking about tough stuff. I do actually care. I'm not a bitch.'

'It's OK,' Jade says.

'I mean, thanks, but it's not,' I say. 'I should grow up and learn how to actually express my emotions, right?' I think I'm making it worse, but how do I make it better? No one teaches you this stuff. 'It was what they used to call cot death? How she died. It was horrible. Just, the worst—' I feel my voice falter in my throat. The memory of that night, the worst night imaginable, rising in my head. I push it away. 'My mum isn't the strongest person. She's always been a bit all over the place, emotionally. And she couldn't deal with it at all, and, I guess, I don't blame her for that. She had a breakdown, and I had to go and live with Caddy's family for a while because she couldn't look after me.'

Jade is nodding, silent, letting me speak.

'I lived there for a few months while she . . . well, I guess she got herself together? I don't actually know *what* she did. No one tells you that sort of stuff when you're eleven, do they? I just got a load of euphemisms. *Taking the time she needs. Getting some help.* That kind of thing. I know her best friend, Janine, stayed at our house with her for a bit while I was living away. I guess she must have got some therapy. I kind of think that maybe she might have . . . you know, hurt herself, but I don't know for sure. No one ever told me, and there's no way to ask that, is there?'

Jade's face is all, *How the fuck should I know*? But what she says is, 'How is your mum now?'

'Much better,' I say. 'She's tried really hard.' It feels important to say this. 'For me, you know. That's what she always said. I know she feels guilty about me having to go and live with Caddy's family. But I get it. I can't even imagine how hard it must have been.' I take a breath, let it out, then say, 'My mum is incredible. I love her more than anyone or anything.'

Jade smiles. 'I'd love to meet her.'

'We'll see how this date goes before we talk about stuff like that,' I say, and she laughs, thank God. 'I'm sorry I turned this into a therapy session instead of a date.'

'You didn't! Stop saying that! This is important; I want to talk about it. Or, I guess, I want you to feel like you can talk about it with me, if you want to. I'm not scared of it.'

I know she's trying to say the right thing, and I appreciate that, even though I know – in the way only those who've grown up with some kind of trauma *can* know – that there is no 'right thing'. Just a load of 'wrong things' in varying degrees of badness. But she's doing better than most.

'What was her name?' Jade asks softly. 'Your sister?'

My sister. My heart stabs.

'Tansy.'

'That's pretty.'

'Isn't it? She'd be seven now. Like, an actual little person.' I reach for my wine again and take another sip that is more like a glug. I don't want to be thinking about this, *my sister*, about this potential other life I could have been living, running parallel with this one. A life where I have a sister, where Mum isn't now on her own at home, where she is still whole, where I don't know what real tragedy is. The truth that I think I'd be a different person if I'd been able to be someone's big sister. A better person.

'I'm sorry,' Jade says.

'I know,' I say. 'Me too.' Now I don't know what to say, and clearly neither does she. The silence builds between us, awkward and uncomfortable. After far too long, I say, 'What's your best thing?'

'We don't have to do that,' Jade says. 'We can talk about anything.'

'Tell me your best thing,' I say. 'Please?'

I watch her look away from me as she reaches for her wine glass again, trying to gauge what she's thinking.

'Coming to uni,' she says eventually, looking back at me with a smile. 'Getting out of my hometown. And away from my family. I love Jasmine more than anyone else in the world, but growing up with a twin sister is a weird thing; I was never really allowed to be my own person, and neither was she. People filtered everything about me through what they knew of her, and vice versa. Coming here was the first time I'd ever really felt free from that. I felt like I really found myself in the first year, who I wanted to be. You know what I mean?'

I nod, even though this is basically the opposite of how I feel about first year.

'And now I've met you,' she adds, very generously, considering I'm still worried I may have thrown a grenade at our fledgling relationship and stopped it from developing into everything it could have been.

'I don't know how to talk about my feelings,' I blurt out, surprising us both. 'I'm sorry. I don't mean to be all weirdly sarcastic about my baby sister dying.'

'That's OK,' she says. 'However you deal with it is legit.'

'I don't think it is, though,' I say. 'Sincerity makes me uncomfortable. That's stupid, isn't it? And I don't . . .' I mean to say that I don't want to be like that with her, not when there could be real feelings involved, but the words don't make it out of my mouth. What I manage is, 'I don't want to put you off.'

'Put me off what?' Jade asks. 'You? Not at all. I like that you're spiky.'

'Really?' I think about that word. *Spiky*. I like it.

'Really,' she says. 'Besides, it was my fault the whole subject came up while we're in an inappropriate place to have a serious conversation.' As if on cue, a table near us bursts into applause as a waitress walks over to them, birthday cake in hand, singing loudly.

Jade and I look at each other, her eyes wide, my lips pressed together, and then start laughing in the same moment. It takes us the full run of 'Happy Birthday' before we calm down, and then we're both smiling, the tension dissipated.

She doesn't tell me about her 'worst thing', and I don't ask. Instead, we eat our food and talk about her parakeet, the surprising discovery that she loves heavy metal music, my lack of cooking ability, how I went through a phase of hating my freckles, then loving them, what we'd each do if we won the lottery, the best place to order takeaway pizza, her summers in Seville with her grandparents, my favourite things about Brighton. It's like talking with a friend, except my eyes keep travelling to her mouth, and her shin has been resting against mine almost the whole time.

Later, when she's walked me to the bus stop and kissed me under a street light and we've posed for our very first selfie, I feel emboldened enough to ask, 'So, how would you rate our first date?'

Jade grins. 'I thought it went very well, personally. You?'

'Very good,' I say, nodding. 'Shame about the tangent into death territory, but still, good.'

'Listen, I'm taking the fact that we got past that as a big plus for us,' she says. 'Lesser lesbians would have balked. But not us!'

'I'm bi,' I say.

'That's not alliterative,' she says. 'Allow me some poetic licence. You're very literal, aren't you?'

'I like things to make sense,' I say.

'OK, so what about us?' she asks, her smile quirking, one eyebrow raised. 'Do we make sense?'

'Oh, yeah,' I say. 'We make a lot of sense.'

13

I spend Sunday at the jewellery shop working a double shift, which is mostly boring until a man comes in with a woman and extravagantly buys her diamond earrings while she beams and blushes, only to return later that afternoon with a different woman, wearing a wedding ring that definitely wasn't on his finger before. I am completely professional about it, obviously, even as the second woman tells me that their anniversary is coming up and he looks – from behind her, out of sight – utterly terrified.

'Lovely,' I say. 'Congratulations.'

When they're gone, the incident is all the rest of us talk about for the rest of the day. 'But why would he come back?' Lukasz asks. 'That's what I don't get. Why come back? There must be a hundred jewellery shops in Norwich.'

'He has an account,' Luisa, the manager, says, rolling her eyes. 'He gets a discount.'

'Oh my God,' Lukasz says. 'So he's not just a cheating toad; he's a *cheap* cheating toad?'

The excitement of the second-hand scandal lasts well into my next shift, when our colleagues who missed the drama demand that Lukasz and I to do a full re-enactment. It's so much fun that I find myself wishing I could just stay at work, that I worked more hours, because university life seems so flat and dull in comparison. Though I tell the story to everyone I know, I keep this final part to myself.

Monday comes back around to start another week too full for me to even find time to think. At least, not about anything other than pharmacy. I have three lectures from 9 a.m. onwards, one after the other, and by lunchtime, I'm about ready to collapse, even just under the weight of my own notes.

After lunch, there's a two-hour workshop on organic reactions, which is good because it's medicinal chemistry, my favourite part of the course, but less good because I have to work with other people, which is exhausting. Luckily, I'm in the same workshop group as Dion, which helps. I even go along when he suggests we all go to the bar together after the workshop finally ends.

'It's just so much,' I say to Dion, beside him at the bar so I can help him carry the round he's ordered back to the table. 'Don't you think? This week is so full on.'

'I know!' he says, so enthusiastically I know he's misunderstood my tone. 'Isn't it great? I feel like I'm . . . all full up with knowledge.' He laughs, embarrassed. 'Doesn't it make you feel . . . bigger? You know?' His eyes are bright. 'I sound like a twat. I don't care. I love it.'

I smile. 'Me too!'

I'm lying.

It's another heavy week in a semester full of heavy weeks. After Monday, it doesn't stop. I have a dispensary workshop, a problem-based learning session, a formative calculations exam, more lectures, more tutorials, and a prep session for next week's kinetics practical in the lab.

I'm so tired.

By Wednesday, after another full morning of lectures, I give myself three hours to knuckle down in my room and concentrate on getting my reading and lab prep done so I can have my whole evening free to see Jade. I'm sat at my desk, trying to concentrate, when there's a knock at my door and I look up in surprise. People rarely come knocking. 'Yeah?'

The door opens and Dawn's head appears. She's smiling. 'Hi!' she says. 'Are you busy? Can I come in?'

'Sure,' I say, turning my music off and spinning in my chair to face her. 'What's up?'

She perches on my bed, the awkwardness of the pose reminding each of us – or, at least, me – that she doesn't ever spend any time in here. But still she tosses her hair in a way that I already think of as Dawnesque, smiles again, then says, 'I was wondering – well, we were wondering – I mean, it was me who was like . . . Well, you don't need to know that bit. I wanted to ask you if you'd decided who you were going to live with yet?'

'Oh,' I say, thrown, and then embarrassed, even though there's no reason to be. 'Um. Why?'

'So, Rika found this amazing-looking house just off The Avenues – right by the uni! – but it's a five-bed, and she was, like, *Do you think we could find someone else who'd want to live with us, as we're only four?* And I was, like –' She's talking fast now, excited and bright-eyed, gesturing with her hands. 'Rosie! I mean, if you haven't found anywhere. And, like, if you wanted to. What do you think? It's a great house. And – oh my God, this is the best bit – the boys are getting a house literally two doors down!' She's pulled out her phone, jabbing at it with her fingers. 'Look, I'll show you some pictures. We have to get it quick because it's definitely going to go. Like, really fast. Because it's so *nice*, not like how I thought a student house would be at *all*.'

She shoves her phone at me and I take it automatically, looking at the screen. There's a picture of a big detached house with a driveway and front garden. I flick through the images, taking in the large kitchen, the garden, the bedrooms. Dawn is right; it really doesn't look like the rundown hovels that people usually joke about when they're talking about student housing.

'The fifth bedroom is smaller than the others,' Dawn adds when I swipe onto a picture of what looks like a box room. 'I should say that. But Rika said we could make the rent cheaper for the person who gets that room. So, like, you could be saving money, too.' She beams at me. 'What do you think?'

My head is spinning. It's a lot of information to take in all at once, especially as Dawn talks so fast. Has Dawn suggested me to be nice, because she somehow knows I don't have anyone else in the picture to live with? Does she feel sorry for me? Or both? Or do she and Rika just *really* want this house, and they're worried it's going to go off the market if they don't drag in the first available person at the first available opportunity? Does it matter in any case?

They've offered me a lifeline, haven't they? I'd been so afraid of having to find somewhere by myself, either by trying to ingratiate myself with some coursemates and hoping we hit it off in time, or by embracing my aloneness and searching through spare room ads until I found somewhere that would take me. Both options seem awful for different reasons. But, I tell myself, it could work out, couldn't it? I could end up, by chance, with some really great people.

Or, I couldn't. It could be like this flat, but worse. I haven't massively bonded with the Dawn and Rika parade, or even really connected in any real way, but at least we just about get along.

Better the devil you know, right?

My head goes, *Come on, be fair. Rika isn't actually the devil*, which makes me smirk to myself. Dawn gives me a funny look, and I quickly try to adjust my face.

'Do you mind if I think about it for a bit?' I ask.

'Sure, of course!' she says, standing up and holding up her hands. 'Take your time! I mean, not too much time, because, like I said, we need to move fast. But take your time! OK, see you later!'

When I see Jade that evening, I'm distracted, even as I try not to be. She's working a shift at the on-campus club later, so we're just meeting for a drink in the bar. After we've talked for a while about some behind-the-scenes drama that's going on at the PharmSoc, I finally ask, as casually as possible, 'Hey, when did you decide about your second-year house when you were a first-year?'

Jade thinks about it. 'God, that feels so long ago. I think we were pretty early. Like, compared to a lot of people. But Vibs, Aisha and me were flatmates, and Saff was already a good friend on our course – she and Vibs actually already knew each other, so they were friends before any of us – and we just knew that we'd stay friends and live together, so there didn't seem to be much point in hanging around. We thought, may as well get ahead of the crowd.'

As she speaks, I'm smiling and nodding, even as my heart sinks. She sounds just like Dawn.

'That's not all that common, though,' Jade adds. 'Second semester is more common, I think? At least, that's when people start scrambling around a bit more, trying to get the right number of people, figure out who they can bear to live with, that kind of thing. Not wanting to end up homeless and alone.' She laughs, so easily, like the idea of this hasn't made the back of my neck prickle with anticipatory anxiety. 'There's no rush, though,' she adds, like an afterthought. 'Why? Are you thinking about it already?'

'A little,' I say, trying to be casual.

'Well, I'd just say, try not to worry about it too much because it'll work out, whatever happens. I know some people who didn't get it sorted until, like, the summer holidays, and they're fine. I'm sure it was pretty stressful for a while, but it worked out.'

Just the idea of still not knowing something as fundamental as where I'd be living as late as the following summer makes me feel ill. Even though her advice seems to basically be the opposite, I decide in that moment that I will say yes to Dawn, because at least then I'll *know*. I don't want to risk ending up 'homeless and alone', and I definitely don't want to leave it all up to chance.

I find Dawn and Rika in the kitchen a couple of hours later, when I go back to the flat. It's just the two of them, both sitting cross-legged on top of the table, playing cards.

'Hey,' Rika calls when I walk in.

'Hey,' I say. 'What are you playing?'

'Slapjack,' Dawn says. 'But there are more games for three, if you want to play?'

'Sure,' I say, and she brightens like I've surprised her. 'One sec.' I go over to my cupboard and pull out my emergency rum, coming back to the table with it in one hand. 'Hey, I thought about what you said earlier.'

Dawn looks up at me from where she's started reshuffling the cards. 'Yeah?'

'About the house,' I say. 'And yeah, I'm in, if the offer is still open.'

'Oh my God, amazing!' Dawn says, beaming. 'I thought you'd say no. That's so cool.'

'We should toast,' I say, lifting the bottle. 'I'll get some glasses.'

'Why bother?' Rika says. 'We're going to be housemates.' She gives me one of her Rika grins, taking the bottle from me and unscrewing the cap. 'We can share the bottle.' She lifts it into the air between us, then says, 'To being housemates!' She takes the first gulp, of course, then hands it to Dawn, who takes a smaller sip before handing it back to me.

'Cheers,' I say. It comes out a little more sarcastically than I'd meant, but they don't seem to notice. I take a sip of rum, and then another. 'So, what's the next step?'

'We've all visited the house already,' Rika says. 'But we can arrange another visit too, if you want to see it properly instead of just in pictures.'

'Do you think I need to?' I ask.

Rika shrugs. 'It's up to you. It looks exactly like it does in the pictures, if that helps.'

I take another swig of rum. 'Let's just go ahead with it, then.'

Dawn claps her hands. 'Yay!'

'That was so much more straightforward than I thought it was going to be,' Rika says.

'Well, you're welcome,' I say, which earns me an eye-roll.

'You have to try harder to be fun, OK?' she says, faux-seriously, pointing at me. It's like a joke and a command at the same time.

I roll my eyes back at her, then turn to Dawn. 'Is she like this with you, too?'

'Now, now,' Rika says. 'No being a bitch now we're going to be housemates.'

'I won't be if you won't be,' I say. We're both using the same tone, safe on the same page, but out of the corner of my eye I see that Dawn looks alarmed, which makes me laugh properly. 'We're joking, Dawn.'

She smiles uncertainly. 'OK . . . ?'

'Don't be so soft,' Rika says to her. 'Rosie gets me. Now, are you going to deal, or what?'

That week, Suze goes to visit Caddy in Warwick. At first, I'm jealous that they get to share this all-important first visit, but that fades pretty quickly when it becomes clear that the trip hasn't gone well. I'm not sure exactly why, or how, because neither of them will actually tell me. All I get from Caddy is that 'things were just . . . off'.

When I try to talk to Suze about it, she's evasive, a little bit distant, almost cold. I try a different tactic – 'OK, so when do I get a visit?' – which is much more successful. She warms up immediately, asking for dates, what we'll do, whether she should get the coach or the train. There's an almost desperate tinge to her enthusiasm, which makes me ache for her. And, in a way, for me, too, because I need to see her almost as much as she seems to want to see me, but I'm not being honest about it, either. We're both talking around our own unhappiness, and who exactly is protecting who?

I end up spending a lot of my time thinking about this, rationalizing my own emotions, trying to decide how best to introduce Suze to my student life without losing face. I'm embarrassed that the life I'm living here is not as full and exciting as Caddy's, but the knowledge that the visit didn't go well is making it all a bit easier for me. (Maybe that's selfish, but it's true.) I've decided that I'm going to be honest with her, when she's here. Tell her that I've not been as happy as I'd expected, maybe even ask for her advice.

And I'll tell her about Jade, obviously. Give her the gift of telling her first, before Caddy, which I know she'll love. The three of us can go for dinner together, maybe even go out with Jade's housemates and friends. Every time I think about it, my excitement rises. I can't wait to see her. I can't wait to have a friend here.

I'm telling Jade about this as we make our way out of the cinema towards the bus stop that evening, thinking aloud about the things we can do in Norwich, what parts of the university will be interesting to a visitor, whether I could sneak her into a lecture.

'Is she interested in pharmacy?' Jade asks, which makes me laugh.

'Not even a little bit. She'd get a kick out of gatecrashing a lecture, though.' We stop at the bus stop, looking up at the live departures board to see that there's not another bus due for eleven minutes. 'She'd probably enjoy it more than me, to be honest.' I mean this as a joke, but Jade looks at me with such alarm on her face that my smile falters. 'I'm kidding.'

'Are you?' she says. 'That's the most excited I've ever heard you sound about a pharmacy lecture. Or . . .' She hesitates. 'Kind of . . . anything uni-related?'

'What? Is it? No, it's not.'

'A little bit,' she says. It might be amusement in her smile, but I think it's in an affectionate way. 'You really don't love it here, do you?'

I feel the smile drop away from my face, right in time with the kick in my chest. 'What does that mean?'

'Hey,' she says, touching my arm. 'That wasn't an attack. Stand down.'

'I'm just happy that I'm having a friend visit,' I say. 'Why would you make that negative?'

Her eyes widen. 'I'm not! I'm sorry, that's not what I meant at all.' Distress has alighted on her face, sudden and surprising. 'Roz, I just meant it was nice to see you get excited, that's all.'

'I get excited about you all the time,' I point out, not quite ready yet to let go of my annoyance. And the high ground.

'Yeah, and I love that, obviously,' Jade says, attempting a smile. 'So long as I'm not, like, the *only* good thing.'

'The best thing,' I say, which is both true and an effective diversion from the actual truth, which is that she really is the only thing I'd count as 'a good thing' about my university experience. 'Do you remember the first time your home friends visited you at uni in first year?'

Jade makes a face. 'No one ever did, to be honest. We weren't that kind of friendship group. Jazz did, though. We didn't start uni at the same time.'

'Did she have a gap year?'

'Kind of. Jazz hasn't . . . well, her academic life hasn't been as straightforward as mine. When I went to uni, she came to visit just to see me and hang out. And then by the time I'd finished the first year, she'd got her place at Cambridge. Shocked the life out of all of us, and trumped me at the same time.' She shakes her head, smiling drily. 'Classic Jasmine.'

'Oh,' I say, thrown by this new information that casts all that came before it in a totally different light. I'm about to say something to this effect, and then I glance at Jade and see the anxiety written all over her face, and I realize that I haven't just not been paying attention this whole time; Jade has kept this part of her life – their life – to herself on purpose, and now she's choosing to share it with me. And there's a lot more to it than what she just said. Carefully, I say, 'Oh, right. And she's studying classics?'

Jade nods. 'An out-of-left-field choice – also classic Jasmine.' She looks at me, then says, 'She's my favourite person in the entire world, and I would die for her, but it's not always easy, me and her. Growing up, she struggled a lot with stuff that was pretty easy for me. She's smarter than me – honestly, don't make that face – but she used to get in a lot of trouble at school, make hell for our parents, and then just . . . ace her exams.' She rolls her eyes. 'She was suspended three times, and she still left school with the highest GCSEs in Somerset. I am not even exaggerating, Rosie. Not even just our school. The *county*. You'd think that would be a good thing, right? But it was sort of . . . unbearable? And then she didn't even want to take A Levels and it was, like, constant arguing between her and my parents, and I was just, like . . . I want out of here at the first opportunity and . . .' She looks at me, lets out a shaky laugh, then says, 'God, I'm sorry. I don't even know where all this came from.'

'No, it's good,' I say. 'I want you to tell me this stuff.' I manage not to ask why she hasn't told me any of it before, and am proud of myself for my uncharacteristic restraint.

'I don't really talk about it much with people,' she says. 'I don't want people to think badly of her. To think she's, like, a bad person, just because she used to get herself in trouble all the time. She was just this little ball of genius that our school didn't know what to do with, and so she'd just, like, explode at random intervals and everyone would look at me, like, Jade, you're the good one. Why are you letting your sister behave this way? All the time, since we were, like, five. Younger even. Oh my gosh, there's this picture—' She stops abruptly. 'Wow, I am just talking and talking, aren't I?'

'Go on!' I say. 'What picture?'

'It's stupid.'

'No, it's not. Tell me,' I say. I've never seen her like this before: almost prickling with energy, like she's finally let it loose after controlling herself for so long. I see that she's hesitating, so I add, 'You saying that you don't talk about it much with other people is sort of how I feel about Suze. She got in a lot of trouble at school, too. Not because she's a genius; just because she was struggling with a lot that no one knew how to deal with, either. But trying to describe her to other people is hard when they don't know her, because she just sounds like a bit of a nightmare.'

'Really?' Jade looks at me properly, her eyes hopeful. 'You've never made her sound like a nightmare to me.'

'That's because I've been holding back all the bad stories,' I say. 'Like – here's one. We both liked the same guy at school and we went to a party and she got with him right in front of me. Like, just to prove that she could? I never even told Caddy that story.'

Jade makes a face. 'A friend who would do that really does sound like a nightmare.'

'I know!' I say. 'She was. Is. Occasionally. I still love her, though, because I know her.'

Jade considers this, nodding slowly. Finally, she smiles. 'I guess you do get it. No one's ever got it before.'

'Not that I'm comparing my friend to your twin sister.'

'No, it's good,' she says. 'I'm glad you did.'

'Tell me about the picture, then.'

'OK, so, we had a proper photo shoot done when we were kids – you know the kind, when your parents get you all dressed up and the photographer is waving a puppet behind the camera to get you to laugh?' I nod, even though this is not something I've ever experienced in my own life. 'We had one done, and Jasmine just went off, a proper tantrum, and we didn't get a single good photo of the two of us. The photographer tried, my gosh, he really did. But there was just photo after photo of me sitting there all smiling nicely and Jasmine next to me really *screaming*, and I remember my grandma saying to me, "Jade, why didn't you help your sister?" Like it was my fault! I was four!' She shakes her head, sighing. 'That's what it was like, growing up together. No one cared that I was doing the right thing, just that I was "letting" Jasmine *not* do the right thing.'

'That sounds really awful,' I say.

'It was, but now, immediately, I feel the need to defend her.' Jade lets out a sad laugh. 'I want to tell you how close we are, and how I'd do anything for her, and how she once got a black eye after she punched a guy for calling me a . . . well, take one guess. She's my best friend. And this might sound weird after everything I just said, but I wouldn't change her. She is who she is.'

I nod. 'I hope I get to meet her one day.'

'Me too!' she says, brightening. 'I think you'll both really get along. And I'm looking forward to meeting Suze. I'm sure it'll be great.'

'It *will* be great.' I feel a swoop of happy excitement in my chest at the thought of it. 'It'll be perfect.'

*

See that? See how I got so excited?

Yeah. Of course, the plan falls through completely.

Really, it was my fault for jinxing it with all my stupid happiness. Suze calls me, distraught and clumsy with apologies, to cancel, just days before she was meant to arrive. Something about a plumbing issue that's left her with no extra money for a trip all the way up to Norfolk. Her guilt and distress are too genuine for me to be angry, so I swallow my disappointment and tell her it's fine, of course it's fine. I remind her that I'll see her at Christmas, that I miss her, but I'll see her soon. I focus hard on making sure she's OK so that I can forget my own disappointment, ignore the ache in my throat.

When I hang up, I stare off into space, blinking, for a while, then walk back into Jade's house through the back door, climb the stairs up to her room and sit down on her bed.

'Everything OK?' Jade asks from where she's sitting cross-legged, notepad and highlighters on her lap, back against the wall. Before I'd gone outside to answer the phone, we'd been studying together.

'Yeah, fine,' I say. 'That was Suze, just saying that . . .' For some reason, my breath catches in my throat. 'Saying that she can't come up to visit.'

'Oh no,' Jade says. 'I'm sorry.'

'Yeah, it's a shame.' I try to keep my voice light, because this isn't a big deal, is it? It's fine. 'But these things happen.'

'Yeah,' Jade says, but she looks worried. 'Are you OK?'

'Yeah!' I say, too quickly. 'I just . . .' I stop, because I don't know what I just. 'It's fine.'

'It's OK if it isn't.' Jade leans forward, reaching for my hand. 'Want to talk about it?'

I try to laugh, but it comes out more like a sob. 'I don't even know why I'm getting so upset. This is so stupid.'

'It's not stupid,' Jade says. She squeezes down gently on my hand. 'Hey. Look at me. It's OK. Talk to me.'

'It's not normal, is it? Being this upset about a friend not visiting you at uni.'

Carefully, she says, 'I think this might be about a bit more than that.' I look away, because I'm suddenly worried I might do something stupid, like cry. 'Roz,' she says. 'You know you can talk to me, right?'

I nod, glancing back at her, trying to answer casually. 'I . . . I'm fine. Really.'

'I know,' she says. 'But also, if you weren't, that would be OK.' She says this like it's so simple.

'I just . . .' I swallow. 'Uni hasn't been what I thought it'd be, that's all.'

She nods, encouraging. There's a silence.

'That's it,' I say, working a smile onto my face. 'I'm still adjusting to it. It's fine. I'm fine.' Have I said that already?

Jade is still looking at me carefully, but she doesn't push. She just waits a beat or two more, then says, brightly, 'Why don't you go there instead?'

'What do you mean? Go where? Brighton?'

'Sure. Why not?'

'It's almost the end of term,' I say. 'I'll be back home for Christmas soon anyway.'

'So what? Get a cheap coach, maybe even an overnight one, and have a couple of days in Brighton. See your mum, see Suze. Maybe it will help, just to have a bit of a break from here.' She smiles. 'Not that I'm trying to get rid of you. But I can tell you're not all that happy here, and sometimes, with homesickness, all you need is that little reminder that it's all still there, and that you can go back. That's kind of how I feel about Jasmine. Sometimes I just need to see her, even for a couple of hours.'

She's making it sound so reasonable. 'Don't you think I should just wait, though?'

'Why?' she says, shrugging. 'If you want to go, go. Be spontaneous. Make it a surprise. Would she like that? Suze?'

Suze would *love* it. In fact, just imagining how she'd react to my unannounced arrival makes me want to do it more than anything else. She'd never expect it from me. I've never been spontaneous.

I look up the coach times and prices as Jade makes us tea, and I find a journey that is less than a fiver each way if I use my student travelcard, which is so cheap it starts to feel like the stupid option would be to *not* go.

'Book it!' Jade says, like a command, waving her fists like silly little pompoms, which makes me laugh. 'Bring me back a stick of rock. Or a pebble, I don't care.' She's grinning. 'So long as it's something Brightony.'

'Do I *have* to bring you back a present?' I ask, teasing.

'Yes!' Jade says. 'What kind of person goes away for a *whole weekend* and doesn't bring a present back for her girlfriend?'

I almost choke on my tea. 'Girlfriend?'

Jade's grin sparkles like light on water. 'Was that not a subtle enough way to bring that up?'

'Maybe a little *too* subtle,' I say. 'A bit blink-and-you'll-miss-it.'

'You're right,' she says, nodding. 'I should probably just ask, right?'

'Probably.'

'OK,' she says, very thoughtfully. 'Good to know.'

We stare at each other. After a full minute, I snort out a laugh. 'Jade!'

She grabs my hand, laughing. 'Will you be my girlfriend?'

'Yes,' I say. 'Will you be *my* girlfriend?'

'Well, I have to say yes now, don't I?' she says, then kisses me. '*Now* will you bring me back a present?'

14

It's a Friday afternoon, and I'm back in Brighton. I'm home. Ever since the coach I was on crossed the Sussex border, I've felt this bubbling, giddy mix of joy and relief. *Home.*

I should probably call or message Suze to let her know I'm here, but I want to have that moment of surprise, to see her face when she realizes where I am. So, I didn't tell her that I was on the coach, homeward bound, and I didn't tell her when I arrived in Brighton, or when I made my way across the city from my house to hers. Now, here I am, on her street, and I'm so excited to see her I can practically taste it, like emotional sherbet on my tongue.

I press the buzzer for her flat, then let go when she answers, hoping it will mean that she'll come down to open the door. It takes three rounds of this – I can hear her getting more and more frustrated, and I have to bite on the inside of my cheek to stop myself laughing – before the front door of the building swings open and there she is, my third-favourite person in the world, wild-haired and stupid-beautiful, her face transforming from an annoyed scowl to a startled gape of happiness.

'Hi!' I yell, way too loud. 'Surprise!'

It feels like a long time since I've felt the pure kind of joy that I feel in this moment, especially when she throws herself at me for a hug and I hug her back. If I could put a pin in the perfect moments on the map of my life, this is where I would put one.

It's so good hanging out with her again. Even though it's really only been a couple of months since we were last together, it feels like so much longer than that. We don't even do anything exciting, just go back to my house to watch films and talk. I finally tell her about Jade, and she's so genuinely, sweetly excited for me that it makes me feel a bit bad for not telling her earlier. She stays over, sleeping on my sofa, and we have breakfast in the morning together before she goes to work.

On Sunday, I spend the day with Mum, just the two of us. We go to Eastbourne, which is what we used to do a lot when I was younger. I know now that this was because we didn't have much money to do anything else, but I never realized that at the time because Mum always made it feel special, making a scavenger hunt for me of items to find in charity shops or a list of people to check off, like we were birdwatching at a nature reserve instead of walking around the centre of Eastbourne.

Today, we have a cream tea in a cafe near the seafront and then walk along the pier together, arm in arm.

'Not to be a traitor to the city of my birth and my heart, but I like Eastbourne Pier a lot better than the Palace Pier in Brighton,' I say.

'Me too,' Mum says. 'Though I like the burned-out old Brighton pier best of all.' She stops to look out over the sea, which is the fifth time she's done it in the last ten minutes.

'The sea looks the same as it just did,' I say. 'Come on, let's get to the end.' I tug on her arm and she stumbles slightly on her feet. 'Oh, sorry.'

She pats my hand and gives a small, light laugh. 'I'm a bit slow on my feet at the moment. You'll have to be patient with me.'

'Why?' I say, surprised but also simultaneously thinking about the last few hours, and how she actually has been a bit slower than usual, and I'd barely noticed.

'Vertigo,' Mum says, sighing. 'It's affecting my balance a little bit.'

'Still?' I ask, frowning. 'Are you *sure* it's vertigo? Maybe you should go back to the doctor.'

'It's fine,' she says, dismissive. 'No sense in fussing, is there? I just have to think a little bit more when I'm out and about, which is probably good for me. Makes me more present in the moment.'

I roll my eyes, then smile despite myself. 'Well, silver lining, then. You're sure you're OK?'

'I'm fine, Rosie,' she says, patting my hand again, like I'm still a child instead of her adult daughter. 'Let's carry on.'

It's very short, a weekend. It's gone by in an instant. I don't ever want to leave, but I have to leave, because I'm paying nine grand a year, plus over a hundred quid a week to study and live at university.

'Everything's OK, isn't it?' Mum asks me from the driver's seat of her car. She's driven me down to the coach station and we're waiting for my coach to arrive.

'Yeah, of course,' I say automatically. 'I was just a bit worried about Suze, like I said.' That was the reason I gave to Mum for my oddly timed visit. *Suze is lonely; she needs a friend.* And it's not a lie. Maybe it's not the whole truth, but it's not *technically* a lie.

'You know you can tell me,' Mum says. 'If you ever want to talk about anything.'

'Yes,' I say, which is also not a lie. I know I *can*, I just don't want to. 'Of course.' I look at her, thinking about that moment on the pier at Eastbourne, the way she'd said, *Vertigo.* The prickle of unease at the back of my neck when I'd watched her hold on to the railing as we walked that I'd pushed away. 'And you can talk to me, too. If there was anything you were, I don't know. Worried about.'

'Yes,' Mum says, exactly like I just had, and I honestly don't know if she's echoed me like this on purpose, or if, even though I said it first, I'd been echoing her in advance, because I'm my mother's daughter. She looks back at me, a small ghost of a smile flickering on her face. 'Of course.'

'Good,' I say.

'Good,' Mum says. She looks for a moment like she's about to say something else, but then the coach is pulling in and she smiles instead, reaching over to kiss my cheek. 'I love you,' she says.

'I love you, too,' I say. 'I'll see you soon.'

15

Jade was completely right about going home making my homesickness better. When I get back to Norwich, I feel lighter, maybe even happier.

It helps that Norwich seems to have been drenched in Christmas over the weekend I was away, and we're now in the final stretch of the term, with Christmas holidays on the horizon. It's very merry. Someone's erected a Christmas tree in the kitchen of my flat, complete with flashing lights and topped with a Pikachu plushie, tinsel-wrapped in place like he's been tethered to a ship.

'Do you like it?' Dawn asks, from where she's writing an essay on her laptop at the kitchen table. Freddie is sitting across from her, but he's got headphones on, an intense frown on his face as he concentrates on his own MacBook screen, ignoring us both.

'I love it,' I say. 'Very festive.'

'Feel free to add your own decorations,' Dawn says. 'It's meant to be for all of us.' She smiles at me. 'Oh, hey, we got our contracts for the house! I put yours under your door. No rush, but we've all signed ours already, so . . . don't, like, take too long with it or anything. And don't forget the deposit.'

'OK, cool,' I say, trying to keep up and also prevent the sudden rise of panic that her words have brought on from showing on my face. 'Um. How much was the deposit again?'

'One month's rent,' she says. 'It's around £500?'

I swallow. 'Can it wait until after our loan comes in? In January?'

Dawn frowns off into the distance, clearly thinking hard. 'It needs to be in by end of term, but I could see if one of us could cover yours until the loan comes in?'

'That would be great, if that's OK,' I say. 'I really don't just have a spare £500 right now.' Or ever. 'Sorry, I didn't realize we'd need to do all this so quickly.'

'You don't,' Freddie says, from where he apparently has been listening this whole time and not ignoring us at all. 'It's still really early.'

'For housing in general,' Dawn replies. 'But for this house, that's what it has to be, if we want to sign the contract. Which we do. You've got your house stuff sorted already, haven't you?'

'Sure,' he says, stretching. 'But Flapjack and Rhino have to wait until the loan comes in before they can pay the deposit, too. It's not a big deal.'

Rhino? I decide not to ask.

When I go back to my room, I find out that I'd left the window partly open, and it's *freezing*. I layer up and then huddle on my bed, wrapped in my covers, looking through the contract. It's very official-sounding. There's a whole section on how we're all *jointly liable* for anything that goes wrong, like if we don't pay our rent or bills, or if we damage the property. I'm not sure how comfortable I really am being *jointly liable* for anything, or with anyone, but I've already made the decision and I don't have an alternative, so I sign the contract right there in my bed with gloves on my hands and three pairs of socks on my feet, thinking, *I am a grown-up. I am responsible.*

The last weeks of term pass quickly and smoothly, which feels like a gift of its own. I go to the Christmassy-themed club night on campus with my flatmates and have one of the best nights I've had in Norwich, maybe even second only to the night of Jade and my first kiss. I wear reindeer antlers and drink 'merry cider' (merry due to the added vodka) and sing loudly along to Christmas songs on the dance floor. I find myself in the middle of group shots for photos, Rika's arm slung around my neck, Freddie gurning behind me, and when I look at them in the morning, I see how well I fit with them, how wide the smile is on my face and think, *See, you're happy. Why are you worrying so much? Everything is fine.*

I'm back in Brighton for three weeks over Christmas, and it somehow manages to be both an anticlimax and everything I'd wanted, all at once. When I get home, Mum takes me out to dinner at one of our favourite vegetarian restaurants, then we walk along the seafront in our winter coats and hats. She's still slow on her feet, but this time I don't mind; there's no need to rush.

Seeing Caddy in person again – the two of us meeting at her house before going on to see Suze – is a blur of laughter, hugs and tears (hers) as she points out that these last few months have been the longest we've ever gone without seeing each other. She looks different, somehow, though I'm not sure exactly why, and I decide to chalk it up to plain old time passing. She changed her hair before she left for uni, and I'd expected she wouldn't keep it up, but she has. Her voice is slightly louder than I remember, more confident. Her smiles are wider and last longer.

'I missed you so much!' she says to me, squeezing my arm as we start to walk to Suze's. 'I didn't even realize how much until I saw you.'

'Same!' I say, though it isn't the same, because I've been actively thinking about how much I miss her almost every day for the last three months.

We don't actually spend as much time together as I'd imagined, because the reality is that Suze and I are both working full time – her in the coffee shop she's worked in since June, and me in the Brighton branch of the jewellers – and Caddy has both her boyfriend and her family to fit in around us. When we are together, it's usually in the evening, and it's rarely just the three of us. There's Kel, Caddy's boyfriend, who I'd expected, but also the surprise of his best friend, Matt, a musician who lives in London and who might be the best-looking guy I've ever seen in real life. He and Suze have been hooking up for the last couple of months, and though she'd told me about this, I'd just assumed it was all a casual-benefits vibe, based on how Suze is generally and also how she'd talked about him. But then I actually see them together, and I realize that my assumptions were completely wrong, because if they aren't already in love, they're at least halfway there. And also in total denial about it. ('It's not a thing!' Suze insists, whenever Caddy and I push her on it. It's cute, really.)

In contrast, Caddy and Kel, who are meant to be the solid ones, are at least halfway *out* of love, which they are also in denial about. (This is not cute at all.) The contrast between Suze's blossoming non-relationship and Caddy's disintegrating actual relationship, and the accompanying denial that makes it impossible to talk about properly, underlined by the fact that Kel and Matt are best friends and so are Caddy and Suze, is the pressure cooker kind of big drama that is obviously going to blow at some point, but everyone is pretending they don't see it simmering. And I just watch, the reluctant fifth wheel to the drama car, and tell Jade about it in messages over the phone. She loves this kind of thing; for all she claims to hate drama in her own life, she clearly enjoys watching other people's.

The whole time I'm at home, even when Mum is winding me up and the cat is sick on my bed and my friends monopolize an entire conversation to talk about their boys, I love it. And I don't miss university. Not at all, not even a little bit. I miss Jade, but that's it. I try to appreciate every moment of the holidays, try to take it all as slowly as possible, but the days and weeks pass so quickly, it feels like I blink and then it's the thirteenth of January and I'm waiting for my coach to arrive at 7 a.m., standing with my rucksack in the cold. Last night, in my room,

I hugged my cat for as long as he'd let me and cried.

Obviously, I have told no one this.

Mum's hands are clasped around her travel mug, and she keeps complaining about how cold and early it is, as if I hadn't said multiple times that she didn't have to come with me. 'How much longer?' she asks me.

'Ten minutes?' I say, shrugging. 'Or less, if it gets in earlier and I can wait on the coach instead of here.'

She sighs. 'If I was rich, I'd be the kind of parent who'd buy you first-class train tickets all the way back.'

This makes me laugh. 'You mean the kind of parent you hate?'

She laughs too. 'Let me dream.' She reaches out an arm to me, and I let her squeeze me in for a hug. 'I'm going to miss you so much,' she says into my hair. 'My little rock.'

'You've been doing just fine without me,' I reply. 'No dramas, no accidents. Seems like you're doing OK.'

'Managing, just about,' she says, releasing me. I glance up to smile, and catch the look on her face, which makes it falter. She notices, gives her head a shake and then smiles back. 'I'm fine.'

'What is it?'

'Nothing.'

'Is it money? Bills? They're not in arrears or anything?'

'No, Rosie!' She looks annoyed. 'We haven't been in arrears for years. Give me some credit.'

'What is it, then?' I can only remember money worries giving Mum that strained, tired look on her face.

'It's nothing. But . . .' She hesitates, and my heart clenches with worry. And also annoyance, because it's so typical of her to leave this clearly important conversation until the very last minute. 'It's this . . . dizziness, this vertigo. It's still giving me a bit of trouble – nothing to worry about, of course – and anyway, I've been referred. That's all.'

'Referred?' I say. In the near distance, I can see a coach approaching, slowing at the traffic lights. 'To where?'

'A neurologist,' she says.

There's a silence. We both look at each other, our subconsciouses having a conversation beyond our awareness, picking up on everything we aren't saying, storing it all for later.

'A neurologist,' I repeat. She nods.

'It's nothing to worry about,' she says again. 'It's a good thing, right? It means I'll finally get an answer.'

'Why did you wait until right now to say this?' I ask, exactly as the door to the coach grinds open. 'Why didn't you tell me earlier, so we could talk about it properly?'

'I didn't want to spoil our Christmas.'

'Didn't want to—' I press my lips together, shaking my head. 'OK. Fine. When is the first appointment?'

'At the end of the month. There was a bit of a wait, of course. Our dear NHS. That's a good thing though, I think, isn't it? If it was urgent, it would have been an emergency referral, but it isn't, so I can wait.'

This seems like some convoluted logic to me, but I don't say so, because if it's helping her cope, then fine. I open my mouth to say something else, but before I can she says, brightly, 'You should get on the coach rather than stand here freezing.' She lifts my rucksack from the pavement and hands it to me. 'Have a good trip back; let me know you got there safely.'

I just stand there, my head spinning. 'I feel like we should talk more about this.'

'We will! I will tell you when I have something worth telling. But right now you need to get on your coach and get back to being a student. No worrying about your dizzy old mother. OK?' She leans forward and kisses me on the cheek. 'I love you very much. Now go away.'

I swear, there's no mother on earth quite like mine.

When the coach has pulled away from the stop and I've waved at Mum until she's out of sight, I look up 'reasons to see a neurologist' on my phone, which is a mistake, because the answers are not, in any way, reassuring. I don't know why I thought they would be. Alzheimer's. A brain tumour. Parkinson's. Multiple sclerosis. Stroke. Spinal infections. Peripheral neuropathy. All these life-changing things. My hands feel cold.

It's just to rule that stuff out, I tell myself. Which doesn't help, because ruling stuff out means ruling something else in. I keep thinking about brain tumours. My mind fast-forwarding to hospital beds, doctors, nurses.

I put my phone back in my rucksack and zip it up. *Stop it.*

For once, thinking about uni seems like the less panic-inducing thing. As Brighton gives way to A roads and motorways, and home slips away behind me, I think about this coming semester. My degree gets more integrated in the second semester, which means that we'll be focusing on one condition and learning everything in relation to that. This semester, the condition is hypertension. By the time May rolls around, I'll basically be an expert in high blood pressure.

What else do I want by May? My birthday month, the start of my exams, when the end of the year will be tantalizingly close. To have made more friends, that would be a good start. To have bonded more with my flatmates and future housemates. I should make more of an effort with them, shouldn't I? Try harder. I should make more of an effort in general, really. It's all in my hands, isn't it? I can make my student life what I want it to be. No one else is going to do it for me.

I nod to myself, like a full stop on my thought sentence. This will be it, I decide. This will be the semester where it all turns around.

*

When I let myself into my flat a few hours later, I expect it to be loud, but it's quiet and still. There's no one in the kitchen, so I head back out into the hall and knock on Dawn's door.

When I hear a 'Hello?' from inside, I duck my head in. 'Hey.'

'Hi!' she says from where she's sitting on her bed, actually looking pleased to see me. She's wearing pyjamas under an oversized Saracens fleece that must belong to Freddie. 'You're back! Happy New Year.'

'Happy New Year,' I echo. 'Just thought I'd say hi. Hi, Rika.'

Rika, sitting at the other end of Dawn's bed, waves. There's a bag of Minstrels between them both, split open down the centre. Rika is wearing odd socks, one with a small hole near the toe. She's not wearing make-up and her hair is in a messy bun. There's something so companionable about how they're sitting together.

'How was your Christmas?' Dawn asks.

'Good,' I say. 'You?'

She nods. 'Yeah, good. So happy to be back, though.'

'Oh, me too,' I say, an outrageous lie. But I want to be part of this. I want to have a space on the bed, an allocation of Minstrels. 'Hey, I can't be bothered to cook tonight. Do you guys want to get pizza or something?'

'Sure,' Rika says, answering for both of them. 'We're rehearsing at the moment, though.' She holds up one of the papers scattered between them; I realize it's a script.

'You can come in,' Dawn adds. 'But it might be boring.'

I'm so determined to try harder that I spend the rest of that afternoon and evening in Dawn's room, listening to the two of them rehearse the same chunk of Shakespeare over and over. By the time I go back to my own room a few hours later, at least some of that determination has left me. Being around them still feels like trying to force my triangle-self into the perfect circle of their friendship. But, I tell myself, there are worse things than being the sidekick who reads the stage directions, right? Like being lonely. Like being alone.

16

The first time I see Jade again, I expect us to greet each other with a running hug and then a bit of passionate kissing, but the moment when we see each other is actually equal parts brilliant and awkward, which I wasn't expecting. I've never had a girlfriend before, and especially not one with whom I was temporarily long distance, so the strange awkwardness that comes with reunion is a surprise.

'It's weird, isn't it?' she says. 'You're like FaceTime brought to life. My head needs to adjust.' She laughs, then kisses me. 'Hi. I missed you. You look gorgeous.'

I'm at her house – I'd resisted the urge to surprise her at the train station, worrying it was too early in our relationship for that kind of gesture – and she'd met me at the door, all smiles, before we headed upstairs to her room. She's had her hair cut since I last saw her in December, and it falls slightly differently around her face. She still smells like vanilla, though, and her kisses feel the same, and . . . well, yeah. The kissing is still amazing.

We lose track of time for a while, the presents we'd saved for each other unopened on the floor beside the bed. When we come up for air, the awkwardness is all gone, and we're both a little breathless, laughing between softer kisses. She curls her fingers around mine. 'You didn't change your mind, then?'

'Definitely didn't,' I say. 'My mind got even more set in its ways.'

She grins. 'Good.'

I wish being back in Norwich could just be all about being back with Jade, but it's not. It's uni, and pharmacy, and exams, and my flat, and club nights on campus, and the newest instalment of my loan, and food shopping and, God, there's so much *life* now. Did life always feel like juggling so much just to keep things stable? I didn't even like school all that much when I was there, but I find myself wishing I could go back, just for the simplicity of it. Someone else making decisions, making grocery lists, telling me what to do and where to be.

It's exhausting, having to do all that myself. And really boring, too. Being able to buy as many boxes of Jaffa Cakes as I like really doesn't feel like as much of a bonus as I once thought it would.

Anyway. My January exams start barely a week after I've come back to Norwich, which seems unfair, especially as the exam period seems to have only a tiny effect on the noise levels in our building. I try to go to the library, but it's *too* quiet, so I just pack up my stuff and go to Jade's. Two of her three housemates are pharmacy students, too, and the house is a companionably peaceful study centre, which I love, except for the designated 'FREEDOM HOUR' at 4 p.m. every day, which starts with the sound of George Michael blasting out from the living room, Jade's groan of annoyance, and then Vibs's voice – 'BREAK TIME!' – which I love even more.

I see a new side of Jade during exam time. The whole time I've known her – which I realize isn't actually that long, only a few months, but in the strange timezone that is student life, feels like much longer – I've only ever seen her calm and collected, the one you look to in a crisis. I'd thought that was her default mode, but it turns out it isn't.

'I'm a *swan*!' she snaps at me when I say this, quite casually, after the first couple of days shared revision time. 'You know? Constantly kicking? Otherwise I will *drown*?'

I laugh. 'Never seen you be dramatic before, either.'

'It's all right for you, fresher,' she says. 'First year is bloody easy. I wish I could do first year again. Third year is *hard*. I'm not joking. I might fail this exam.' She shakes her head, which is when I realize that she's actually a bit annoyed. 'Can you stop asking me to explain everything to you? I need to concentrate.'

Thoroughly chastised, I tug my notebook back towards me from where I'd angled it towards her while she talked me through a calculation problem, biting down on my lip. 'Sorry.'

'*I'm* sorry,' she says, but her voice is still more irritated than contrite. 'I do want to help you, really. But this module is stressing me out and I can't be sitting in the exam thinking about first year stuff instead of clinical therapeutics, OK?'

'OK,' I say. There's a sort of dread building in my stomach. Not because she snapped at me for the first time in our relationship – I have a high tolerance for other people being annoyed, and I'm not insecure enough to think it means our relationship is in trouble – but because of what she said about first year being 'bloody easy'. It hasn't felt easy. It's not exactly that I've found it *hard* – it is hard, obviously, but manageably so – but it's more like it's taking up most of my time just to stay on top of it. I'm handling it all, but I'm handling it in the same kind of way you can just about carry a cup of tea that's full to the brim if you walk really slowly and put all of your concentration into not spilling it. I can't take more tea. I have no capacity for more tea.

So what happens when there is more, unavoidable, tea? I mean, pharmacy. Second-year pharmacy, and then third year, then fourth.

'Hey,' Jade says, her voice soft and contrite. 'I'm really sorry.'

'It's fine,' I say. 'I wasn't thinking about that. My head is all pharmaceutical calculations right now. I'd actually forgotten you were there.'

This makes her laugh. 'Thanks?'

'Let's take a break in ten,' I say.

'Very decisive,' Jade says, smiling. 'Take-charge Roz. I like it.'

'Shush,' I say, putting my finger to my lips. 'No talking.'

As soon as the exam period is over, the weight disappears from Jade's shoulders and she's back, almost instantly, to her warm, calm self. She meets me in the main square after her last exam with two coffees, a wide smile and an apology.

'For what?' I ask.

'Being a stressy bitch,' she says. 'Exam-mode-me is not fun. Vibs tells me that all the time.'

'I liked it,' I say, taking a sip of coffee, smiling. 'Good to see the flappy bit of the swan.'

She grimaces, pressing her knuckles to her forehead. 'Oh my *God*. I'm sorry. I said the thing about being a swan, didn't I? How mortifying.'

'It's good,' I say, enjoying this way too much. 'It wasn't healthy of me to think you were perfect. This is better.'

She laughs, sliding her arm through mine. 'How was your exam?'

'Fine,' I say. 'Glad it's over. Can we do something fun?'

'Yes!' she says, sweet with enthusiasm. 'I've been thinking about exactly that. I've been making a plan.'

'A plan?'

'A plan! A project, in fact. Project Make-Rosie-Love-Norwich,' she says.

I splutter out a laugh. 'Oh my God. You came up with that this afternoon?'

'Yes! Not just for today, obviously. This is a semester project.'

'I do like Norwich,' I say, laughing. 'Norwich isn't the problem.'

'*Love* Norwich,' she corrects. 'I'm going to make us a map. All the places Jade and Rosie are going to kiss before May.'

'I like that idea,' I say, then correct myself. 'Love. I love that idea.'

She grins. 'I thought you would. Ask me what the first stop is.'

'What's the first stop?' I ask obediently, lifting my cup for another sip of coffee.

'My bed,' she says, straight-faced, not even attempting to lower her voice.

I choke on the coffee, feeling my face blaze an immediate red, and her grin widens, like she's enjoying herself.

'No?' she asks, very innocently.

'I thought you meant new places in Norwich,' I say, trying to regain my composure. 'I know your bed pretty well.'

'Not well enough,' she says, her eyes on mine, and my stomach flips right over. There's a twist to the way she's smiling, the kind of twist that's doing things to every nerve ending in my body. 'Speaking of places we haven't been . . .'

Oh my God. Oh my *God*. It's not just my face on fire any more, because I know what she means. I know *exactly* what she means. I feel like I might just about burst into flame. She holds my gaze for a moment more, then laughs a warm, teasing laugh, full of promise and also, in her Jade way, reassurance. She gives my arm a squeeze.

'So, this first stop,' I say. I'm aiming for casual, but it comes out a bit strangled. 'When were you thinking?'

'Whenever you're ready,' Jade says. 'But there are a lot of places on my list, so we should get started soon, don't you think?'

I get my exam results the following week, all solid passes. This should make me happy, but it doesn't. It doesn't even make me unhappy. It's just . . . OK. Like a mental shrug. I used to care so much about my results, back in the days when I was working my arse off to get *exactly here*, to university, to a place on a pharmacy course. Now I'm here, I apparently don't care. What's wrong with me?

Maybe it's because they're all passes, I tell myself. That's all I need. Maybe if I was failing, I'd worry. Let's be honest, I'd *definitely* worry if I was failing. I'd be panicking, even.

I try and will that into my mind when I meet with my personal tutor to discuss my results and my progress on the course, which is compulsory. I can tell from the moment I sit down that I'm one of the middle people; the kind of student for whom this kind of meeting is perfunctory, but not important. I'm not dazzling at the top of the pile, nor flailing at the bottom of it. I'm doing fine. Just fine.

'You must be pleased,' she says to me with a smile. 'You're doing well.'

I nod. 'Yep.'

She asks me a few questions about what I like about the course, how I'm balancing my paid work with my studying, how I feel generally, and I know I say all the right things because she nods and smiles and so do I and the whole thing barely lasts ten minutes.

When I'm done, I head across the concrete to the Hive, where I'm meeting Dion to compare notes ahead of our upcoming lab session tomorrow. I'm early, because I'd expected the meeting to take longer, so I get a hot chocolate for myself and settle down to wait for him. I open my lab notebook to read over my notes, but I just stare at the page instead, and then at my boots. I'm thinking about a time when I was a kid, when Mum and I were running late for getting me to school. In the mad rush I grabbed what I thought was a pair of shoes, shoving them onto my feet on the way out of the door. I realized something was wrong before we were even at the end of our road, but I couldn't say anything, because Mum was so stressed she was almost crying, half dragging me along the road, cursing under her breath.

It was only after she'd delivered me to my teacher – 'Good morning, Rosie! How lovely to see you. Hello, Shell. No, don't worry at all!' – and I was sitting in my seat, hiccuping, that I discovered the problem. In my seven-year-old haste, I'd grabbed not a pair of shoes, but a *non*-pair of shoes. I was wearing two left feet.

The shoes were similar enough to look at that you couldn't tell, just at a glance, that there was anything wrong. And it turns out, people don't really look closer than a glance, so nobody knew. But I felt it with every step, a distinct wrongness I couldn't ignore. Not painful, just a bit uncomfortable, just . . . *wrong.*

I think about this, a tiny version of myself trying to run across the playground in the wrong shoes, hoping desperately that someone would notice and also that no one would, as January turns into February during my second semester of university. That feeling of something being off, not enough to actually be a problem but enough that you feel it with every step. A day is a long time to a seven-year-old; it feels like for ever. But it ended, and I could take those shoes off, tell my mum, cry to her while she hugged me.

Can't do that, now. And this isn't about a day, and let's be honest, it's not about shoes, either. Talk about for ever; this is my entire life, isn't it? The first few miles of a road I'll be travelling on until the road ends.

'Rosie!'

I look up, startled, and there's Dion in his big woollen black coat, smiling at me.

'Hi! I'm just going to grab myself a coffee, and then we can get started, OK?'

Dion is a nice person. I'm lucky he's my lab partner, lucky he's my friend. My problem is that I keep focusing on the negatives of it all, instead of everything that is going right. What I should remember about that whole two-left-feet thing is that even though it was uncomfortable, I could still walk, couldn't I? *And for God's sake, Rosie, you're an adult now. Buy a new pair of damn shoes.*

'So how did it go with your tutor?' Dion asks. Either he's got back really quickly, or I've been stuck in my head for longer than I realized.

'Fine,' I say. And fine is good enough, isn't it? It's definitional. 'Yeah, just fine.'

17

I'd known Jade was the practical, organized type – her revision timetable for her exams was a thing of colour-coordinated, scheduled beauty – but I watch her come into her own when she plans out her Make-Rosie-Love-Norwich project. She's made a list of places to visit, together with 'feasibility' marks out of ten for things like accessibility by public transport and unique-to-Norfolk-ness. She prints out a map and marks it with little crosses, beaming away to herself the whole time. It's both adorable and extremely sexy.

'You don't think it's weird?' she asks, with an unusual flash of vulnerability, when I say this to her. (Or some version of it; I don't actually use the word 'sexy', because it seems like one I couldn't pull off if I tried to say it out loud.)

'Oh, it's very weird,' I say, and she laughs. 'But I like it. A lot. Give me the coordinates of the zoo again.'

She laughs again, smacking my arm gently with her notepad. 'I didn't give coordinates! I'm not that bad!'

The plan involves a trip or two per week for the rest of the semester. When I look at the map she's made for us – she's sketched in little cartoon versions of lions and trains and sandcastles – I see a roadmap for me to navigate, like she's created little lily-pads just for me on a pond I'd been drowning in. She doesn't say it like that, and neither do I, but that's what it is. It's such a *relief*.

Over the next few weeks, between the grey haze of lectures, the lab, my flat and my job, there are bursts of colour and fun. Usually it's just Jade and me, but occasionally her housemates come along too, sometimes making use of Vibs's car and all cramming in for a trip across Norfolk to the places we can't reach so easily by train or bus.

We start with what Jade calls the 'beach triad', which means the three beaches we can reach from Norwich by train: Cromer, Sheringham and Great Yarmouth. One beach per Saturday for three weeks. 'It will remind us both of home!' Jade says, which makes me smile. I love that we're both British beach girls, born and raised among the pebbles and sand and bitter seaside winds, hardy and wholesome.

We do Cromer, with its pier and sandy beach and sprawling town, alone, eating chips against the wind and talking. When we get back to her student house, we watch *Never Let Me Go*, and she cries. In Sheringham, with its pebble beach that reminds me of home, it rains, and the two of us spend most of our time huddled together under an umbrella, teeth chattering, fingertips pink with cold. A group of her friends come with us to Yarmouth on a beautiful clear day – still bitterly cold, but sunny – and we spend a chaotic few hours playing in the arcades, attempting a barbecue on the beach, eating ice cream and drinking bottled ciders. It is the closest I've felt to home since I've been away, and I love it so purely it makes me a bit weepy, which would be mortifying if I couldn't so easily blame it on the wind.

In February, we see the seals at Blakeney, wander around Banham Zoo hand in hand, spend a ridiculous day at a dinosaur adventure park taking photos of each other trying to pose like a T. rex. When we don't have time for what Jade calls 'big trips', we walk around the lake on campus or go to Earlham Park together, or even just take the bus into the city centre to get salted caramel waffles and bubble tea.

'Is it working?' she asks me at random intervals, her eyes wide and hopeful. 'Are you falling in love with Norfolk?'

Every time, I laugh and say yes, even as my heart skips at the word 'love' and I wonder, *Is this it? Is this the moment?* Because I feel it coming, in those early weeks of the year, with Valentine's Day a big heart-shaped elephant in the room, as our relationship solidifies around us. I know I love her for a while before I say it. I even know the exact moment I realize: Jade in Blakeney, turning to me with a huge grin, hair flying all over the place in the wind, raising her hands to her head and pulling a ridiculous face to mimic the seal that was at that moment yawning on the shore. *Oh, I love you*, I thought, the realization landing like the world's most obvious surprise.

It didn't feel anything like I always thought it would, falling in love. I'd always read about it being like a loss of control, something that happens to you, a wave you get swept up in. But with Jade, that's not how it feels at all. It's more like an active decision I'm making, a deliberate step into love, one we're making together. Every time she takes my hand and tugs me beside her, I feel it. Whenever it's me that kisses her, I feel the way she smiles as she kisses me back. I'm not being swept away; I'm being collected.

The moment on the beach with the seals isn't when I say the words. That happens a couple of weeks later, when the two of us are in the city centre together, browsing in Waterstones in the last few minutes before I have to go to work. She calls over to me, gesturing, and then shows me a collector's edition of *His Dark Materials*, all three of the books in one volume, and says, 'Can you believe how gorgeous this book jacket is?' She opens the cover and then closes it again, beaming. As she slides the book back into position on the shelf, she glances over at me to say, happily, 'Isn't it cute that books have jackets? Like little people. Or potatoes.'

'I love you,' I say.

I expect her to look startled, or even just surprised, but she just smiles a little wider, nods, and says, 'I love you, too.'

Just like that.

*

So, that's the bit that's going well.

Jade is great. Me and Jade is great. Me and Jade in her lovely student house with her lovely housemates, having movie nights, playing board games, sampling different flavours of schnapps is great. If this was all my life was, my God, I'd be so happy.

But it's not. Because in between all this loveliness, and our trips around Norfolk, and kissing and tipping over the brink into sex ('great' is not big enough of a word for this), between all of this is what I'm actually meant to be here for: my course. I am not a Jade student; I am a pharmacy student.

Last semester, I spent a lot of my thought-time moping about how I wasn't enjoying pharmacy as much as I thought I would, that I wasn't finding it as interesting or stimulating as other people around me clearly did. But I'd been able to tell myself that this was because it was just the first semester, the transition from A Levels to degree level, just a taster, even. The second semester would be when it all kicked into gear and it would all, as a consequence, fall into place.

Turns out . . . nope.

At my university, the pharmacy degree is fully integrated, which means that we learn everything in relation to a specific disease. The first semester is mostly about getting everyone to the same basic level of scientific knowledge and ability, with a bit of an introduction to pharmacy practice thrown in, but the second semester is when the integration part kicks in. So, basically, it's when the actual degree starts, at least in the form that it will take for the rest of the programme. This semester, all of the material we study is related to hypertension, which is high blood pressure. So, for example, when we learn about drug design, it's by looking at drugs that treat hypertension.

And I hate it. I *hate* it. But I can't hate it because I *need* this, I told everyone I wanted this, I told *myself* I wanted this, and the sole reason I like being in Norwich at all is my brilliant girlfriend, who is inextricably tied to this place and this life. It is not an exaggeration to say that if I don't somehow learn how to care about my degree, I will lose everything. *Everything.* I will be back in Brighton with much lighter pockets, no girlfriend and no future. Nothing but the bitter taste of failure in my mouth and the awful stomach churn of knowing I've let down my mother.

Last week, after a full day of lectures and a two hour workshop, I went back to my flat instead of to the pub with my coursemates and only just made it inside my bedroom before I had a panic attack. I think it was a panic attack, anyway. I'd never had anything like it before, so I didn't have anything to compare it to, but I certainly *felt* panicked. Like the panic had climbed up inside my body and started screaming.

I didn't tell a single person. Not Jade, not my personal tutor, not my friends, not my mother. I just waited until it was over, drank some water, wiped my eyes, picked up my bag and headed out for the next lecture.

So, I'm coping, right? This is what coping looks like.

Speaking of coping, Mum says she's doing just fine. Her appointment with the neurologist in February was 'fine', her symptoms are 'fine', she's feeling 'fine' and any potential prognosis is 'still on hold, but that's fine'. Her voice when she tells me these things is upbeat, determinedly so, as if it's all just water flying off her ducky back. The only time I get a hint of the truth is when she calls me, tearful, and I'm instantly on high alert until I realize that she's happy. 'They've ruled out Parkinson's,' she says. 'It's not Parkinson's, Rosie.'

Which is the first I'd heard of it even being a possibility, let alone one that was so high on the list that having it ruled out was cause for celebration. (Janine was with her, the two of them drinking mimosas and watching *Mamma Mia*.)

'Why didn't you tell me that you thought you might?' I asked, frustrated.

'The important thing is that I don't any more,' she said.

When I relay this story to Jade, intending it to be an example of how bad my mum's communication skills are when she wants them to be, Jade looks a little alarmed, but like she's trying not to show it.

'But if it's not that, does that mean the remaining possibilities are worse?' And then she sees my face, and tries to take it back. 'I'm really glad, Roz. Thank God. Your poor mum; she must have been scared!'

Jade is the only person I tell. Voicing it to my friends feels too close to making it real in a way I don't even really understand, and there really isn't anyone else *to* tell here in Norwich.

At the beginning of the semester, I'd fully intended to spend more time with my flatmates, but the truth is I think I'm actually spending less even than I did last term. I went out with them for Dawn's birthday at the beginning of February and it was fine. I brought Jade with me, which was the first time she'd met them after hearing enough about them over the last few months. ('So *you're* the reason why Ro is never around!' Rika said. 'I thought it was us.') There was a large enough crowd there – Dawn has a lot of friends – that my lack of closeness with her and Rika (at least in the kind of closeness you're meant to have with people you're choosing to live with) was unnoticeable.

I tell myself it doesn't matter anyway. I probably won't spend much time in the house, will I? I'm just glad I have somewhere to live, that they've saved me from the panic of having to find somewhere by myself. And it helps a lot, when Caddy and I talk about our student lives, that I can talk up the house, and them, as if I'm actually excited, the way she is and does.

This is on my mind because it's currently just after 5 p.m. on a Tuesday, and I'm meeting my future housemates in the Blue Bar 'to sort out logistics', as Dawn puts it. It's the first time all five of us have properly met and I'm putting on my best smile for Louisa and Tam, who seem friendly enough. Not very interested in me, but fair enough, really.

'Rosie probably won't be around much,' Rika says to them. 'You might want to take a picture of her face so you can remember it.'

'So long as she pays rent, that's fine with me,' Tammy says, even though I'm sitting right there, and this is so rude even Rika looks surprised.

'She's very reliable,' Rika says, a little frown on her forehead, like she's not sure what to say, as if she's fighting with an instinct to defend me. She looks at me. 'Aren't you, Ro?'

'That's me,' I say.

'I'm sure we'll all, like, come and go a lot,' Louisa says. 'And that's good, right? No pressure for anyone to be social.' She smiles at me, and I smile back, because thank God someone is nice.

I can't quite visualize the five of us living together in an actual house. Though I haven't loved the slightly hotel-esque feeling of being in a flat with everyone, it makes the lack of closeness I feel with them easier to deal with. How would that feel in a house? I try to imagine sitting in a living room with these four girls, watching something on someone's TV, maybe. Sharing drinks. Even in my own head, the only way I can visualize it is to be standing in the doorway, watching the four of them. Even in my own head, I can't make myself be part of it.

18

At the beginning of March, I bring Jade home to Brighton for a few days, which we both know is a big deal but try to play down as much as possible, to keep the pressure off. I've organized it with Caddy to coincide with her Reading Week, so the two of us can be in Brighton at the same time to see Suze and make the whole thing like an event. Caddy is bringing a few of her friends who are sharing an Airbnb, which makes me worry – needlessly – that she's going to wonder why I haven't brought any of my own friends. I'd worried about this so much that I'd even suggested to Jade that we invite Vibs, Saff and Aisha to come along with us, but she'd just looked at me with such pure bafflement and said, 'Why?' Which was the end of that.

When we get to Brighton – we go by coach to save money, which is stuffy and long and boring, even with Jade beside me – we spend a bit of time on the beach together, breathing in the sea air and laughing at how happy the other is to be back on a beach, then head up to my house.

Mum is at work, so she's not there to greet us, but she's left a note on the kitchen table:

My lovely Rosie, WELCOME HOME, and Jade, WELCOME! There is cake in the fridge. Have fun with the girls today, and don't worry about fitting me in. I'll see you tomorrow morning with breakfast and many questions about every detail of your day, night and lives. Love to you both, Shell (Mum) xxx

'Oh my God,' Jade says. 'You didn't tell me your mum is adorable.'

I smile, embarrassed and proud. 'She tries.'

I'd been nursing a secret worry that the house would be a mess, because Mum's never been great at keeping on top of stuff like that, and though she still hasn't really talked to me about how good (or not) her health is, I'm pretty sure it's been bad enough to stop her keeping up with stuff like vacuuming and cleaning the toilet. But the house is spotless, maybe even cleaner than I've ever seen it. Even the kitchen is sparkling. It makes me feel bad for doubting Mum – who has obviously made an effort because she knew I'd be bringing Jade home – and also relieved. I've clearly been worrying about nothing if she's well enough to clean like this.

I give Jade a tour of my house, which doesn't take long on account of it being so small, before we head out to go to the train station to meet Caddy and her cohort. Kel, Caddy's boyfriend, is already there when we arrive. I introduce him and Jade, realizing for the first time that they're both third-years, and therefore not only the same age but also the only two older ones in our group, which seems like an obvious bonding opportunity.

Caddy arrives in a running shriek of a hug, her assortment of friends behind her. She surprises me by greeting me first, before Kel, hugging me tight and then turning with a grin to Jade. 'Hi!' she says. 'I'm Caddy.'

For as long as I can remember, I've always been the forward one, introducing Caddy to people I know, sometimes even having to almost force her out of her shell to be sociable with my friends. Maybe it's the surprise of this that makes me stand there watching instead of doing the same and introducing myself to her friends, but for whatever reason, I must take too long, because Caddy has turned back to me, taking my arm, turning me towards her friends.

'This is Rosie,' she tells them. The way she says this makes it clear that she doesn't need to give them any more information; they already know about me. My heart swells three sizes. 'Roz, this is Owen, Sam and Tess.'

Tess beams at me. 'I'm so excited to meet you!' she says. 'Caddy talks about you all the time.'

'Does she?' I say, grinning at Caddy, who grins back.

'All good things,' Caddy says. 'Mostly.'

'Hi,' Kel says.

Caddy swings towards him, beaming. 'Hi.' She puts her arms out and the two of them hug, then kiss very briefly, and it's extremely awkward, though I'm not sure why. Maybe it's the PDA thing. She turns back to me. 'Have you heard from Suze?'

I nod. 'She says she finishes work at six, and she's good to meet us at your Airbnb later.'

'Great,' Caddy says. 'Where shall we go first? Pavilion?'

Meeting your best friend's friends is always a bit weird, and this Brighton trip is no exception, especially with the added new element that is Jade. I can't figure out whether I should be focusing on her, who I see most of the time but is new to Brighton, or Caddy, who I rarely see any more but knows this city as well as I do. Or whether I should be sociable and get to know Tess, or friendly and chat to Sam and Owen, or kind and talk to Kel, who seems a bit confused, a bit lost.

I end up trying to do all of these things at once, probably quite badly, as we spend time at the Pavilion, wander through the Lanes and then head to the beach, and it's exhausting. We're queuing for chips on the beach and I'm watching Kel and Caddy have a quiet gritted-teeth not-quite argument when Jade puts her arm around my neck and murmurs into my ear, 'You worry too much about other people.'

'Do I?' I say in surprise. It's not the kind of accusation I usually hear. More often, it's that I'm emotionally cold, that I don't care enough, that I'm too blunt.

'Way too much,' Jade says. She squeezes me into her. 'Relax. Look at the seagulls. Aren't they *massive*? Which one is your favourite? I like that one, see there, with the grey bit on its wing? He's majestic.'

'Could be a she,' I say.

'They're majestic,' Jade says promptly. 'A majestic non-binary seagull of dreams.'

I turn on the spot and kiss her, right there on the beach in front of everyone. I can feel her smile against mine. 'I'm so glad you're here,' I say.

That moment of happiness turns out to be just that, though. Momentary. By the time we make it onto the pier, Caddy and Kel are bickering openly, so much so that Caddy's university friends have dropped back to group up with Jade and me instead of them.

'Are they always like that?' Tess asks me, voice low, when we all pause at a smoothie stand.

'No,' I say. 'I've never seen them like this, ever.'

She frowns. 'She's been nervous about this trip for ages. Now I understand why.'

'Nervous how?' I ask.

'About Kel?' Tess says, like a prompt, as if I've forgotten my lines rather than being entirely new to this script. 'Because of them having problems?'

I knew they'd had problems, obviously, but it hadn't even occurred to me that those problems could spill over into a group setting. Caddy just isn't the kind of person to have fights in public. She'd chew off her own arm before letting that happen.

Except it is happening. I watch as Caddy turns to us with a determined, wide smile. 'What rides shall we go on?' she asks, a little too loudly. 'You know what, I think I'm brave enough for the Booster.'

'Really?' I blurt out in surprise, which is a mistake, because I say it at exactly the same time, and in exactly the same tone, as Kel. But since when has Caddy been *brave*?

Caddy whips round to look at me, hurt and startled, and I want to apologize, but I think it might make it worse, so I laugh instead and say, 'Wow, Cads! What do they put in the water in Warwick?'

'Which one is the Booster?' Jade asks, calmly but louder than usual, drawing the attention her way. She looks around, then laughs. 'Oh, the one that says BOOSTER in massive letters?'

'Let's start smaller,' Kel says. 'We can build up to it. Let's do Wild River first.' He reaches out and touches Caddy's shoulder, gentle and sweet. Something about the gesture, the hope and anxiety mixed on his face, makes me feel suddenly sad for him.

'Is that a scary one?' Tess asks, her eyes travelling anxiously over the steep inclines of some of the rides.

'No, just fun,' Kel says. 'One of the water ones. See the log flumes?' He points. 'They're two a car. It'll be great.'

'I'll go in it with you, Tess,' Caddy says. Kel lets out a cough, and she ignores him. 'It's not even that high.'

Kel turns slightly so his back is to the rest of us, dropping his voice so we don't hear what he says to Caddy. I watch as she shakes her head, says something back, rolls her eyes. The air feels suddenly thick with tension, like something overdue is about to spark.

'Do you think—' Jade starts to say, but she stops herself when Kel jerks back, throwing his arms up in frustration and turning away from Caddy, shaking his head.

Caddy's voice is raised. 'I told you not to come if you were going to be like this.'

'Be like what?' he yells back. Yells. My whole body tenses

tight with reflexive, protective anxiety. 'Wanting to spend time with you? You're my fucking girlfriend. Why is anyone else even here?'

'Hey, mate,' Owen says, stepping forward. 'Don't shout at her, OK? That's not cool.'

Kel's head jerks towards him. 'I'm not your mate. Mate.'

'Kel!' Caddy snaps. 'What is *wrong* with you?' She waits a beat, like she expects him to have an answer to this, then continues. 'You want to know why everyone else is here? Because of *you*! Because of this!' Her voice has picked up with each word, and now she's yelling, too. My quiet, careful friend. Yelling in the middle of Brighton Pier. People are staring. 'Just back off for once, OK? You don't own me.'

'Fine. Fine.' Kel puts his hands up as if in defeat, except his voice is too hard for that, almost snide. 'You want space that badly? Have it.'

He walks away in large, determined steps, shoving his hands into his jacket pockets as he goes, not looking at any of us on the way. I look at Caddy, who hasn't moved. She's just watching him leave. Tess looks at me expectantly, but Owen is already stepping forward, reaching out an arm to Caddy and pulling her in for a hug. I watch him rub her back for a few seconds before she abruptly pulls away, spinning to face us all with a wide smile.

'So!' she sings out, way too brightly. 'Who's feeling brave enough for the Booster?'

This is how it continues for the rest of the day. Enthusiastic, determined denial. On each ride, through multiple greasy pier doughnuts, at the beach, across the city to the pizza place for dinner and into the evening, which is when Jade and I separate off to pop home and change before meeting them again later at the Airbnb Caddy's friends are sharing. (Presumably, Caddy had planned to stay with Kel, but that all seems very up in the air now.)

'Do you think it'll be OK tonight?' Jade asks as she helps zip up my top, her fingers light against my skin.

'Yeah,' I say. 'Cads probably just needs to let off some steam. She'll maybe drink a bit, cry a bit, and then we can look after her, and it'll be fine. Sometimes Cads bottles stuff up, but it always comes out eventually. I'm actually glad I'm here for it – and Suze, obviously. God, I'm so glad she'll be here too. And that you'll finally get to meet her.'

'Me too,' Jade says. 'It's a shame she couldn't be around earlier.'

I think about how Suze would have reacted if she'd seen Kel shout in Caddy's face like he did. 'I don't know,' I say. 'It might be a good thing she missed all that drama.'

'Does she not like drama?' Jade asks, which makes me laugh, very loudly.

'Suze invented drama,' I say. There's a flicker of worry on her face, so I add, 'But it'll be fine. We can all just have fun together.' I tap at my phone for the time. 'We should go. Are you ready?'

'Yeah,' Jade says. 'You're sure it's going to be OK?'

'Of course!' I say with a laugh. I lean over to kiss her – just softly, because if we start kissing properly, we'll probably never leave the room, let alone the house – and give her my best winning smile. 'It's going to be great.'

19

The night is a disaster.

An unmitigated, bona fide disaster. The kind of night that would probably be really entertaining, if it happened to someone else's friends.

But it happens to mine, and it's just *bad*. It's not even that much of a surprise; I feel it coming from the earliest hours of the evening, when Suze arrives and her excited, puppylike energy is all off in the rigid awkwardness of the Airbnb. Caddy refuses to talk about what happened with Kel, but she's never been good at hiding her emotions, and her hurt and confusion and pain is written all over her face, even when she's smiling. Jade, who'd been upbeat for most of the day even when things weren't going all that well, seems to grow tired of everyone before we've even got to the club. Which is fair enough, to be honest. *I'm* tired of everyone. It's tiring, trying to be normal when everyone around you is being off.

Everyone else seems to deal with this by getting drunk, but Jade sticks to lime and soda, so I do, too, which is maybe part of the reason why I feel like I'm watching the night happen rather than being part of it myself. Because that is what it feels like. Watching Caddy get drunk far too quickly, dancing like I've never seen her dance – I love her, but she's not a natural dancer, and the alcohol doesn't help – flirting with Owen so brazenly that Suze keeps looking at me like, *Are you seeing this?* And I am, and it's awful, but I don't know what I can do that will make any of it right.

I'm still trying to figure out the answer to this when Suze, queen of bad decisions, champion of the self-destructive, decides to throw petrol onto the flames of the evening because she operates on her own plane of logic and maybe in her head it makes sense to burn everything down if fixing it seems too hard? That's the only reason I can think of as to why she'd think it was a good idea to kiss Owen like she does that night, right in the middle of the dance floor, in front of Caddy.

The fallout is as predictable as it is horrendous. My two best friends, yelling at each other outside a club, Caddy in tears, Suze all ice – Owen already slunk away like it had nothing to do with him – until Suze finally turns and walks away from all of us without another word, even to me, disappearing into the crowd while Caddy crumples.

I wish that none of it had happened. And I *really* wish that none of it had happened in front of my girlfriend, who'd patiently listened to me banging on about how great my best friends are for the last few months. I'm embarrassed; that's the truth. Mortified, even. Especially because I waste ten minutes of my life looking for Suze in and around the club before I finally realize that she's actually left.

Jade is leaning against the wall of the club, arms crossed, mouth set in a grim line, when I rejoin her. She doesn't even say anything, just raises one hard eyebrow at me, like, *Are we done now? Are you finished?*

'She just left,' I say.

'Clearly,' Jade says, in a very un-Jade-like voice.

'I can't believe she just . . . left.'

'Why not? I can. That is exactly how this night was going. Can it be over now?'

'She's not answering her phone,' I say. I'm almost in tears myself now. 'She shouldn't go home on her own like this. What if something happens? I should find Caddy; she might—'

'*Hey.*' Jade's voice is so sharp it cuts through my head noise and I look at her, startled. 'Do you need me to be brutal right now?' I don't say anything, and she must take this – or whatever is on my face – as the answer because she says, hard and firm, eyes fixed on mine, 'This is not your drama. It's theirs. OK? Leave them to it. There is literally nothing you can do for either of them right now except stay out of it. Here.' She reaches for my hand, gesturing to my phone. 'Give me your phone, OK? Let's go back to yours.'

I hand my phone over to her mostly because she sounds so firm and commanding. I watch as she slides it into her bag, shaking her head a little, then smiles a determined, strained smile. I don't think I've ever seen her this annoyed before, and I'm more aware of the two-year age gap between us than I've ever been.

'OK,' I say. 'Let's go home.'

Mum is already in bed and asleep when we get home that night, so it isn't until the following morning that I get to introduce her to Jade. She's up and waiting for us in the kitchen, a large paper bag in front of her.

'Hello!' she calls out as we walk in, beaming. 'Good morning.' She reaches out a hand to me and I go over for a hug. 'I got you pancakes.'

'Pancakes?' I repeat in surprise, stepping back to look into the bag.

'Deliveroo,' she says. She looks so proud of herself. 'A treat for my girls. Can I call you mine, yet, Jade? Hello.' She beams. 'I'm Shell.'

'Hi,' Jade says, coming over and sitting on the nearest stool, her hand out. Mum grabs it, squeezing. 'It's so nice to meet you.'

'And to meet you!' Mum says. 'I hope you like pancakes. I was guessing, but doesn't everyone like pancakes?'

'I love them,' Jade confirms.

'Good,' Mum says, reaching into the bag and pulling out plastic trays, handing them to me to sort out. 'Now, tell me everything about yesterday and last night. How did you find Brighton, Jade? And how are the girls, Rosie?'

I let Jade talk as I slide into my seat, watching Mum nodding and smiling, digging into her pancakes with her fork. Is it just a coincidence that she's been sat on that chair the whole time, that she didn't get up to greet us like I'd expected her to, or is she trying to disguise the fact that her mobility has got worse? She looks pale. Tired. There are lines on her face I haven't noticed before.

'I really liked the Pavilion,' Jade is saying. 'It wasn't what I was expecting. The beach and pier were pretty busy, and that's when things went a bit . . .' She looks at me with a question on her face, unsure if she should share, which makes me smile because there's little Mum likes more than to revel in the drama of my friends.

'Things went a bit wrong,' I say.

I tell her what happened on the pier, and then later in the club. She's thrilled, demanding more details, shaking her head with the kind of affection for my friends she's allowed to feel from a distance, peppering my story with variations of 'Oh no!' and 'She didn't!' and 'Oh, Suzanne!' which makes Jade laugh. I move on to the aftermath, which I know only via the medium of WhatsApp; confusing, scattered messages from the early morning through to the actual morning. 'Kel and Caddy broke up.'

'Oh no!' Mum says again, but sadly this time. 'Poor Caddy.'

'I think it's been a long time coming,' I say. 'She's gone back to Warwick already.' This stings, even as I understand why, because I wish I could have seen her and spoken to her properly before she disappeared off again.

'And how about Suze?' Mum asks.

'I haven't spoken to her, either,' I say. 'But she's been online, which means she's still alive. That's the important thing.'

The fallout from last night is going to be *bad*, especially as Caddy's already left and the two of them won't have the chance to talk it all over. The last thing I want is to be stuck in the middle, so I message Suze with a command to **Keep me out of this**, and then take Jade's advice and mute WhatsApp for the rest of the day. I'm not sure if it's mature or cowardly but, either way, it's necessary.

Jade and I arrange to meet Mum in town for a late lunch, and then head out into the city together. I take her on my own personal tour of Brighton, showing her my old school, the park Mum used to take me to when I was tiny, the graffiti walls in North Laine, the playground that Caddy and I used to meet in after school before we got too old for it, the pub Suze charmed us both into when we were still underage.

'How do you like it?' I ask, when we're on our way to meet Mum. 'Brighton?'

Jade smiles. 'Much better today,' she says. She squeezes my hand, which she's holding lightly between us. 'You're so happy here. It's nice.'

'It's home,' I say.

The two of us get to the vegetarian cafe first, which doesn't seem unusual until I realize Jade and I have been talking for fifteen minutes and there's still no sign of Mum.

I'm just starting to think that I should call her when she finally appears in the doorway to the cafe. I'm relieved until I register that she's moving very slowly, clearly unsteady on her feet, face all anxiety. People are actually moving out of the way for her; someone even offers an arm.

A cold feeling is spreading through my chest, even as I slide out of my seat and hurry across the length of the cafe to get to her.

When she notices me, her face sinks with relief.

'Oh, Rosie!' she says. 'I'm sorry I'm late. It took me a while to get going.'

'What's the matter?' I ask, a little more aggressively than I'd intended. But my heart is pounding so hard, and the fear that has taken hold of me feels urgent and relentless.

'Nothing, I'm just a bit slow today,' Mum says.

'Mum, I'm not an idiot,' I say.

'Don't make a scene,' she says. 'Hello, Jade!' We've just about reached the table. 'How are you?'

'Fine,' Jade says, glancing at me as if to check that this is the right response. 'How are you?'

'Tired,' Mum says, sinking with a sigh into a chair. 'Rosie, stop making that face and sit down.'

'Why didn't you tell me things were this bad?' I ask, not moving. 'You can barely walk.'

'I'm just going to see what cakes they have,' Jade says, then makes her very graceful escape from the table.

Mum sighs again. 'You made Jade feel uncomfortable.'

'She's just giving us some privacy,' I say. 'So you can tell me what the fuck is going on.'

'Rosie!' Mum says sharply. 'Don't use that tone with me, please. I don't know why you're acting like this is some giant surprise. You know that I've been having tests.'

'Actually, what you told me was that there'd be tests, and then you gave no extra information.'

'That's because I don't have any,' she says, tensely. 'It's very frustrating, not getting any answers.'

'So what tests have you had? What do they think might be wrong?'

'Rosie, for goodness' sake, I don't want to have this conversation here.'

'You clearly don't want to have the conversation at all,' I point out. 'Or we would have had it already. And you've just been trying to hide it the whole time I've been . . . Wait.' Something occurs to me, suddenly, as obvious as it is unlikely. 'The house. It's so clean.'

Mum looks instantly cornered, which is an answer in itself, but still she says, 'What about it? Is that so strange?' We stare at each other for a moment, before she sighs again, louder this time, a little annoyed. 'OK, fine, I hired a cleaner.'

'What?' I honestly can't believe it. The Mum I know would never pay to have someone do the cleaning for her. '*Why?*'

'Because I didn't want you to be ashamed of me,' she says, and for a moment, seeing the look on her face when she says this, a piece of my heart breaks.

'Mum.'

'In front of Jade,' she adds. 'OK? Please, I don't want to talk about all of this now. Sit down. Choose what you're going to have for lunch.'

I feel like crying. 'It's bad, isn't it? Whatever's wrong. It's bad.'

There's a long, painful silence. Finally, she says. 'I think so, yes.'

I bite down hard on my lip. 'Why didn't you tell me?'

'Because I'm your mother,' she says, which makes no sense. 'Sit down. Choose your lunch.'

Jade gives it a few more minutes before she comes back to us, talking casually about the cakes on display, and how she's thinking about having the carrot cake later. She takes my hand under the table and squeezes it, then lets go.

Mum seems to perk up a bit after we've eaten, which makes me feel a tiny bit better. Maybe she just needed a boost of energy. Maybe . . . I can't convince myself.

'Is it just this?' I ask, when Jade has gone to the bathroom. 'Like, a fatigue? And the dizzy spells? Or is there something else?'

Mum sighs, rubbing at her forehead. 'There are other symptoms that are part of . . . whatever this is.'

'Like what?'

'You know how I lose words sometimes? And I don't remember things?'

'That's just you,' I say, and I'm surprised by how defensive my voice sounds, almost fierce with it. 'That's not an illness.'

'There's a chance it might be,' she says, very gently.

'You've always been scatty.'

'Yes, but . . . Rosie . . .'

'I've put up with this for years and you're suddenly telling me it's actually a symptom for something?'

There's a silence. I bite down hard on my top lip.

'I'm sorry,' I say.

She sighs. 'I know I'm not always the ideal mother.'

'That's not—'

'I know there have been times when you've been more taking care of me than the other way around. You've been very patient.'

'OK, stop,' I say. 'I said I was sorry.' Jade appears from around the corner, clearly walking slowly, trying to gauge from a distance whether it's OK to come over. I smile at her to let her know it's fine.

'Jade, it was so lovely to spend a bit more time with you,' Mum says when Jade reaches the table. 'I'm sorry I'm not quite my usual self.'

'That's OK,' Jade says. 'I really don't mind.' It occurs to me that it's not like she has anything to compare it to. That for her, this version of Mum is the only version of Mum. It's a strange thing to think.

'I need to be getting back to work,' Mum says. 'I'll see you both later tonight? I can't see you for dinner, I'm afraid; I've got an event at the Dome with Janine.'

'Feminism?' I ask.

Mum beams. 'Feminism.' She leans over and gives me a kiss on the cheek. 'I love you. I'll see you later.'

Jade and I are quiet when we leave the cafe. I'm thinking about all the little quirks Mum has had for basically as long as I can remember, the kind of things I barely register any more. I'm so used to supplying a word when she loses track mid-sentence, reminding her about bills and appointments and people's names. Now, those quirks have a different name: *symptoms*.

'Do you have any idea at all what it could be?' Jade asks me finally, when we've been walking in silence for five minutes.

'No,' I say. 'I know it isn't Parkinson's.'

'That's all?' Jade asks, looking baffled. 'That's all they know?'

'It's all *I* know,' I say. 'She's not really telling me stuff, clearly.'

'Isn't that a bit . . . weird?' she asks.

'It's hard, with me being away.'

'Yeah, but . . .' She's shaking her head. 'My family and I fight all the time, but we'd tell each other if we were ill.'

My instinctive defensiveness flames, immediate and hot. 'This isn't your family. Don't judge her, or me.' I hate it when anyone criticizes Mum and me and our tiny little family, especially when it's from the safety of a nuclear family like Jade's.

'I wasn't,' Jade says. 'I'm sorry. I was just a bit surprised. You and your mum are so close.'

'Yeah, we're close. That doesn't mean things can't be hard. Or that sometimes it's not easy to talk.' It suddenly feels like I'm talking about more than just Mum's illness, so I stop. 'Can we talk about something else?'

'OK,' Jade says, a little hesitantly. 'What's next on the tour?'

*

Later, when we're all Brightoned out and Jade has had her fill of the Lanes and the beach, I let myself look at my phone again. Caddy has messaged to assure me that she's fine – **just need to cry it out for a while** – and promised to call in a couple of days for a proper talk. I reply, telling her that I'm sorry about how it all went down, that she'll be fine, that it's for the best, and she never has to worry about breaking up with me. She sends me hearts and tells me she loves me.

I add, **Suze, too.**

She replies with a cold, **Don't talk to me about Suze.**

For her part, Suze has at least listened to my command to not involve me in the drama. She hasn't messaged me again since this morning.

'Is it OK if I invite Suze out for dinner with us tonight?' I ask Jade. 'She might have got it in the neck from Cads today, and I'm a bit worried that I haven't talked to her since last night.'

'OK,' Jade says, her expression unreadable.

'Are you sure? I promise she'll be a much better version of herself when it's just us.'

'I said OK,' Jade says. 'It's fine.'

I message Suze, who responds immediately, like she's been waiting by her phone. As we make arrangements for dinner over WhatsApp, I say to Jade, 'By the way, Suze doesn't know about the tests and things that Mum's having, so don't mention it, OK? Just so I can tell her properly at some point.'

Jade pauses from where she's been brushing her hair in front of my mirror, her hand suspended above her hair. She frowns at me. 'Does Caddy know?'

I shake my head.

'Roz! Why not?'

'Because I just . . . It hasn't come up. There's enough going on, anyway.'

Jade's face scrunches, incredulous. 'Yeah, stuff about *them* and *their* lives. Yours matters too, you know. You're allowed to also have problems.'

'I know that.'

'Do you? Do they?'

'That's not fair,' I say. 'They'd be the first to support me if I needed it.'

'Then why aren't you telling them you *do* need it?'

'Because I don't!' It comes out too harsh, more like a snap, and she doesn't flinch but instead makes a face like I've just proved some kind of a point.

There's a moment of silence. I wait for her to do what I'm sure she's going to do, which is start pushing me harder, force me to admit something out loud, but she doesn't. She resumes brushing her hair, her eyes travelling back to her reflection. 'OK,' she says mildly. 'I won't mention it.'

20

Jade is quiet on the coach back to Norwich. The last day and a half of our trip had gone well, by which I basically mean they were drama free. Even the dinner with Suze had been nice and low-key – save a maddening tangent about Matt telling her he loved her and the subsequent, inevitable breaking of his heart, which made me want to strangle her for giving in to the self-sabotaging power of her own denial – and Jade was certainly warmer towards her when we said goodbye than when we'd said hello, which was a relief. The two of us spent the next day taking the train up the coast, and it had been great, even perfect.

But now, the two of us side by side, Jade is silent. At first I think she's fallen asleep, but I realize after a while that she's just staring out the window, deep in thought, her head tilted away from me.

'Are you OK?' I ask eventually.

She starts, then turns to me with a smile. 'Sure. Are you?'

I nod, though I'm actually feeling really sad, like a combination of grief and homesickness that even I know is ridiculous, given that we've only just left.

'Did you like Brighton?' I ask.

She hesitates, glancing back out of the window and then back at me. 'Yeah,' she says. 'It lived up to expectations. But there were a lot of distractions.'

I wince. 'I'm sorry about that.'

'One, you don't have to be. And two, it's OK. But I just . . . I feel a bit weird.'

'Weird? About what?'

'I don't know. I'm trying to figure it out myself.' She looks at me, her eyes moving over my face. 'It's just . . . you're obviously so much happier there. In Brighton, at home.'

I don't know what to do with my face. I try to smile. 'Well, yeah, of course. It's home.'

'It's more than that,' she says. 'Even though things didn't go as you planned – which I know you hate – and even though there was all that drama and arguments, and we didn't really get to hang out with your friends properly, you were just . . . happier. Not even happy; maybe that's not the word. Like, comfortable? More relaxed. And I realized that I've never seen you like that. At uni you're always tense; I just didn't realize how much.'

My skin feels tight and hot. I feel so exposed, even though her voice is so calm and mild. Where is this going?

'I don't really know what you're trying to say. Are you saying that's a bad thing?'

'No, it was nice,' she says. 'To see you like that. But it makes me sad that you can't be like that at uni. And . . . honestly, Roz, if we're talking like this, it was kind of unsettling to see that you're not being honest with your friends.'

'How am I not being—'

'Your mum being ill? They'd want to know, Roz. And it's like, if you can lie to them so easily, maybe you're not being honest with me either.'

'About what?'

'Well, I don't know, do I?' From anyone else, this might sound combative, but Jade is still talking quietly, more contemplative than anything else, like she's thinking aloud.

'I am being honest with you,' I say. It's the truth, isn't it?

'You would tell me, wouldn't you?' she says. 'If you were unhappy?'

'Yes,' I say. 'Of course.'

She lets it drop, and then she actually does sleep for a while, and I try to listen to a podcast but keep getting distracted by my own thoughts and realizing that I haven't taken in a word anyone has said. When she wakes up, we talk about the placement in a community pharmacy that I have coming up on my course, and on the surface it's all fine, but because I know her by now as well as I do, I can tell something is still off. And whatever that something is, it's getting bigger and bigger between us with each mile we travel. By the time we get to Norwich, it's huge, and impossible to ignore.

We get off the bus at Unthank Road so we can go to her house rather than the campus as planned, even though we're barely talking by this point, and she's walking slightly ahead of me, which is really annoying.

'Can you just say what's wrong?' I say, when she's let us into the house, we've said hi to her housemates and headed up to the privacy of her room. I drop my rucksack on her floor, pushing it away from me with my foot. 'I can't deal with this weird passive-aggressive thing you've got going on.'

She sighs, reaching up to rub her forehead with her index finger and thumb. 'I really don't want to fight right now.'

'And I don't want the silent treatment,' I say. 'So just say it. Please.'

'It's not . . .' She sighs again, sharper and more frustrated, then sits down heavily on her bed. 'It's not your fault; I know that. I don't want to fight about it. But if we talk about this now, that's what will happen.'

'What isn't my fault?'

'What we talked about on the coach. All of it. I know you're not happy here, OK? I've worried about that for a while, but now . . . now I've seen that version of you, the home version, I can't ignore it any more.'

'OK, so I'm not happy, whatever,' I say. Usually, at this point, I'd have sat down beside her on the bed, but I find myself staying where I am, hovering by my rucksack in the centre of the room. 'Why is that making you mad?'

'I'm not mad; I'm . . .' She groans, putting her hand to her forehead again. 'God, do we really have to do this now?'

'Yes, stop saying that. Yes. We have to do this right now.'

'Don't you get that it's not a good thing for you to only be happy with me?' She finally looks at me properly, her hand falling back to her side. 'Because what does that make me? Just a distraction?'

'You're obviously not a distraction. If that's why you're upset, it's really stupid.'

'Call me stupid, great. That's going to help. Don't be a bitch to me right now, Roz, seriously. If you want to talk about this, let's talk.'

'Fine, we're talking.' We're not talking. We're arguing. At some point, I realize I've crossed my arms. 'You think I called you stupid, even though I didn't, but you did just call me a bitch, so it's clearly going really well so far.'

'For God's sake!' she snaps, raking her hand through her hair. 'Maybe you should just go, and we'll talk about it tomorrow.'

'Why does it bother you so much?' I ask, not moving. 'You make me happy. That's a good thing.'

'Not if it's the only thing. I can't be your only source of happiness.'

'Why not?'

She shakes her head, closing her eyes momentarily. 'Because it's like none of it's real. I saw how you were there, in Brighton, when you were actually happy and comfortable, how you were with your friends, even when they were acting like brats. It was like I actually saw you for the first time.'

My heart drops. 'And . . . and you didn't like me?'

'*No*, Roz! The opposite, if anything. I loved seeing you like that; it just hurts that it's taken this long. And if you're not yourself here, in Norwich, where our bit is, what does that make us? I don't want to be part of your half-life. And I don't want to be the only good thing in a life you hate. It's not healthy. Not for you, not for me. Especially when . . .' She stops herself, then lets out a slow breath. 'Never mind.'

'Sure, never mind,' I say, rolling my eyes, which seems like a smarter option than crying, which is what I suddenly feel like I might do. 'That'll stop me asking you to finish whatever that sentence was going to be.'

'It doesn't matter. I'm tired. I don't want to do this now; I said that already. ' She stands, reaching up to pull her hair loose from its ponytail. 'If you push this, it's on you, OK? You need to learn when to stop.'

'Oh my God,' I say, dropping my arms back down to my sides. 'Do you want to patronize me a little bit more?'

'No, I want us to not be fighting right now. If you can't do that, then you should go.' She leans past me to put her hair tie on her desk.

'Or you should stop being so passive aggressive,' I say. 'I'm not going anywhere.'

'Of course not,' she mutters, gritting her teeth like the words have slipped out, like she regrets them already.

'What does that mean?'

'Well, you're always here, aren't you?' She raises her chin when she says this, almost defiant.

The words land hard, like I know she meant them to. Something unspoken, something previously safe, wielded like a weapon. I don't need to ask what she means; we both already know.

'I like it here,' I say. 'And so do you. It's nicer than my flat. You said that.'

'It's *all the time*, Roz.'

My throat is so tight, but I still manage to speak, which I'm proud of. 'You can't tell me that you find freshers really annoying, and you're glad we hang out here, and then throw that back in my face like that. That's such a shitty thing to do to me.'

'It's not just that! You know it isn't. Maybe I just said that to make you feel better, I don't know. Freshers *are* annoying, but of course I'd put up with them for you. But this . . . It's like you want to make it yours. But this is my house, and these are my friends, and this is my life.'

It is taking everything in me to not start crying. My hands are actually balled into fists at my sides. My teeth are clenched so hard, my jaw hurts.

'I love you,' she says. Her voice is tight, like maybe she wants to cry, too. 'But we both need to have our lives, not share one. It's too unbalanced.'

'We've barely been together a few months,' I say. 'And even that is only, like, a month or so longer than I've even been in Norwich. Of course you've got more of a life here than I have. Of course I want to share it with you, because it's good, and I don't feel shit about myself when I'm with you. I'm sorry that's annoying for you, or whatever—'

'That's obviously not what I said—'

'And I'm sorry that seeing me happy at home with my friends has changed what you think of me for some reason—'

'Rosie! For God's sake—'

'I guess it must be annoying to have to listen to me all the time—'

'Are you done?' she almost shouts. 'Twisting everything I'm saying even though you know – you *know* – that I only want what's best for you?'

'There you go, patronizing me again.'

'Oh my God!' She throws her hands up, shaking her head. 'This is so childish. This is why I shouldn't have gone with a fresher.'

'That's what you're going to go with, now? Me being a fresher?'

'No, not just that,' she says, and she's properly snapping now, just as angry as me. I've never seen her angry. 'A baby lesbian.'

'I'm not a lesbian,' I say. 'I'm bisexual.'

'For God's sake, Roz, I *know*. You know what I meant. Why do you have to be so literal all the time?'

'Because words matter, and bi and lesbian are two different things. You always talk about them like they're the same.'

'In all the important ways, they are. And obsessing over labels is *such* a baby lesbian thing to do. Baby bi. Whatever.' She actually shrugs, like it doesn't matter.

'Can you stop calling me a fucking baby?'

'Can you not swear at me?'

'You can't stand the word "fucking" and I'm the immature one?' I have a sudden flash that this is a very stupid argument we're having, which is a shame, because it's the first one we've ever had and should therefore have more gravitas.

Jade grinds her teeth together, her eyes closing. 'Maybe you should go.'

'You were the one who said we should come back here.'

Her eyes open again. 'I changed my mind.'

We stare at each other for a moment, her mouth set in a grim line. I reach over and pick up my rucksack. 'Fine.' There's a jolt of alarm on her face, like she thought I would argue, maybe even beg. So much for her knowing me. 'Bye.'

I turn and go, throwing my rucksack over my shoulder, and clatter down the stairs. Vibs and Aisha look up in confusion when I walk past – I wave and call out a cheery 'Bye, guys!' which probably confuses them even more – and I head back out into the street, down the road and to the bus stop.

The two of us aren't meant to be *drama*, but I feel pretty dramatic now. Dramatic and annoyed, and sad. I thought we were better than petty arguments, but apparently not. Although, maybe it isn't petty. That whole thing about me spending all my time at the house instead of my own flat; she's clearly been sitting on that for a while, hasn't she?

The bus arrives almost immediately – small mercies – and I wave my pass at the driver before swinging myself into a seat. I try and think back over the last few months of our relationship, where I've been aware that I've been spending more time at hers than mine, but hadn't thought she'd noticed. Maybe that was just self-centred of me. Maybe I should pay more attention.

I'm so lost in my thoughts that I barely notice that we're back at the university until the doors swish open. I get off the bus, regretting my bravado, because now I have to face up to the unBrightonness of Norwich, which was easier to do with Jade than without. God, she's right, isn't she? I am leaning on her, way too much.

'Rosie!' someone yells, and I look up, confused, to see Rika, Dawn, Freddie and Matteo standing at the opposite bus stop. Automatically, I wave. 'Holy shit!' Rika yells, at twice the necessary volume, bearing in mind I'm only on the other side of the road. 'The Enigma, live and in person!'

Thankfully, the bus they're waiting for arrives at this moment, and I'm saved having to reply. I watch them clamber on, climbing to the top deck, where they collect at the windows and wave at me like they're going off to war.

The Enigma. Freshers seems like such a long time ago. I carry on waving as their bus pulls away, even managing a grin, like this is all just a big joke, one I'm in on.

I walk back to the flat alone.

*

By the next morning, Jade and I have both cooled off. She meets me on campus for lunch, bringing with her a single rose, a hopeful smile and an apology.

'This isn't fair,' I say. 'I didn't have time to get you a piece of jade.'

She laughs. 'Next time. Maybe get one to have in reserve, for our next fight.'

'Was that really a fight?' I ask. 'It was quite low-key, for a fight.'

'It felt like a fight to me,' she says. 'I felt horrible after you left. I almost went after you, but then I thought you'd think that was pathetic.'

'I would have done,' I agree, even though I think I would actually have quite liked it if she'd come after me. 'I'm sorry, too.'

'Should we talk about it?' Jade asks. She clearly wants to, so I nod, a little reluctantly. 'The last few days just really threw me,' she says. 'The whole thing, it just . . . I wanted to talk about it, but it was the wrong time. I shouldn't have let it ruin the night. It's not what I wanted.'

'Me neither,' I say.

'I'm sorry I blindsided you with a lot of stuff that's maybe been weighing on me a bit,' she says. 'I should have given you a bit of warning on that.'

'Maybe a little,' I say. 'But was it really that bad? Brighton?'

'Of course not,' she says. 'I'm sorry if I made it sound like it was. And I'm sorry that I called your friends brats. I keep thinking about how I said that; it was really out of line.'

This makes me smile despite myself. 'That's OK. They were being a bit bratty. You were right, about that and the bit about me always being at yours.'

'I like that, though,' she says quickly.

'I know, but still. I should work on that.'

'*We*,' she says. 'We can work on that, together. I want you to be happy so we can be happy. Very selfish, really.'

'So selfish,' I agree, reaching out tentatively for her hand. She lets me take it. 'So, are we OK?'

She nods. 'I'm OK if you're OK.'

I nod back. 'I'm OK.'

She squeezes my hand. 'OK.'

21

There's another month left of term before the Easter holidays, which seems like a long time when I think about how much I want to be in the holidays, and a really short time when it comes to how much I'm supposed to have learned and done by then. My timetable is still relentless. Every time I see the word 'hypertension' I want to scream.

I've had a vague idea all term that I'll probably go home over the Easter holidays, but when I call Mum a week after my trip home, she talks me out of it.

In fact, 'Don't bother!' is what she actually says, cheerfully. 'Brighton is just the same as it was when you visited, I promise, and you'll be home for the summer soon. Spend the extra time with Jade. And studying, of course.' She says this vaguely – I think she's still not sure exactly what it is I do at university that doesn't involve Jade – but with confidence.

'What about your tests, though?' I ask. 'I thought I'd be there to help out.'

'There aren't any coming up over Easter,' she says. 'And even if there were, I wouldn't want you giving up your time to traipse to the hospital to watch them poke and prod your tired old mother.'

'Old? You're forty.'

'Exactly! So old. So tired. Oh, Rosie, please be wild and young on my behalf. Get drunk and film yourself trying to say the alphabet backwards. I miss being young.'

This makes me laugh. 'You're ridiculous. I miss you.'

'Well, don't. I'm very boring. Oh! How are the girls? Have they made up yet?'

She means, of course, Suze and Caddy, and the answer is no. Caddy is still stubbornly refusing to even talk to Suze, let alone make up with her, and the weird three-way seesaw of our friendship is completely unbalanced.

'Just leave them to it!' Jade insists, as the drama stretches into its second week, and I've asked her, again, if she thinks I should do something. She says this with all the patience and understanding of someone who hasn't lived the unique triangle of having two best friends. 'Why is it anything to do with you? Is someone paying you to be mediator?'

No, and it's a good thing they aren't, because I'm clearly not doing a very good job of it.

The distraction comes from this particular drama the next Friday, when I finally have my first placement at a community pharmacy in Norwich. Placements will become much more of a regular thing next year and throughout my degree, but in first year, this is the only placement I'll have, and I've been waiting for it for a long time. I'm excited to finally be in a real pharmacy, behind the counter, actually living my degree instead of hearing about it in a lecture theatre or a lab. I can't wait for all the confusion and uncertainty I've felt about pharmacy to finally solidify into actual experience, to be able to visualize myself and the rest of my life like I've planned.

But that's not what happens.

Why? I don't even know. Nothing goes wrong. I don't make any mistakes. No one is horrible to me. I don't have to really even do much except observe the pharmacist, Vivien Saini, and the other members of staff, who are clearly very used to having pharmacy students around. The whole point of this exercise is to get some real-world experience, to be able to see how what we learn in theory translates into real-world practice.

But after about ten minutes, I know that something is off.

Is it me? Is it the pharmacy? Is it the fellow student I'm on the placement with, Leoš, who won't stop talking? No. I think it's me. (I know it's me.) For the whole time I'm in there – it's the first of three two-hour shifts I'll have over consecutive Fridays – the vague feeling of wrongness fills my throat, then my chest, then all of me. When I look around, I can't visualize myself standing here, qualified and fully grown, an Actual Real-Life Pharmacist . . .

Why can't I? I'm here, in the actual environment. The pharmacy team are friendly and patient. When they ask me questions, I know the answers. *So what the fuck is wrong?* I'm so frustrated with myself, I want to claw out my own brain to stop the constant questioning. I'd expected to find it daunting, but this is more than that, this is—

'Are you OK?' Talia, the pharmacy technician, asks me, looking a little alarmed, and I realize I'm breathing really loudly. I think I might be having a minor existential crisis.

'Do you have asthma?' Leoš asks, a little too hopefully, clearly hoping he might get some bonus real-world experience.

I shake my head. 'I just need some water.'

'No worries,' the pharmacy assistant, Cleo, says cheerfully, handing me a cup of water. 'Take your time.'

Later, when I try to tell Jade about this experience, hoping it's the kind of thing that happens a lot, I can see by her face that it isn't.

'Not everyone likes the placements all that much,' she says finally, which is clearly the best she can do. 'It's probably just that. You're quite an impatient person, aren't you? It's probably just your brain wanting to skip this bit and get to the actual job, you know?'

This doesn't make me feel better. In fact, when I go back to the flat that night, I give in to the swirling panic in my head and my throat and cry. Something is so wrong, and I can't ignore it any more. What am I going to do? Should I think about dropping out? *No! Obviously not. That's not an option.* Maybe I should talk to my personal tutor. But what's she going to say? I try and think rationally. She'll say, *Your grades are very good; we have no concerns. This is just first-year stress.* Or maybe, *Perhaps you should speak to a student counsellor?*

Why waste her time or mine? No, I just need to calm down. Focus on the facts, the certainties. Which are: the fact that I'm passing every exam I take; that I know the answers to the questions; that I clearly *can* do this, even if for some reason I feel like I can't. (Or, not even that I *can't*, so much as that I *won't*, which is really strange and doesn't make sense, even in my own head.)

Honestly, the ongoing Suze and Caddy drama feels like taking a break from my own head-drama. At least I can convince myself that I'm not burying my head in the sand if I'm concentrating on their problems instead of my own. It makes me think about the three of us in year eleven, when Suze and I stopped talking after an argument, and Caddy was the one left to try and play mediator. Maybe we haven't grown up much in three years. Maybe nothing has really changed, including me.

I've just entered the third week of it, starting to seriously worry that it's never going to be fixed, when the drama is eclipsed by a bigger, more serious, *actual* drama. Suze is given a notice of eviction from her bedsit, which means that she is essentially, and imminently, homeless. She messages us both in an uncharacteristic panic and – even more uncharacteristic – asks for our help. Which may actually be a first.

Not that we can help, not really, though we try. We can't fix the situation – 'So I kind of have a dog and apparently I'm not allowed to have a dog?' – because we didn't even know there was a dog, and the only further context she provides is that getting rid of this random dog ('Clarence!') is not an option, even though the landlord is evicting her over it. ('Him! Not it!') It would be funny if it wasn't so scary.

What's amazing is how effectively an actual crisis will cut through the childish bullshit of an argument. By the time the whole issue is resolved a few days later – Suze is moving in with her aunt (and keeping the dog) – she and Caddy are friends again. I didn't even need to do anything.

At first, the most overwhelming thing about the whole situation is how shockingly easy it is for someone's life to implode, but then, within a couple of days, the surprise is how quickly and capably Suze rallies. It's not even just the housing issue that she resolves; it's a bunch of other problems at the same time. The whole time I've known her, she's always been reluctant to talk about her future – if pushed, she'd make the kinds of jokes about not having one that scared me in a way I tried not to show – but when I speak to her over the phone a few days after the storm has passed, she has a whole plan. A whole future for herself mapped out, bright and full of hope. She wants to be a nurse and is going to apply for an Access course to make up for the A Levels she doesn't have.

'*How?*' I ask, almost laughing. 'How have you just . . . suddenly got a plan? You've never had a plan. Who *are* you?'

'I thought I'd try out something new,' she says. 'Like knowing what I'm doing for once. You and Caddy make it look so good. Worth a try, right?' There's a bounce in her voice. 'Are you proud?'

'Let's see how you get on with the course first,' I say. I'm *so* proud. It's making my throat hurt. 'Don't get carried away.'

I can hear that she's smiling. 'OK, Roz.'

She sounds happier than I've heard her in . . . well, possibly ever.

The truth is, though, I'm a little shell-shocked. Proud, yes, obviously, but also thrown in a way I hadn't expected. I've wanted stability for Suze the whole time we've been friends, of course I have, but . . . OK, I know how awful this sounds. I wouldn't admit it out loud to anyone, even Jade. But . . . does her life have to start coming together at exactly the time mine starts to feel so out of control? I know it's small and bitter and mean, but I think it. And also that now I *really* have to push aside all the doubts I've been having about university, because if Suze is going, I really can't drop out.

I don't know why I think it. I don't want to think it. It makes me worry I might actually be quite a terrible person.

I bury the thoughts as far down as I can, in the part of my mind where I'm storing all the other worries I don't want to look at, like I think I may be living a mistake, and I shouldn't have chosen this course but it's too late to turn back, and I think I might be a failure.

Jade says, that evening when we're eating dinner in her bedroom, after I've told her all of this with a happy smile on my face, 'Are you OK?'

And I think, *God, no.* And I say, 'Yes.'

22

Easter finally arrives, a dizzying relief. Finally, a break from the constant stress of my timetable, just for a handful of weeks. (Yes, next term means end-of-year exams, but I'm trying not to worry about that too much yet.)

Most of my flat goes home at some point over the holidays, so it's unusually quiet and utterly blissful. I spend actual periods of time in the kitchen not cooking dinner or eating, just reading at the table or looking out the window, sometimes with Jade – who comes over more during those couple of weeks of quiet than she does the whole rest of the year – but often on my own, too. I even have a few friendly conversations with some of my other flatmates that I so rarely see because they spend about as much time here as I do.

It's not just my flat; the whole campus is quieter, less full on. I feel like I have time and space to think for once.

'I wish it was like this all the time,' I say to Jade, who smiles in bemusement.

'I don't think it would count as a university if it was like this all the time,' she says. 'Isn't that a bit like saying you only love an airport when you're not flying anywhere?'

'Incorrect,' I say. 'It's more like saying I love an airport without any tourists, which sounds pretty great to me, sure.' She laughs. 'And also, haven't you been to an airport when you're not the one flying? It's great. One time, Mum and me went to pick up Janine – that's her friend – from Gatwick after a trip, and her plane was delayed, so we got to spend, like, three or four hours just sitting drinking hot chocolate and watching the planes on the runway and talking. No stress about having to get somewhere, no luggage to carry around. It was nice.'

She's frowning, confused. 'But wasn't it a waste of time? What if you'd had somewhere to be?'

I shrug, smiling. 'Never mind.'

The lovely quiet calm doesn't last for long. Over the last week of the holidays, the campus starts slowly filling up again, and so does my flat. Rika, Freddie and the Jacks all return on the same Wednesday, loud and boisterously happy about it. Dawn isn't due back for another few days, which means I'm spared the noise of her and Freddie's reunion sex for a little while longer. Small mercies.

On Friday night, when Jade is working a bar shift, I make the most of the last hours of relative peace and do two loads of laundry in the campus launderette. While I wait, I drink vending-machine Dr Pepper and work my way through a few practice papers with my course texts open beside me.

I'm concentrating so hard on the work, getting up only to move clothes from washer to dryer, that it's late when I remember to look at the time, almost 2 a.m. I've timed it badly, because it's exactly the time the clubs start closing, and the campus is full of returning students falling over each other, arguing, shrieking with laughter, kissing. It's one of the moments that I feel most alienated from the people around me and the experience I feel like I should be having. This is what I thought student life would look like, and it does.

For everyone else.

I let myself into my flat, dump the clothes in my room and head to the kitchen to make a toasted cheese sandwich. As I shuffle around, I hear the loud bang of the main door slamming open, loud voices, the stumble of drunken figures making their way down the hall.

After a few minutes, when the noise has died down and my sandwich is happily toasting away, I head to the bathroom, wondering if it's a mistake to have cheese so late at night, or if the thing about cheese dreams is—

'FUCK!' I shriek, my hand fumbling to turn off the bathroom light that I had innocently – mistake of mistakes – turned on, revealing the half-naked, entwined figures of – *fuck!* – Rika and Freddie.

'FUCK!' Rika also shrieks. In the second before I get the light off and merciful darkness cloaks us all, I see her panicked eyes, her hands pushing Freddie away from her, him almost tripping over his own boxers.

'Sorry, sorry, sorry,' I gabber, for some reason, as if any of this is even remotely my fault.

'You didn't lock the fucking door!' Rika is snarling to Freddie as I make my escape.

As the door closes behind me, I hear him snap back, 'Neither did you, bitch!'

Classy. On all levels. My brain is actually struggling to comprehend them all. One, sex in a shared bathroom without bothering to lock the door. Two, cheating on your girlfriend. Three, shagging your friend's boyfriend. Four . . .

'Rosie!'

Oh, shit. Rika is stumbling after me, still tugging her top down over her torso. I glance back at her from the open doorway of the kitchen, expecting to see panic on her face, but there's no trace of it. She just looks really annoyed. Not ashamed, or contrite. Just pissed off.

'You didn't see anything, right?' she says, with no preamble. She's stayed in the doorway as I've gone over to the sandwich toaster, holding the door open with her back.

I'm confused for a second, thinking she means 'see anything' as in, body parts, which is surely the least important thing to be worrying about. And then I get it. It's not a question; it's a command.

Stalling, I flip the switch on the toaster and open the lid.

'Right?' Rika says.

'Look, I'm just making dinner,' I say, shrugging, without turning round.

There's a silence, long and loaded. I lift the toasted sandwich onto the waiting plate and cut it carefully in half. When I finally let myself glance back, the doorway is empty, and Rika is gone.

23

Rosie:

Moral dilemma. Are you both in attendance?

Suze:

PRESENT.

Caddy:

Intrigue!

Rosie:

OK. So. There's a couple in my flat. I know the guy cheated on the girl with the girl's best friend. Do I tell the friend? Yes or no?

Suze is typing . . .

Caddy is typing . . .

Rosie:

No need to write an essay!

Suze:

Hmmmmmmm.

Caddy:

How do you know? Is it just a rumour?

Rosie:

No, I unfortunately have the empirical evidence of my own eyes. So do I tell Dawn? One-word answer, please.

Suze:

Yes.

Caddy:

No.

Rosie:

OK, that is not the answer I would've guessed for either of you. Expand, please?

Suze:

Girl Code, right? You have to tell. Doesn't she deserve to know?

Caddy:

Why get involved, though? Isn't it best to stay out of it instead of get dragged in?

Rosie:

:/ both good points.

Suze:

Cads, wouldn't you want to know?

Caddy:

Yeah? Maybe? I don't know, though. I think you should stay out of other people's relationship drama. You only make it worse getting involved.

Suze:

...

Caddy:

What?

Suze:

👀

Caddy:

I wasn't talking about you.

Suze:

I said I was sorry.

Caddy:

You're not sorry though, are you.

Rosie:

Guys.

Suze:

Not really, no.

Rosie:

Suze!

Caddy:

OK.

Rosie:

I thought you'd sorted this out already.

Suze:

So did I.

Caddy:

We did.

Rosie:

Good, well God forbid a conversation is about my issue for longer than two minutes.

Suze:

Sorry, Roz. I think you should tell the girl. Yeah, it'll be shit, but better for her to know so she can cut it off with the guy and not waste time during her first year of uni tied to some shithead who isn't worth it.

Caddy:

What if he is worth it?

Suze:

Then knowing won't change that.

Caddy:

True.

What if it ruins the friendship though?
Roz, did you say they were friends?

Rosie:

Yeah.

Suze:

Don't sound like very good friends. The friendship is ruined already, even if she doesn't know it yet.

Caddy:

Also true.

Rosie:

Wait are we still passive aggressively talking in code?

Suze:

WHAT? NO!

Caddy:

NO!

Suze:

I love you both to death for ever.

Caddy:

ME TOO.

Suze:

Don't ever leave me.

Caddy:

Chained for life xxx

Suze:

Oh thank God xxxxx

Rosie:
You are both ridiculous and I love you too.

Suze:
Did we help?

Rosie:
Yes. Also no.

Caddy:
Let us know what you decide?

Rosie:
I will. Thanks xxx

Later, I will wonder why I didn't include the pretty crucial detail of our future living situation in the WhatsApp conversation with Caddy and Suze. It might be because it didn't seem relevant to include any kind of a potential selfish motive into the ethical dilemma. Or it might be because the whole thing is actually a monumental act of self-sabotage on my part. That's probably more likely, especially as I don't raise the so-called ethical dilemma with Jade, whose opinion I value so highly, and who doesn't exactly know Rika or Dawn, but at least has actually met them.

Yeah. Let's call it self-sabotage.

At first, I convince myself that Freddie and Dawn were actually broken up, and I just hadn't realized because I was so rarely around. But this possibility is disproved, very quickly, when I hear them through the wall on the Sunday night that Dawn arrives back on campus. Anyone would think I was prudish, based on the grimace I can feel on my face, but my disgust is all aimed at Freddie, not Dawn, and it's because he is a dick, not because of what he's doing with it. A weasel dick, if that's a thing. A dickish weasel. Poor Dawn.

I dither for another twelve hours, but I know, really, that I've already made up my mind. Dawn deserves my loyalty a lot more than Rika, and she definitely doesn't deserve to be treated like this by someone she considers a friend. And I've given Rika plenty of time to talk to Dawn herself, haven't I? She knows I saw them. Why is she just assuming that I'll follow her orders to keep her secrets for her? I don't owe her anything.

On Monday afternoon, I knock gently on Dawn's door, half hoping there'll be no response. But a chirpy 'Yup!' sounds from within, and I open it.

'Oh,' Dawn says, when she sees it's me, like she was expecting someone else. But she smiles when she says, 'Hi, Rosie.'

She's sitting at her desk in front of an open laptop, and she's wearing glasses. I didn't even know she needed glasses.

'Can I come in for a sec?' I ask.

'Sure,' she says, leaning back in her chair. 'Everything OK?'

'Sort of, no,' I say, nonsensically. I perch on the end of her bed. 'I kind of . . . need to tell you something.'

'OK . . .' she says, making a face. 'Should I be worried?'

'It's about Freddie,' I say, and this time her face drops. 'So . . . I'm really sorry about telling you this, but I think you deserve to know. He cheated on you while you were away. With Rika.'

I don't know what I expect from her, but she barely reacts when I say this. She's silent, watching me, her face set but unflinching. Finally, after far too long, she says, 'How—'

'I saw them,' I say. 'I walked in on them, actually.'

'Right,' Dawn says, nodding. I'd always thought of her as expressive, maybe even to an annoying degree, but right now she's utterly inscrutable. 'Why are you telling me this?'

'Because . . . I thought you deserved to know?'

'You thought I deserved to hear something really shit?' she asks. 'That's what I deserved? To feel like this?'

'No, I mean . . . the truth. You deserve the truth.'

'Why do you care?' she says. 'Like, who even are you? We're not friends. This has got fuck all to do with you.'

'We are friends,' I say, stung.

'No, we're not,' she says. She's less inscrutable now; more very obviously extremely angry, but she's sitting on it with a restraint I'd never have expected from her. She's like a simmering pot, the steam visible but controlled, blazing in her eyes and her unnaturally steady voice. 'We could have been. But you're literally never around. You couldn't make it more obvious that you don't give a shit. I tried. I tried when Rika was all, *Fuck her, she thinks she's above us all*. But she was right. You think you know me and Rika? *Rika* is my friend. Rika has been my friend this whole time you've been . . .' She's clearly trying to think of the right word, frustrated with herself that she has to flail for it. 'The fucking *Enigma*.'

I'm trying to keep myself as steady as she is. 'Rika just fucked you over, and I really was just trying to do the decent thing. For you. I was trying to be your friend.'

'You don't know anything.' She's all ice now, even as her eyes are still blazing. 'And you're not my friend. You don't have any friends. You don't know how to be a friend.'

I bite my lips together. I think my hands might be shaking. 'None of this is my fault.'

'If you were my friend,' Dawn says, with emphasis, like I haven't spoken at all, 'I could have at least thought you were doing it because you cared about me. But you don't, and we're not. So fuck you for thinking you know best and getting involved. Fuck you.'

I open the door and leave without another word, as if I don't care. But I do care. I care so much my eyes are stinging and my throat feels tight and I'm clenching my hands into tight fists with it. *'Fuck you.'* No one has ever said that to me before and meant it.

I shut the door to my room, my heart pounding thick and hard. *'You don't know how to be a friend.'* My hand spasms with pain and I look down to see that I'm clutching my phone so hard, the edge of the case has dug into my palm. I unlock the screen and message Caddy.

Rosie:

Just want to remind you that you're the best and I love you.

I'm crying. Embarrassed about it even though I'm alone in my room.

I message Suze.

Rosie:

Have I ever told you that I'm really proud of you? You're kind of the best.

Caddy:

Are you OK?!

Suze:

What the fuck, are you dying??

I sit down on my bed, drop my phone onto my lap and cry. Hard crying, the kind I have to mute by crushing my hand over my mouth.

Look at this, Rosie. Look who you are. You say something honest to your friends and they think it's strange. You saying something nice is unusual to them.

Sometimes, someone will hand you a mirror to really look at yourself and it's not a pretty sight. Maybe Dawn is right. Maybe I don't know how to be a friend.

I don't know how long I sit there in this spiral of self-hatred, rethinking every friendship I've ever had through this new lens, all the ways I've let people down, all the times I could have been better.

When I look at my phone again, there are more messages.

Caddy:

I hope you are OK! Call me! I love you too!

Suze:

The fact that you're proud of me is the reason I'm still alive, Roz. I love you too xxx

My heart, still jagged and painful in my chest, finally starts to calm. They were joking. They were joking because they know me, because they love me. They must have messaged each other – **Did you just get a weird message from Roz?!** – worried, then replied with love, just in case that was what I needed. I do have friends. I am a friend. A good one. I must be, because I am theirs. They love me and they know me.

I call Jade. She says, 'Come over here, right now, don't wait. Just walk out of there, Roz. I'm here.'

She's on my side, of course.

'Of course you did the right thing!' she says, over and over, squeezing my arm, hugging me close when I cry. We have dinner with her housemates and they all agree. *Of course*, they say. *Of course it was the right thing.* It helps, even when Vibs rolls his eyes, calling it 'fresher drama'.

If I could, I'd spend the next few weeks hiding out there, but I can't. I go back to the flat the next afternoon, my heart pounding with nerves I wish I was too cool to feel. I can hear voices in the kitchen, but I walk past without pausing, heading for my room. I'm safely inside, and just wondering whether I can relax, when there's a knock at the door. Sharp and cold. Three short raps.

I could ignore it, but whoever it is has clearly seen me walk in here, so I say, 'Yeah?' It actually comes out level and steady, even a little bit bored.

But then the door opens and it's Rika, stony-faced. *Fuck.* 'You came back, then,' she says.

'All my stuff is here,' I say.

She crosses her arms. 'Sort of pathetic to run away, don't you think?' she says. 'You could have stayed to deal with the fallout. It was a proper shitshow here last night.'

'I think me being here would've made it worse,' I say.

She shrugs. 'Maybe. You know, you could have told me that you wanted to tell Dawn. Just a little heads up. That would have been decent.'

'Decent?' I repeat. 'I'm not the one in the wrong here.'

'I know I'm in the wrong,' she says. 'That doesn't mean what you did is OK. The thing you don't seem to get is that Dawn and I are actually friends? So, yeah, we have to deal with this somehow, but we *will* figure out how to do that.'

I don't really understand what she's trying to say. 'You're just expecting her to forgive you for fucking her over?'

She almost laughs. 'No. But can you take a second to think about the fact that you don't know everything? You don't know very much about me, or Dawn, or even Freddie? But we know about each other. Do you get where I'm going with this?'

'I really don't,' I say.

Rika lets out a long sigh. 'Did you really think you could just live in our house after this?'

Immediately, too late, I *do* see where she's going with this. And it is not anywhere good. 'What?'

'Loyalty matters,' she says, with no apparent hint of irony. 'We were already putting up with a lot, what with you never being around and everything. Dawn was trying to be nice, inviting you to live with us. Did you know that? But you were just a bitch about it, and maybe that could have been OK, but now this? Forget it. Find somewhere else to live.'

'You can't do that,' I say. 'I signed a contract.'

'Sure, a contract that we're all jointly liable for. We just need to replace you, and we already have. Ivy is really happy that she can come and live with us now. She's already sent me the deposit.' She waits for me to say something, but I've lost the power of speech. 'You'll get your deposit back in a few days,' she says. 'So you won't be out of pocket. And I'm sure you won't have any trouble finding somewhere else, right? What with all those friends you have.'

I finally find my voice. 'You're a class-A bitch, Rika.'

'Maybe,' she says. 'But I have friends and a house to live in, so . . .' She shrugs. 'I can live with myself.'

I take a step towards her and she flinches backwards, which gives me the tiniest hint of satisfaction that she isn't quite as untouchable as she seems. I walk past her, down the hall to the kitchen. 'Dawn,' I say, when I open the door.

Dawn is sitting at the table with Freddie and Flapjack. She doesn't say anything, just looks at me. Flapjack lets out a nervous cough.

'You're not serious, are you?' I say. 'You're seriously going to kick me out of the house for something Rika did? And not even talk to me about it?'

'Can you guys get lost for a sec?' Dawn says to the boys, in a very unDawnlike voice. It actually throws me a little, hearing the assertive tone in her voice for the first time all year. Even more surprising, the two of them obey.

I glance behind me, expecting to see Rika standing there, watching, but it's just me and Dawn, alone in the kitchen.

'Rosie, you don't even want to live with us,' she says. I hesitate, then, because her voice has got softer, I go to sit beside her. She looks tired. 'Do you?' She looks expectantly at me, and I have to look away. 'I don't know what's been going on with you this whole year, but I thought it would help, offering you a place with us. And you kind of just threw it right back in my face.'

'But I was trying to help!' I say. It comes out more irritated than I intended, more irritated than I even feel. 'I was trying to help *you*. What am I supposed to do now?'

'Find somewhere else to live,' she says, almost flatly. 'Or just leave. I don't know.'

My heart clenches at the unexpected meanness. 'I don't understand why it doesn't matter to you.'

She frowns. 'What doesn't? You not living with us?'

'No, Rika. That you're just OK with what she did to you.'

Dawn sighs, putting her fist to her forehead. 'Remember that you don't know everything, OK? You don't know what's actually gone on or what we've talked about, me and her.'

'But you just forgave her. Like, straight away.'

She looks away, shaking her head. 'Look, we all do what we have to do to get through, OK?' When she looks back at me, she seems so sad that I feel the first flush of guilt that I had anything to do with her feeling like this. 'If it helps, I am sorry about the house. I'm sorry it hasn't worked out. I get why you're pissed off. But this is just how it is, OK? Rika is just . . .'

'Queen?'

The surprise of a half-smile on her face. 'Yeah. But there's a lot you don't know about her. Or me.'

'Are you still with Freddie?'

'Yes.'

'Why?'

Dawn makes eye contact with me, steady and firm. 'That's really none of your business, Rosie.'

The conversation is unmistakeably over. I go to my room, the door still wide open, and walk inside. My heart is racing. What the fuck am I going to do? *What the fuck am I going to do?*

The answer doesn't come to me over the next few days. Not even a tiny little bit of one. No matter how much I think, and google, and panic, there's nothing. How could I have been so stupid, when I had so much to lose? It's so unlike me. I'm a planner, aren't I? I'm meant to think everything through. What's happened to me?

'Can you just put that aside for now?' Jade asks, the fourth time we have this conversation.

She has been very, very patient with me.

'For how long, though?' I ask. 'I can't just not have somewhere to live next year.'

'No, but you don't have to find it *now*,' she says. 'This is the worst time of year to try and find somewhere. Wait until the summer, when there'll be more options and you won't still be in the stress bubble of what happened.'

'Isn't it going to be too late, waiting for the summer?'

She shakes her head. 'That's when there'll be more single rooms in houses around. From, like, people who drop out at the end of the first year.' She says this casually, and my heart clenches. 'Right now, you should be focusing on preparing for next month's exams, and your scary schedule.' She makes a face. 'I remember the end of first year. I stress-ate a lot of cereal bars.

How *are* you feeling about your schedule? Is it OK?'

I shrug. 'It's fine.' It isn't fine. It's so stressful I keep having anxiety dreams.

'Are you sure?' Jade asks, her forehead crinkling. 'How do you feel about your placement now it's over?'

My heart clenches again, more painfully this time. The pharmacist had made a comment on my observation sheet about how I hadn't seemed as 'engaged' as other students, which had made me feel exposed and ashamed in a way I hadn't been able to articulate to anyone, especially Jade.

'I think maybe I'll be better in a hospital pharmacy setting,' I say. It's what I've been telling myself. 'I guess I'll find out next year, when I have a placement at the hospital.'

She nods. 'Yeah, probably. No need to rush that kind of decision, anyway. You've got years to figure all that stuff out.'

This is clearly meant to be reassuring, but all my head hears is *years*. I suddenly feel really, really tired. She looks at me, worry in her eyes, and reaches out to touch my hand.

'It'll be OK,' she says. 'I know it's hard at the moment, but it will be OK. Honestly.'

I breathe in a sigh. 'Do you promise?'

'No,' she says, and I laugh despite myself. 'But I promise that I'll be here, even if it isn't.'

I smile, leaning over to rest my forehead against her shoulder. 'Thank you.'

'Does that help?'

'Yes. It helps a lot.'

I don't tell Mum about any of this, of course. Partly because I don't want to, but mostly because I find out, when I speak to her a week after the fallout, that she's just had an MRI scan.

'Why didn't you tell me you were booked in for one of those?'

I demand. 'I need to know this stuff. I could have come home to help you with it.'

'I don't need any help with it,' she says, sounding almost irritated. 'And of course you shouldn't have to be coming home all the time just because no one can figure out what's wrong with me. It's enough I have to deal with it; I don't want any of it put on you.'

'But I want to be there,' I say. 'And it's hardly coming back "all the time" when I haven't even – Wait.' I stop, my mouth falling open. 'Is *that* why you told me not to come home for Easter?'

'No,' she says, unconvincingly.

'*Mum!*' I snap. 'For God's sake! I want to help!'

'And I don't need you to help! I just said that. Janine was with me. She drove me there, and afterwards we went to Sprinkles and had pancakes.'

'I would have liked pancakes.'

She goes quiet. I can hear her breath through the phone. Finally, softly, she says, 'I'm sorry. I'm not trying to make this hard for you; quite the opposite.'

'I know that, but is there anything else you aren't telling me?'

'No. Is there anything *you* aren't telling *me*?'

This silences me. Where has she got that from? Has she guessed something, or is she just throwing my own question back at me? Dawn's face comes into my mind, her mouth forming the words, *Fuck you.* 'No. How was it, anyway? The MRI?'

'It was fine,' she says. 'Uncomfortable, but fine. It took about half an hour and I was allowed to wear headphones.'

'What did you listen to?'

'Take That,' she says. When I laugh in surprise, she says, 'When you're my age, you'll find the music you loved when you were young soothing, too. I'm not ashamed. It helped a lot. I just closed my eyes and pretended I was nineteen again. Oh! Speaking of being nineteen. Are you looking forward to your birthday?'

'Nice segue,' I say. 'Smooth. And yeah, I guess? It's the same week as the start of the exam period, though, so it's not going to be, like, wild or anything.' Not that it would have been anyway. I'm kind of glad to have the excuse not to have any exciting plans. It'll be just Jade and me, and that will be all I need.

24

The only good thing about April is that it passes quickly. There's so much going on, and so much to worry about, that it's over before it even sinks in that it's almost May. Month of my birth, and also the month of exams. This has happened to me for the last few years, from my end-of-year exams in year ten, to my GCSEs, to my A Levels.

I'm actually quite glad, in a way, that I have the excuse of my upcoming exams – the first is two days after my actual birthday – to distract me from the strangeness that comes with having so few people to celebrate a birthday with. Much as I love Jade, it will be the first year I haven't been able to see Mum – ever – or Caddy – since I was five – and the thought makes me feel a little lonely, a little sad.

'I'll make it special,' Jade promises. 'Don't worry, I have a plan.'

'Can I have a clue?' I ask.

She smiles. 'Just that it's a surprise.'

She remains tight-lipped in the run-up to my birthday, and even on the actual day, though she's so excited by this point she's practically bouncing on her feet. She's greeted me with a kiss and a 'Happy birthday!' and is, right now, leading me towards Earlham Park.

'Obviously, I wanted it to be special,' she's saying, the words bubbly, her smile wide. 'And, like, an extra to your actual present – obviously I've got you an actual present too – because this is your first birthday with me – with any girlfriend! – and so I want it to be, like, perfect, and so . . . Roz, are you listening?'

'Listening to what?' I ask, teasing. 'You babbling?'

'Be excited,' she commands. 'This took some organizing, you know.'

'Oh God, it's not something public, is it?' I ask, suddenly nervous, looking around the calm, quiet park. There are groups clustered around on blankets, having picnics, talking, laughing. 'Tell me you haven't arranged a flash mob.'

'That was my first idea,' she says, deadpan. 'But then I changed my mind. This way.' She takes my hand, tugging me alongside her, across the grass, to nowhere specific.

'I might need you to give me a clue at this point,' I say. 'Because otherwise I'm going to worry that—'

I stop abruptly, because Jade has stopped me. So suddenly, in fact, that I've almost tripped over my feet. She grins at me, puts both her hands on my shoulders, then turns me in a deliberate half-circle.

And there, sitting on a picnic blanket, beaming, are Caddy and Suze.

'What the fuck!' I shriek.

'Happy birthday!' all three of them yell out, in perfect unison, like they'd been practising. Caddy lifts a party horn to her lips and toots it. Suze moves her hand from behind her back, causing two bright helium balloons to bounce into the air over her shoulder.

'What the fuck!' I say again, a little more quietly.

Caddy leaps to her feet and hugs me, and I'm so surprised I let her, even when Suze throws her arms around us both from the other side, and I find myself at the centre of some kind of hug sandwich.

'OK, I love you, get off,' I say, laughing, trying to disentangle myself. But they're here. They're *here*.

'Oh my God, Suze, you let go of the balloons,' Caddy scolds. We all look up to see the two balloons bobbing up and away.

'Seriously, you had one job.'

'Oh no,' Suze says, looking momentarily heartbroken. She turns her wide eyes to me. 'I'm sorry.'

'I don't care about a couple of balloons,' I say, laughing. 'What are you doing here? *How* are you here? I mean . . . what?!'

They explain as we all sit together on the blanket, Jade taking my hand to tug me down beside her. They're excitable, talking over each other, their voices a giddy mix of pride and happiness. Caddy has produced a cake tin from a bag and is pulling off the lid, beaming. It was Suze's idea; she and Caddy had talked about them both coming together and had messaged Jade for her help in coordinating their 'amazing surprise'.

'Jade was amazing,' Suze says. 'She didn't even say, like, *Give me more details* when all we said was, *We're going to surprise Roz on her birthday.* She was just all, *When can you get here?*' She grins at her. 'Right?'

'To be fair, I didn't need to do much,' Jade says, smiling. 'The planning was all you guys.'

'How did you get here?' I ask Suze, thinking about how much the train costs. 'The coach?'

'Matt drove,' she says. My eyebrows shoot up, and she adds quickly, 'Don't get excited. Not like that; just a friend helping out a friend. A friend of his has a gig somewhere in Norwich on Thursday night, so he offered to drive a few days early so I could be here for you, and he could hang out with his friends. It worked out really well. Cads got the train.'

'But don't you have exams?' I ask Caddy. She's moved on from the cake tin and is now holding a bottle of Prosecco. Suze leans over and pulls out some cups from the bag in preparation.

'Yeah, but not until next week,' Caddy says, popping the Prosecco and pouring it out into the cups. 'I did a load of reading on the train, and I'll do more on the way back. This actually works out really well.' She grins at me, handing over a cup. 'Don't worry, Roz. We wanted to be here.'

'But where are you staying?' I press. 'My room isn't big enough for—'

'We've got a hotel room,' Caddy breaks in patiently. 'Suze and me. Two nights. We'd love it if you stayed with us there, but you don't have to, of course. Obviously, you've got your exams. It's totally OK if you can only, like, have dinner with us. We get it. We just . . .' She half laughs, like she knows she's about to repeat herself. 'We just really wanted to be here.'

They wanted to be here. With me. On my birthday. They really do love me, still. Out of nowhere, I want to cry.

'But why?' I ask.

'One, that is a stupid question,' Suze says. 'Very below you. You know why. And two, we know we kind of fucked up last time we were all together, and we're sorry about that. This is making it up to you, a little bit.'

I look at Jade, questioning. *Did you tell them?*

'We do have a little bit of self-awareness, occasionally,' Suze says, clearly reading the look. 'Right, Cads?'

Caddy nods, and I wonder which of them had this particular realization; who shared it with who.

'Anyway, we're sorry it all went a bit chaotic last time,' Suze continues. 'This time, it's just about us.'

'Is that the word you'd choose?' I ask. '*Chaotic?*'

'It's accurate, right?' she says.

'No boys this time,' Caddy contributes. 'This is a male-free zone.'

Jade raises her cup in a faux-toast, and they laugh, reaching their own cups towards hers to cheers.

'Except Matt?' I say.

'Matt's not hanging out with us,' Suze says. 'He's got his own thing going on. It just worked out for the driving. Honest, this is about the three of us. And Jade,' she adds quickly.

'Less of me,' Jade says, smiling. 'My exams start earlier than Roz's, so I'll need to be very boring and bow out early.'

'Not too early!' Caddy says. 'Cake first?'

'Definitely cake!' Jade says. 'I've been dreaming about it ever since you sent that picture. I've got a couple of hours, anyway. Roz, shall we stay here for a bit and then go to the bar? Do the full tour of the campus?'

I feel a sudden jolt of anxiety. A full tour will include my flat, won't it? Of course they'll want to see where I've been living, and expect to meet my flatmates.

'Roz?' Jade prompts.

'Sounds great,' I say.

We stay at Earlham Park for another hour, drinking Prosecco and eating the cake – chocolate, from a bakery in the city – then Suze and Caddy gather up the stuff they've brought into one bag so we can head into the main campus and go to the bar for a drink. Jade puts her arm through mine and ducks her head close, saying quietly, 'Is this OK? That we did this? I know you don't always love surprises.'

I touch my head to hers. 'Extremely OK. Thank you.'

She kisses my cheek. 'Love you.'

I lead the way, carefully choosing a route that takes us far away from my flat. I can tell Jade has noticed, but she doesn't say anything about it. Instead, she asks Suze about her dog – Suze's whole face lights up at this – and Caddy takes a hold of my arm, squeezing. When I look at her, she smiles, and I think about the time when we were six years old and she told everyone we were sisters, and when her actual older sister tried to patiently explain why we *weren't* sisters, she got annoyed and snapped, 'But blood doesn't *matter!*'

Now, we're both nineteen, and here we are.

The bar is relatively quiet, which is probably something to do with the beginning of the exam period, so we get a booth to ourselves. Jade insists on getting a round in first, and Suze helps her carry the drinks over.

'I have to say,' I say, laughing, 'it's really weird to see you here in the Blue Bar. You're not meant to exist in this world.'

'Does it suit me?' Suze asks with a grin. 'I could be a student here, right?'

'It's uncanny,' I say. 'Get a hoodie and you'll fit right in.'

'Roz,' Caddy says. 'Obviously, this was really short notice from your point of view, but we can meet your friends, right?'

I feel Jade's eyes on me, and it occurs to me for the first time that Jade helped them orchestrate this whole thing with the full knowledge that I haven't been entirely honest with them about what kind of life I have here. Is that part of why she's done it? Surely not. She's not that cynical.

'Probably not,' I say, shrugging. 'It's exam time, so . . . you know. Everyone's busy.'

'But it's your birthday,' Caddy points out, looking confused. 'We thought we could just tag along to whatever thing you had planned. If that's OK, obviously.'

Fuck. Of course they'd assume I'd have plans for my birthday. My skin is starting to heat up; my throat feels tight. How can I admit to them that I haven't made the kind of friends that you spend birthdays with? I've been able to convince myself that it's enough just having Jade, and in a lot of ways it is, but with my two best friends sitting opposite me, expectant smiles on their faces, I suddenly feel the lack like a hole carved into my chest.

'Nothing's planned,' I say. I'm trying to keep my voice light, but there's an ache in it, and I'm sure they'll be able to hear it. 'It's just too . . . you know. Exams.'

There's a silence. Suze is frowning now, the first hint of realization on her face, and I can't stand it.

'You came to see me, right?' I say. 'So . . .' I wave my hands around. 'Here I am.'

'And me,' Jade pipes up, and I'm so grateful and relieved that I take her hand under the table, squeezing tight.

'Roz—' Suze begins.

'Remember how we couldn't do anything for my birthday when we had our GCSEs?' I interrupt, a little desperately, looking at Caddy. 'We were both in revision hell? Remember? Such a sucky time to have a birthday.'

'Roz,' Suze says again, more firmly this time. 'Are you OK?'

It's not what I expected her to say. I was preparing myself for a demand to explain myself, to list my friends by name, to prove my emotional worth by the number of people who'd care about it being my birthday. But when she asks me this, such understanding in her voice, though she can't possibly understand any of this, I feel myself crumple under the weight of it.

'No,' I say. 'I just . . . There's a lot going on, OK?'

'OK,' Caddy says immediately. 'That's OK, Roz. Whatever it is, you can tell us. And if you want us to go, we can go.'

'Of course I don't want you to go!' My voice catches, surprising me. For a second, I think I am going to start crying in front of them, but I'm fine. Good. 'But I don't know how to even start. Mum, she's . . .' Where did *that* come from? This is how I'm going to tell them about Mum? I look at Jade, who smiles her most reassuring Jade smile. 'She's not well, and . . . I'm sorry I haven't told you earlier, but—'

'What?' Caddy looks horrified. 'What do you mean, not well? What's wrong?'

'We don't know yet, that's the thing,' I say. 'It's nothing serious.' I know this isn't true. But I need it to be true. I want to will it into truth just by saying it.

'But what's wrong?' Caddy asks, anxious. 'What are her symptoms?'

'Mostly mobility related,' I say. 'Balance issues, dizziness. That kind of thing. She's been referred to a neurologist and it's all just . . . tests, tests, tests.'

'Poor Shell,' Caddy says. 'And poor *you*! That must be so scary.'

'Are you sure it isn't serious?' Suze asks uncertainly. 'Neurology, that's . . . that's a big deal, right?' She glances nervously at Caddy.

I swallow. 'The longer it goes on, the more likely it is, yeah. Mum thinks it's going to be serious. Or, like . . . long term.'

They're both staring at me, silent and worried, and I wish I hadn't told them. People say talking about things will make it better, but giving it all a voice is making it more real, which is worse. And it's also making me even more aware of how little I know, how little there is to tell, reminding me that it's been so long with nothing definitive to say. The longer it goes on, the worse the possibilities get.

Neither of them gives me any heat for not telling them earlier, though I can tell that they're hurt that it's taken me so long. They just alternate between asking me questions, reassuring me that it will be OK, telling me that 'whatever happens' they're here for me. ('Even when "here" is, like, far away,' Suze says.)

They also don't ask me anything more about my friends or my university experience, and they don't ask to see my flat. I feel simultaneously guilty and relieved that this conversation has stopped that conversation from happening, at least for now, though I know that makes me a bad person, using my own mother's illness – however accidentally – as some kind of shield. When the conversation does move on, it's to ask Jade questions about her life, how third year is going, if she liked Brighton, if she'll come back over the summer.

Jade ends up staying with us an hour later than she'd planned, but eventually she shakes her head and sighs. 'I wish I could stay, really, but exam panic awaits.' She kisses me on the cheek and waves at Suze and Caddy as she gathers up her bag.

'Good luck with your exams,' Caddy says. 'And thanks for helping us with all of this.'

Jade grins at them, dropping her hand to my shoulder to give it a squeeze. 'Thanks for letting me help. It's been great. See you guys.'

After she's gone, the three of us have another drink, and then revert to tradition: we go to Nando's.

We don't talk about anything serious; we don't even talk about university at all. We reminisce over our shared history (only the good bits) and tease each other about the heat of our chosen spice. Caddy carefully cuts a pastel de nata into thirds. Suze fills a bowl with frozen yoghurt and comes back with three spoons.

It's the kind of low-key evening you have with either people you don't know very well, or people you know and love better than anyone. We even lapse into quiet when we leave the restaurant, each of us momentarily lost in our own thoughts, and it's as comfortable as quiet can ever get.

I decide to go back to my flat to sleep rather than stay with them, partly because I really do have to fit as much studying as I can around their surprise visit, and also because I'm worried that, at some point, they'll ask me again about my friends, or lack of friends.

'We're just going to look around Norwich tomorrow,' Caddy says. 'Nothing major. So do you just want to spend the day studying and then meet us for dinner?'

'Sounds great,' I say, almost dizzy with relief. They've let me off the hook. They're not going to make me explain myself or admit any more of my unhappiness. Thank God.

*

But of course they do.

There are friends, and then there are best friends, and then there are *my* best friends. Of course they know that there's more wrong than I'm letting on, and of course they haven't let me off the hook.

We meet by the cathedral the next evening so I can do one tourist thing with them before we all get dinner together. I am the least religious person I know, but I still love cathedrals, and the Norwich one is pretty special. Suze is completely quiet as we walk around, her eyes on the ceiling, thoughtful. When I ask her if she's OK, she widens her eyes at me and then shushes me like she's my grandmother, which makes me laugh.

Dinner is an Italian chain this time – Caddy has a voucher – and we're guided towards a table by the window, looking out over Tombland, which is one of my favourite parts of Norwich. At this point, I'm still high on the relief of the knowledge that we won't have time to go back to campus and I won't ever have to show them the flat where I am, once again, the Enigma, with no friends to speak of and nothing but shame. I'm still enjoying this illusion right up until after we order drinks and olives, when I'm watching the waitress disappear around a corner and Caddy says, 'Roz?' and I turn to her with a smile.

'Yeah?'

'Who are you going to live with next year?'

The thing is, this is probably a question she's chosen to start with because she thinks it's innocuous. A way into a more difficult conversation. They have both clearly talked about this in my absence; they want to know why I hadn't made plans for my birthday, why I haven't mentioned friends. And so they're starting with something that should be very simple, but isn't.

I feel my face go an immediate, flaming red. 'Why?' I ask,

which is a stupid response, one that barely makes sense.

Caddy just stares at me, confused.

'That's, um . . .' I clear my throat. 'That's kind of a complicated question.'

'Why?' Caddy asks, reasonably.

'Because we . . . um. It kind of fell through? The housing plan I had. You know how I told you about it at Christmas? Well, we had an argument and they . . .' Caddy is already looking alarmed, and I haven't even really said anything yet. I wish I had my drink already. 'Well, I'm not living with them any more.'

They both look so confused, staring at me, waiting for me to say something that makes sense.

'It's fine,' I say, attempting a carefree laugh. 'I mean, it wasn't great, but . . . it'll be fine.'

'You mean you don't know where you're going to live?' Caddy asks, in her very calm clarifying voice.

'I'm still working on it,' I say.

'Is that bad?' Suze asks. 'When do people normally get that kind of thing sorted?'

'Before now,' Caddy says.

'Oh,' Suze says. She's frowning, mostly with confusion but also a hint of frustration, too. 'Well, what was the argument about?'

'Well,' I say, then stop. 'Um, you remember that moral dilemma I had?'

Caddy's eyes go wide with understanding. 'That was your future *housemates*? Roz! Why didn't you tell us that bit?'

'So you did tell the other girl?' Suze is already saying, while I shrug a helpless shrug. 'And now they've chucked *you* out?'

'Pretty much, yeah,' I say. Seeing their faces, I suddenly want to start crying. I reach for my cutlery, rearranging it against the napkin until the feeling passes.

'*Fuckers*,' Suze says, vehement with loyal rage.

'I mean,' I say, swallowing. 'I get it. It was my fault, getting involved. And we weren't really friends anyway, to be honest. It was just a . . . What do you call it? Like, a mutually beneficial kind of thing.'

'But not any more,' Suze says, a statement and a question in one.

'Right,' I say.

'And they've decided that, not you.'

I nod and she shakes her head, looking at Caddy, who shakes her head back. There's a silence. Finally, Caddy says, very cautiously, like she's trying to figure out how best to word the obvious. 'Do your other friends already have their housing sorted?'

I take in a breath. 'I don't really have any other friends. Not ones I can live with. When I finally get this sorted, it'll probably be with strangers. OK? You got me. Well done.' I wish our drinks had already arrived so I could have something to do with my hands, somewhere to look that isn't so obviously anywhere but their faces.

'Oh, Roz,' Caddy says, softly. 'That's . . . I'm sorry.'

I shrug. 'It's fine.' My eyes are stinging. 'Like, it's fine.'

This is when the drinks arrive, the waitress smiling into the space above our heads as she deposits the glasses in front of us, the olives in front of Caddy. We're all silent until she leaves.

'We didn't come here to try and catch you out,' Caddy says. 'Really. We just wanted to see you.'

'But you should have told us,' Suze says. 'Why didn't you tell us?'

'Because . . .' I don't even know how to start the sentence, let alone finish it. 'How could I?'

They both look confused. 'You can tell us anything,' Suze says.

'Oh my God,' I say. 'Don't be a hypocrite.'

'What do you mean?'

'Suze, I *know* that a bunch of stuff has happened in your

life – just in the past few months, even! – that you haven't told us about. You can't expect me to tell you everything when you give me nothing back.'

'OK,' Caddy says, like the mediator she is. 'Let's not get distracted.'

'By what?' Suze says. There's a set in her jaw that hints at her annoyance. 'My crappy life?'

'You disappear,' I snap. 'You take yourself offline. It's really fucking annoying.'

'So you agree?' Suze says, her eyes sharp. 'You agree that not being told things you should know about your friend's life is annoying?'

I frown, trying to keep up. 'Yes. No. What?'

'If you're blaming Suze,' Caddy says, very calmly, very firmly. 'Then why didn't you tell *me*?'

I wait for Suze to get annoyed about this, but she doesn't, just raises her eyebrows at me, like, *Good question.* The one time she decides not to get upset about being the 'new friend', always slightly outside our best-friend twosome.

'Cads . . .' I start to say, but I don't know how to finish that, either. Neither of them says anything, forcing me to speak into the silence. 'You're having the best time. You've made this amazing group of friends. I just feel so . . . stupid and embarrassed, OK?'

'About what?' she asks, bewildered.

'About not being, like . . . happy.' I hate how thin my voice sounds. 'About not having friends.'

'But why does it make a difference, *me* having friends?'

I look at Suze for help, but she's just looking at me blankly. There's a long silence.

'So . . . just to be clear . . .' Caddy says, in a tone of voice I can't quite read. 'Me being happy means . . . you can't talk to me any more?'

'No, that's obviously not what I'm saying.'

'Are you sure? Because that's what it sounds like.'

'No, it's . . . I don't know how to explain this.'

'Roz, I'm sorry you're unhappy here. I hate that you've been going through all of this and for some reason you think you can't talk to me. Us. But you can't put that on me, OK? Not now, not after all these years when you've been secure and I've been floundering around trying to find a place somewhere.'

'You haven't been—'

'Roz, I've watched you for years not ever having to doubt yourself. You've always been sure of who you are and what you want. I finally feel that way in my own life, and yes, I love it, OK? I love my life at Warwick, and I'm not going to be sorry about that. It doesn't mean I love you any less, and it doesn't mean I've stopped worrying about Suze and missing you both every day, but I'm *happy* there. I've been overshadowed by you both for years. I'm finally my own person, *with* people who *like* that person. Can't I have that without having to feel bad about it?'

When she finally finishes talking, a little breathless, her eyes wet and blinking, all three of us sit there in silence. I think we're all a little stunned.

'I wasn't saying that at all,' I say, when I find my voice. 'But . . . wow, Cads. I'm glad you've finally found friends who like you properly, or something?'

She closes her eyes, clenching her jaw in frustration. 'And *that* wasn't what *I* was saying.'

'Sounds like it,' I say, looking at Suze.

'It kind of did sound like it, yeah,' she says.

Caddy shakes her head. 'The two of you, you totally take it for granted that you're both the confident ones. Maybe you don't realize that's what you're doing, but you do it all the time. Make me feel stupid for trying to be funny or not being cool for some stupid reason.'

'We don't—' Suze starts to say.

'Yeah, you do. Even just on WhatsApp. My friends at uni don't do that. They've never thought of me as the quiet one. So I'm just . . . not that. With them. Like magic. Don't you understand what a difference that makes?' She lets out a growl of frustration, raking her hand through her hair. 'I'm not saying they're better than you both because of it. Obviously they're not. They're just different. *I'm* different, with them. And I like that—'

'You want to talk about being taken for granted?' I say, and I'm surprised by how annoyed my voice sounds. They both look at me, almost alarmed. '*Hello?!* The two of you spend so much time obsessing over each other and worrying about each other, it's like you forget I'm even around.'

'We never—' Caddy tries.

'*Always.* And it's not because I'm forgettable – this isn't me being insecure about myself – it's because you *always think I'm fine*. That's it, isn't it? I'm the OK one. You both get all the worry, especially you, Suze, but me? You don't even ask.'

'Excuse me, we do fucking ask,' Suze says, her voice a full snap now. The 'especially you' was a mistake. 'I ask all the time, and you literally say that you're fine. That's not me taking you for granted. And also, it *sucks* being the shit one. The one everyone worries about. I'm sorry I'm such a fuck-up, but it would be great if that wasn't the first thing you assumed every time anything happens to me.'

This silences all of us. For what could be a full minute we all just stare at each other, jaws clenched (me), eyes glistening (Caddy) and arms crossed (Suze).

'Well,' Caddy says finally. 'This surprise trip is going really well so far.'

'Oh yes, really well,' I agree. 'Happy birthday, me.'

'Your birthday was yesterday,' Suze says, her voice a petulant sulk, which makes me laugh, and then Caddy is laughing, and then all three of us are in hysterics.

'Fuck you,' I manage, and she flicks an olive stone at me, which is exactly the moment the waitress arrives at the table, looking bewildered.

'Hi . . .' she says. 'You guys ready to order, or . . . should I come back?'

We gather ourselves enough to order, which also gives us enough time that, by the time the waitress leaves, we're all calm again. In fact, we're so calm that no one seems to know what to say.

Finally, cautiously, Suze says, 'Matt says all friendships change when university happens. He said something like, true friendship is seeing it through. So I guess it makes sense if we've all found this hard in some way or other. Right?' She looks at me like she needs me to agree.

I hesitate, then nod. We go quiet again. I sip at my water. Caddy fiddles with her napkin.

'We're always going to be fine,' I say eventually.

'Always,' Caddy says. 'But, Roz, I think we got a bit distracted then, because this is meant to be about you, and you being unhappy. Stop letting Suze take over everything.'

'Hey!' Suze's mouth drops open. 'That's not fair—'

'One, you're doing it again, and two, I was obviously joking.' Caddy gives her a sly grin, which makes me laugh, especially as Suze looks so thrown. 'Roz,' Caddy says to me. 'Let's go back to the bit where you're unhappy.'

'I'm not actually *unhappy*,' I start to say. Start to lie.

'That's not what you—'

'I have Jade,' I say. 'I don't want you guys thinking I've just been . . . wallowing in my lonely misery or something, the whole time I've been here. I haven't.'

'Jade's great. I really like her,' Caddy says. 'But is she the *only* happy thing you have here?' I open my mouth, and she says quickly, 'Obviously Jade isn't a "thing". You know what I mean.' When I don't answer, she says, 'Roz, I just . . . I don't want to say anything that's going to annoy you, but this whole time we've been in Norwich you haven't said anything about, like, the campus, or your lectures, or even . . . I don't know, uni nights out, you know? Pub crawls? Socials? Derby day. That kind of thing.'

I don't say anything, because I'm not sure what I can say.

'You don't have to be here,' Caddy says quietly. 'People drop out of uni because it's not right for them. It's—'

'I'm not *dropping out*,' I say, appalled. 'I'm not failing. I'm fine. Why would I drop out?'

'Four years is a long time,' Caddy says. 'To be unhappy. To be in the wrong place.'

'That's easy for you to say,' I say. 'When you *are* happy.'

She shrugs, undeterred. 'Someone in my flat dropped out. She was miserable; she said she hated Warwick. She spent every weekend going home, and eventually she just didn't come back. Someone else, on my course, transferred onto a different course because they found out they didn't like linguistics. It happens. It's totally normal.'

'It's not going to happen to me,' I say. 'I've put in all this time, all this work. For what? Nothing? No. No way. I'm not going to be a dropout. That's pathetic. It's not me.'

Caddy's eyes have gone alarmingly, significantly wide, and still it takes me far too many seconds to realize why. Suze's face has gone rigid, her fingers tight around her fork.

Shit. Suze dropped out of school. It's so easy to forget, because of everything that's happened since, but she did. Less than three months before our GCSEs, she was out. Gone.

'That's not . . .' I try to say, but the words feel clumsy in my mouth. *Shit.* 'I didn't mean . . . Uni's just different from . . .'

'Pathetic,' Suze says, stiffly. 'That's what you think?'

'Not of you,' I say. 'I'm talking about uni.'

'If you think dropping out of uni is pathetic, what do you think of someone who couldn't even make it to her GCSEs?'

'That's a completely different situation, Suze.'

'Why? Because I tried to kill myself first?'

There's a loud, dangerous silence. We've never talked about Suze's suicide attempt, not ever, even though it was a bomb going off in all our lives, even though it changed everything for all three of us.

'Talk about pathetic, right?' Suze says, choking out a flat, humourless laugh. 'Trying to drop out of *life*.'

Oh God, I don't know what to say. This is such a hideous tangent, and I'm not quite sure how we got here, and I don't know what to do. I look at Caddy, almost frantic. *Help.*

'You're not pathetic,' Caddy says, her voice soft. 'You've never been pathetic. Hey.' She reaches over and takes Suze's hand. Suze looks away, squeezing down tight. I watch her eyes close, then open again, before she lets go of Caddy's hand and takes a step back away from the table.

'I'll be back in a minute.'

'Suze,' I start to say, but she's already walking away. '*Fuck.*'

'It's OK,' Caddy says. 'Let her have a minute if she needs it. That was kind of a shit thing you said.'

'I didn't mean to!'

'I know. It'll be fine. Just give it a minute.'

'I wasn't actually calling her pathetic. You get that, right?'

This is the moment the waitress returns with a tray full of

plates. By the time she's finished arranging them in front of us, asking about pepper, sprinkling parmesan, Suze has slid back into her seat, her face placid. She's still, I realize, holding her fork.

'I'm sorry,' I say as soon as the waitress is gone, getting it out before she can speak.

'It's fine,' she says.

'Are you OK?' Caddy asks.

She nods, then turns to me, ignoring the carbonara in front of her. 'Why do you think you can't drop out of your course if it's not right for you?'

It's much harder to stay belligerent about this line of questioning now she has the moral high ground.

'Because . . .' I try and think of a different angle I can take, anticipating their responses to everything I say. 'Because I made a plan.'

'So?'

'So I want to stick to the plan.'

'Why?'

'OK,' Caddy breaks in, before I answer/scream with frustration. 'Let's go with a hypothetical. If – *if* – you didn't complete a pharmacy degree, what kind of thing *could* you do instead?' I shrug helplessly, so she adds, 'Imagine you could start over. Like, from scratch. What would you do? Would you still choose pharmacy?'

No. The answer is immediate, and it makes me want to throw up. I hate this conversation. I hate it. I hate it.

'It's just a hypothetical,' Caddy says. 'A thought exercise.'

'Uni has made you very annoying,' I say.

'Roz,' Suze says, very sharp, so sharp it almost makes me jump. It's not usually Suze 'Roz-ing' me like that.

'That's OK,' Caddy says, shrugging. 'I can deal with bitch-Roz. It just means she knows I'm right.' She rolls her eyes at me.

'We're not twelve years old any more.'

I cross my arms, like a child. They both just stare at me, waiting. Finally, Suze squints at me and says, 'You know how you waste so much of your brain energy worrying about my mental health?'

'I wouldn't call it wasting—'

'Maybe you should direct some of that attention towards your own.'

'My own? What do you mean?'

She raises both her eyebrows. Like, *Come on, Roz.*

'My mental health is fine.'

'Great, add denial to the list, too.'

Despite myself, I laugh. 'Suze. I'm fine.'

'You know it's not all big dramatic explosions and suicidal thoughts, right? It sounds to me like you've been unhappy and stressed for a long time. Maybe the whole time you've been at uni? And anxious, too. That's mental health stuff too, Roz. I'm allowed to be worried about you, as your friend.'

'And I appreciate that,' I say. 'But I really am fine. I have Jade.'

'Again,' she says, patiently. 'Having low mental health doesn't mean *everything* is, like, all miserable all the time. Or that *nothing* is good. It's great that you have Jade, but that doesn't cancel out the unhappy bit.' She looks at Caddy. 'Back me up, here.'

Caddy laughs. 'You don't need me to back you up. You're doing just fine.'

'Back me up, anyway.'

'Suze is right, Roz,' Caddy says, obediently. 'But you already know that, don't you?'

I do. 'OK, I think we've gone way too far on this tangent,' I say, sitting up straight and reaching randomly for the bottle of chilli oil and shaking it out over my pizza, even though I don't like chilli oil. 'Like I said, I'm finishing my degree. I can't turn back now. I've put in so much time – and money. This is what I'm doing.' Caddy opens her mouth, so I deliver my final conversation-ending blow. 'I'm literally about to start my exams. Do we maybe want to think about how helpful this conversation is right now?'

This quietens them both. Caddy makes a face. 'You're right, I'm sorry. I forgot about that.'

'Also,' I add. 'Remember how it's my birthday?' Suze opens her mouth, so I say quickly, 'Yesterday.'

Mercifully, they let it drop. We spend the rest of the meal talking about how Caddy feels about her break-up with Kel – fine; she hopes they can still be friends – and how Suze and Matt have agreed to stay friends but nothing else, even though he's in love with her (he has said this out loud) and she is in love with him (she has still not admitted this to anyone, even us). I tell them about Jade, her Make-Rosie-Love-Norwich project, how happy I am with her, despite everything else.

We decide to skip dessert and go on to a bar for a single drink before I have to go back to my flat to study for my first exam tomorrow.

'Shit, I didn't realize it was actually tomorrow,' Suze says. 'Are you sure you can stay out?'

'For one, sure,' I say. 'I've done all the prep and revision for it, so it will just be going over that. I can manage one drink.'

'That is impressively chilled of you,' she says. She glances down at her phone as the screen lights up. 'Oh hey, Matt wants to stop by and say happy birthday. Is that OK? At the bar? You can say no. We said this would be a girls-only trip.'

'No, that'd be nice,' I say, actually a little bit touched.

'Will he mind any atmosphere?' Caddy asks, raising her eyebrows at me as she unwraps one of the sweets that came with the bill. 'Maybe you should warn him that it's been fraught.'

'Only briefly fraught,' Suze says, eyes on her phone.

'Title of your autobiography,' Caddy says, which makes Suze

bark out a laugh of genuine surprise.

'Cads!' she says, widening her eyes at her. 'You *are* funny!'

Caddy flips her off, and I have a sudden flash of them at sixteen, still uncertain of each other, connected only through their mutual friendship with me. I try to think about how I'd describe this scene to those versions of them. I don't even know what words I'd use.

'Let's go,' I say. 'If we leave now, I might even fit *two* drinks in.'

'Push the boat out, why not,' Suze says, standing. 'You're only nineteen yesterday once.'

Matt arrives at our table in the cocktail bar with a broad smile and a flourish – my favourite cocktail, a Black Russian.

'How did you know?' I ask, pleased. 'Thank you!'

'Someone might have given me a hint,' he says, glancing at Suze to grin.

'Well, thank you,' I say again. 'And cheers.'

We all clink glasses as Caddy shuffles along the bench to give Matt room to slide in beside Suze. I see the way his hand touches her leg in a second quiet hello, how she quirks a smaller smile that is just for him.

'So how's your birthday been?' Matt asks me. 'Was it a good surprise, these two?' He points at Suze and Caddy, then smiles.

'The best surprise,' I say, indulging them, and they beam.

'Matt,' Suze says, 'You should tell Roz about how you dropped out of uni.'

He looks at me. 'Is that relevant?'

'Roz isn't happy,' Suze says.

'Suze!' I snap.

'She's also in denial,' she adds. 'Seriously, Matt is really glad he dropped out.' She looks at him. 'Right?'

He nods. 'Completely.'

'It might help to talk to someone who made that decision,' Suze says.

'I already know people who dropped out,' I say, thinking of Laini for the first time in months. I wonder how she's doing. 'And I'm not dropping out, so it's irrelevant.'

'You not being happy is very relevant,' Suze insists.

'Drop it,' I say.

'Not everyone loves uni,' Matt says. 'Maybe people don't talk about it much, but some people don't like it. The lifestyle, the work, the people; lots of things. Uni wasn't for me, and that's OK.'

'Why not?'

He thinks about it, lifting his shoulders in a slow shrug. 'More the studying side of things than anything else. Academia just isn't for me. I wanted music; it's what I've always wanted. And, like now, working in a bar and doing session work on the side, I'm happy. Really happy. I've never regretted leaving uni.'

'Never?'

'Not once.'

'What about the money?'

'It would have cost a lot more if I'd stayed for another two years,' he says. 'Sunk cost fallacy, right? And you can't put a price on that kind of unhappiness. It just isn't worth it.'

'*Exactly*,' Suze says. 'That's what I keep saying.'

'Not everything is about being happy,' I point out.

'Sure, but it still *matters*,' Matt says. 'Especially if you're talking about *the rest of your life*. Why set yourself up for a future you don't want? I don't get that.'

'That's because you're a creative,' I say, only half teasing. 'A dreamer.'

'Guilty as charged,' he says, smiling. 'What's the alternative? Plan everything and then have no surprises?'

'Yes,' I say. 'Exactly that. No nasty surprises, thanks.'

'No way,' Suze says, frowning. 'You can't really think that. No surprises, ever? What about the good ones?'

'You must understand, though,' I respond, frustrated. 'You just made a plan for, like, the first time in your life. Imagine if it went wrong? You wouldn't just give up on it, would you?'

Suze shrugs, tapping her fingers against the side of her glass. 'If it went wrong, it wouldn't be "giving up", would it? It would just be that the plan wasn't the right one. So, I'd make another one, or try something else.'

'You would not be that relaxed about it,' I say, trying not to get annoyed. 'It would be horrible.'

'Maybe,' she says. 'But it wouldn't be the end of the world. Things change. You've got to be able to adapt to that, otherwise you'll just end up stuck. And that's way worse, isn't it?' She takes in my face, then shakes her head. 'Roz, you can't make a plan and just expect it to happen.'

'Why not? That's exactly why people make plans.'

'Because so much of the world and life is just out of your control. And you're being way too hard on yourself. Why should a life plan you came up with at, what, seventeen . . . ?' She looks at me for confirmation, and I nod reluctantly. 'Why should that be exactly right? You need to be more flexible.'

'It's because so much of life is out of my control that I wanted to plan what *is* in my control,' I say. 'I'm not giving up on that yet just because it's hard. Giving up is bad. Trying harder is good.'

They're all shaking their heads. 'I don't think that's right,' Caddy says.

'If at first you don't succeed,' I say, 'try, try again?'

'Know when to stop,' Suze returns. 'Anyway, whatever, look at it this way. When you think about, like, the best things in your life, what do you think of? And were they things you'd planned?

Mine aren't. Totally the opposite.' She looks at me expectantly.

'Roz doesn't have to stop making plans,' Matt says when I don't say anything, and I smile at him gratefully. 'Just leave a little wiggle room, that's all. A space for a maybe.'

25

I end up staying with them for three drinks, and then lead them on a detour to Pulls Ferry, a medieval water gate for the cathedral, which looks like something out of a fairy tale, even in the dark. And then the train station is in sight, and so is their hotel and the bus stop, and the night and their visit is over. Reality beckons.

I should have been back at my desk hours ago. I should be focused on tomorrow's exam. I should care more about the fact that I'm not.

I just feel really tired.

'Have a good trip back to Warwick,' I say to Caddy. 'And good luck with your exams.'

'You too!' she says. She smiles at me with her special brand of quiet understanding. 'We'll all be back in Brighton soon, OK?'

Six weeks, that's all. No time at all, right? As I sit alone on the bus back to the university, I think about Brighton, every familiar street leading down to the sea. I wish I could just . . . be there. Everything would be easier.

But I can't be there, because I am here, and it's exam time.

I wake up the following morning feeling determined, maybe even a little bullish, annoyed with myself for staying out for too long last night, for losing focus. Caddy's right – we'll all be back in Brighton soon. So why pine?

I spend the couple of hours before my exam going over the material, which I already know by heart. This is reassuring, and by the time I'm actually in the exam, with the paper open in front of me, I'm back to feeling confident again. Of course I know this stuff. What am I worrying about? Why did I let Caddy and Suze lead me off on a tangent about dropping out? Look, see? I'm fine; I can do this. I don't need to drop out. I just need to stop whining.

When I walk outside of the exam hall, I find that the early morning rain has cleared and the sun's come out. Mum would say it was a sign, and thinking that makes me smile. I swing my bag up over my shoulder and start walking back to my flat, pulling out my phone as I go to see if I've got any messages.

I stop dead, so abruptly someone knocks into the back of me. They say something, but I don't even register the words.

Twelve missed calls from Janine Buchrest.

One message: **Call me when you can, Rosie.**

There is no panic in the world like the panic that comes from twelve missed calls left from a person who would only call you in an emergency. And that message, both soft and hard at the same time. No warm kisses, but my name.

Mum. Something has happened to Mum.

'Rosie,' Janine answers the phone in a breathless gasp, on my third attempt at calling. 'I'm sorry, I had to get out of the hospital to answer the phone. I shouldn't have had it on, but I knew you'd call—'

'What's happened?' It comes out like a shout. *Hospital.*

'There was an accident,' she says. 'Shell, she – oh, Rosie, I'm sorry to scare you like this. I'm at the hospital with her. She fell down the stairs at the beach. The ones . . . you know, the ones down to the promenade? She was on a lunchtime walk with a colleague. The hospital called me; I'm her emergency contact.'

Even in the midst of my all-encompassing terror, my brain finds a spare cluster of cells with which to be upset that I, her adult daughter, am apparently not her emergency contact.

Not that I feel much like an adult, not right now.

'Is she OK?' I say.

There is a pause. Just a second or two. Milliseconds, probably. But it's an air pocket of forever, that pause. A black hole. I fall into it, and time stops.

'Can you come home?' Janine says. She doesn't say, *Yes.* 'I think you need to come home.'

She says more, of course. She doesn't say that and then hang up. She says things like '*emergency surgery*' and '*possible swelling in the brain*' and '*I'm sorry, Rosie.*'

But that's all I hear, really. '*I think you need to come home.*'

I walk on autopilot to my flat, trying to figure out my fastest route home. The coach will take hours, but so will the train. Why did I have to come to Norfolk? *Why?* Why don't I have a car? Why can't I drive? Why did I never think, in all those months of planning, what I would do in an emergency? I'll have to get the train. Throw my stuff in a bag, wait for a bus, half an hour to the train station, wait for a train, four hours to Brighton, taxi to the hospital . . . God, if I could drive, I'd be there in—

A blinding flash of realization. Suze. Suze and Matt – and Matt's car. They're in Norfolk. Aren't they in Norfolk? I look down at my phone, still clutched in my hand.

'Hey!' Suze's voice is disarmingly, confusingly cheerful. 'How was the exam?'

In the background, I can hear music playing. Car sounds. Have they already left? Am I too late? I don't even know what day it is.

'Roz?' Suze says, expectant. She waits. Then, 'Are you there?'

'Suze.' This is when the tears come. I hadn't even realized I was holding them back until that moment.

'Hey,' Suze says, and her voice is alert now. I hear the music stop, a voice in the background. Matt, probably, asking what's wrong. 'Are you OK? What's happened? Is it the exam?'

I try to gather myself into coherence, forcing myself to breathe.

God, it's hard talking during a meltdown. 'It's Mum. I need to go home.'

'OK, we'll come and get you,' Suze says immediately. Not even the slightest pause. 'We'll come right now, OK?' Her voice muffles. 'How long will it take—? OK. OK, Roz? We can be at the uni in half an hour. We'll pick you up. Is that what you need?'

I nod, as if she can see me. I manage, 'Thank you.'

Somehow, my flat looks the same as it did this morning. I think, vaguely, that I need to pack, but I don't know what I need and I can't summon the brain space to actually think about it.

Jade. I should message Jade. When I look at my phone, I see that my hands are shaking.

What do I say? Then I remember that she'll already be in her exam. She won't even be able to see a message from me for . . . I check the time. Another two hours. Two hours. I put my phone back into my pocket and bite my thumb to stop myself sobbing.

When I walk out of the university entrance to find Matt's car waiting for me on the side of the road, I'm still carrying the bag I took to the exam hall. Suze is standing beside the car, arms crossed, sunglasses on. When she sees me, she leaps into action, moving as if to hug me then stopping, remembering that it's me.

'Here,' she says instead, handing over a water bottle. 'Drink some of that before we do anything else, OK?'

She pushes the sunglasses up over her hair as I obey, her eyes focused on me, a slight frown in her forehead. When I hand over the bottle, she touches my arm, gently, just once.

'Can we go now?' I say.

Matt says he can get us back to Brighton in two and a half hours. Suze tells him to put Passenger on, which immediately makes me think of Mum saying, every single time 'Let Her Go' came on the radio, 'He's from Brighton, you know!' Tears rise fresh and stinging in my eyes.

Suze sits in the back seat with me, all of her attention focused on me, listening as I tell her – in barely articulate snatches of words between sobs – what Janine had said on the phone. She tells me that it will be fine, that the doctors at the Royal Sussex are amazing, reminding me that they saved her life, and Caddy's, and that I don't need to worry about anything. There's such confidence in her voice when she says this that part of me actually believes her.

As she talks, she stays cuddled beside me, far closer than I'd usually let her go, resting her head on my shoulder, holding my hand.

It's really, really nice.

'Is this your way of showing me how I'm supposed to act when you have one of your breakdowns?' I ask.

She doesn't take the bait; doesn't tell me not to be a bitch; doesn't let go of my hand. She just says, very calmly, 'This isn't about me.'

'Makes a change,' I say.

This makes her smile. I feel it against my neck, and I hear it in her voice when she speaks. 'OK, Roz.' An indulgent, affectionate smile from someone who knows me, and loves me anyway.

We're both quiet for a while. Finally, I say, 'You know I'm trying to say thanks, right?'

She squeezes my hand. 'Yep.'

26

We arrive in Brighton in the late afternoon. I've called Janine to let her know I'm almost there, so she's waiting outside the hospital when Matt pulls up to drop me off.

'Let us know——' Suze begins, but I'm already clambering out of the car, desperate to get this part over, to be there, to *know*.

'Thank you,' I manage to throw over my shoulder. 'Thanks. Bye.'

I'll probably feel bad about that later, but all my thoughts are concentrated on one thing, and that is Janine, hurrying over to me. She squeezes me into a hug, and I'm so frazzled with anxiety I let her.

'I'm so sorry,' she says. 'Calling you like that, making you panic. I wish there could have been a way to make it less frightening. I'm sorry.'

'Don't be sorry,' I say, impatiently, because why does that matter right now? 'Of course you had to call me. How is she? *Where* is she?'

'Stable,' Janine says. 'I'll take you to see her now, and you can talk to her doctor.'

'Is she awake?' I ask, and when Janine nods I feel a surge of relief so powerful I almost lose my balance. 'Oh thank God.' I don't even believe in God. 'Thank God. Thank God.'

'She's not particularly lucid,' Janine says, half smiling. 'But she's awake, and that's what's important.'

She leads me towards the hospital entrance. I glance behind me to see that Matt's car is still there, idling at the kerbside.

'You got here so fast,' Janine is saying.

'My friends,' I say. It's all I can manage.

We walk along corridors, wait for lifts, walk along more corridors. I'm not even sure where we're going, except the knowledge that it isn't A&E, which must be a good sign. By the time we get to the right ward – I can tell because Janine's steps have slowed – she's holding my hand, which she hasn't done since I was eleven, the last time the world ended, and I'm trying not to cry.

The curtain pulls back and there's Mum, looking small and delicate and fragile on the bed. There's a vicious-looking bruise across one side of her face, a bandage wrapped tight around her arm. She is alive; she is still here. I am five years old and eleven years old and eighteen and nineteen and this is my mother, and she is still alive. I have a vague sense that I should be crying, but I feel so beyond crying. I feel like I lost everything, and it's just been handed back.

Her eyes are closed, but they open when I sit on the chair beside the bed. I reach to touch her hand, not quite taking it, just in case it will hurt her. There are a million things I should say.

I say, 'Hi.'

'Rosie,' she says, very hoarsely. 'Oh, Rosie.' She closes her eyes again. 'Good.'

I wait for more, but she stays quiet, her face creased with what I hope is something fleeting, like confusion, rather than pain.

Janine squats beside me and says, very softly, 'The doctor said she'll be like this for a few more hours; you're not likely to get much out of her. I know she'll be glad you're here, though. I'll give you some time.' She squeezes my shoulder.

'Thanks,' I say, because there's nothing else to say.

When she's gone, I look back at Mum, hoping she'll open her eyes again. I wish, for the first time in my entire life, that I had a second parent. Someone to sit on the other side of the bed, holding

Mum's other hand. To talk to the doctors, reassure me in a way I can believe, shoulder the strain, or at least share it.

I've been there for ten, maybe fifteen minutes, when I hear my name. The voice is assured, confusingly familiar, and I turn to see Caddy's dad, of all people, parting the curtain and pulling up a chair beside me. 'Hello.'

'Hi,' I say, more bewildered than I probably should be, given that I know that Caddy's dad is a doctor that works in this very hospital. But still, it takes my head a minute to catch up to reality.

'I've been checking in for the last couple of hours, in case you arrived,' Dr Oliver says.

'Are you her doctor?' I ask.

'I was part of the team that treated her when she came into A&E,' he explains. 'And I've since spoken to the consultant to explain that I know you and that you might benefit from a familiar face. Is that all right? Would you rather speak with the consultant?'

'I just want to know if she's going to be OK.'

Dr Oliver glances at Mum, then back at me, gesturing with his head. I follow him into the corridor. 'She's going to be just fine,' he says. 'Broken bones, concussion, a nasty shock to the system – all treatable, all will pass.' He gives me a warm, reassuring smile.

I shake my head. 'No, she's been having problems like this for a while.' Maybe this happening, as awful as it is, can be the thing that finally gets Mum the attention she needs. Finally, a diagnosis. 'Something's wrong, and we need to get an answer on what it is.' I'm proud of how I say this: like an adult. 'Do you have her notes? You know what kind of tests she's had and stuff?'

Dr Oliver is nodding. 'Yes, we're well aware. These kinds of accidents can happen at this stage, unfortunately. Even after a diagnosis, even after starting a treatment plan, it's still an adjustment. Your mother was quite unlucky, but when she's more used to managing her symptoms – she may want to think about stability training at some point in the near future – and when she's made some lifestyle changes, perhaps, this will be far less likely to happen.'

'What do you mean?' I ask, frowning.

'I can't guarantee it, I'm afraid,' he says, misunderstanding my confusion. 'That this won't happen again. MS is manageable – very manageable these days – but it is lifelong. We can maintain it, treat problems as they arise, but we can't fix it. I'm sorry, Rosie.'

I'm staring at him. My chest feels funny. Tight and hot. 'MS?'

'Yes,' he says.

'MS,' I say again. I search for the acronym in my mind, feeling a familiarity, knowing I've read about it somewhere. 'Multiple sclerosis?'

I must say this in a particular way, because understanding dawns on his face. The confused horror of a doctor that is also a family friend who assumed, because of course he did, that I would know if my mother had been diagnosed with a progressive illness. 'Rosie, I'm sorry,' he says immediately. 'I'm sorry. I thought you would know, and this was extremely careless of me.'

'How did *you* know?' I ask.

'Her emergency contact, Janine, told us,' he says. 'In case it affected how we treated her.'

So Janine knew. Of course Dr Oliver had assumed I'd know, if she did.

'And it's in her notes, of course,' he adds. 'In her medical history.'

'Do you know when she got the diagnosis?' I ask.

He hesitates. 'I think at this point you need to speak to your mother, Rosie.' When I don't say anything, a silence stretches between us, long and awkward. Finally, gently, he says, 'I'm sure she had her reasons for not telling you yet.'

For a moment, I think I'm about to start crying again. Wild, wailing sobs, like a child. I think I'm going to collapse onto the floor, beating my hand against the linoleum. Instead, what comes out is a very calm, 'Thank you.'

I know it's too late to confront Mum about any of this, even if she were lucid enough for a conversation. If it was any other circumstance than her lying bruised and battered in a hospital bed, I would. I'd go in all guns blazing, demanding an explanation.

Instead, I corner Janine. Well, not really 'corner' so much as go with her to the hospital canteen, wait until we are both sitting at a table with tea, and then say, 'So. MS?'

Janine jolts, startled. Tea sloshes onto the table, over her fingers, and she winces.

'Sorry,' I say. 'But yeah. Didn't you think I'd probably find out at some point over the last few hours?'

She nods, wiping at her fingers with a napkin. 'I did, as it happens. But I thought it would be from Shell. I thought it *should* be from Shell, not me. Did one of the doctors tell you?'

'Yeah. He assumed I already knew.'

'Well, that's quite unprofessional,' she says, frowning. 'But if it's done, I suppose it's too late. I'm sorry that's how you found out. I know that's not what Shell wanted.'

'What *did* she want?' I ask. 'Why didn't she tell me? And when did she find out?'

'A couple of weeks ago,' Janine says. 'I was with her, if that helps at all. I'm sorry, Rosie. You've every right to feel angry. But this was your mother's choice, and of course I honoured that. It wouldn't have been right for me to tell you, would it?'

It wouldn't, but that doesn't make the betrayal sting any less.

'She wanted to wait until you'd finished your first year,' Janine says, when I don't speak. 'Until after your exams. You can understand that, can't you? She was only thinking of you.'

'So what if I've got exams?' I demand. 'She's obviously more important than anything else. I would have come home.'

'Exactly,' Janine says. 'That's exactly why, Rosie. Because she knows that's how you would have reacted. And she so desperately wanted to protect you from it, for as long as she could.'

'Protect me?' I repeat, the words an almost hysterical splutter. 'Like I haven't spent most of my life dealing with . . .' I swallow, not sure what words to use. 'Now I'm finally old enough to actually deal with things, she shuts me out? *Now* she wants to protect me?'

Janine just gives me a small, understanding smile, but doesn't reply. I guess there's really nothing she can say.

I look down into my hospital tea, which I can tell will be too strong, not enough milk. I think about how it's someone's job to order tea bags for this canteen, for the whole hospital. How many tea bags will they get through in one day? A week? How many people have sat like I have, digesting life-changing news, with no room for anything else in their heads except, *Tea. I'll have a cup of tea.*

I take a sip. It helps.

'Do you know much about MS?' Janine asks.

I shrug, because I don't want to have this conversation, but I know I have to. 'It's neurological. It's progressive. What else matters?'

She gives me another one of her understanding smiles. 'I didn't know anything at all. I'd heard of it, but that was all. I had no idea that it was about the immune system. It actually attacks the coating of the nerves in the brain and spinal cord, did you know that? I thought it was all more . . . I don't know.' She lets out a soft, embarrassed laugh. 'More abstract. Nerves, you know?'

I don't know. I don't even really know what she's talking

about. The immune system? I'd thought neurological meant the nervous system.

'And there's just *so much* they don't know. That took me by surprise. I thought a diagnosis meant knowing more, but . . .' She shakes her head. 'The symptoms can vary so wildly. The thing is, from my very limited understanding, nerves travel all over your body, and this illness can affect any of them, anywhere, essentially at any time. And there are a *lot* of them.'

I try to take in what she's saying, but I can't make it make sense. She must see the confusion all over my face, because she continues.

'Think of it like . . . the road system in the UK. All those roads, all interconnected. It's like knowing that there's a problem with the . . . ' She searches in the air, her eyes travelling left and then right. 'With the tarmac! And the road people know that this is a problem, but they can't know when or where it will cause problems.'

'Road people,' I say flatly. She deflates, and I immediately feel bad. 'That was a good analogy. Thank you.'

When I let myself in to my house that night, just a couple of hours later, the cat comes barrelling across the carpet, yowling in pure outrage. He rolls on the floor in front of me, spitting at me when I reach for his lovely, fluffy belly.

'All right, fine!' I snap, withdrawing my hand. 'You haven't been fed, I get it. I'm sorry no one was thinking about your stomach while Mum was trying *not to die*.'

I go to the kitchen and fill his bowl with food, adding some Dreamies to the mix as an extra treat. While he eats noisily, I look around the kitchen. Forget the unnatural neatness of my last visit here with Jade; now it's messy and lived-in – very Mum. Or, more accurately, Mum without Rosie. It's late, and I should go to bed, but instead I start cleaning. I wash up the dishes that are piled in the sink, clean the counters, go through the fridge on a hunt for anything out of date. When I'm done, I feel a bit better, my heart a little calmer. If nothing else, at least Mum will come home to a sparkling kitchen.

I walk through the home I grew up in, so quiet and so familiar. It's been a long time since I spent a night here alone. I wander around, letting memories surface around every corner. But even as the past presses in, the future – now so completely changed – threatens in all its uncertainty. Will we need to move from here? This house surely isn't suitable for someone with a disability, with its narrow doorways and sharp corners and steep, deep stairs. But won't it break Mum's heart to leave here? And where would she go? *We*, I remind myself. It's just the two of us, and so along with the spectre of 'progressive', there's another word: 'carer'.

There's a framed photo hanging on the square of wall above the kitchen doorway. Mum with one arm around me, the other on the small but noticeable bump protruding from under her dress. Her smile is radiant; mine is too. Mum calls this the only picture of 'the three of us'. Mum, baby and me. It's sacred to Mum, this picture. When I was younger, sometimes I'd walk down the stairs to see her just standing there, staring at it.

It's after midnight when I plug my dead phone in to charge. I go to have a shower and return to a screen full of messages. I scroll through them, trying to focus my attention long enough to take them in. The gist is that Suze has spoken to Caddy and to Jade – **Just keeping them up to date, no details. I hope that's OK? xxxx** – and that everyone loves me. The love from them radiates out of the screen.

I should message them all back.

I call Jade.

'Roz!' She answers the phone in an exclamation of hope and

worry and love, and it makes fresh tears rise in my eyes, stealing my voice away. 'Are you OK? I'm so sorry. How is your mum? I spoke to Suze – did she tell you that?'

I try to gather myself. 'I'm sorry I didn't call—'

'Oh my God, don't be! Don't be at all. You had enough to be thinking about. Roz, how are you? Where are you right now?'

There's so much to say. Too much.

'I'm at home,' I say. My throat closes, and no more words come.

'How's your mum?'

'She's OK,' I say, imagining Jade's eyes closing briefly in relief, the *Thank you, God* that will have passed through her mind. 'She's stable. Awake, but not all that lucid yet. There won't be any lasting damage from the fall. A few broken bones, concussion, that kind of thing.'

'Thank God,' Jade says, out loud this time. 'Oh, thank God, Roz. I'm so relieved for you.'

'There's . . .' My voice gives out. I try again. 'There's something else.'

I tell her in juddering snatches of words, each accompanied by painful twists of my heart. Because she's Jade, she stays calm: no drama, no sympathy tears, no elaborate gasps. She tells me that she's sorry, that she loves me, that she's here for me. She once did a paper on neurological conditions, so she knows 'a little' about MS.

'How long are you going to stay?' she asks, tentative, like she's not sure it's the right question to ask.

'A few days?' I say, though the truth is that I hadn't given any thought at all to how long I'd stay. God, I've still got exams, haven't I? I just . . . upped and left. I didn't even tell anyone.

'Do you want me to speak to your personal tutor? Explain what's happened? Would that help?'

'Oh my God, yes, it would help so much, thank you.'

'I'll do that tomorrow. They might want to speak to you as well, but don't worry about that now. It'll be fine. Obviously your mum is more important than some exams.' There's a pause that I don't know how to fill. I'm just nodding, as if she can see me. Eventually she says, very softly, 'How do you feel?'

'I . . .' What is the answer to this? I search myself, but the question just spirals in my head, senseless. 'I don't know.'

Later, I go to sleep in Mum's bed. Maybe it's childish, but I don't care. I want to sleep under sheets that smell like her, with Bartholomew curled on the pillow beside me, and cry in the warm safety of it. There's a book on the bedside table, *Little Tremors: My Life With MS*, cracked open at the spine. A pile of papers beside it, some topped with an NHS logo. I want to read them, but I'm too tired. Tired and sad. It kills me to think that she's been reading stuff like this and she hasn't told me. Something this huge is happening to her and she just . . . didn't tell me.

Well, you haven't exactly been honest with her, either, have you?

I close my eyes, sighing. There's no point in taking myself down this road. All that matters is right now. Being here now. I reach out a hand and touch my fingers to Bartholomew's warm, fuzzy cheek. He purrs. I go to sleep.

27

In films, people always have big, heartfelt conversations after an accident. The hospital bed seems to be *the* place for revelations and emotional epiphanies. That's what I'm expecting when I go to the hospital the following morning with Janine and slide into the seat beside Mum's bed.

Instead, I find out that the reality is slower, and more confusing. Mum knows I'm there and is happy to see me, but she's still not lucid enough for a proper conversation. She just wants to know if I'm OK, as if it's me hooked up to monitors instead of her. She asks about Bartholomew. She doesn't seem to remember that I'm meant to be at university, that I have exams. I don't remind her, just hold her hand, repeat patiently that I'm fine every time she asks.

At lunchtime, I go to the hospital canteen while she rests. Suze, who'd messaged me this morning telling me she'd taken the day off work 'just in case', is waiting for me at a table as planned, an anxious, hopeful smile on her face.

'Hi,' I say, in a normal voice, then surprise us both by taking not the seat opposite her but the one beside her and pressing my face into her shoulder.

'Oh,' I hear her say, but she rallies herself quickly, putting a hesitant arm around me and squeezing. 'It's OK,' she says. 'It'll be OK.'

I sit up, wiping my eyes. 'You, of all people, know that's a totally empty thing to say.'

'I do, but this whole thing has made me realize why people say it anyway.'

'So they have something to say?'

'No, because if they can't know it will be true, they *hope* it will be. Which is the next best thing, isn't it?'

'How?'

'Well, like . . .' She considers. 'If you can't be certain about what's going to happen, at least you have people who care about you. That's not going away. And that's really what it means, isn't it?'

I grind my teeth together to stop myself from bursting into tears. 'Yeah, OK. Thanks for coming.'

'Of course! You'll tell me if there's anything I can do, right? Anything you need?'

I nod. 'Thanks for talking to Cads and Jade for me.'

'That's OK,' she says. 'I was a bit worried you'd be annoyed.'

'No, it helped a lot,' I say. 'Sorry you had to be my secretary.'

'Your emotional secretary,' Suze amends promptly, looking pleased with herself. 'And it's an honour.'

'You can ask.'

'What?'

'What's wrong with Mum. You can ask.'

For a moment, she looks cornered, then shakes her head, looking me right in the eye. 'Or you can just tell me.'

We stare at each other. 'Or that,' I say.

'Get your lunch first,' she says. 'If you need a minute. I'll wait here at the table, OK?'

For someone who has historically handled her own crises so badly, Suze is really, really good in a crisis that belongs to someone else. It's a good thing to find out.

I stand up, tapping my pocket to check my wallet is there. 'You're going to make a great nurse.'

She pinkens with pleased surprise. 'You think?'

I nod. 'I know.'

'Rosie, hello.'

I turn at the familiar voice to see Dr Oliver coming up behind me, smiling. And then he clocks Suze sitting at the table, and it drops.

'Oh,' he says. 'Hello, Suzanne.'

'Hi,' Suze says, her voice drained of its usual bounce and energy. She looks down at her cup, like she's trying to shrink herself. Clearly, Dr Oliver still sees her as the sixteen-year-old troublemaker she was when he first knew her, as if whole worlds haven't changed since then.

I hate seeing her cowed, so I guide Dr Oliver away from the table towards the fridge of sandwiches.

'How is your mother today?' he asks me.

'OK,' I say, reaching for a cheese and pickle sandwich. 'Better. Not at proper conversation level yet, but hopefully this afternoon.'

'Good!' he says. 'That's good. I'll try to stop by later today. I assume you'll still be here then?'

I nod, taking a bottle of orange juice from the bottom of the fridge. I turn to him. 'So what's going to happen?' I ask.

He hesitates, which makes me uneasy, because I've never seen Caddy's dad be anything but totally sure of everything he says and does. 'Happen?'

'With Mum,' I say. I realize that I'm almost hugging the sandwich and juice to my chest, even though their coldness is already starting to numb my arms. Janine gave me the medical basics, but Dr Oliver has a medical *degree*. He'll know. He can tell me for certain. 'What kind of thing should we expect? What's the prognosis?'

'Rosie,' he says, 'I'm not . . . I'm not the person you should be having this conversation with. Your mother will have a neurologist who will be in a much better position than me to—'

'Generally,' I interrupt. 'If I was a student asking you about MS for a project. Just give me a general idea.'

'I can't do that, Rosie, I'm sorry,' he says, lowering his voice as a woman in scrubs leans around us to get to the fridge. Dr Oliver and I step aside, out of the way. 'MS is a very . . . challenging illness, at least in that respect. It affects people differently, so it's just not possible to predict how it will progress for one individual.'

'But that's not good enough,' I say. It comes out like a snap. 'How can I . . . How can anyone plan their lives with that kind of uncertainty? It's just the two of us; me and Mum, on our own. I need to know what's coming. You must know something. At least tell me how it affects life expectancy.' My voice wavers on the final word, betraying me. I'd wanted to sound confident and firm, but I sound like what I am: my mother's child, asking for answers that don't exist.

'There are ways to plan,' Dr Oliver says quickly. 'Your mother will have a treatment plan. She'll have lots of support. And in terms of life expectancy . . . this isn't my specialism, Rosie. But my understanding is that it doesn't have the impact on life expectancy it once did. It's lifelong, yes, but not life-shortening. Does that help at all?' He makes a face, like a wince. 'I shouldn't be talking to you like this. It's unprofessional of me.'

'I don't care about that,' I say.

'Why don't you speak to your mother when she's more stable?' he says. ' And then you can contact me whenever you want if you have questions that she or a specialist can't answer. How does that sound?'

It sounds like he's closing a door, but taking care to open a window. 'Thank you,' I say.

He smiles at me – he seems a bit relieved – and gestures towards the door. 'I need to get back to A&E now. You'll let me know if you need anything?'

I nod and he turns to leave.

'You should be nicer to Suze,' I say, and he looks back at me, blinking in surprise.

'I'm sorry?'

'She's not going anywhere,' I say. *Not any more.* 'And she's pretty amazing, you know? She's going to be a nurse. Maybe one day she'll even work here. You should be proud of her. And Cads.'

Dr Oliver looks at me for a long moment, his face completely unreadable. I wait for him to say something polite but distancing, a gentle reminder that, to him, I'll always be just a kid.

He says, 'I'm proud of all of you.'

He walks away before I can even think of how to reply.

Mum regains her lucidity and coherence gradually over that afternoon and the following morning. She seems to mark each stage of her cognitive recovery with another apology. That I have to be here, that I had to leave Norwich, that I've missed exams. For worrying me, for keeping things from me. In her head, it's a long list. Even though, for every one, I tell her it's fine. It's fine. It's fine.

'Not the lying, though,' I say, when I'm confident she's strong enough for this conversation.

'I didn't lie,' she says, shifting against her pillows so she's sitting more upright. 'I just decided to delay telling you something that could wait.'

I bite my tongue, then shake my head. 'Well, I'm here now. So tell me. You have MS.'

'I do have MS, yes. Primary progressive MS. That's the rarer kind.' She closes her eyes and breathes in a sigh through her nose, letting it out through her mouth. 'What do you want to know? I'm becoming quite the expert already. I've done a lot of reading.'

'I want to know why you didn't tell me.'

'You know why,' she says, opening her eyes. 'Let's not go over it again. Please. If I'd known this was going to happen, I would, of course, have told you earlier. But this is not what I planned, quite obviously.'

'OK, fine,' I say. 'Well, how do you feel? About the diagnosis?'

She's quiet for a long time. 'People keep asking me that,' she says eventually. 'As if there's an answer. The truth is, I don't know, Rosie. Sad. Confused. Less worried than I was, now I at least know what it is. And I . . . I keep thinking about all the things I thought I'd do when I was a kid. The person I thought I'd be. Or maybe, all the people I thought I could be; maybe that's more accurate.' She pauses, then repeats, quietly, 'All the things I'd do.'

'You can still do anything,' I say, frowning. 'This won't stop you doing things. Even if—'

'No, I don't mean in any real way,' Mum says, and she makes a face at the same time I do, both of us hearing how little sense the words make. 'It's not about accessibility, or logistics. I don't mean physically. Maybe I mean . . . sort of, metaphysically. Oh, Rosie, I don't know.' She sighs. 'I'm so tired. I just feel heavy in myself; I don't know how to explain it. Like I've finally become the person I am, and there aren't any other options any more, not like there were once. Maybe that's not something you can understand at your age, when you're still all potential. Maybe that's the way to describe it. That's how I feel. Like the potential has gone; like maybe it went a while ago, quietly, and I didn't notice until my neurologist said, *Michelle*. Not even the diagnosis, Rosie – isn't that strange? Just how he said my name. And I thought, *Oh, that's me. This is my life.*'

I let her talk. I watch her eyes close even as the words keep coming, her forehead creasing and then clearing. When she reaches out her hand, I take it and squeeze.

'You need to go back,' she says, switching gears so abruptly it confuses me for a moment. 'As soon as you can.'

'Oh my God, don't even start with that,' I say, rolling my eyes. 'It's not a problem, me being here. Not at all.'

'I'm glad you're here, of course I am,' she says, wincing as if pain has flared in her head, then passed. 'But you're so close to the end of term. You have to go back. I will be fine; I'm being well taken care of, and I'll talk to you every day if that's what you need to feel more at ease.'

'But who's going to look after you?'

'Janine is going to stay with me for a few days, at least,' she says. 'To make sure I'm getting back on my feet. So to speak. I promise you I won't be flailing around on my own, crying for you. Is that what you need to hear?'

I can't help laughing. 'At moments like this, it's really clear to me where all my sentimentality comes from.'

A grin breaks on her face for the first time. 'I raised a good, tough girl. I'm proud of that.'

I raise my hands in fists, like I'm preparing to box, which gets a laugh out of her. I lower them, smiling. 'It'll only be for a few weeks, and then I'll be back for the summer.'

She nods, slow, as if to stop it hurting too much. 'By then, I'll be much stronger, and we can talk properly. Figure this all out.'

This all. This huge life change that is going to swallow us both up. I smile for her, even as my heart clenches with what could be dread or hope or love or fear.

She says, 'I love you.'

And I say, 'I know.'

28

I stay in Brighton for two more days, then get the coach back to Norwich. It feels like I've been gone for weeks, but still everything is exactly the same. I walk to my flat almost on autopilot, not even bothering to look into the kitchen on the way in. The heaviness of being back here is already starting to weigh on me, and it's making me want to climb into my bed and stay there. I wish I could have just stayed in Brighton, even if it was hard.

I'm thinking about this, staring out my window at the groups of students clustered over the grass while I empty my bag, when there's a knock at the door and I turn, frowning in confusion. Who would come knocking at my door? When I open it, I'm still holding a wad of T-shirts. Of all people, it's Rika, biting her lip.

'Um, hi,' I say.

'Hey,' she says. 'You're back. Are you OK?'

Whatever I was expecting her to say, it wasn't that. *She noticed I was gone? She's asking if I'm OK?*

'We were worried,' she adds, probably because I haven't replied.

They were *worried*?!

'I'm . . .' I can't bring myself to say that I'm OK, even though that's the polite, British response I'm meant to give right now. I shrug. 'Yeah, I'm back. How come you knew I was gone?'

'We saw you leaving,' she says. 'You seemed really upset. And then you didn't come back. I thought you might've dropped out or something. What happened?'

I can barely remember being in the flat before Suze and Matt picked me up to take me home. I must have been completely out of it, my entire brain space already in Brighton, with Mum. No wonder I forgot to pack anything useful.

'My mum . . .' I say, though I'm not sure why. It's not like I need to explain myself to Rika. 'She had an accident and I . . . I had to go back in a bit of a rush.'

'I'm sorry,' Rika says. 'That must have been really scary. Is she OK?'

I look at her, focusing on her face properly for the first time. She seems sincere. Who is this Rika, and where has she come from?

'Yeah, but . . .' I'm going to have to figure out how to talk about this, aren't I? Maybe Rika is good practice. 'She's OK after the fall, but it turns out she . . . well, she's ill; just diagnosed. Long term.'

'With what?' This is such an inappropriate, rude question to ask, but delivered with such calmness, that I'm completely thrown. I must have made a face, because she adds, still calmly, 'My dad has Huntington's disease.'

'Oh!' I say, shocked and understanding all at once. 'Oh, shit, OK. I'm sorry.'

'Yeah, it's shit,' she says, shrugging.

'I didn't . . . know.'

'No, why would you? I don't shout about it. The bit after diagnosis is weird, though, isn't it? So, yeah. Now you know that I know. I mean, I get it. What's your mum got?'

'MS,' I say.

There's a faint smile on her face when she nods, then shakes her head. 'Not to be massively inappropriate, but you're lucky. I know you won't hear that a lot. I know it's probably not the "right" thing to say, or whatever, but I wish to fuck my dad had MS. You can think I'm a bitch for saying that; I don't care. Perspective, right? There's mine.'

I don't know what to say. I'm annoyed and relieved and

offended and grateful all at once. How many people in the world but Rika would be responding this way? So matter of fact, so honest.

Me? God, that's a weird thing to think.

'Anyway,' Rika says, taking a small step back. 'I'm, like, glad you're OK. Like I said, we were worried.' She raises a hand in a kind of half-wave, then walks away without waiting for a response.

I watch her go, speechless. They were worried about me. *Rika* was worried about me. Talk about perspective. I feel completely thrown, like the Rika I've had in my head might not have been the whole story, just like Dawn had said.

I close my door with a sigh. The end of first year is so close now, and after we've moved out we'll probably never see each other again. Maybe this is what I'll remember, though. That after everything, it was Rika who came to my door to check I was OK. That's something.

Jade comes over and hugs me so tight – right in the doorway, not even pausing to come inside – it makes me cry into her shoulder. She's brought what I will later find out is a bag of treats – doughnuts, popcorn, eclairs, jelly – but leaves it on the floor while we curl together on the bed so she can stroke my hair and tell me she loves me while I cry. She smells so purely of Jade that it almost hurts my heart.

'I missed you,' I say, wiping my eyes. 'I feel like I shouldn't say that, because obviously there was so much going on that was massively serious, but I really did. I missed you.'

'I missed you, too!' she says. 'And I was *worried*. I should have got on a train, shouldn't I? I'm sorry.'

'No, it's good you didn't,' I say. 'I probably wouldn't have managed to come back if you weren't here to come back to, anyway.' I mean this to come out like a joke, but through my cracked, teary voice, it sounds as serious as it is. I try to smile. 'Everything is so fucked.'

She doesn't tell me it's not, which I appreciate. She just reaches over and squeezes my hand. 'Do you want to tell me about it?' she asks.

'I probably said it all on the phone.'

'That's OK,' she says. 'If you want to talk about it again, now you've had some time to process it, maybe. It's OK.'

I start to tell her it all in summary, trying to be quick about it, but after a few sentences I stop trying and just let it all come out. I tell her about the car journey with Suze and Matt, the hospital, Janine, Caddy's dad and how horrified he'd looked when he realized how he'd fucked up. I tell her about my cat, the way the house smelt, the fact that it didn't rain. I show her the booklets and factsheets on MS that I got from the hospital.

And then she tells me that she's spent the last two days researching MS herself, talking on the phone to someone at an MS charity, contacting the pharmacist at the hospital pharmacy where she did her placement last term. All of it so she could talk to me about it, so she'd know. If I was crying before, this makes me absolutely *bawl*, and that's when she starts crying, too.

It takes us both a while to calm down – me especially – and when I'm done crying, all I want is to be out of my room and the flat. Jade suggests a walk around the lake, which makes me smile. 'Perfect,' I say.

The following morning, I go to speak to my personal tutor about the exams I missed. I still feel weirdly removed from the whole situation; like, I *know* that the exams are important, and that I *should* feel panicky that disappearing like I did might have a significant impact on my first-year grade. But honestly, I don't care. I really don't. (I care about not caring, though, which is even stranger. I *should* care, and it worries me that I don't.)

The first thing my personal tutor asks, very kindly, is, 'How is your mother?'

I'm still not sure how to answer this question. None of the obvious answers seem right, not when the diagnosis is lifelong and progressive. 'She . . . well, she . . .' I suddenly feel like I'm about to start crying, which would be hideously embarrassing. 'She's OK. Thanks.'

'She's getting the help she needs?'

I nod.

'That's good. And how are you, Rosie?'

'I'm . . . I'm OK.' I shrug and try to smile.

'It must have been a shock.'

'Yeah.'

She waits, but I don't say anything else.

Finally, she says, 'If you felt you needed to take the time to be at home with your mother, we would support you in that. I don't want you to feel like you had to come back because of your exams, or even because of your course. We understand that sometimes things will happen that will . . .' She considers, like she's trying to find the right phrase. 'That will put this part of your life to the back of your mind. Sometimes life throws out some surprises.'

'Surprises' isn't the word I would have used. Maybe 'shocks'. Or 'sledgehammers to your happiness'.

'If you're needed at home,' she continues, 'please don't feel that you can't say so. We have policies in place to help support students who are dealing with crises.'

'My mum's friend is staying with her for a while, so she isn't on her own. And I'm going to go back home after my last exam,' I say. 'To check in that everything is OK, basically. And then I'll come back for the last week or so of my accommodation contract before the proper end of the year.'

She smiles an understanding smile. 'I see. You have a plan.'

I nod. 'It's important to my mum that I'm here for my exams.'

'I see,' she says again.

'I can handle it,' I say, possibly unnecessarily. 'It's only, like, a month or so. And then I'll be back home for the summer.'

This time, she nods. 'And next year? How are you feeling about coming back to us in September?'

My heart drops. Right through my chest, my stomach, down to the floor. September feels so far away. I don't want to think about it now.

'Fine.'

There's another silence. I know she's reading my face, which is a little unnerving.

'Why don't you and I talk through your options?' she suggests, so gently. 'Your emotional well-being is very important, Rosie. I know it can be hard to see that, sometimes, but it's even more important than an exam, or your course.'

I surprise myself by laughing, which is embarrassing, but she just smiles, like she understands.

'The first year of university can be an overwhelming experience,' she says. 'That's why we have support services set up. Have you made use of them at all?'

I shake my head. 'I'm fine.'

'And how *have* you felt about this year?'

'I thought this was about the exams I missed.'

She's quiet for a while, looking from my face to her notes, which makes me wonder what they say. I'm just starting to feel uneasy when she says, 'Of course. Well, it's quite straightforward if you feel able to continue with the rest of your exams as normal. Resits always take place in August. This year, they'll be . . .' She frowns at her screen. 'Let me just find out . . . yes, the second week of August. So you'll just need to be back here for those few days. Will you have moved into your second-year accommodation by then? Most contracts do start in July or August, but if not, we can help you make arrangements.'

She carries on talking, explaining the resit process, but I'm barely listening. My throat has tightened, my fingers feel tingly. *Resits?* Coming back here in August? Why?

I'd expected that they would just write off the exams I missed, because it's only three out of the countless times I've been graded on something over the last year, and my average is good enough that I could take the hit of missing them. The idea of resits is . . . well, it's not good. The thought of having to come back to campus in August makes me feel vaguely nauseous.

'How does that sound?' she asks, her eyebrows lifting in expectation.

I swallow. 'I guess . . . fine, yeah.'

'Good,' she says. 'Now, if you'll just indulge me, Rosie – if you don't have to rush off anywhere – I'd like to just talk you through the options we have for students who find their first year impacted in some way. Just so you're aware. I'll feel better about how I'm doing my job if I know I've said it all, so it's really for me.' She gives me a wide smile that I can't quite return. I think I know what she's doing. I think she's seen through me. 'OK?'

'OK,' I say.

29

When I turned eighteen, I went on one of those treetop adventure days with my friends. It was the kind of thing that seemed like a good idea in theory, until the day actually came, and it was pouring with rain, and I realized that I was actually really scared of heights, and the harness we had to wear dug into my leg.

Everything that was meant to be good about it, that I'd thought I was excited about, either fell flat or was, in actuality, just really scary. The final zip line, which was the reason I'd picked the course in the first place, was so much higher in real life than it had looked in photos and videos online, the harness suddenly flimsier, the ground so solid and far away. I did it because I had to do it, because not doing it wasn't an option, and when my feet touched the ground – safely, as intended – what I felt was an overwhelming, almost dizzying relief. Just, *Thank God that's over; thank God I get to walk around normally on the ground now; thank God I don't have to pretend I'm enjoying myself any more.*

That's how I feel when the coach has deposited me back in Brighton after the end of my exams, and I've hoisted my rucksack over my shoulders again and heaved myself up Brighton's hilly streets to my own front door. Even though I'm so worried about what I'm about to find, even though everything is still so uncertain, even though I still have to go back to campus before the year actually ends and there are resits in August and decisions, decisions, decisions. It's still just . . . sheer relief. *Thank God.*

I let myself in and call, 'Hello?'

I wait for Mum's voice to sound from somewhere else in the house, probably weak and tremulous, and I can go to her and—

'Hello!'

But no. Mum's voice is loud and cheerful, sounding from the kitchen.

'Come to me!' she calls, and I hear laughter.

I'm disorientated, still standing in the doorway. I drop my rucksack, close the door and head into the kitchen, where I find my wonderful, infuriating mother, bright-eyed and smiling, sitting at the kitchen table with Janine.

'Hello!' Mum says again when she sees me. 'Rosie, my love. Come and hug me.'

Janine is smiling at me as I go to Mum's side and give her a proper, rare hug. She smells like Mum. She feels like Mum. I look her over, so obviously that Mum laughs, rolling her eyes.

'Yes, I'm still me,' she says. Her arm is still around me, and she gives me another squeeze. 'What were you expecting?'

I just shake my head. 'I don't know.'

'Well, welcome home,' she says. 'I'm so happy to see you.'

'How do you feel, Rosie?' Janine asks. 'Now your exams are finished.'

Relieved. Tired. Wishing I could just stay here. 'Good,' I say.

'How understated of you,' Mum says. 'Well, that's fine. I can be proud enough of you for the both of us.' She grins at us both, releasing me to clasp her hands around her mug.

'And how are you?' I ask. 'How are *you* feeling?'

'Better,' she says. 'Like I've said every time you've asked.' She throws me an affectionate smile, and I smile back. It's true that each time we've spoken on the phone since she left the hospital – every day at first, then every few days – she's insisted that she's doing well, but I've been uncertain about how much I believe her. I'm still not OK with how long she kept her diagnosis a secret from me. 'I'll be happy to have you home properly, though,' she adds.

'Me too!' I say. 'Anything you need doing, just tell me.'

'I meant because you're my daughter and I love you,' she says, amused. She glances at me, then lets out a small laugh. 'What did you think? That you were coming home to immediately become my carer? Oh, Rosie, we're not there yet, thank God. A long way from it. The accident has made some things difficult, yes, but only over the short term. My consultant says the progression of my MS should be comparatively slow, and that I'll have time to adjust to each change.'

'Comparative to what?' I ask.

Janine stands, smiling at us both. 'I'm going to leave you to it,' she says. 'You've both got a lot to talk about.' She leans over and gives my mother a kiss on the cheek. 'Love you, Shelly. I'll see you later. Call me if you need anything.' She doesn't try and hug or kiss me, because she knows me well enough for that. 'Bye, Rosie.'

When she's gone, Mum and I are both silent for a minute in her absence, looking at each other. Though my initial thought had been that she looked a lot better than I'd expected, now I'm looking closer I can see that she's still pale, her hair still uneven from where it was partially shaved after her accident, her eyes tired despite their brightness. There's a purple walking stick resting against the wall beside her, which I know from our phone calls she's named 'Betty' and is her 'new best friend'.

'So,' I say. 'Comparative to what?'

It takes her a moment to catch up. She sighs, stretching her neck, then sighs again. 'I don't know, actually. I didn't ask. There's been so much information to take in over the last couple of months. So many people to meet, lots of them with MS. That's been very helpful. Actually, one of them, Jo, said that the mental adjustment was harder for her in the time after diagnosis than the physical adjustment was. But that's been easier for me than I expected. I feel very . . .' She considers. 'Resigned to it. That's not quite the word, but it's close enough. I've accepted it.'

'How very stoic of you,' I say.

'Oh, there you are,' Mum says, surprising me with a smile. 'There's that Rosie snark. I thought you'd been far too nice to me these last few weeks.'

'I've just been worried.'

'I know, my love, and I appreciate that. We've got so much to talk about, haven't we? I've missed you.'

'I've missed you too. But, like, we've got to start making plans, right? Like, what are you going to do about work?'

'Work?' she repeats, confused. 'What do you mean?'

'Well, you're not working, are you?'

'I haven't been recently, no,' she says. 'Because I fell down some concrete steps and spent some time in hospital making sure I hadn't permanently damaged my *brain*.'

'But the MS—'

'Rosie.' She cuts me off, her voice an odd mix of amusement and annoyance. 'I'm not leaving my job. Of course I'm not leaving my job. Why on earth would you think that's a possibility?'

I don't say anything, because I'm not sure what to say.

'I'm sorry you saw me at such a low point,' she says. 'No one wants to see their mother in a hospital bed, let alone on the back of the revelation of a progressive illness. But that was an unfortunate combination of events, not a starting point for the rest of my life. I am still competent, Rosie. I don't plan to stop working for many, many years. In fact, I've never been so happy at the prospect of being *able* to work for many years. The bank have been very understanding, my manager especially. I'm planning on going back next week to do three days a week until I'm confident I can handle all five. Does that make you feel better?'

I don't know what I'm feeling.

'You're free this summer,' she adds. 'As much as you want to be. Spend time with the girls; go and stay with Jade. So long as you tell me all about it, I'll be happy. And your student escapades, of course; I want to hear about those, too.'

'Pretty sure I've told you all those already,' I say, as if there are any. 'And I'll probably spend most of this summer working, anyway, so I can save as much money as I can.'

'Very sensible,' Mum says, a little drily. 'Please remember to try and have fun, too. Now, are you hungry yet? I thought I'd make us a Thai green curry. I got us a chunky cauliflower to roast with it. Does that sound good?'

'Sure,' I say. 'But I can make it. You can just talk to me.'

'About what?'

I give her my very best stare, then repeat flatly, 'About what.'

She lets out a guilty sigh, 'OK, OK. I know I haven't been entirely honest with you this year—'

'*Entirely honest!*'

'But I had very legitimate reasons for that. Preheat the oven to about one hundred and eighty. Prep the veg first. I knew my health situation was going to be the same whether you knew the details of it or not. Did you see the green beans? They're in the fridge drawer. And honestly, like I said, I really did want to protect you from it as long as I could. Why spoil your first year?'

'You weren't going to spoil—' I bite my lip in frustration. With her, and with myself. This is my fault, isn't it? If I'd just been honest about how unhappy I've been, she wouldn't have felt there was anything to spoil. But then, if I *had* told her that, she would have worried about me, and that might have made her own health worse. So who is in the wrong here? Both of us? 'Look, whatever, let's not talk about that now. I want to know about the diagnosis. All of it. And what's been happening since.'

Finally, she tells me. All the stuff she'd kept from me over the last weeks and months. I'd known she was keeping some of it from me, but it's a shock to hear just how much. So many tests. How scared she'd been. How she'd googled herself 'into panic attacks'. The lumbar puncture she'd had just before diagnosis – 'which was horrible, Rosie, just horrible' – the diagnosis itself, which she said was so long coming it felt more like a relief. That she hadn't even cried. She tells me about the aftermath, how many people she's met, how 'wonderful' everyone has been. Her MS nurse, Mika, the support group she's joined in Brighton, the MS yoga class she's signed up for.

'It won't just be us,' she says to me. 'That was a worry I had, that I'd have to depend on you, which would be . . .' She trails off, like she can't even bear to finish the sentence. 'But there are so many people involved. I'll have a whole support network. Isn't that lovely?'

She's quiet for a moment, then goes off on a tangent about Janine, talking about how nice it was to live with her for a little while, the conversations they'd had. 'We watched *Beaches*,' she says. 'The Bette Midler film. Have you seen it? You should watch it with the girls. You'd love it.'

I've filled a bowl with cauliflower florets and covered them with olive oil and turmeric as she's talked and have just started mixing it all together when she says, out of nowhere, 'Do you know what I've been thinking about? Your sister.'

I freeze, my hands deep in the bowl, fingers staining ever more orange with every second that passes. Mum and I don't talk about Tansy, not any more. She did at first, a lot – constantly, even – but she stopped when I was about thirteen and never brought her up again, so of course neither did I. Now, I don't even know what to say.

'Rosie?' she prompts, as if I may just not have heard.

'What . . . what about her?' I ask carefully.

'How I would have felt about all this if she was still with us.

Having a dependent instead of one grown daughter.'

I glance over to see that she's smiling at me, though her eyes are glistening.

'And how would you have felt?'

'I don't know. I can't know, can I? But I think it would have been harder. I never worry about you, because you're so tough and strong and independent, but an eight- or nine-year-old would have been quite different.' There's a long pause, and then she says, 'I used to think I was being punished.'

'Punished? For what? And how?'

'A lot of things. Some things you know about, some things you don't. But mostly for letting the both of you down.'

'You didn't . . .' This is so ridiculous, I don't even know what to say. 'Let us down? What does that even mean?'

'Tansy, for dying. And you, for what you lost. A sister, and your mother, in a way. Part of me went with her, I know. The best part, I think.'

'For God's sake!' I snap. 'Why would you bring this up when I've got turmeric and oil all over my hands? I can't even hug you.'

Mum stands up, a little shaky but determinedly, half laughing, and I take a couple of steps towards her so she doesn't have to come to me. She wipes at my eyes with her own thumbs, like I'm still just a kid myself. 'Maybe I chose this moment for that reason,' she says, soft and teasing. She puts an arm around my shoulder and pulls me closer to her, resting my head against her chest. I hear and feel her sigh. 'What I meant to say is that I don't feel like that any more. That's funny, isn't it? You'd think I'd think this was the ultimate punishment. But, actually, what I realized . . . it's all arbitrary. What happens to us. You can't find reasons for everything. And you can't plan everything, either. Before Tansy was born I was planning out our whole lives, the three of us. I was going to move us to Scotland. I never told you that.'

'Scotland?' I repeat, the word muffled by her shirt.

'We had that holiday there, in Edinburgh, you and me, when I found out I was pregnant,' she says. 'That's where I took the test. I thought it was a sign. But it turns out that it wasn't, and here we are, still in Brighton, and she's long gone and you're so wonderful.'

I break free, trying to wipe my eyes with the side of my wrist. An entire alternate life has sprung up in my head, one where I've developed a Scottish accent, where my little sister sleeps in my bed while I'm at uni because she misses me and messages me every day complaining about our mother, where Caddy is just an old friend I have on Facebook, where I never met Suze and so neither did she, where there is no Jade because I never thought to take pharmacy, and I just came home from a course I love, where I am still myself but also totally someone else, someone familiar but unrecognizable.

I feel a bit dizzy.

'I still have dreams about that,' Mum says softly, like a confession. 'Where the three of us are in Scotland. But what I meant to say, what I'm trying to say, is that this life is what *is*. Everything else is . . . just dreams. That's something I understand now. It's taken me a long time, but I'm here now.' There's a silence, and then she adds, 'The therapist I started seeing after my diagnosis has really helped.'

This makes me laugh, louder and for longer than maybe it should, until there are different tears in my eyes and I wipe them away with my fingers, forgetting that they're sticky and orange. 'I can tell.'

'Let me finish dinner,' Mum says, gentle but firm. 'Go and wash your face. I'll tell you when it's ready.'

I look at the bowl. 'I've barely started.'

'That's OK,' Mum says. 'I can finish.'

30

It feels like Mum and I have been out of step for a long time now. Not exactly lying to each other, but keeping our own pain a secret, telling ourselves it was because we were protecting the other. And for what? We've both ended up worse off, and without the other's support to help deal with it. Now, at least, I can be here for Mum. She can talk to me properly, without any of that pointless worry that she was somehow going to spoil my imagined perfect first year.

Except she can't really do that, can she? Because even though her truth has come out now, mine is still hidden. One elephant down, but still another in the corner, towering over us both. It was hard enough to justify my own reticence about how I was really feeling before, but now, knowing she's been honest with me, I can't do it any more. I know I need to talk to her.

But still, when I try, the words don't make it out of my throat. Not that first day, nor the second. When she asks me about my exams, I say truthfully that they went fine. I can talk about Jade for hours. But anything deeper, anything painful, stays stuck inside me.

On the last evening before I'm due to go back up to Norwich to see out the last few days of my contract, I force myself, finally, to say, 'I kind of have to tell you something.'

We're sitting on the sofa together, our cat purring contentedly between us. 'Oh?' Mum says, pointing at her cup of tea. I hand it to her, carefully.

'I haven't really had the best year at uni,' I say.

'OK,' Mum says uncertainly. So far, she mostly seems a bit

confused. 'I'm not sure what you mean, my love.'

I take in a breath. 'I haven't told you because I didn't want to worry you. But this whole time, I really haven't . . . I've been pretty miserable, to be honest. About everything but Jade.'

She's frowning now, like she's trying to understand. 'Everything?' she repeats. 'Do you mean . . . student life? You love your course, don't you?'

'No,' I say. 'I really don't.'

'But I don't understand,' she says. 'Why wouldn't you tell me that you were unhappy?'

This, at least, is easy to answer. 'For the same reason *you* didn't tell *me* anything about you being ill except the absolute bare minimum.'

'That's not the same,' Mum says. 'I'm your mother. I was trying to protect you because that's my job.'

'*I* try to protect *you*,' I say. Out of nowhere, there are tears in my throat and my voice. 'That's *my* job.'

'Rosie,' she says, looking like she's about to start crying herself. 'Oh no. Rosie. No.' She takes in a breath. 'You know you can always talk to me, especially about something like this. Tell me what's been going on. Why are you so unhappy?'

I tell her – or try to – the lowlights of the year. How Freshers Week hadn't gone how I'd expected, which in the end had set the tone for the entire year. Everything that had gone wrong with my flatmates, even losing the house. How I've never felt anything click into place, the way it was meant to. How my early ambivalence towards the course hadn't bloomed into a love or even an interest, but more into something like hatred. How when I think about the next three years, I get panicky.

'Then stop,' Mum says, when I get to this point. 'You stop, Rosie. This is when you stop.'

I half laugh, wiping at my eyes, which are wet. 'I can't stop.'

'Why not? Of course you can.'

'No, I can't. I made a plan; I have to stick to it. And it's all this money, and it'll be worth it, anyway. In the end, when I'm qualified.'

She's staring at me like she doesn't even know who I am. 'Rosie,' she says again.

'And especially now,' I add, before she can continue.

'Especially—'

'I want to be able to help you,' I say. 'And I'll be able to do that better, as a qualified pharmacist.'

'Absolutely not,' she says, surprising me.

'What?'

'Don't put any of the blame on me,' she says. 'Or my illness. If you want to be a pharmacist because you want to be a pharmacist, then fantastic! I'm thrilled for you. But if you've decided that you *have* to be one because I've had this diagnosis, even though it's already making you this unhappy, then that's nonsense, Rosie. It's nonsense.'

'But I want to be able to help you.'

'You *are* going to help me. You help me every day. But I'm going to have any number of professionals helping me in whatever my future is going to be; I don't need you to be one of them. Do you understand that? You're my daughter. Even if you were . . . I don't know, the most qualified doctor in the country, I wouldn't want you to be *my* doctor. Just yourself.' This is a lovely, comforting thing to say, and I'm about to get all choked up again, when she adds, 'Sometimes I think you forget how well I know you. And I know that you are very stubborn, and you have a tendency towards denial. And an absolute refusal to show any vulnerability. I love you for all those things as well as the good, but don't you use me as your excuse not to face your own reality. If you don't like your course, leave.'

'But it's not that simple.'

'Of course it's that simple. Multiple sclerosis is not simple. People are not simple. Trauma is not simple. But this? This is simple.'

'But I don't know what to do instead,' I say. 'If I leave, I'll have nothing. I don't have a back-up plan, I don't—'

'So what? Do you think everyone does everything with a back-up plan? Of course they don't. But they manage. Do you want my advice? Embrace that. Take some time to figure it out. Take a year out. Take two years out, or three. There's no rush, Rosie. I know it feels like there is, but there isn't. You only get to live your life once. Don't waste a decade trying to convince yourself that the wrong thing is right, when you could take a couple of years trusting yourself to find out what the right thing actually is. It'll be worth it.'

'But that's such a waste of time,' I say, frustrated. '*Years*? Wasting *years* just trying to figure it out? I want to *do* something. I want to know where I'm going. I don't want to just be stuck somewhere, just getting by. I don't want to waste my life, like—' I stop myself, just in time.

Mum's lips have fallen into a thin line. 'Like what? Or who?'

'Never mind.'

'No, go on,' she says, her voice a little louder. 'Waste your life like me – that's what you were going to say, isn't it? You think I've wasted my life because I never went to university, because I don't have some exciting career you could have been proud of. I've just struggled through life and raised a child and somehow survived all these terrible things, and that's not enough, is it? I never got to throw a graduation cap in the air. I've never not worried about money. That makes me a failure, does it?'

'Of course it doesn't.'

'Then what are you saying?' She's staring at me, hard. When I don't say anything, she shakes her head and says, 'My God, Rosie, I want the world for you, you know that I do. But I would be proud of you if you went back to that jewellery shop you worked in last summer and stayed there for the next thirty years. And I would not be proud of you if you became one of those people who think success is about letters after your name and numbers on a payslip. I would be ashamed of you.'

Mum so rarely speaks to me like this. Hard and firm, even angry. The parent.

'Do you know something I never told you? I used to worry about your friendship with Caddy. Not because of her, that sweet girl, but that life she had. I used to worry it was what you wanted; that you thought that was what life was supposed to be. Private school and that big house and big plans. That you would look at our life differently. I worried about that for years, especially after you had to live with them, after you saw it from the inside. And then you met your Suze, and there was this girl with *nothing*, nothing but pain and trauma, and I was so proud of you, Rosie, for choosing her, that that was the kind of friend you wanted to be. I was proud of *myself*, for raising a girl like that. Someone who sees the heart of people and all their potential and doesn't care about what they don't have. And you choosing pharmacy! I thought you wanted to help people! But it's just about the *money* you might make? The title?'

'It's not just that,' I try to say, but it's hard to form a sentence when I'm still trying to catch up with everything she's said. She worried about my friendship with Caddy? She saw Suze as someone who had nothing? For me, Caddy's friendship had always been the best thing about my life, the thing that saved me. And Suze has had more spirit and fire and warmth in her than anyone I've ever met the whole time I've known her, even when things were hard. How can Mum have seen it all so differently from me?

Does being an adult really change perspective that much?

'Then what is it?' Mum demands, and I have to try really hard to remember what she's talking about. 'Tell me, why did you want to be a pharmacist? Try and explain it without using the words "career" or "money".'

'But that is what it was,' I say. 'And that's not a bad thing. It's sensible.'

'It's blinkered,' she says. 'It's tunnel vision. Those are the bits you grow to, not the place you start from. You're trying to go too fast. If you're not happy at that university, you have to listen to yourself and figure out why. Listen to your unhappiness; don't just ignore it. You have to be able to trust yourself in life, and that starts with being honest with yourself.'

'I am being honest with myself.'

'Are you?' She looks at me, hard. '*Are you?*'

Am I? In the silence that follows, I feel my innermost self cringing away from the question, shaking her head.

'I don't know,' I say, finally. My voice comes out very quiet. 'Maybe I'm not.'

'Maybe you're not,' she agrees, her voice calmer now, softer. 'Have you spoken to your friends about this?'

'A little,' I say, thinking about Suze and Caddy in Norwich, their confusion and their worry.

'And what do they say?'

Reluctantly, I admit, 'Basically the same as you.'

She smiles. 'Maybe you should listen to us, then.'

'Maybe.'

We're both quiet for a while. Bartholomew rolls onto his back between us, exposing his fluffy belly. Mum rubs his fur and he shifts contentedly.

'So you think I should just leave?' I ask. 'Drop out?'

'I think that you need to answer that question yourself. And stop looking for reasons not to do that. I'm not going to tell you what to do. The whole point is that this isn't my decision to make. It's your choice. But make it for *you*, not for anyone else, and certainly not me.' She thinks for what feels like a long time, then says, 'There's something I think I need to say, because I don't think you know this, and that worries me. Even if I had wanted you to carry on, and I was telling you that you had to stick with it for one reason or another, and my pride in you *was* dependent on it, it would still be the right thing for you to leave. Do you understand? You can't make life choices for other people – even if you love them – if the choice is the wrong one, or if it will make you unhappy. You have to make these decisions for yourself, not for anyone else. Even your mother. I know you love me, Rosie, and I love you, more than anything or anyone. But this choice is for you to make regardless of that.'

'But . . . you do support it?'

'Of course I do. I want you to be happy. Does it surprise me that you don't know exactly what that will look like right now? No, not at all. You're nineteen. I had no idea what I was doing at nineteen. One year on, I was pregnant with you. Now, that's certainly not something I saw coming. Not anything I planned for. And look at you! The greatest thing I ever did. My pride and joy. My rock.'

'Ok, you can stop now.'

She smiles at me, so full of love, but so understanding, too. 'Please don't ever think you need to make yourself unhappy for my sake. Like I said, I'm not going to make this decision for you, but if worrying about me has been what's holding you back, then . . .' She trails off, gesturing with her hand, like, *OK?*

'It's not just that,' I say. 'It's such a huge thing to even consider.'

'Then consider it,' she says, shrugging. 'Go ahead. Take your time. And when you tell me what you've decided, we'll open a bottle of wine. How does that sound?'

I'm not sure whether I want to laugh or cry. I hug her instead. 'Sounds great.'

31

When I get back to Norwich, there are six days left of term. Six days left of my accommodation contract. Six days left of this life. I have two shifts at work, but the rest of the time I plan to fill with Jade. In the few days that I was back in Brighton, she's been in Cambridge visiting her sister. Before Mum's accident, the two of us had talked about making that trip together, so I could meet Jasmine, but that, like a lot of things, will have to wait.

I'm happy to see Jade again, but also strangely nervous. My head is so full of the conversations I had with Mum, and also the conversations I had with Caddy and Suze before the world almost ended. Three of the people I love and trust most, unequivocally telling me the same thing, which is, basically, to leave. From their points of view, there's no reason to stay.

But Jade.

'Oh my God, I missed you so much,' she says, sweeping me into a hug, sticking her nose into my hair like a cat. We've met on campus at the Sainsbury Centre because there's an exhibition she wants to see, something about art and light that I hadn't quite taken in. 'I know it was, like, four days or something, but I just kept thinking, the *whole summer*, you know? I'll have to get used to missing you.'

I hug her back, probably too tight, but she doesn't complain. We head inside together, her hand finding mine. The main exhibition space is filled with panels of stained glass, which are illuminated by the light streaming through the floor-to-ceiling windows.

'Oh, wow,' Jade says.

'Definitely wow,' I agree, though the truth is, I'm too distracted to really take it in. I'd been nervous before, but the strange thing is that *she* seems a bit nervous too, which is weird. I keep feeling her eyes on me, like she's studying my face, either like she's about to broach something, or like she thinks I am. As we walk around, our conversation becomes more and more stilted until it stops entirely, and we're just silent, surrounded by colourful glass.

'What's the matter?' I say finally.

She blinks. 'What? Nothing.'

'You keep looking at me funny. And you're not talking.'

'No, I . . .' She stops herself, rolling her eyes with a sigh. 'OK, sorry. I know.'

'Is everything OK?'

'Yes. No. I don't know.' As she shakes her head, the light flickers over her face. 'Roz, I think we need to talk.'

'Oh my God,' I say, my heart plummeting. 'Did you really just use that actual phrase? Are you trying to give me a heart attack?'

She half smiles, but she still looks too serious. 'You know we do.'

'Here?' I deliberately lower my voice, gesturing around. An art exhibition is surely the worst place to have a 'we need to talk' conversation.

'No one's listening,' she says, which is true. The exhibition space is huge and, right now, practically empty. No one in the small scatter of people is within hearing distance, unless I start shouting. 'Listen,' she continues, her voice soft. 'While you were away and I was with Jazz, I did a lot of thinking. And I was talking to her about you – obviously I was; I did that a lot – anyway, I was telling her about how your first year has gone, and I realized, I mean, I guess I always knew this, we've even talked about it, but . . .'

'But what?!' My heart is about ready to thump right out of my chest, it's going so hard. I can't believe this is happening, right here among the stained glass and light.

'The only good thing is me. And I thought that was bad because it makes our relationship unbalanced, but that's selfish of me. It's bad because it's bad for *you*. I realized that maybe I . . . maybe I'm the reason you're unhappy, because I'm confusing things. If it wasn't for me, maybe you'd have had to face up to the fact that you're unhappy.' She looks so worried, her whole face a crease of anxiety. 'Roz, I love you. I don't want you to be unhappy. I'm sorry. I should have talked to you about this earlier, instead of playing pretend and just forcing you to be happy with all that stupid Norfolk stuff.'

'I loved the Norfolk stuff!' It comes out too loud, and I bite my lip, embarrassed. More quietly, I repeat, 'I loved the Norfolk stuff.'

She shakes her head. 'But I should have let you be unhappy instead of waving it away. I hate that you might have thought you couldn't talk to me because I'd just be all, *La la la let's go on a boat trip to the Broads! Isn't Norfolk the best?'*

This makes me laugh, even though my stomach is somersaulting with real fear, though my throat feels so tight it might choke me. 'You were never like that. I know I can talk to you, about anything.'

'Then talk to me! Be honest with me.' Her anxious eyes are trained on me, like she's trying to read me. Quietly, she adds, '*Please.*'

I look away, towards a blue glass panel with yellow leaves, casting coloured, flickering shadows on the floor. 'This isn't the right place,' I say.

'Then let's go outside,' she says. 'Let's go to the lake.'

She's not going to let me off, that much is clear. This is going to happen. I follow her out of the Sainsbury Centre and across the grass, the two of us completely silent. I'm waiting for her, and she's waiting for me.

After whole minutes have gone by, I stop still and say, abruptly, 'I am unhappy.' I'm not looking at her, staring fixedly out over the lake. 'I've been unhappy for a long time, since I got here. About everything except you.' I know I'm going to start crying, very soon. 'I think . . . I think maybe I'm not supposed to be here.' Saying it out loud is like a deadweight has been momentarily lifted from my chest. I actually gasp out a breath. 'I think I made a mistake.'

She hugs me, sudden and close and tight, and I do start crying then. I hear her tell me that it's OK, even though it obviously isn't. Even though everything is about to come apart.

When she breaks away from me, she asks, so gently, 'Do you want to leave?'

'*No*,' I say, hearing how my breath shudders. 'Of course I don't. I don't want to fail. I don't want to be a failure. All I wanted was to come here and do my degree and become a pharmacist. But it's not . . . it's not . . .' I cast around for the words, but they don't come.

Jade is nodding, her eyes steady on me. She curves a gentle hand around my elbow and we start walking again. After another couple of minutes, she says, 'Can I ask you something?' When I nod, she says, 'Why do you think you'd be a failure?'

'You know why! Putting a year into a course, paying all that money, and then having to admit it's too hard and packing it in and going home with nothing to show for it? Of course that's a failure. You can't dress it up as anything else.'

'As opposed to what?' She stops again and looks at me, dead on, eyebrows rising as she speaks. 'Putting five years into a course, paying way *more* money, never admitting to anyone how hard you're finding it, and finally going home with a degree in something you hate, preparing you to start a career you don't want? What do you call that? Success?'

I open my mouth, then close it again.

'Honestly, think about it. Really think about it. Admitting you're on the wrong path and doubling back on yourself is way better than just carrying on because you're too proud to turn around. You're smart, Roz. You know that's true.'

I do know it's true. But. 'But . . .'

'But what?' she asks, forehead creasing. 'Why would you think you had to put yourself through that? Is it just the money and thinking you'll be a failure?' Her eyes go suddenly wide. 'It's not *me*, is it? Because forget me. Pretend I'm not a factor.'

'Oh great,' I say, more snappishly than I'd intended, wiping at my cheeks, which are still wet. 'Just like that? Is that how easy it would be for you?'

'What do you mean?'

'You said yourself long distance never works. So if you want me to drop out, it means—'

'What? When did I say that?'

'Ages ago. You were talking about Marie, and you said long distance is a scam.'

She looks at me for a moment, confused, before her eyes go wide. 'Shit, Roz! I was being flippant! I wasn't talking about us. You and me are nothing like Marie and me. She cheated on me. She told me she was bored of me. She said I was only fun when I was the only option.'

'*What?!* Oh my God.'

'You are not Marie. And I'm not who I was then, either. This is us now, Roz. I love what we have. I love you. Is that what you think this has all been about – me asking you about this? That it's an ending conversation?'

'Isn't it?'

'No! Of course not! Do you think I'd be this calm if this was *that*? I'd be hyperventilating. I'd have three boxes of tissues.'

'You don't want this to be over?'

'*No!*' She looks so horrified. 'No, that's not what I'm saying. I'm trying to say – and clearly, I'm making a mess of it – is that I want you to know that I've thought about it,' she says. 'A lot. Just in case. I made a plan.'

My heart skips. 'You made a plan?'

An affectionate grin spreads over her face. 'I made a plan. Want to hear it?' I nod. 'Well, we'll have to be long distance for one more year, but I can do my pre-registration year anywhere, so I'll come down to Brighton for it. And then we'll be together, and we can figure out where to go from there, together. It'll only be one year actually apart, and that's nothing in the grand scheme of things, right?'

I shake my head, half crying, half laughing. 'Right.'

As we continue around the lake, she tells me more about the plan, how often we'd be able to see each other while we were apart, the holidays we could take. She sounds so bright about it, so confident.

'Can we go back to the exhibition?' she asks, when we've completed a circuit of the lake. 'I kind of wasn't really taking it in earlier.'

This makes me laugh. 'Me neither. Sure.'

It's only been about half an hour, but the light has already changed inside the Sainsbury Centre. It's brighter, sharper; it's almost dancing through the coloured glass. Jade takes my hand as we walk around, squeezing. When I look at her, there's a wide smile on her face.

'Jade?'

'Yeah?'

'Do you think we can make it?'

Her reply is immediate, emphatic. 'Of course!'

'How do you know?'

I expect her to reply seriously but instead she laughs, pulls me into her and points us towards the clear glass panel to our left, which is reflecting us back at ourselves in glittering gold. 'Because look at us! We're fucking adorable!' She kisses my cheek. 'I love you. And I'm all in.' She grins at our reflection. 'Are you?'

I never knew love could be like this – that's what I'm thinking. That it can be every emotion at once, even the bad ones, and that that can be something good. That's how I feel with Jade right now, in this moment, in the light. Everything at once.

'I'm all in,' I say, turning to her so we're face to face. She has the best face. 'Totally, completely, all in.'

32

For all the conversations and the tears and the encouragement and tough love and soft love and plans and plan Bs, I make the decision on my own.

I get up early on my last Wednesday in Norwich and sit in the empty kitchen for a while, watching the mist move over the lake. I open up the email my personal tutor sent me after our meeting a few weeks ago, where she'd written down everything we'd talked about, all my options 'just in case, Rosie'. I'm thinking about how kind she was to me in that half an hour, how patient with my sullen refusal to have the conversation she knew I needed to have.

I read through the information she'd included about dropping out, forcing myself through the immediate instinct to turn away from it. I used to think there were two options: drop out, or don't drop out. But that's not actually true. I can pause, if I want to. Take some time away, a year out, even, to give myself the breathing room to figure out what it is I actually want, away from the noise of a flat I don't like and a girlfriend I love and a course that has confused my head since I first arrived. My personal tutor has added a comment, one I didn't see because I didn't read the email properly when it first arrived: *Sometimes time is all you need. And permission to take it.*

I rest my head against the window, looking back out at the lake, which is probably my favourite thing about this campus. Last night, I'd messaged Laini to ask how she was. I thought she might not reply, but she did, enthusiastically, asking me how the year had gone, telling me about the culinary school she'd applied to in Switzerland – **freaking SWITZERLAND, Rosie!** – and how she still had **weird dreams about being in a pharmacy lecture, and then I wake up and I'm so relieved lol**. I'd planned to ask her if she'd ever regretted her decision, but there was no need. I told her I was glad it was going so well, that I was sorry I hadn't been more supportive of her decision at the time.

Laini:

Damn, that's OK! We barely knew each other.

Rosie:

I think I was a bit judgey?

LOL if you were you def didn't say so. Fun to hear that now, though! ;)

God, sorry. The thing that I'm trying to say is that I wish I'd done the same.

Fuck, what? Seriously?

Yeah. I'm not happy.

Call me.

It had been months and months since we'd last seen each other, and we'd really only spent a few hours together in total, but I decided to go ahead and call her, and we ended up talking for an hour. I'd remembered her as downbeat and sad, even a little bit dour, but on the phone she was bright and enthusiastic, asking about my year, every detail that had made me get to this point. It was like talking to a friend. It *was* talking to a friend.

'Come to Kent!' she said. 'Over the summer. We'll hang out.

And I'll make you a cake.'

I thought I hadn't made friends at uni. But there was Dion, cheerful and kind. Dawn, if I'd tried that little bit harder, maybe. Laini, brief but still real. Maybe they didn't look like I'd imagined in the plans I'd made in the months before university, but they were still there, they still made a difference, even though that difference hasn't been enough.

I *had* been judgemental about the choice Laini made at the time, but I was the one who was wrong. She had the intelligence and self-awareness to know, in two weeks – less, even – what it's taken me an entire academic year to realize. *This is not right for me. I am in the wrong place.* I'd thought – and told her – that she just needed to give it time, but she knew that wasn't the problem, and she was right. What has all this extra time given me, except tuition fees and a mountain of accommodation costs I could have just avoided?

Jade.

It has given me Jade.

I take a deep breath and close my eyes. *Calm down. You are not Laini. You could never have made a decision like that in such a tiny amount of time. You wanted to give it all a chance, and that's still smart, even if it hasn't worked out this time.*

I leave my flat and take myself on a walk around the quiet campus, thinking about that phone call with Laini, the email from my personal tutor. Caddy's support and Suze's advice and Jade's love. Mum, with all three, the backbone of my entire life. There's nothing left for me to hang my denial on. No one else to hide behind. Just me and this campus that I now know so well, months on from when I first arrived.

What surprises me is how, when I strip away all the dithering and shame and anxiety, it's so easy to pin down exactly what my problems are. Which is funny, because I'd genuinely thought I didn't know; it's like I've been keeping secrets from myself.

I pause by the Sainsbury Centre to send a quick email reply to my personal tutor, asking for a meeting, then continue, planning out in my head what I'll say to explain. I don't think she really will ask me to explain, but thinking it through helps, anyway.

I think I might have chosen the course too quickly, and that I need to give myself space to figure out if it's really what I want. That basically sums it up, doesn't it?

There's a thing I always believed – I didn't realize, but I did – which is that the older you get, the clearer life gets. The clearer everything gets. Twelve-year-old me thought nineteen-year-old me would know it all by now.

But the weird thing is, life was a lot clearer to that twelve-year-old than it is to me. At least then I still believed I'd understand things one day. That the things I didn't know were still there to be known.

Now, it's just uncertainty. Around and ahead. Maybe that's what adulthood is: learning to live with uncertainty, probably for ever.

And that's OK, I tell myself. Sometimes things will go wrong, and when they do, what matters is how you deal with that. And for me, that means no more distractions, no more excuses. It means trusting the people around me to love me through it all, because they do, and they will.

33

It's the last day of fresherhood. Last day on my accommodation contract. Last day of the year.

The strange thing is that it feels weirdly similar to the first day of all of that, too. Doors all over the flat are wedged open, parents – incongruously unfamiliar, older, cheerier – are walking in and out, carrying boxes, introducing themselves to one another, smiling with indulgent affection at their emotional offspring, who are hugging each other and crying about the end of something special.

Not me, obviously. I'm not hugging anyone and I'm not crying, either. I'm beaming. Jade is with me, helping me pack up what remains of my stuff, talking happily about the coming summer. When we'll see each other – next month, when we meet in Cambridge for the weekend to celebrate her and Jasmine's birthday; August, when I come back to Norwich for my resits; and September, when she comes to Brighton to stay for a week – and what she expects from her summer placement in a hospital pharmacy in North Norfolk.

'And we'll talk every day,' she says, for the fourth or fifth time. 'Even if we're tired.'

'Every day,' I confirm, for the fourth or fifth time, smiling. 'It'll be like we're not even apart.'

She stands up from where she's been piling up books in a box and winds an arm around my neck, pulling me towards her and kissing my hair. She squeezes me tight, and I give myself a moment of pure emotional indulgence, breathing in the vanilla scent of this amazing person, my *girlfriend*, the biggest gift I could ever have had out of this cold, dark year. For her, I would do it all again.

I pull back and look at the stripped mattress, the empty desk, the bare walls. I try to remember how I felt the first time I stood there, but mostly I'm just feeling so happy that it's time to leave. Far happier, on leaving, than I was to arrive.

My rucksack is heavy, but I don't mind. I close my door behind me, Jade slightly ahead, glancing back to smile, and I knock the wood twice, just lightly, with my knuckles. Silently, I wish the next occupant a better year than mine.

Part of me wants to just leave, but I stop in the kitchen on the way out, anyway. Dawn and Freddie are sorting through the fridge, laughing about something.

'Bye,' I say.

They both look up, their smiles fading. After a pause that lasts too long, Dawn says, 'Bye, Rosie.'

And that's that.

Outside, the sun is bright. Jade and I walk side by side to the bus stop, where the coach that will take me home has already pulled in, the door opening. Jade and I hug one more time, neither of us the type for a big emotional goodbye, especially not in public. And we've said it all already, anyway.

I climb up into the coach, find my seat and look out at my smiling girlfriend, waving up at me. I'm lifting my hand to wave back as the coach pulls away, and then Jade is out of view, the university campus is sliding by my window, moving into the past. I sit back, letting my head rest against the seat, closing my eyes for a second, just to let myself feel it. And then I open my eyes again, pull out my phone and connect my headphones as I tap on Spotify, searching for a playlist I haven't thought about for ten months.

Day One.

I bite my lip, feeling the kind of smile my September self would not have understood fill my face. I press play.

EPILOGUE
Summer

It's July, and the afternoon is just starting to turn into evening when the three of us meet outside Shakeaway. Caddy is the first to arrive, waiting for us with a patient smile – Suze with her dog, Clarence, tucked under her arm, only slightly ahead of me. We get milkshakes and take a long route through the Lanes on our way to the beach, stopping at Paperchase so Suze can find a birthday card for Matt. Caddy volunteers to wait outside with Clarence – she has taken to the dog in a way I definitely haven't – and I follow Suze into the air-conditioned cool of the shop.

'When's his birthday?' I ask.

'This Friday,' she says, pausing at a display to scan the cards. 'Cancer.'

It takes me a second. 'Oh my God,' I say. 'Horoscopes? Really?'

'You can say it's all bullshit, but you are a *classic* Taurus.' She's grinning as she reaches up to take a card featuring a cartoon cat playing the guitar. 'You don't have to believe in things for them to be true.'

'And vice versa,' I say, which makes her laugh again. 'What's a classic Taurus, anyway?'

'Bullish. Like, stubborn,' she says, half her attention on the card, squinting in concentration. It's quite sweet how much this card seems to matter to her. She puts it back and carries on looking. 'Loyal. Dependable.' She throws me a grin. 'All the good things.'

'I really didn't have you down as a horoscope person.'

'Well, good,' she says. 'Nearly four years down and I can still surprise you.'

I smile, shaking my head, and leave her to search through the cards for something perfect. I don't have any cards to buy, so I stop at a rotating display of postcards, browsing contentedly. They're the whimsical kind: a neon llama in sunglasses; an Andy Warhol'd cat; platitudes of all kinds in all different fonts. There's an urban sunset behind THE BEST IS YET TO COME in bold block letters. I stare at it for a while, letting my eyes travel over the words, the saturated colours. **The best is yet to come.** *Is it?* I think, with an almost distant curiosity. How could you ever know, at least enough to buy a postcard that states it so confidently? Or maybe it's just a hope rather than a promise. Maybe I should buy it, just to remind myself. Mum would say it was a sign, me seeing it right now, at this point in my life.

A hand slides around my waist, a chin tucks into my shoulder. A voice in my ear, playful and teasing. 'Wotcha looking at?'

'Get off, weirdo,' I say, making no move to shake Suze loose. She gives me a squeeze before she lets go. I point to the postcard. 'This.'

'*The best is yet to come,*' she reads aloud. There's a pause. 'Optimistic.'

'Do you think it's true?' I ask.

'Yes,' she says, so definitive, which makes me smile. 'Do you?'

'I don't know,' I say. 'Maybe.'

'That's good enough,' she says. 'I'll get it for you.' She counts out three of the postcards and pulls them free from the display. 'One for each of us. I'm ready. Let's go.'

When she's paid and we walk back outside, Clarence reacts like he thought he'd never see Suze again, which even I have to admit is cute. Caddy hands my milkshake back to me and we continue on to the beach. It's busy when we get there – a sunny July evening on Brighton beach is always busy – but we find a spot for the three of us near the old pier, arranging jackets to sit on, adjusting sunglasses. The air smells like disposable barbecues and salt. It's loud with voices and laughter and music. The sea stretches out before us, as far as the distance will go.

I take my moment. 'So,' I say. 'I've decided to drop out of uni.'

They both react like I've just announced I've won the lottery. They cheer and hug me, telling me how great it is, how happy they are for me. It's ridiculous and adorable, and I love them for being so perfectly who they are with me. When they've calmed down, I explain about how I'd known for a couple of weeks, but that I'd been having conversations with the university to confirm everything, and had wanted to wait until I was certain. I tell them how it's not technically dropping out – not yet – more a leave of absence, which is what I want and need; plenty of time to make a proper, long-term decision.

'I'm still going to go back to Norwich next month to do my resits from May,' I finish. 'So I can know that I've completed the year.'

'Is that so you can decide to carry on with pharmacy?' Suze asks.

'For anything, really,' I say. 'There's no harm in being able to say I passed first year, whatever I decide to do, and it'll be better if I decide later to just transfer unis or move to a different course. Or both.'

'Is that what you think you'll do?' Caddy asks. 'Transfer?'

I shrug. 'Maybe? I'm really not sure, but I want to take the time to figure it out. I can't see myself going back to study in Norwich, or wanting to go away from home again, what with Mum and everything. But that's OK either way. My personal tutor said that the point of it is so I can decide, and that just taking the pressure off might make things clearer. Like, maybe I'll realize I actually *do* want to carry on with pharmacy, if I don't feel like I'm forcing myself to do it. It's all just . . .' I think about it. 'It's a big maybe.

I'm trying to be comfortable with that.'

'That's good,' Caddy says. 'Do you feel better now you've made that decision?'

I nod. 'Loads. Even if I eventually decide to go back, it'll be good to have a year off. Mum and I have got a lot to figure out, so having proper time for that is going to be good, too.'

'What are you going to do instead?' Suze asks. 'For the year, I mean. Work?'

'Yeah. Maybe at the jewellery shop, but I'm hoping to get something full time somewhere else, to get some different experience and to see how that feels.'

'How about you and Jade?' Caddy asks, a little cautiously.

I feel the smile spread on my face. 'We're good. We've got a plan.'

Some plans, I've decided, are still OK. So long as you've left a little room for the maybe.

Caddy asks me more questions about Mum, then more about the last year of my life. Suze asks her about how she's feeling being single and back in Brighton, then me about being newly long distance. We both ask her how she feels about being estranged from her family, and she actually tells us. We talk for a long time, pausing for trips to get fish and chips, to open ciders, to paddle in the sea.

At one point, when the sky is starting to pinken, Caddy says, 'Do you remember the first time we came here together?' and I realize I actually don't. She describes a September afternoon after school, the three of us in school uniform, Suze all brand new, Caddy her mousy former self, and as she talks it comes to life in my head, when there was so much we didn't know, about each other and where we were going.

I try and imagine us in four more years, or eight, or ten, or twenty. Will we remember this evening, be able to pick it out of a sea of almost identical moments, and remember ourselves younger, greener, from the certainty of a future present? I'll know, then, how this decision I made as an uncertain nineteen-year-old turned out. Maybe I'll have a degree, or a career, or both. Or neither. Maybe Mum will still be using her stick, or need a wheelchair, or better, or worse. She'll still be Mum, and she'll still love me the same. Maybe Jade will be a face from the past, or my favourite face in the present, still. In either scenario, the way she kept me together this year will always be true, will always make me feel happy, and grateful, and loved.

Maybe I'll have travelled the world by then, or learned how to speak Spanish, or left home for another in the same city I grew up in. Maybe I'll have studied dentistry, or microbiology, or forensic science, or something I've never even heard of. It doesn't seem scary any more. Maybe Suze will become a nurse. Maybe it will all fall apart again, and I'll watch her build it all back up, again, and carry on, always summoning that smile from somewhere, always looking up, trying again. Maybe Caddy will become a speech therapist like she's planned. Maybe she'll make a life in the Midlands, or find a new home somewhere else. Maybe she'll come back again, because Brighton is always home, and so am I. Maybe we'll be closer than sisters our whole lives.

Maybe all three of us will drift apart, then come together again, over and over again, like a tide that is constantly changing but is also, constantly, dependable.

Maybe the best really is yet to come.

Acknowledgements

My first thanks have to go to Claire Wilson and Rachel Petty, for believing in both me and these girls right at the beginning of the journey. None of this would have been possible without you both. I hope we've made you proud.

Thank you to Cate Augustin for being the best thing that could have happened to Rosie and this book. Your insight, enthusiasm and warmth made this book better than I hoped it could be. Thank you also to the wider team at Macmillan, both for this book and those that came before. No paragraph in an acknowledgements section could be too effusive, or long enough.

Thank you to the University of East Anglia, especially between the years 2006 and 2010, and everyone who shared it with me. From my first flatmates, who made that first year so magical, to the School of American Studies, who opened up the world for me, to the boy with the long hair across the room in the US Contemporary Foreign Policy seminars that I went on to marry on a sunny day in March, many years later. UEA truly is wonderful. Thank you.

Thank you, Sam Davenhill-Lyon MPharm, for giving so much of your time and knowledge to help me understand the first year of a pharmacy degree. This book truly wouldn't have been possible without you, and I'm so very grateful!

Thank you, Christian Donlan, for your brilliant book, *The Unmapped Mind*, which helped me to finally begin to understand multiple sclerosis, after over a decade of confusion. You're an incredible writer. Thank you.

Thank you to all the friends who have made my life, the old

and new, those who came and went, and those who stayed – I love and appreciate all of you.

Thank you to James and Monika, and to Anna, Richard, Arthur, Harry and Stanley – my favourite hairy family. I wish I lived next door.

Thank you to my parents, for being my parents, but also for being so generous with your stories and memories of diagnosis and of living with MS, and so gracious in allowing me to sift through them and spin them into fiction. So much is different, but the love is all true.

And thank you, as ever and always, to Tom, for being my heart and home in Norfolk and Sussex, and everywhere we go.

About the Author

Sara Barnard lives in Brighton and does all her best writing on trains. She loves books, book people and book things. She has been writing ever since she was too small to reach the 'on' switch on the family's Amstrad computer. She gets her love of words from her dad, who made sure she always had books to read and introduced her to the wonders of second-hand bookshops at a young age.

Sara is trying to visit every country in Europe, and has managed to reach thirteen with her best friend. She has also lived in Canada and worked in India.